Jessica Blair grew up in Middlesbrough, trained as a teacher and now lives in Ampleforth. She became a full-time writer in 1977 and has written more than 50 books under various pseudonyms including *The Red Shawl, A Distant Harbour, Storm Bay, The Other Side of the River, The Seaweed Gatherers, Portrait of Charlotte, The Locket, The Long Way Home, The Restless Heart, Time & Tide, Echoes of the Past, Secrets of the Sea, Yesterday's Dreams, Reach for Tomorrow, Dangerous Shores, Wings of Sorrow, Stay With Me* and *Sealed Secrets*, all published by Piatkus.

For more information about the author visit: www. jessicablair.co.uk

The Restless Spirit

Jessica Blair

piatkus

PIATKUS

First published in Great Britain in 1996 by Judy Piatkus (Publishers) Ltd
This paperback edition published in 2010 by Piatkus

A CIP catalogue record for this book is available from the British Library.

ISBN 978 0 7515 4536 4

Typeset in Sabon by Hewer Text UK Ltd, Edinburgh
Printed and bound in Great Britain by Clays Ltd, St Ives plc

Papers used by Piatkus are natural, renewable and recyclable products
sourced from well-managed forests and certified in accordance with
the rules of the Forest Stewardship Council.

Mixed Sources
Product group from well-managed
forests and other controlled sources
www.fsc.org Cert no. SGS-COC-004081
© 1996 Forest Stewardship Council

FSC

Piatkus
An imprint of
Little, Brown Book Group
100 Victoria Embankment
London EC4Y 0DY

An Hachette UK Company
www.hachette.co.uk

www.piatkus.co.uk

For
my favourite grandchild
Dominic, Paul, Joe, Alexandra

and for
Joan
who lived 'The White Cliffs'

Acknowledgements

For help with background material I sincerely thank Dominic Hudson, Roy Knox, Malcolm Collier, Princess Mary's Royal Air Force Nursing Service, the Imperial War Museum, Whitby Archives and Whitby Public Library.

I thank my family for their critical advice and patient support and my editor, Lynn Curtis, for her expertise, continued guidance and valuable encouragement.

Prologue

1945

The sea!

Jean Lawson's eyes widened with pleasure. She inched nearer the carriage window as if that would bring it closer, but only her spirit could reach out and touch the gentle waves.

Until now, with the first glimpse of the sea as the train left the confines of Scarborough, heading north towards Whitby, she had not realised how much she had missed it. Not for six years had she even glimpsed it, not since the day she had walked out of home and climbed the steep bank between the houses of Robin Hood's Bay on the Yorkshire coast, to join the WAAFs, the Women's Auxiliary Air Force.

She ran her long, delicate fingers through her light-brown hair in a gesture of momentary contentment. Her blue eyes, matching the colour of the sea, sparkled beneath thin, arched eyebrows.

Far away three fishing boats plied their trade on a sea of glass, bringing memories of life before the war. It was a scene of calm normality which seemed to be trying to convince her that, in this world returned to peace, all would be well.

The cliffs steepened. Smoke from the engine billowed past to be left drifting lazily in the still air. Patches of grass beside the track, blackened by sparks, marked the progress of previous trains. The clickety-clack of turning wheels beat a rhythm of 'welcome home, welcome home'.

Born and bred in the tiny coastal village, the only girl in a family of fishermen, she had the sea in her blood. It would have been natural for her to join the naval service, the Wrens, but she had chosen otherwise. The WAAF had offered a means of escape from this tight-knit, isolated village and perhaps her only chance to see another way of life. More than anything, it had been an act of defiance, a rebellion against the narrow views of her father, who had refused to give her leaving his blessing.

Now, as the engine, puffing hard, climbed high along the edge of the precipitous cliffs, she felt the pull of the sea once more. She had known it in all its moods: calm and peaceful on still, moonlit nights when the waves found it an effort to lap the sand; at other times ferociously pounding that same sand and the mighty cliffs with such strength that it seemed it would tear the land apart. It brought joy when the fishing was good, anxiety when a boat was overdue and fear when the cobles – small fishing boats – had to run before a storm. She had seen big ships torn to pieces on the rocky coast and people dragged to a watery grave when attempts at rescue proved useless. But above all she remembered its tranquillity, the soothing balm it could bring to a troubled mind, as it had done when she was trying to decide whether she should leave or not. One starlit night she had listened to the waves and in the swish of their movement, as they ran to their limit on the beach, they seemed to say, 'Go, go, go . . .'

Now she was returning, having crammed a whole lifetime into six years.

She had left in a mixture of emotions: excitement at embracing a different life, sadness at leaving her family, especially Sarah, her mother.

At five foot four, Jean's compact, shapely figure gave the impression of bustling control effervescent with life. Although well able to cope, she had experienced times when her vulnerability was exposed. There had been moments when she had cried out to be mothered, to feel those comforting arms enfold her in loving care. She knew that her mother in her heart of hearts gave her daughter her blessing when she volunteered for the WAAFs, but dared not voice it openly for it would have brought scorn and anger from her husband.

Jonas Lawson was a stubborn man, always had been, but Sarah had married him when the zest for living had been upon him. He and Sam Harland had been the village beaux. Bosom pals, they had wooed all the girls, their banter friendly, their attitude mischievous but respectful. At times they threw out audacious hints, which in retelling grew out of all proportion until their exploits became the hushed talk of the village.

Sarah had been the envy of many a girl when she had married Jonas, though later some were thankful for their escape when they saw the embittered man he had become. But he did not let his bitterness touch his love for Sarah. She understood it, tolerated it, loved him deeply, but regretted when it touched his children, who had never known him any other way.

Apprehension about her homecoming ran nervously in Jean's mind. Could she expect her father to welcome her with open arms? She had never heard from him during the six years she had been away, not even when her mother had died. She would not have known but for her dear friend Gabrielle. Jean had written to her father but her words, crying out for the love she had lost, had brought no response. The bitterness he had felt about her departing had not been curbed by her sorrow. Was that bitterness still ingrained in his heart?

Jean had always known it was there. It had puzzled her when she was young but her mother had reassured her that it had nothing to do with her or her brothers. Indeed her father, though stern and unbending, showed flashes of love which were hastily brought under the control of a harsh exterior. He was not a man to cross, as she found out when she announced she had signed up to join the WAAFs. That day the bitterness, engendered long before she was born, was turned on her and she felt the wrath which had burned in her father's soul for so long – from the day in 1919 when Sam Harland returned from France, from the war to end all wars.

Chapter One

1915

Jonas Lawson and Sam Harland lurched out of the Black
Bull on Whitby's Church Street. They were not drunk,
nor were they cold sober. They were in that state in which
senses are real though sometimes blurred, a state where
something impinges on the mind to be recalled in vivid
images or tossed away, never to be remembered.

At twenty-four, they had been bosom pals since their
school days in Robin Hood's Bay. Their families, inshore
fishermen, were close. They always had been, in living
memory and beyond. Tales were told of great-grandpar-
ents and great-great-grandparents, of their exploits to
wrest a livelihood from the sea, of trials, disasters, heroic
deeds and through them all a love of the sea which had
been passed on from generation to generation to the two
men through whom their fathers looked to the future.

But that future was in jeopardy. Where once thirty-five
cobles put to sea from the beach at Baytown, the local

name for the village, now, in 1915, there were only two families plying the trade, the Lawsons and the Harlands. Even before the outbreak of war, men had been walking the five miles to Whitby to join the deep-sea trawlers and a regular income. Hostilities took volunteers on a wave of patriotic zeal, or as an escape from nagging wives or a bleak future.

Unmarried, Jonas Lawson and Sam Harland had stayed. They were ingrained with their fathers' outlook: 'Lawsons and Harlands have allus fished from Bay and allus will.' But, at times, Sam had sensed a change in his father's attitude, especially since the outbreak of war.

They started down Church Street a little unsteadily. Sam stopped and clasped Jonas round the shoulders. His eyes narrowed trying to focus on his friend.

'What . . .' He drew a deep breath, swallowed hard, bringing words from his slightly muddled mind. 'What if we gan to the White Horse . . . get a couple of pints and then find a couple of lasses?'

Jonas straightened his broad, six-foot-two frame and frowned, about to speak. He turned his brown gaze skywards, first one way and then the other, before bringing it back to Sam, who, never liking Jonas to tower over him, tried to push himself taller than his six foot.

'Sam,' chuckled Jonas, 'thee's a one for the lasses.'

'Aye, I is.' His mirth rumbled from deep in his chest. His face went serious. 'But it's all innocent fun, thee knows.'

'I hope it is,' replied Jonas. 'I wouldn't want our Mary to think otherwise.'

A grin spread across Sam's face. 'Your sister's a fine lass, Jonas, a fine lass.'

'Aye, and she thinks a lot about thee.'

'Don't all the lasses in Baytown?' There was a touch of pride in his voice. Sam was handsome and he knew it. There was the hint of a dimple in the cheeks, which ran to a firm jaw. A touch of attractive ruggedness was enhanced with the browning of sun and wind. His thick, dark hair held just sufficient wave to make a girl look twice until her attention was drawn to his eyes. It was riveted there by their vitality. There was something venturesome and challenging about them, a wildness which tempted.

'Thee's a downright flirt,' Jonas commented.

'Thee wants to take a leaf out of my book,' Sam slurred, swaying a little.

'Nay, there's only one lass for me, Sarah Duggleby,' replied Jonas.

Sam licked his lips, focusing his eyes on his pal. 'Thee asked her to marry thee yet?'

'Thee knows I haven't.'

'Thee'll lose her.' Sam wagged his finger under Jonas's nose.

'Nay. We have an understanding.'

'Understanding?' Sam's voice thickened with mockery.

'Aye, and thee knows why. Her ma's ill, can't leave her.'

'She's been ill for ages.'

'Two years.'

'Two years thee's missed.'

Jonas was beginning to be irritated by Sam's line of talk. He took hold of his arm and turned him round. 'We'd better be going home. It'll be dark before we get there.'

The June sky was cloudless, allowing the western light to linger longer, and Jonas reckoned they'd be halfway home before it was dark. He started off along Church Street in the direction of the Church Stairs, one hundred and ninety-nine steps which led to the church on top of the cliffs from where they could follow a track to Robin Hood's Bay.

Their pace was not quick and their direction not always in a straight line. Jonas, the less inebriated of the two, had to act as navigator. There was strength in his arms, acquired through years of fishing, pulling in lines, handling fish, and hauling cobles up the beach since the day he had first helped launch his father's boat when he was ten. The wind, rain, sun and sea had marked his rugged features. He loved the life of an inshore fisherman and set a determined chin against anything or anyone who would alter the rhythm of his life. He held his own opinions and little would budge him once his mind was made up. He had been told more than once that his stubborn streak would bring him trouble, but he laughed the warnings off, saying he could handle life. And so it seemed, for he was a big man, powerful, muscular without an ounce of fat. He was fiercely loyal to his family; father, mother, two brothers, and sister Mary, a year younger than himself.

Light still filtered into Church Street. Its shops were closed and the dwellings seemingly settling down for the night, but the inns were doing a sharp trade. Narrow openings led to the staithes beside the river, which ran between soaring cliffs to reach the sea. On the opposite side of the street, similar openings led to 'yards' lined by small cottages climbing the cliffside so that they seemed to stand one on top of the other.

Few people were on the street, most having reached

home after a day's work. Noisy chatter, mingled with raucous laughter, came in waves from the inns to which individuals hurried for one last drink. Three urchins in full chase burst from one of the yards and cannoned into Sam, almost knocking him over. Only Jonas's quick reaction prevented a heavy fall. Sam yelled abuse after the boys, whose bare feet hurtled them in a weaving run along Church Street.

As he straightened up and started to move off, Sam stopped. 'Who's that pointing at me?' he slurred, his head jutting forward, his eyes peering at a wall.

'No one,' replied Jonas.

'There is. He's there pointing at me.' He waved an arm in the direction of the wall.

'There's no one,' Jonas returned sharply.

Sam shook off Jonas's grip and stumbled towards the wall. 'I tell thee, there is,' he called irritably. 'I'll knock his block off for pointing at me.' He raised his fist in a gesture of defiance.

'Don't be a fool, Sam. Thee's worse for your drink than I thought thee were. That's just a recruiting poster.'

Sam swung round to face his friend, his lips drawn into an expression of doubt. 'Recruiting poster?'

'Aye, there's a war on, thee knows.'

Sam turned sharply to face the wall. He swayed, then leaned forward to peer more closely at the poster. He saw a military man with a peaked flat hat, insignia at the front of the band. The man had a huge moustache dropping in a sweeping curve from the nose and ending in a neat point beyond his cheeks.

Sam reached out and touched him. 'I'm sorry,' he

apologised, putting on a serious voice. 'I didn't know it was thee.' He stepped back a little, his eyes drawn to the arm which seemed to be reaching out from the poster. The fingers were clenched, all except the index finger, which was pointing straight at him. Sam was mesmerised by it.

Jonas took Sam's arms. 'Come on, time we were getting home.'

Sam started. He half turned, then looked back at the picture. 'Wait a minute. It says YOU on there and he's pointing at me.' He went close to the poster and saw three words in smaller letters above the large YOU. 'It says, "Your country needs".' He looked a little puzzled for a moment. ' "Your country needs YOU." And he's pointing at me.'

'It's only a poster.' Jonas sounded annoyed, wanting to be on his way.

Sam ignored his friend and read more. ' "Men can enlist in the new army for the duration of the war".' He paused, scanned a few words, then went on, ' "Seven shillings per week with food, clothing et cetera".' He swallowed. 'Not bad, not bad,' he commented. 'And it says that's the lowest scale.' He nodded. 'Fighting men! Fall in!' He straightened, pulled his shoulders back and stepped backwards. He stared at the poster man, who seemed to be looking at him more intently than ever. Sam threw him a mock salute, turned sharply and with a 'Quick march!' set off for the Church Stairs.

Jonas shook his head and grinned to himself as he watched Sam's effort to march in a straight line. He wasn't doing too badly, either, and he was keeping in step with the

10

marching tune he was whistling. Jonas took a few quick strides and fell into step beside his pal.

Sam opened his eyes and shut them quickly against the bright light which seared his sight. He groaned and turned over, pulling the sheet across his bare shoulder. Someone was pounding an anvil in his brain.

He opened his eyes slowly. They focused on the wallpaper but he did not see the small blue flower motif his mother had chosen for his bedroom. All he saw was a man pointing at him. That same man had haunted his sleeping hours, ever there, pointing, and he had not gone away with daylight. He seemed to be both calling him and accusing him: calling him to join the army and accusing him for not doing so. His stare was compulsive and Sam knew he had to do something about it.

He rolled on to his back and stared at the ceiling. His head cleared, leaving only a dull ache, the result of the beer he had drunk the night before. Other times when he had been like this, the ache had quickly disappeared when he had a cold wash, a good breakfast and went out to breathe the salty fresh air. He had no doubt it would do the same today.

But this man troubled him. He could not get him out of his mind. He was still there after Sam swilled his face in cold water from the ewer which stood in a bowl on the small wooden table beside the window from which he could glimpse the sea. He remained vivid while Sam dressed, and he accompanied him to breakfast.

The small kitchen in which the Harland family spent their time, using the 'holy of holies' only on very special

11

occasions, was comfortable and cosy. A sofa of black leather stood with its curving mahogany back against one wall. Two matching chairs, one for his mother and one for his father, stood on either side of the fireplace. A table with four chairs occupied the middle of the room, seeming to make it shrink even smaller. The black range with its oven, a copper for heating water, and a reckon, the iron hook from which hung a kettle puffing steam from its spout, was kept spotless by his mother. Even though it was summer, a fire burned in the grate, for it was the family's only means of cooking.

Sam arrived to find his father and brother Mark already tucking into bacon and egg. His two sisters, Doris and Ruth, were laying a place for him and his mother was conjuring an appetising smell from the frying pan on the fire. He sat down without a word and replied in monosyllables when anyone spoke to him. They all exchanged glances on these occasions, and their raised eyebrows imparted the assumption that Sam had had a little too much to drink last night. Had they known the real reason for his preoccupation, they might have wondered about the future.

Breakfast finished, the three men reached for their caps and left the house for the women to have their meal.

Once outside, Luke Harland paused and started his usual routine of examining the sky, grunting at his thoughts about the weather and filling his pipe while his sons waited. Once it was charged and lit to his liking, they would be on their way to the coble to prepare for fishing later in the day.

But today that routine was broken. Before Luke had applied a match to the tobacco, Sam interfered.

'Want to see Jonas, be with thee later,' he said sharply and was off before his father could comment.

'Want to see if he's a head like yours?' Mark shouted after him, but Sam ignored the mockery and hurried to the end of the narrow street, along which houses faced each other within touching distance. He crossed the Openings, skirted Sunny Place, leaped down Bakehouse Steps and reached Silver Street. He saw Bob Lawson and his three sons – Jonas, Cliff and Bruce – emerge from one of the houses and set off for their coble.

'Jonas!' Sam's call stopped his friend.

'Catch thee up, Pa,' said Jonas when he saw Sam hurrying after them.

His father said nothing and did not alter his stride, and his two younger sons knew to do likewise.

Jonas waited, quizzically wondering why Sam had sought him out so early in the morning, even before they had reached the Dock and their cobles.

'Glad I caught thee,' panted Sam as he reached Jonas.

'What is it?' asked Jonas, concerned at the trouble he read in his friend's face.

'That fella who was pointing at me, he's been doing it all night,' Sam gasped.

A puzzled frown marked Jonas's forehead. 'What's thee talking about?'

'Thee remember him,' snapped Sam, irritated by his pal's mystified expression. 'After we came out of the Black Bull.'

'Nobody stopped us,' returned Jonas. 'Thee'll have to watch thissen, the drink's getting to thee.'

'I can take my drink as good as thee and thee knows it,'

13

growled Sam. 'That chap on the wall, soldier pointing his finger.'

Jonas gave a short laugh of derision when he realised to what Sam was referring. 'That was only a poster. Thee been having nightmares about that?'

'He became real enough to me during the night. And those words, "Your country needs YOU", he kept saying them.'

Jonas glanced sideways at his pal with a quirk of his eyebrow. 'The booze sure got to thee.' He grinned. 'Come on, let's get to the boats.' He started to walk away.

Sam skittered after him and fell into step beside him. He looked anxiously at Jonas. 'No, look, I'm serious. I'm going to volunteer.'

Jonas stopped in his tracks. He stared in amazement at his friend. He searched his face with a quick glance. 'Thee's in earnest, isn't thee?' He knew the answer before it came.

'I am,' Sam replied firmly. His face wore a worried expression, anxious for Jonas to understand. 'That poster did it. I just feel I should be doing more. Didn't thee feel that way?'

Jonas's face tightened. 'No, it didn't affect me. Besides, we're doing our bit bringing fish in, feeding folk.'

'The little we catch is nothing. It's the trawlers that are helping to feed the nation, not us. Inshore fishing is finished.'

'Never,' said Jonas, a venomous snap to his voice. 'There'll allus be fishing from Bay as long as there's a Lawson to do it. Thee should feel that way about the Harlands. It's up to us to keep it going.'

'Pa says it'll be different after the war. He can see the

day when there won't be a coble leaving Bay. He says he'll understand if we lads want to leave for better things.'

'Well, my pa doesn't feel the same, nor do I. I'll fish out of Bay as long as I live,' replied Jonas.

'Thee wants to get your head out of the sand. Look to the future. There's a big world out there. Here's a chance to see it. Come with me, Jonas. Let's get in this together.'

Jonas shook his head. 'Nay. It's thee that's the fool.'

'Thee'll have to go eventually. It'll become compulsory. Volunteering now will be better than being forced to go. Think on it, Jonas. Come with me.'

'Your pa know about this?'

'Not yet. Thee's the first I've told.'

'Not Mary?'

'No.'

'She isn't going to like it.'

'Maybe. But it's my life. And I'll be back, with better prospects than inshore fishing.' Sam put enthusiasm into his voice to try to convince Jonas.

'What about the fishing now?'

'Pa and Mark will manage, just as yours will. Come with me!'

Jonas shook his head slowly. 'Nay. If thee wants your head shot off, thee get on with it.' He set off for the boats, his stride long.

Sam stared after him. He could sense annoyance in the tautness of Jonas's body, though annoyance at what he was not sure. Upset because he was leaving, breaking up their comradeship, or irritated because he did not feel the same way? Sam shrugged his shoulders and followed, but he made no attempt to catch up with his friend.

Reaching the area known as the Dock, where the cobles were drawn up from the beach, Sam glanced at Jonas, who was busy checking the oars and did not look in his direction. Sam's father and brother were already baiting the lines when he reached the Harland coble. He hesitated.

His father looked up, eyed his son for a moment and, without taking his pipe from his mouth, said, 'Get on with it, lad.'

Sam looked apprehensive and licked his lips.

Luke knew his son. Something was bothering him. 'Spit it out, lad. It'll do no good bottled up.'

Sam started at the remark. He saw his father's eyes intent upon him. His brother, wondering what was coming, had paused in his job.

'I'm going to join up, Pa,' Sam blurted out. 'Volunteer for the army.'

Stunned by the announcement, Luke stared at Sam for a moment, then slowly took his pipe from his mouth. He tried to sort out his reactions while he gazed into its bowl. Sam waited uneasily. Mark sat like a statue, wondering what his father would say.

When Luke raised his eyes to his son, Sam felt relief surge over him, for he saw understanding in them. 'If that's what thee wants, son, then so be it.'

Sam relaxed. A broad smile spread across his face. This had been easier than he had thought. He had expected some opposition. 'Thanks, Pa.' He caught Mark's wink and grinned back.

Luke's mouth set in a hard line. 'It'll upset your ma, so break it to her gently.'

'I will, Pa.'

'Another thing, son, I can't guarantee there'll be a boat for thee when thee gets back.'

'I know. Things have changed and, like thee says, the future might be with the trawlers.'

'Aye, things will be different after the war.' Luke shook his head sadly as if mourning a life past. He looked up and turned his head to call, 'Bob, our Sam's going to join up.'

Bob barely raised his eyebrows. 'More fool him! Hope he ain't smitten our Jonas.' He shot his son a sharp glance.

'He hasn't, Pa,' muttered Jonas.

'Good. There's the fishing to think on.' He looked across at Luke. 'What'll thee do? Thee'll be a man short.'

'Some lad in the village will help out. But like I've told thee before, fishing from Bay is finished.'

'There'll allus be a place for us,' Bob argued. 'Besides, some of us like our independence, go and come as we please, beholden to no man. That's worth a lot. Thee all think on that.' His words took in not only his own sons but Luke's family as well. He turned his gaze on Sam. 'But I wish thee well, lad. Come back safe to us.' He turned his attention to the baiting, putting an end to the matter as far as he was concerned.

Luke looked at Sam. 'When will thee go?'

'I've to visit the recruiting office yet, Pa. I'll do that tomorrow.'

'Ah, away with thee now. If thee's decided to do something, then get on with it.'

'What about today's fishing?'

'We'll manage. Ask young Fred Wood if he'll give us a hand. Reckon he won't say no to earning a copper or two.'

'Right, Pa.' Sam nodded to Mark, who gave him a

reassuring smile. He knew his young brother would keep an eye on his father.

Sam paused as he reached the Lawson coble. 'Coming, Jonas?' He put the question firmly.

Jonas fixed his eyes on the bait, determinedly avoiding the question. He looked up only when he felt his father's penetrating gaze upon him. From drooped eyelids Jonas glanced at him and saw hard, pursed lips, eyes cold without understanding but with a flare that defied opposition to his views. Jonas went on with his baiting.

'And I'm glad to see thee got no fool notions from Sam Harland,' said Bob as the four Lawson men walked into the cottage just before midday.

The lines were all ready, the boats prepared. They would put out in the early afternoon and return late in the evening. Now they would have a fortifying meal of broth, roast beef and Yorkshire pudding, followed by apple pie, before they sailed.

'There's a good smell, Rachel, lass,' Bob commented with a smile at his wife. The tempting aroma of cooking meat came from the oven beside the fire. A kettle boiled on the reckon and the apple pies sat on the table waiting to be warmed in the oven when the meat was taken out.

'And what's Sam Harland been up to?' she enquired, as she straightened from stirring a pan of gravy.

'Fool's gone off to join the army.'

'Nivver!' Rachel was astounded by the news.

'It's as reet as I'm standing here,' replied Bob.

Rachel shot a glance filled with questioning alarm at Jonas. Knowing what pals he and Sam were, she dreaded the thought that Sam might have influenced her son to do the same. He looked away and pulled out a chair to sit at the table. She knew from the morose look in his eyes that he was not going, and that he had been hurt by Sam's decision, feeling that it had shown him up for not following suit.

'Ah, well, if that's what he wants, I suppose there's no holding him.' She shrugged her shoulders and was about to turn back to her pan when her attention was drawn to her daughter.

Mary, who had been setting the table when the men returned, was gripping the back of the chair with hands which showed white at the knuckles. It was a grip of someone trying hard to hold her feelings in check. Her face had lost its colour. Her eyes stared unseeingly through her father but his words were ringing in her mind. Sam was joining the army. He could be killed in the bloody fields of Flanders. The vision of him lying dead in the mud was vivid.

'Oh, no!' The cry came as a long-drawn-out whisper. The overpowering calamity of her father's announcement hit her. She turned and ran from the cottage.

Bob looked after her in surprise. 'What the . . . ?' He turned to his wife, his eyes wide, seeking an explanation.

'She's smitten with Sam Harland, didn't thee know?'

'Smitten?'

'Ah, thee men, thee can see nowt.'

'Has he given her any reason to be smitten?' Bob frowned.

'Not what thee's thinking,' said Rachel, her sharp look condemning him for even considering the worst. 'Have thee forgotten what it's like to be smitten? Now sit thee

19

down and get your dinner, there's fishing to be done this afternoon. Our Mary'll be all right. She'll get used to it.'

Mary ran down the narrow street, her white apron still tied around her blue, ankle-length skirt. Her copper-coloured hair, free of any encumbrance, fell to her shoulders, which were covered by a white blouse with full sleeves. Reaching Bridge End, she turned up the Bank and raced up the steep incline, negotiating the uneven steps with sure-footedness. She was oblivious to the exertion and to people who stared at her; she saw no one, heard nothing. She must catch Sam and stop him doing this fool thing. He must have gone to Whitby.

At the top of the Bank she pulled to a stop, her chest heaving. She gulped air into her lungs as she stared into the distance, hoping to catch a sight of Sam striding towards Whitby. No one! Her heart sank. She bit her lip and brushed back the unruly hair which had fallen forwards over her shoulder. The train! Maybe he had gone for a train. Maybe he was still at the station.

Still breathing heavily, she hurried past the new houses at the banktop to the brick-built station. In the ticket office, the shutter at the booking point was down. No train was due. She ran on to the platform and looked hopefully right and left. There was no one. Despair threatened to overwhelm her as she looked about, needing someone who could tell her what she wanted to know.

A figure appeared further along the platform and walked briskly in her direction. She started towards the trim figure, with neat official jacket carefully brushed, trousers with a sharp crease, black tie knotted on a blue

20

shirt, peaked hat with the letters NER flamboyantly worked at the front.

The stationmaster's friendly face broke into a smile when he recognised her. He took his pipe from his mouth and said, 'Miss Lawson, nice to see you, but what brings you here at this time? There's no train yet for a couple of hours.' He noted the concerned look on her face and it troubled him. 'Something the matter?'

'I was trying to catch Sam Harland, Mr Newton. Did he go to Whitby by train?' she asked, unable to keep the note of disquiet from her voice.

'Aye,' replied Will Newton. 'Went on the ten o'clock, just caught it.'

Mary's lips tightened, trying to hold back the tears which threatened to flow. Her shoulders drooped with disappointment. She knew she would never be able to catch him, never be able to stop him signing up.

'Something wrong, Mary?' asked Will with a note of concern.

Mary looked into a kindly face. She had known Will Newton all her life, a friendly, amiable man who loved his station and encouraged the village children to come and see the trains he admired so much.

'Sam's gone to join the army.' The words jerked from her and their impact brought a flood of tears.

He put his arm round her shoulders, heaving with sobs. 'Now, don't take on so, Mary.'

'I don't want him to go,' she cried. 'I wanted to stop him. I'm too late.'

'I'm afraid you are,' Will agreed sympathetically as he eased her gently from his shoulder. He looked into her

21

tear-filled eyes. 'But you know, it isn't the end of the world.'

'Oh, but it is. It is.' Mary shook her head.

'Now, now, it isn't,' he said gently but firmly.

'He'll be killed, Mr Newton, I know it.'

'Mary, that's nonsense. There's no reason why he should.' A tiny smile flicked the corners of his lips. 'If I know Sam Harland, he'll bear a charmed life.' He turned Mary slowly and, with his arm still comfortingly round her shoulder, started along the platform. 'Let's find you a cup of tea. I'm sure Mrs Newton will have the kettle on. Then you can wait for Sam. He got a return ticket.'

By the time the three-o'clock train from Whitby arrived at Robin Hood's Bay, Mary was much more in control of herself, though she still felt despair at Sam's leaving. Mrs Newton had been sympathetic and had offered Mary a cup of tea and then a bite to eat when she and Will sat down to their dinner. She chattered constantly, keeping Mary from dwelling too much on what she saw as a world-shaking catastrophe.

But all Mary's anxiety returned as she watched the pointers on the clock on the mantelpiece move nearer and nearer three o'clock. She fidgeted, screwed her hands together and bit her nails. Eventually she could bear the mounting tension no longer. She jumped from her chair and called to Mrs Newton, who was in the kitchen, that she was going on to the platform.

Emerging from the house into the sunlight, she glanced in the direction from which the train must come but she could see no telltale smoke. She inclined her head, listening intently, trying to catch the sound of its coming. But there was nothing. Instead there was a charged calm as if these moments were held in timeless suspension awaiting a signal to move on.

It came a few moments later. The whistle, the clickety-clack, the smoke, footsteps on the platform. The world was in motion again and the news Mary did not want to hear was crowding in on her.

The train, puffing and hissing, rumbled towards the station. Will Newton, his jacket pulled straight, his hat set firm, was standing importantly by the WAY OUT sign, ready to receive passengers' tickets and exchange greetings which would make locals pleased to be home and strangers sense the friendliness of the quiet village. His porter was further along the platform, waiting to exchange messages with the train crew and to assist any passengers who needed help. As the train slowed, Will Newton's sonorous voice called out, 'Robin Hood's Bay' with a lilt which raised it above the ordinary.

Mary glanced at the passing carriages until the train jerked and finally came to a halt. Three doors swung open. Her gaze passed over them quickly. A lady and two children emerged from one. Further along, a figure she recognised as Mrs Batty alighted. A gentleman stepped out of a third and turned to help two ladies to the platform – strangers. Mary grew anxious. Hadn't Sam returned? She turned to look behind her towards the front of the train. A carriage door opened and her heart leaped with relief when Sam stepped out and swung the door shut behind him. She realised that he had set out to make an impression at the recruiting office, for he was wearing his best dark-blue jacket and charcoal-grey flannels. His plain white shirt with stiff collar sported a subdued grey tie, and his brown shoes were highly polished.

Mary rushed towards him.

Seeing her, he opened the carriage door again. 'Thee gallivanting?' He grinned. 'Where to?'

'I'm not going anywhere. I've come to meet thee,' she replied, irritated that he should treat her presence so lightly.

'Me?' Sam raised his eyebrows in surprise, and closed the carriage door again.

'I tried to catch thee before thee went to Whitby,' Mary explained. 'Wanted to stop thee doing the fool thing I expect thee's done.'

Sam nodded his head slowly. His eyes narrowed slightly and the cheerful smile was replaced by a sober expression. 'So thee's heard. How long have thee been here?'

'Since Pa told us when he came for dinner.'

'Oh, I left much earlier than that.'

'I'd hoped maybe thee hadn't. I hoped I could stop thee.'

They were oblivious to the activity on the platform, of the passengers leaving the station, the checking of doors, the whistle, the waving of the green flag and the train pulling away with its wheels spinning momentarily on the metal rails until they made a firm grip.

Sam's mind was confused. He had never expected her to want to stop him, nor wait for him as she had done. He stared at her, his eyes serious. His mind was latching on fast to the situation.

Mary was seeing their friendship as something more

serious. True, he had been out with her, sometimes just the two of them but more often than not six of them, three and three; they had gone about together, walks on the cliffs, picnics on the shore, visits to Whitby to see the trawlers or explore the ancient abbey, high on the cliff. Oh, he had flirted with her just as he had with many other village girls but he had never indicated that there was anything serious between them. He felt sure he hadn't. He racked his brain to isolate a moment but he could find none. There had been kisses and cuddles but he had meant it all in good fun. There had been times when the physical contact might have gone further but they had always drawn back. Surely she hadn't taken those moments to mean much more?

'Ticket, young man? Or is you two going to stand here the rest of the day now that she's found you?' The station-master eyed Sam. 'She was right upset that you'd gone.'

They started when Will Newton's voice broke into their thoughts.

'Sorry,' Sam spluttered and thrust out the small green stub.

'We'd better be going,' said Mary. She gave the station-master a smile and added, 'Thanks, Mr Newton.'

As they walked along the platform, Mary slipped her arm through Sam's. She would soon lose him to the army but she had him here now, so she must not look on the black side. She would make the best of the days that were left, make them exciting, leaving memories for him to take with him and for her to live on until his return.

Sam bit his lip and frowned to himself. The linking of arms in this situation felt too possessive.

25

They left the station and started towards the village. He summoned words to put things right, as he saw them, but a glance at Mary stopped him. He could not find it in his heart to destroy the pleasure that showed on her face. He realised she was in love with him. How could he tell her he did not feel the same? Oh, he liked being with her, they'd had good times together, but he did not feel as deeply as she did. He would soon be gone and maybe separation would resolve the situation and Mary would forget him.

'Why did thee have to do it, Sam?' she asked. 'Thee needn't have volunteered.'

His eyes narrowed as if seeing the future. 'You know, there's more to life than Baytown. And I want to see it.' He was moved to excitement. 'This war, terrible as it is, gives me the chance to see what's beyond that bay out there.'

Alarm at the enthusiasm in his voice fluttered at Mary's heart. It was as if he couldn't get away soon enough, as if breaking a lifelong tie was important to him. 'But thee'll be back?'

'Who knows?' he replied. 'Who knows what awaits me out there?'

'Maybe death on a muddy battlefield.' The words came sharply from Mary, almost before she knew what she was saying, and yet behind them was the attempt to jolt him into seeing sense.

'If that's the fate awaiting Sam Harland, then so be it,' he replied lightly. 'At least he'll have stepped out of the shadow of Baytown, if only for a short while.'

This treatment of the matter clouded Mary's eyes with tears. He did not want her breaking down, so laughed frivolously and brushed her cheeks with his lips. 'Don't look so solemn, Mary. I might not pass my medical but if I do, there'll be a little while before I go.'

Blinded by her feelings for Sam, Mary read in those words only what she wanted to, whereas he saw no commitment in them.

During the fortnight that followed, Sam had his medical and was declared fit. He awaited his call-up buoyed by the thought of the 'adventure' that awaited him and also by the fact that he would escape from Mary, who had taken on the role of possessor more and more. She blazed a warning eye at any girl who would have butted in when Sam cast his glad eye in her direction. More than once he came to a point where he was tempted to tell her outright that they should not be serious, but he knew she would be hurt. They had been friends since their school days and she was the sister of his best friend. He did not want to fall out with Jonas because of her. So he let the situation ride, expecting it to change once he had gone. It wasn't that he disliked her; on the contrary, he thought a lot of her. She was pretty, good fun, had an enthusiasm for life and was probably the only girl in the village who could match his dancing ability. More than one person said they made a handsome couple, and the village expected them to marry one day. There were those who said it should be before he joined up; others frowned upon the idea, knowing that Mary might be left a widow. But Sam enjoyed his freedom too much to get tied down to married life in Baytown just yet.

Fred Mills, postman in Baytown, knew the type of

envelope, so most of the village heard at once that Sam Harland had got his call-up papers.

When that news hit the Lawson household, Mary plucked her shawl from the peg beside the door and left the house without a word. Dreading the parting, she ran quickly to the Harland cottage, her inside churning. Tears welled in her eyes and tension gripped her whole body in fear at what might happen to Sam.

She had almost reached the cottage when Sam came out. Instantly recognising the state she was in, he grabbed her arm and whisked her round. 'Can't have two of you blubbering in there,' he said brusquely. 'Ma's bad enough. Let's walk.'

Mary fell into step beside him and linked her arm with his. She fought back the tears, determined not to spoil the few precious hours they would have together.

'When do thee go?' she asked.

'Tomorrow.'

Mary gasped. She had thought he would have a few more days at home. 'So soon?'

'Aye.' He moved to treat the matter lightly. 'Seems as though they want Sam Harland to finish the war for them.'

She squeezed his arm. 'Come on, let's walk on the cliffs.'

Folk called out their good wishes to Sam as they walked through the village. They left its confines and took the path to the clifftop. The sun shone from a blue sky dotted with cotton-wool clouds. It was a day made for enjoyment, a time that shouldn't be marred by thoughts of Sam's leaving. Mary resolved to make this a day to remember.

They kept their talk away from Sam's leaving and got

lost in reminiscences, laughing at their recollections of school days, of tricking their teacher and playing truant. They remembered collecting crabs on the beach, picnics on the cliffs at Ravenscar, taking part in the May Queen procession, and all the excitement of Lifeboat Day when the crowds paid tribute to the volunteers ever ready to launch the boat when the occasion demanded. Lawsons and Harlands had always been among them.

Lost in their chatter, they were unaware that their steps had taken them away from the path along the cliff edge to a hollow sheltered from the north by an arc of oaks. It drew the warmth and held it invitingly from the breeze. Sam took off his jacket and laid it on the ground. He held her hand as they sat down. He leaned forward and kissed her gently on the lips. They sank on to their backs, fingers entwined and faces to the sun. The war was far away.

They lay without speaking, watching clouds, but each could sense the rising desire in the other. There was no need for words to express the longing which was taking them over.

Sam did not fight it as he had done before when he had suspected that Mary wished to go on further than a kiss and a cuddle. Now he was conscious of a response so strong that he knew he could take something he had always desired to take. And tomorrow he would be gone.

He turned to her, raising himself on his elbow. He met the invitation in her eyes and lowered his mouth to hers. She felt a quiver go through her. Her arms came round his neck, pulling him close, and as his lips swept into passion she matched him kiss for kiss.

'Take me, Sam, take me,' she gasped through hungry

kisses. Her voice was hoarse as she added, 'But be gentle, it's the first time.'

'I will,' he gulped as he looked down at her face shining with anticipation. 'And it'll be safe,' he reassured her.

She was already reaching for the buttons on her skirt.

As they walked back to Baytown, Mary felt that her inner joy would burst for all the world to see. She had given her body willingly and, after the first tentative time, when doubtful moments of a strange new experience mingled with and sometimes detracted from the pleasures, she had been overwhelmed by the joy and satisfaction which had enveloped her. Then she had lain and, her pulse beating with desire to be taken again, she had tempted Sam once more.

Now life would never be the same. It had taken a new turn, brought her into a new world, and memories of these last two hours would sustain her until Sam returned and took her again and again, but this time in wedlock. Sam would be hers. To her there was nothing more binding than the love they had just shared. They would marry when he returned from war. Now there was no thought that he might be killed, and throughout their time apart they would still be together in the memory of the ecstasy they had just shared.

They reached the narrow street where Mary lived. Sam stopped.

'Mary, please don't come to see me off tomorrow,' he said.

'Why not?' A frown of disappointment creased her forehead.

'I want no fuss, no tears. I want to go quietly.'

She hesitated.

'Please,' he urged.

'Very well,' she agreed reluctantly. 'If that's what thee wants.'

He glanced up and down the main street. There was no one in sight. He kissed her quickly on the cheek. 'Thanks.'

'Take care, Sam. And write.'

'I will,' he said.

Mary smiled at him and held back the tears, for nothing must spoil the joys of this day. She turned and hurried with a light step towards home. When Sam returned she would be Mrs Sam Harland.

Chapter Two

1919

The Reverend George Stone bustled breathlessly into the Congregational Hall. The ruddy complexion of his chubby face had been heightened by rushing on this warm spring day. Sweeping his wide-brimmed, low-crowned black hat from his head, he dropped it on the nearest table. He smoothed his silvery hair, pulled a snow-white handkerchief from the pocket of his thigh-length black coat and mopped his brow.

'My apologies, ladies and gentlemen.' His mutton-chop whiskers quivered as his eyes swept across the ten people already sitting round the table awaiting his arrival.

All eyes had turned in the minister's direction when he entered the room and remained riveted on him.

He caught his breath and sat down in the high-backed chair at the head of the table, his customary position as chairman of the specially formed Peace Celebration Day Committee. They had been meeting since December to plan an enjoyable day in a week's time on the sports field alongside Thorpe Lane above the village.

'I was delayed on my way here,' he explained. There was a delightful twinkle in his brown eyes and the five men and five women gathered round the table waited expectantly for him to go on.

George tucked his handkerchief into his pocket and with a broad smile leaned back in his chair and surveyed the members of his committee. He revelled in the atmosphere of suspense a moment longer and then said, 'I have wonderful news! The timing couldn't be better if we had planned it.' His eyes flashed across them all. 'Sam Harland will be arriving home next Wednesday!'

A gasp rippled round the table. Eager glances and whispered words were quickly exchanged, by all except Mary Lawson. She felt numb, yet her heart fluttered with excitement – Sam was coming home. Why hadn't he let her know? She had had only four postcards in four years. Occasionally she had received news from his sisters but his letters home were also few and far between and they were not very forthcoming. The messages on her postcards were but a few words: 'Am well', 'Enjoying much appreciated leave.' And they always ended, 'Sincerely, Sam.' Never the one word she hoped to see, but maybe Sam was bashful at putting it on a postcard. So why hadn't he ever written a letter? But Mary clung to the memory of their loving the day before he left and still saw it as a pledge for the future.

The Reverend Stone was speaking again, breaking into her thoughts. 'I've just had the news from his mother. We'll have our hero, our own VC, returning home on the very day of our peace celebrations! What could be more fitting? And to think we all thought he was still in France, when this past week he's been in this country. I think this calls for some new ideas for our celebrations.'

Chattering broke out among the committee and eyes turned on Mary.

'It'll be a great day for thee,' someone said, and heads nodded in agreement.

'Aye, absence makes the heart grow fonder, lass.'

Mary blushed and smiled wanly at the eyes staring at her. She was relieved when the Reverend George tapped the table sharply. 'I know this is exciting news, but please let us have ideas through the chair.'

The butcher, the baker, the schoolteacher, the fisherman, the grocer, the stationmaster, the housewife, the unattached, all went quiet and looked sheepish.

'Reverend,' said a tiny voice. All eyes turned on the diminutive figure of the middle-aged spinster who nervously played with her fingers on the table. 'Oh.' She shot a nervous glance round the gathering and went quiet.

'Well, Miss Kemp?' The minister encouraged her to go on.

'I . . . I . . . think maybe we should meet him at the station.'

'Splendid idea!' George beamed. He looked round his committee for their approval.

There was a nodding of heads and little grunts of agreement.

'We're having the band, so let's have it at the station.' The suggestion boomed from Mr Potter, whose hands rested comfortably on his stomach.

'Aye, good idea, Bert,' agreed the baker, whose complexion always seemed to indicate he had just emerged from the hot bakehouse. 'They can play "Hail, the Conquering Hero".'

'There'll be crowds there when they know Sam's arriving,' added Bert. 'We can all march to the sports field in procession.'

'Who'll make the speech on his arrival?' asked one of the housewives.

'Well,' said the Reverend Stone, 'as he's arriving by train and that station is the domain of Mr Newton, I suppose he, as the official of that little bit of territory, should do the honours.'

Will Newton cleared his throat. 'You're right, it is my little kingdom and nothing should go on there without my full approval as I see the railway authorities would allow. Dignitaries arriving at the big stations are always met by the stationmaster even if he is not in the official party, so I suppose I should do it. I'll say a few words, if you want me to, but if you'd rather Lord Derwent—'

'Not possible,' George cut in. 'Lord Derwent has another engagement in the morning and will arrive just a few minutes before two to open the official celebrations. I understand from Mrs Harland that Sam will be arriving on the one-thirty.'

'Couldn't be better,' chuckled Bert Potter. 'Will to greet Sam back on home soil, then along to the sports field for Lord Derwent's official welcome and the opening of the celebrations.'

All murmured their approval, the committee got down to making the final arrangements, checking and rechecking that everyone had done what they had promised and that everything was under way to make the celebration something special, a day to be recalled by the folk of Robin Hood's Bay – the day Sam Harland, VC, arrived home.

Mary left the Congregational Hall without lingering. She had gone through the meeting in a daze, adding a word when necessary and, when asked, making a comment on how the organisation of the refreshments was going. Her mind was constantly turning to the thought that next week Sam would be home. Soon there would be another celebration – their marriage.

Mary hugged herself with glee as she hurried to her brother's cottage in Sunny Place. Jonas had stayed fishing with his father until he was called up. He had left to join a minesweeper with a promise that he would be back to take up the family trade of inshore fishing, even though they were now the only ones trying to earn a living from it out of Robin Hood's Bay. He had married his Sarah before he had left. John had been born in 1917, James the following year, and, after Jonas's early release from the navy because of an injury to his left arm, Sarah was pregnant again.

Mary knocked on the door of the cottage, opened it and walked in. She knew she was always welcome. She liked Sarah and adored the two babies, looking forward to the time when she would have Sam's children. She loved helping Sarah with them, saying laughingly that it was good practice for the future.

The cottage was sparsely furnished but comfortable and bore the marks of a feminine hand, making it attractive.

Mary admired Sarah for being able to keep it so spotless with two babies to look after. The table in the centre of the room was covered with a pure white tablecloth and two places were set neatly for tea. Nothing rough and ready for Sarah. She had been brought up 'proper' and 'proper' she would remain.

'Hello, Mary.' Sarah, teapot in hand, greeted her with a smile.

'Thee's timed it right, lass.' Jonas grinned.

'Get another cup and saucer and plate, Jonas,' said Sarah as she went to the kettle on the reckon. Careful to keep the scalding water away from the two babies in their home-made cradles beside the fire, she filled the teapot.

Mary went to the cradles. James was asleep but John was awake. He gurgled when she tickled him and his smile responded broadly to the extra joy on her face.

'Something seems to have pleased thee, lass,' her brother commented as he laid a place for her at the table.

'Aye. Just heard Sam's arriving home next week, the day of the celebrations.'

'What?' Jonas gasped.

Sarah paused in pouring the tea and looked questioningly at her sister-in-law as if seeking further confirmation.

'The Reverend Stone told us at our committee meeting for the peace celebrations,' explained Mary.

'That's great news!' Jonas exclaimed. 'It'll be good to have Sam back – but will he stay? He's no boat to come to.'

'I'll see that he does,' said Mary thoughtfully.

'Wedding bells soon?' said Sarah, continuing to pour the tea.

Mary blushed. 'Maybe,' she said quietly.

'Sam can't complain,' Jonas commented. 'Thee's waited in spite of his not writing.'

'I've had postcards,' she pointed out as she sat down at the table.

'Four,' said Jonas, a touch of disgust in his voice.

'Thee did little better,' said Sarah, glancing at her husband as she handed a plate of ham sandwiches to Mary.

'Well, I was married,' Jonas said with a grin. 'He was supposed to be still courting. Besides, I came home on leave – little James there can bear witness to that.'

'Jonas!' Embarrassed by his flippancy, Sarah frowned at her husband. 'Another thing, when Sam gets home—'

'There'll be a lot of celebrating for us to do,' Jonas broke in.

'Now don't thee be letting Sam Harland lead thee on. Don't be coming home the worse for drink.'

'I won't, my love.' He glanced at his sister. 'Mary's more likely to take up his time.'

Will Newton had got out his best uniform for the occasion. He adjusted it and looked at his watch for the umpteenth time as he paced the platform. His familiar pipe had been put aside, he could not be seen smoking before the great event. And there were plenty to see him if he did. Almost all the village had gathered at the station.

Anticipating such a crowd, Will had made the necessary preparations. A small area of the platform had been roped off and he made sure that Sam's carriage would stop at that spot by having a word with the engine driver who he knew would be on duty. Before leaving Scarborough, he would discreetly ascertain which coach Sam was in and stop at the appointed position. The band had been allocated a place on the platform and were already tuned up, determined to play their best for the returning hero. For the rest it was a free-for-all, but Will had made sure that Sam's family, Mary Lawson and her brother Jonas had front positions.

The weather could not have been better. The spring day was warm, the sky was blue and the world was at peace.

The platform was crowded. People swarmed around the entrance to the station and spilled along the road. The buzz of conversation filled the air but was suddenly hushed by the train's whistle. People jostled for a better position. Those on the platform looked in the direction from which the train would come. Smoke rose skywards to be left in a long trail. The clatter of the wheels grew louder. Another whistle. The train began to slow.

The conductor cast his eyes over his band, making sure that everyone was ready. He wanted no one coming in a fraction of a beat after the others. He half turned to watch the train and judge the right moment. As the engine reached the end of the platform, the conductor turned to face his men. His baton moved and the band struck up together with all the vim and vigour they could muster.

The train slowed. Steam hissed. Against the clanking and rumbling, the band, determined to be heard and not miss these moments of glory, played even more loudly.

A hush of anticipation had descended on the crowd. Mary's heart was aflutter. Realising she was trembling with excitement, she tried to control it but then gave up. Calm would come when she felt Sam's arms around her. It would be hard to wait until he had greeted his family.

She ran her hands nervously down her calf-length chemise dress, which she had made herself for Sam's homecoming. Knowing he liked yellow, she had chosen that colour as the background to the attractive green leaf motifs patterning the dress from the waist down. The wide, white collar supported a large yellow bow at the throat, matching the yellow court shoes she was wearing for the first time. She had taken particular care over her hair, now bobbed in the new style of the modern young woman. Sam couldn't help noticing her.

A carriage window opened and a head appeared. Sam Harland! A cheer split the air. His surprise disappeared into a broad smile. The train stopped. Judging the moment to perfection, the conductor stopped the music in mid-flow. They would take up again when Will Newton had made his speech.

Sam ducked back in and at the same time let the carriage door swing open. He stood there, wreathed in a wide grin. Mary's heart missed a beat. He was more handsome than ever, taller, a fine figure in his uniform, sergeant's stripes on his arms and ribbons on his chest, including the highest honour he could be given. He looked well. Mary had half expected him to look harrowed after his experiences but she might have known Sam Harland would not. His face was brown, his thick dark hair had an extra wave to it, but it was his eyes that held her. They sparkled even more than she remembered; there was a new joy in them. Was it just that he was revelling in this homecoming, in the rapturous welcome of so many people, or was there something else? Whatever it was did not matter – she would be proud to walk beside this man as Mrs Harland.

He was smiling and waving. She wanted to rush up to him and hug him and thank God for his safe deliverance from the bloody battlefields of Europe.

'Stay where you are, Sam.' Will Newton's quiet word was presented firmly and Sam stayed put. Will turned and held up his hands. Quietness spread through the crowd. Will half turned so that he could direct his words to Sam.

'Sergeant Sam Harland, on behalf of all your friends in Robin Hood's Bay, may I welcome you home? We thank God that you have returned to us safe and sound. We are all proud of the heroic deed which earned you the Victoria Cross.' A cheer rang out. 'The timing of your arrival couldn't have been better, for we have been planning peace celebrations in the sports field for this very day. Welcome home, Sam, we are all proud of you.' He held out his hand and took Sam's in a firm grip.

Cheering broke out again. Sam held up his hands for silence. Still standing in the carriage door, he said, 'Thank you all for your welcome. I don't deserve it.'

'Thee does!' 'Don't be modest!' 'You showed 'em, Sam!' Shouts from the crowd subsided only when Sam raised his hands again.

'No, I don't,' he went on. 'I was lucky, I survived. There were a lot who didn't and many of them deserved the award I was given, but no one will ever know the deeds they did before they died.' He paused. 'But enough of the sombre note. You've planned to celebrate the peace and nothing should mar that. So let's away and celebrate. But before we do –' he raised his voice to still the cheer that started among the crowd – 'but before we do, I want you all to –' he half turned into the carriage and held out his hand – 'meet my wife, Colette!'

He stepped out of the carriage, helping her to the door. As she stopped, a great cheer rose from the crowd. She paused with a shy smile at the reception she was receiving, and glanced at Sam. He gave a wink, an action which she had found reassuring since they married three months ago. She had been apprehensive about coming to England, where she knew she would be a foreigner in a small, close-knit community. She realised that she would face the jealousy of local girls who must have had their eyes on the handsome Sam, but with him beside her she was prepared to face anything.

Mary was numb. This couldn't be true. This couldn't be happening. She was oblivious to the noise around her. Her face had drained of all its colour as she stared unbelievingly at the petite figure who stood beside the man she had expected to marry. Confused as her tumbling thoughts were, she somehow saw Colette clearly, taking in every detail. Large, bright eyes with long lashes were set in a gentle face with a petite, perfectly shaped nose and bowed lips. They were red, and rouge had been rubbed on both cheeks complementing a touch of make-up around the eyes. Mary did not hear the under-the-breath comments which came from women close by. Colette's fair, bobbed hair had a natural-looking wave and seemed to tumble in attractive disarray around her ears. Her red chemise dress was simply cut with a lightly marked waistline. Instead of the usual round neck, hers came to a V with a small lace collar. The dress came to the lower half of her calves and revealed slim ankles. Her high-heeled, brightly polished

42

shoes accentuated what Mary thought must be shapely legs. No wonder Sam had fallen for her. But he should have been hers – hadn't she given herself to him on the cliffs the day before he left?

The thought suddenly burst in her mind and she shuddered. Jonas glanced at her. Alarm struck him when he saw her face. 'Thee all right, lass?' he asked. He saw her staring straight at Sam, who was now being greeted by his family. There was loathing in her eyes. Jonas recalled his sister's expectations when Sam returned and he realised the shock of the announcement had more than upset her.

'He should be mine!' she hissed. 'What happened on the cliffs made him mine!'

Jonas caught the words as they strangled in her throat. He stared unbelievingly at her. The implication of her words hit him hard. Not his little sister . . . ? She wouldn't! But from the look on her face he knew she had and she had been naive enough to think Sam would take it as a sign that they should marry. And Sam had taken advantage of her. Sam, his best pal! A chill came across Jonas. Sam had come back a married man and it had devastated his sister.

The crowds around the station were still cheering. The band was getting ready for the parade to the sports field. Sam and Colette were being fussed over by his relatives. Jonas turned to say something to Mary, but she had gone. Alarmed, he looked round for her but could not see her in the mass of people. His gaze came back to Sam and at that moment Sam spotted him.

'Jonas, my old pal!' Beaming, Sam held out his hand.

Jonas ignored it. His clenched fist took Sam clean on

the jaw. Stopped in full step, Sam staggered. 'You bastard!' Jonas snarled and hit him again. Sam fell heavily to the ground.

A startled hush came to the nearby crowd. Everyone stared in amazement. Colette's cry split the air and she rushed forward to her husband, falling to her knees beside him. 'Sam, Sam!' she cried.

Although dazed by the blows and confused by Jonas's action, Sam tried to muster a smile to reassure her that he was all right.

With anger blazing in her eyes, Colette looked up for the man who had spoiled Sam's homecoming, but he had gone.

Jonas, his heart pounding with anxiety, was already pushing his way through the crowd, looking for Mary.

Mary squirmed her way through the press of people, pushing and shoving if her way was blocked. She had to get away from there as quickly as possible. The horror of Sam's homecoming would haunt her for ever. He was mine! Mine! Mine! The words kept screaming in her mind. She was unaware of the hush which had descended on the crowd and of the murmur as the news that Jonas Lawson had hit Sam spread like fire. She did not notice the glances cast at her as she struggled to the edge of the crowd.

Then she was free, running away from the people, away from the station, away from the destroyer of her life. Her world was shattered, never to be put together again. In such a small community she would be pointed at as the girl whose dreams were false, who thought she would be Mrs Sam Harland but never made it. There would be those who would laugh at her. Even if it was behind her back she would know, for there were old rivals who would make sure she did. She would be pointed at, scorned and teased. The horror of what life would be like began to overpower her mind. She couldn't face it. She couldn't bear to be around with Sam living in Robin Hood's Bay. With the thought of him came the pain of rejection. It hit like the barb of a fish hook, tearing at her very being.

Tears misted her eyes. She did not know where she ran, only turning along this street or that alley whenever someone came in sight. She did not want to meet anyone, and was thankful that most people were at the station or the sports field on this day of celebration.

Mary found herself on the beach. Her steps did not slow, though the soft sand dragged at her. She moved to firmer ground nearer the sea. Waves rolled in, crashing on to the beach with the ferocity which matched the tumult in her mind. She went on round the bay towards the towering cliffs of Ravenscar, sensing their brooding atmosphere even in the strong sunlight. They seemed to bear down on her as if trying to press her into the ground to relieve her of any more pain. Then the sea was joining in, its pounding on the beach constantly reminding her that it could offer escape.

She stopped and turned to face the waves. They ran in strongly, broke with a roar and sent water hissing across the sand around her feet. They offered solace from a threatening world, a world in which she had no part.

Slowly she walked into the sea.

* * *

45

Jonas did not hear his name running through the crowd like the breeze ruffling the corn. It spread outwards from those who had been close to the incident until it reached the perimeter of the gathering. By then all sorts of rumours had linked themselves to his name as questions were asked and the answers grew in their telling.

Jonas hurried, pushing and shoving to get beyond the crowd, with the hope of seeing his sister. His rough passage brought looks of annoyance and sharp words but he ignored them in the urgency of his search.

He tried to recall what she was wearing but could not. He cursed himself for not being more observant. His eyes, filled with disquiet, combed the throng which pressed around him but did not catch even a glimpse of Mary. As he cleared the edge of the crowd, he turned this way and that, but she had vanished. She had been too quick. Or was she still among the press of people? He swung round but his search was in vain. She must have gone. Where? Home?

He ran towards the village, his pace quickening when he reached the slope. His eyes were everywhere but he saw no sign of her. He burst into his mother's house. 'Mary! Mary!' The words died without an answer. He took the stairs two at a time to Mary's room but she was not there. He was thankful that his mother and father had gone straight to the sports field for the celebrations. They had been spared Mary's anguish. Maybe he could reason with her so that the impact of the news on their parents would be lessened.

He tore from the house and raced to Sunny Place. His sudden intrusion into the peaceful atmosphere startled

Sarah who was getting the children ready to go to the sports field. Jonas's heart sank. Mary was not there.

'Have thee seen Mary?' he cried.

Sarah was shocked by the tone of his voice and the anguish on his face.

'No, I thought she was with you at the station,' she replied, pausing as she was helping John into his jersey. 'What's wrong?'

'She ran off when Sam arrived with his wife!' His statement hung in the air.

'What? Sam married?' Sarah knew that Mary had expected to marry him on his return. She must be devastated.

'Aye. Announced it after Will Newton's speech of welcome, then turned round and helped her from the carriage. Pretty thing, French. Mary was flabbergasted. Sam spotted us. Mary ran. I hit him.'

'Jonas!' Sarah was aghast, but she could understand her husband's reaction for she knew how close he and his sister were. Hurt one and you hurt the other.

'I'm not sorry. Bastard deserved it, running out on Mary like that with never a word of explanation before his arrival. He must have known it would be a terrible shock to her. I must find her. She mustn't be alone at a time like this.'

'I'd help, love, but . . .'

'No, thee's got the bairns. Thee go to the sports field. I'll find her.' He hurried from the house.

Running through the streets, he visited the likely places but found no trace of her. With each failure his anxiety mounted. He could easily miss her in the warren of streets

47

which ran up and down and across the cliff face. The cliffs? Could she have gone there? The beach? Would she try to come to terms with the situation there? He bit his lip in consideration. Which should it be? He was nearer the beach and he would be able to view its full sweep from Wayfoot.

He raced down New Road, past Tyson's Steps, his stride lengthening with the slope. His feet barely touched the ground as he tore across the open space known as the Dock and down on to Wayfoot and the scaur-marked beach. Panting hard, he pulled up and cast his eyes along the expanse, willing Mary to be there.

Relief flooded over him when he spotted a figure far round the bay. Mary! It must be. Some of the tension gripping him drained away as he started out quickly after her. His mind tried hard to find the right approach. He must ease the pain, make her see that losing Sam was not the end of the world. He quickened his pace as much as he could on the seaweed-covered scaurs, eager to be on the sand where he would have a surer footing.

He had made three paces on the better ground when he stopped. His eyes widened in horror. 'Mary!' His cry rent the air. She made no sign of hearing. 'Mary!' He started to run, his legs driven by the need to reach her, to stop her walking into the sea.

'Mary!' His shouts grew in desperation as he realised that she was going deeper and deeper. 'Don't! He's not worth it!' She waded further. Soon she would be beyond her depth. 'Don't, Mary! This is Jonas. Thee's got us!'

She disappeared. Jonas split the air with a cry of horror. The sand slid beneath the urgent drive of his legs. The waves raised her up. He saw her, he cried out her name. For one moment he thought she raised her hand, but he was wrong. She disappeared again.

As he ran the final yards towards the spot where he had seen her enter the water, he threw off his jacket. He dashed into the sea, his powerful body charging against the waves. He could not see her but he struck out, tireless in his search.

How long it was before he found her he never knew, but she was dead when his arms closed round her.

With his heart and mind torn by anguish, he swam with her to the shore. As his feet touched the sand, he stumbled and fell to his knees. His chest heaved as he gulped air into his lungs. Waves broke around him and tried to drag his sister from him but he held on. The sea had taken her once, it would not do so again. He struggled to his feet and dragged her further up the beach until the pull of the sea lessened and he was able to scoop her into his arms.

He stood there, the water swirling around his feet, and looked down at the pale features which had held such a zest for life and such hopes for the future. Mary's head lolled back. Water ran from her lank hair and her arms hung lifeless as Jonas held her close.

Silent tears streamed down his cheeks, mingling with the water which ran from his hair. He raised his eyes to the sky. It was deep blue and tranquil. Death should not mar such a day. The sound of distant music and revelry drifted from the cliffs above the village. It bore into Jonas, reminding him of Sam and the reason he was standing here holding his beloved sister.

Jonas screwed up his eyes, tightened his lips and shook his head as if he could get rid of the horror, but Mary still lay silently in his arms. A cry from deep in the soul rent the air and the bitterness was born that was to mark his life.

Chapter Three

1936

Jean Lawson's feet barely touched the ground as she raced home from school. Nothing could mar the excitement which had gripped her when her best friend, Gabrielle Harland, had invited her to a party for her fifteenth birthday.

Her father must let her go. He really must. Surely he would retract his antagonism towards the Harlands just this once. Growing older, Jean had begun to wonder about the reasons for her father's hostility. He had forbidden his children to have anything to do with the Harland children but they had taken little notice of his ban; after all, they met at school, they played on the beach together and walked on the cliffs, away from their father's condemning eye.

Jean and Gabrielle had both been born the same year, 1921. There had been rejoicing in both families at the birth of a daughter. Jonas and Sarah had welcomed Jean as sister to John, James and Martin, and Sam and Colette had a sister for Colin. But no congratulations passed between the two men.

Jonas was unmoving in his view that Sam was really a murderer. If he had struck with his own hands he could not more surely have killed Mary than the way he drove her into the sea. Jonas would not accept Sam's word that there never had been an agreement between himself and Mary. Sam denied that her expectations were well founded, even when Jonas confronted him with the knowledge of what happened on the cliffs the day before he left for the army. 'Your sister was more than willing; in fact, she begged for it.' These words stunned Jonas, who tried to ram them back down Sam's throat with a blow which put him in hospital with a broken jaw.

From that moment on it had been silent enmity, especially from Jonas, whose bitterness deepened. He lost friends through it, for Sam was the local hero and in many eyes could do no wrong. They were pleased when he prospered after using the mechanical knowledge gained in the army to set up a garage business. 'The motorcar's a coming thing, most folks will own one one day. There'll be cars to sell, they'll need petrol to run on and they'll need repairing,' he had said and set about making his prophecy work for his benefit. So successful had he become that he had built himself a big house on top of the cliffs overlooking the village with fine views across the sea. The sea was still very much at his heart for he had been born to it and a man such as he would never eliminate it from his blood. He still had his father's coble, fixed it up with an engine and loved to sail in the bay, accompanied by his family or friends or alone in a reflective mood.

From his garden he would watch Jonas and his three sons put out in their coble to fish, and he wished they were still friends so that he could join them.

Sam's house on the cliffs seemed to haunt Jonas. Wherever he was in the bay, he could see it. Not only was it a reminder of what had happened to Mary but of the man who had driven her to her doom, a man who had made a success of his life, who had a happy marriage which should have been Mary's. It also recalled Sam's warning before the war that inshore fishing from Baytown was finished. Jonas wasn't going to agree. He held to tradition, making only one concession to progress. At John's constant badgering he had finally agreed, just a couple of months ago, to fit an engine to his coble, though he 'would never understand mechanical goings-on'. Start it up, let it run, stop it, was all he chose to know. He could still catch fish but, whereas once the catch would be taken by train into Whitby and sold there, now the trawlers had killed that trade, and Jonas could sell his fish only locally. It brought him a bare living, sufficient to keep his family comfortable, but without the luxuries there were in the house on the cliffs. Though he sometimes envied Sam's success, he drew comfort from the fact that his independence was something special, born in the sea. He would always have it, nature would see to that, for there would always be fish to catch and the sea to sail, whereas Sam's depended on mechanical things without deep roots.

Both men were content but occasionally, when they caught sight of each other, they wished for the far-off days when they were inseparable.

Sam saw a possibility to break down the barrier

between them through their children, especially when they started to go to school, where the Harlands and the Lawsons would have to mix. He viewed with some pleasure from a distance the friendship which grew up between Gabrielle and Jean. But inevitably one day he was faced with the question, 'Jean says her father tells her to get other friends, not me. Why?'

His anger roused, Sam wanted to confront Jonas and tell him to keep his bitterness to himself and not let it affect the lives of their children. But Colette, knowing the outcome might be violence, prevailed upon him to do nothing, saying that Jonas could not keep his eye on the children all the time, that they would see each other at school and could do so at other times unbeknown to him. There was no need for their friendship to be marred by his stubbornness.

So today Jean hoped her father might relax his opposition just a little. Maybe her mother could persuade him. Sarah was much more tolerant than her husband. Though outwardly she supported him as he expected she would, she was careful to see that her children were not affected. She wanted nothing to mar their lives. Questions had been asked but Jonas always said it was none of their business, they should just do as they were told and keep away from the Harland children. Sarah agreed with him but out of his hearing told her children she saw no reason for them not to be friendly with Gabrielle and her brother Colin as long as Jonas did not know.

With her mind buoyed by the invitation, Jean was oblivious to the subtle change in the weather which brought with it a strengthening wind.

'Mum! Mum!' Jean cried as she burst into the cottage, where her mother was preparing a meal for her husband and sons when they returned from the fishing. A pan of stew was plopping appetisingly on the fire. Potatoes were cooking in the oven and a teapot warmed on the hearth. 'Gabrielle's asked me to her birthday party a week on Saturday. Can I go?' Her eyes were bright with anticipation. 'Oh, say I can. Please!'

Sarah laughed at her daughter's enthusiasm as she danced around the kitchen, unable to keep still. She recalled the excitement she had always felt whenever she was asked to a party. She knew what going would mean to her.

'Calm down, Jean, calm down. Thee knows we'll have to see what your father says.'

Jean stopped her rush. She frowned as childish worry crossed her face. 'Must he know, Mum?' she pleaded, fearing his refusal.

'He'd see thee all dressed up and want to know why,' Sarah pointed out.

'Can't we say I'm going somewhere else?' Jean suggested, seeing the delight of sharing Gabrielle's birthday vanishing.

'Maybe we're deceiving your father about being friendly with Gabrielle, but I'll have no downright lies about where thee's going.' From the touch of sternness in her mother's voice, Jean knew it was no use arguing.

She pouted. 'I don't see why Dad being unfriendly with Mr Harland should affect us.'

Sarah looked sympathetically at her daughter. Maybe now was the time to tell her. She was growing quickly, both physically and psychologically, though childish traits were sometimes still evident. She was old enough to know and understand what caused her father's attitude to the Harlands.

The wind howled in the chimney. Sarah glanced at the fire, then turned to her daughter.

'Sit down, Jean. I think it's time thee knew about something that happened before thee was born.'

The serious expression on her mother's face held Jean's attention. She sat down on a wooden chair beside the table. The familiar kitchen surroundings faded in the knowledge that she was about to hear something momentous, something that had influenced her father's outlook. As her mother started to speak, she was aware of nothing but her words.

'Your father and Mr Harland were once great friends, before the Great War. A group of us went about together. Your aunt Mary –' she glanced at the sepia photograph which stood on the sideboard – 'was smitten with Mr Harland . . .'

Sarah told Jean the whole story of the day of the drowning.

A charged silence hung in the kitchen, broken only when the wind rattled the windows.

'And Dad blamed Mr Harland?' said Jean in a hoarse whisper.

Sarah nodded. 'Aye.'

'Was he to blame?' asked Jean.

'Who knows?' Sarah sighed. 'He says he had never promised to marry Aunt Mary, that she had only assumed they would. There had been nothing binding about their friendship.'

'Do you think he was telling the truth?'

Sarah shrugged her shoulders. 'Happen he was. I think we'd have known if he had proposed. I'm sure there would have been an announcement, certainly from your aunt. But you never know, maybe they wanted to keep it quiet until after the war, maybe they had an understanding. At least your father thinks so. He says if there hadn't been, your aunt wouldn't have held such hopes.'

'And Dad's held that grudge all these years?'

'Aye.' Sarah nodded her head sadly. 'It's been hard at times to see the bitterness eating into him, especially when they were such good pals. And that's why he says you shouldn't mix with Gabrielle and Colin.'

'But you think we may?' Jean's eyes were hopeful.

'I see no harm in it, never have, but there are times when it's hard for a wife to go against her husband. I hope you understand that.'

'Yes, Mum, I do. Like now, if Dad says I can't go to the party.'

Sarah gave a wan smile. She nodded. 'But I'll do my best to persuade him.'

'Thanks, Mum.' She looked appreciatively at the mother she loved, who, through this shared confidence, now seemed much closer. Anguish momentarily touched her face. 'Oh, he's just got to let me go! He must!'

Sam Harland, armed with binoculars, walked briskly to the end of his long garden where he had constructed a comfortable shelter from which he could look out to sea. The wind was freshening from the northeast. He breathed in the crisp air deeply and enjoyed the cool sharpness in

57

his lungs. It gave him a sense of well-being, of exhilaration and pleasure that he still had an affinity with the sea even though he was not deriving a living from it.

He sat down on the wooden seat behind an eight-foot stone wall built partly into the slope of the land. He had constructed a projecting roof to give extra protection and had plans to erect a glass front so that he could use it in all weathers. Now he pulled his woollen thigh-length jacket more tightly around him and raised his binoculars to his eyes.

He swept his vision across the bay to focus on the coble lying at sea beyond the protective cover of the cliffs. He recognised it immediately as Jonas's.

'Thee's further out today,' Sam commented to himself.

As he watched Jonas and his three sons, he was mindful of the days before the war when he had fished with his father and brother. Jonas, cradling the tiller boom under his right arm, ever ready to exert the right pressure, looked a commanding figure and Sam knew he would be watchful and alert, ready to direct and advise his crew. John at nineteen had the mechanical bent of mind which his father lacked but even to him the workings of the engine were new. Sam saw him at the engine, hand on throttle, ready to control the power at a touch. James at eighteen had inherited his father's skills and Sam watched with fascination through his binoculars as the young man threw the coils of line, carrying the deadly hooks, with unerring accuracy into the sea. His actions were laced with a poetic motion matched to the undulations of the coble so that no hook was fouled. Sam watched until all the line was out and then, turning his gaze on seventeen-year-old Martin, recalled the days when he, too, as the youngest member of a crew, was there to watch and learn and help when the lines were hauled in.

Sam sighed with a touch of envy. They had been good days. Jonas's independence founded on the sea was something special. 'Aye, it is,' he muttered to himself, 'but it's now mighty hard work for little return. I told thee before the war what it would be like. Thee should have come into the garage business with me when I offered thee a partnership.' There was regret in Sam's voice that Jonas had turned down the olive branch.

He lowered his binoculars and sat back, his eyes watching the running sea sending its waves in white-topped rows to break on the beach and run on until, their energy spent, they slid back to be united with the oncoming water. It was a sight which always pleased him and from which he drew an unfathomable comfort.

He sat entranced by the sea until a sudden buffeting from the wind roused him. He sat up and blinked. The sea was running stronger. The waves had grown and their crests, torn by the wind, sent spray in a thin cloud across the bay. Sam frowned. Any increase in strength could be a matter of concern when coming ashore, for the menacing scaurs, which could tear the bottom from a boat, needed careful watching even in the calmest of weather. Avoiding them could be tricky, with rough seas breaking across them and at times obscuring the guide posts to the landing at Wayfoot.

Sam raised his binoculars. Jonas was still there. They were starting to haul in the lines. He stood up and turned his binoculars to the horizon as far towards the northeast as he could before the towering rise of Ness Point obscured his view. But he saw enough to send a chill to his bones.

The sky was dark with cloud. Grey-bellied outriders were being driven by the wind, portents of what was to come. The metal-grey sea beneath them was heaving as if gathering strength for some momentous upheaval. He swung his binoculars back across the bay. The waves were bigger, pounding the coast with vicious strength. The bay would take a beating when the storm hit. No boat should be on the water then.

Sam turned his gaze to the coble. They had stopped hauling. Jonas's place at the tiller had been taken by young Martin. Something was wrong. The other three members of the family were gathered round the engine. He could see them gesticulating and he interpreted annoyance and concern in their movements. Sam stiffened. The boat was drifting! Martin was leaning heavily on the tiller, trying to keep the bow into the waves. He saw Jonas hurry to relieve him, leaving his other sons bent over the engine. If that engine was not going to start before the storm hit, they were in serious trouble.

Sam dropped his binoculars and started to run to the village. His feet flew as he tore down the Bank, along Bridge End and the length of New Road to the open space of the Dock. The alarm in his race and his shouts had attracted attention so that by the time he reached the old lifeboat station he had recruited help from Nathan, Lance, Len and Keith, along with many hands to help launch his boat. Word had spread quickly that Jonas Lawson and his boys were in danger.

The crowd hung back, buzzing with concerned excitement, as Sam unlocked the doors of the building which he had bought for his own use when the lifeboat station had been decommissioned in 1931. Eager hands helped to pull the doors open and then push the coble out and across the Dock and down Wayfoot to the sea. Sam and his willing four-man crew were already aboard by the time the boat was released to the sea.

In a matter of seconds Sam had the engine running and Nathan was at the tiller, guiding the vessel between the markers which indicated the safe route from the shore. Stray either way and the sharp scaurs could rip the boat. The bow met the first wave and cleaved through it with the engine driving the boat on. They slid into the trough, climbed and sent spray flying around them as they crested the next rise.

Sam cast his eyes to the northeast. The sky was darkening. Clouds, juggled by the wind, matched the heavings of the sea as if both were determined to obliterate everything and everyone in their path.

Each time they crested a wave, Sam, in the bow, shielded his eyes against the wind and spray, trying to catch a glimpse of Jonas's coble. Lance and Len braced their legs to the plunge and sway of the boat, Len at the engine, Lance on the port side, eyes narrowed in search, while Keith stood close to Nathan, ready to add pressure on the tiller when necessary.

The wind strengthened, piling more water into the oncoming waves. The first of these giants struck, and the boat shuddered. For one moment the engine seemed to falter, but Len's experienced, delicate touch on the throttle brought the right amount of extra power to keep the vessel moving as Nathan made a slight adjustment to bring the bow head on to the next roller. They got through it and the next, and were then beyond the power of the breakers and able to ride the strengthening rises with more assurance.

'There!' Lance's shout split the shrieking wind.

Sam spun round to see his arm pointing stiffly to approximately two points on the port bow. He was beside him in a moment, his eyes piercing the gloom which obscured Jonas from view. The boat climbed from a trough and topped the wave.

'Got her!' Sam yelled as he caught a glimpse of Jonas's coble. 'Bring her round, Nathan! Bring her round!'

He knew he need give no more instructions to him. They had sailed together many a time and Sam had quickly realised he was an expert.

Nathan leaned on the tiller. The boat came round. He watched the huge undulations moving on with unrelenting motion. He rode the heights and plunged into the troughs with expertise, all the while watching for Sam's signals, which came with each glimpse of Jonas's coble, still at the mercy of the waves and currents, drifting helplessly with only Jonas at the tiller to save it from being swamped.

Gradually the distance between the two boats narrowed. Sam eyed the approaching storm. They wouldn't have long.

He stiffened. James was still hauling in the lines, plucking fish from the hooks. 'Why the hell hasn't he cut the lines?' Even as he posed the question, he knew the answer lay in Jonas's stubbornness.

Sam braced himself, cupped his hands around his mouth

and with Jonas's boat now continuously in sight yelled, 'Ahoy, Jonas! Ahoy, there!'

Jonas turned his head. Sam sensed him stiffen. He knew what he would be thinking – What the hell's this bastard doing here? He heard Jonas shout, 'John, get that bloody engine started,' and John's reply, 'Can't, Dad. Don't know what's wrong.' Sam sensed the frustration and helplessness in the young man's voice.

Sam signalled Nathan to close the gap between the boats.

Jonas saw the alteration of movement. 'Stand off!' he yelled.

'Coming aboard,' shouted Sam.

'Like hell thee's not,' bellowed Jonas, anger and rage in his voice.

'I am! Thee needs me.' He signalled Nathan to take the boat nearer.

Nathan nodded to Keith, who came beside him, ready to lend a steadying hand when the two vessels were close enough for Sam to jump between them. Skilfully he eased his boat closer, riding the waves with certainty, defying their attempts to nullify his manoeuvres.

Jonas, though he abhorred taking help from Sam, knew that John needed him and if the engine could be put right, Sam Harland could do it. His reputation with engines was widely known.

Sam moved to the starboard gunwale. The boats were close. He glanced at Nathan and with a downward sweep of his hand signalled that he would try to jump as they reached the bottom of the next trough.

Nathan nodded his understanding. Keith also saw the

signal and knew that Nathan would require him to throw his weight on the tiller if the boats struck too hard.

Jonas recognised Sam's intention and subdued his hostility to concentrate on his skill as a sailor.

The boats rode the crest of the huge rise side by side. They slid over the top and plunged down, faster and faster until it seemed they must plunge into the depths of the sea. They touched, the men at the tillers guiding the movement. They reached the bottom together and, in that moment of hesitancy before climbing the next wall of water, Sam jumped. He seemed to hang in the air. The boats moved apart. Sam's feet hit the bottom of Jonas's boat. He rocked, doubled himself, his arm flailing to keep his balance. Then he straightened with a grin. He did not look at Jonas but in a couple of strides was beside John.

He gave the young man a slap on the shoulder and accompanied his 'Let's have a look, lad' with a wink of assurance.

The moment Sam was safely aboard the other vessel, Nathan and Keith leaned on the tiller and, with Len opening the throttle, the gap between the boats widened to a safe distance.

They rode the waves in unison while Sam cast his eyes quickly over the offending engine.

'Spanner!' he called.

John thrust one into his hand. With a few quick movements he had loosened a pipe and drained the petrol. He tightened the nuts to rejoin the pipes.

'Petrol!'

In an instant John passed him the spare can carried for emergencies.

Sam poured the petrol into the tank.

'Try it!'

The engine spluttered and broke into a steady hum. Sam grinned at the relief which came over John's face.

'Water in the petrol,' Sam informed him as he glanced in Jonas's direction. There was no acknowledgement. Jonas's face remained impassive. Sam waved to Nathan and the boat headed off towards the shore.

James was still hauling in the lines. The catch looked good. He worked quickly, with a dexterity which his brother Martin tried to copy. Sam eyed the coming storm. The sky was darkening rapidly as the shrieking wind battered them with ever increasing strength. The sea was taking on a solid appearance as if building an overwhelming power to destroy.

Alarm seized Sam. They must run for it now. He looked at Jonas, but Jonas was still at the tiller, guiding the coble on the best course for James to bring in the catch. His face was set in stony immobility as if he had not seen the danger or did not want to. Sam was shaken by the look of belief that he could win, that he could defeat nature. Steadying himself against the sway of the plunging boat, riding the deeping troughs and growing waves, he reached Jonas's side without mishap.

'Cut the lines and head for shore,' he yelled in Jonas's ear.

Jonas took no notice.

Anger mounted in Sam. 'Thee'll get us all killed!'

Thunder rumbled. Lightning streaked to the sea. Sam weighed up the distance. They could just make it if they ran before the storm now. As if to remind them of impending disaster, a wave broke across the boat, leaving water sloshing in the bottom.

'Shore,' Sam shouted. 'Shore!'

Jonas ignored him. His eyes glinted with defiance. His face bore the insane joy of a man possessed, a man determined to challenge the elements.

Sam's gaze swept across the Lawson boys. He saw terror in young Martin's eyes. He had stopped plucking fish from the hooks and was staring at the black clouds and heaving sea. James had slowed his hauling and cast anxious glances in the direction of his father, while John, standing by the engine, frowned in anxious disbelief that his father had not ordered them home.

The sway of the boat became wilder as the sea struck time after time. Sam, matching his steps to it, moved quickly to James's side. He snatched the knife which lay beside him and in one swift movement slashed the line, making sure that no hook snagged the side of the boat as the line was taken by the sea.

A howl of fury swept over the vessel and Sam met Jonas's glare of hate with a cold indifference. But his action had broken Jonas's defiance. No more fish could be taken. There was nothing now but to turn for the shore. That reality hit Jonas as the first, cold rain stung his face. He leaned on the tiller and brought the boat round to run before the storm.

The wind was gusting hard, driving mountains of water after them. Lightning broke the gathering darkness with vivid flashes to add its own terror to the scene. Thunder crashed, drawing ever nearer and nearer. Sam moved back beside Jonas. He might want a hand at the tiller to combat the growing strength of the sea.

The wind flecked the furrowed sea with whitecaps which trailed spray as they raced in towards the coast. Sam had lost sight of his own boat but he knew it was in Nathan's capable hands; besides, this was not the time to worry about that. He was concerned about the waves breaking across the scaurs, hoping the boat would reach them before they obscured the posts marking the safe passage. He glanced at Jonas. It would need all his skill to save the boat from being torn on the knifelike rock.

The rain came faster, casting a veil over the way ahead as if it wanted to blot out all hope of seeing the markers. But Sam realised that Jonas had already picked his spot and was holding the tiller with all his strength to keep the vessel on the right course. The boat shuddered as a wave took it from behind and hurried it forwards. John eased the throttle, then gunned it again as the boat slowed in the aftermath of the running wave. Sam admired his skill. John might not be a mechanic but he certainly had learned quickly how to use an engine in adverse circumstances.

Another wave rolled in behind them, bigger than ever. It carried them up and up, seeming to hold the coble immobile on its crest before leaving them to battle in its boiling wake.

As they came to the crest of the next one, Sam saw that Jonas still had his direction right. Then they were plunging forwards, racing between the markers and finding calmer water as they ran in through the gap between the scaurs, invisible on either side. John cut the engine. The boat's momentum took it to the beach. The bow touched the sand. By the time the boat stopped, many willing hands, oblivious of the lashing rain, were grasping the gunwales and dragging the vessel higher up the shore alongside Sam's, which, to his relief, was already beached.

Not a word was spoken as the Lawson boys, exhausted by the anxiety and pounding, were helped out of the boat. Jonas shook off all aid and stepped ashore as if he had just been out for a sail on a calm summer's day.

'Stubborn bastard,' muttered Sam to himself as Colette, Gabrielle and Colin, water streaming down their rain-coats, embraced him with heartfelt relief.

Sarah and Jean, who had been drawn by the shouts as people hurried to the beach, had waited anxiously, praying that their menfolk would be brought safely from the encroaching storm. Now Sarah, sobbing with relief, flung her arms round Jonas, ignoring the cold of his saturated clothes.

'I'm all right, lass,' he said, his voice gentle but strong with reassurance. Churned as he was about Sam's part in what had happened, he showed nothing but understanding for his wife's feelings. Holding her with one arm, he released the other to embrace his daughter, who clung to him with a fierceness which betrayed the anxiety and fear she had been feeling. He patted her comfortingly. Then he looked beyond them and saw Sam embracing Colette. His mind spun. That should have been Mary. Even after all these years, he could still visualise her and Sam together.

He pushed his wife and daughter gently to one side, and stepped towards Sam. Sarah held her breath. Could he be going to put things right between them? After all, Sam had saved not only his life but those of their sons.

Jonas's eyes narrowed as he faced Sam. The rain beat at them, streaming down their faces from hair made lank.

Lightning's vivid brightness lit up the crowd around the two old enemies. Waves crashed with a pounding roar, sending spray high, throwing a mist across the scene.

Those who expected a shake of the hand, a word of thanks, the healing of a rift, were disappointed as Jonas hissed, 'Thee cut my lines, bastard! Cut off my living!' He lashed out, hitting Sam high on the cheek. Sam staggered backwards and would have fallen, had it not been for the closeness of the crowd. Dazed by the blow and shocked by the unexpected attitude, Sam could only stare as Jonas swung round and pushed his way through the crowd.

Startled by his action, Sarah gaped after him. The comments that started through the crowd jerked her back to reality and, as much as she abhorred his action, she knew she should be by her husband's side. She looked at Colette, who had eyes only for Sam. She started towards her, wanting to apologise but, knowing it would have no effect, turned and hurried after Jonas.

Jean, devastated by what her father had done, stared at Gabrielle, who met her gaze. There was understanding between the two friends. Despite the strong feelings they must have for their own families, they must not take sides or let what had happened destroy their deep friendship. Gabrielle nodded and gave a reassuring smile. Jean half raised her hand in a signal of affection and ran after her mother. Her heart was heavy. How could she get her father's permission to go to Gabrielle's party after what had happened?

'Good heavens, man, thee's still letting Mary eat into our lives even after all this time. Sam saved—'

'Don't mention that name in this house!' Jonas glared as he swung round from the fire.

Sarah straightened, bristling with defiance. Her eyes met his unflinchingly. 'Jonas Lawson, I'll say it if I want. I've never disregarded your wishes but this time thee's gone too far. Sam saved thee and our sons today. If it hadn't been for him I'd have been a widow and Jean fatherless and I'd have had no sons to turn to.'

'We were never in danger,' hissed Jonas.

Sarah's lips tightened. 'Thee's a fool if thee believes that. There's none so blind as those that don't want to see.'

'Bloody hell, woman, he destroyed our living out there. Cut our lines. How the hell can I afford to buy more?'

Sarah's eyes darkened. 'Don't swear at me, Jonas Lawson. Don't ever do that again. Better to lose those lines than four lives. Bitterness has eaten into thee so much that there are times when I don't recognise the man I married. It's affected all our lives.'

'I've held nothing against thee nor the kids,' Jonas protested.

'I know that,' agreed Sarah, 'but thee's blind if thee don't see that it's changed people's attitudes towards us, that at times your moroseness eats into this very house. Now, Jonas, thee's going to apologise to Sam for what thee did today.'

Jonas's eyes flared with anger. 'I'll not, and don't ever think I will.'

The sharpness in her husband's voice told her it would be no use pursuing the matter.

'Very well,' Sarah conceded, 'but there's two things I'm going to insist on.' Jonas eyed her with curiosity laced

70

with suspicion. 'First, John gets Sam to teach him all he knows about engines.' Jonas opened his mouth to protest but she raised a hand to silence him. 'If John had been trained with engines there would have been no danger today. He's going to learn.'

Although he wanted to scotch the association between his son and Sam, Jonas knew Sarah had a point. It would be better if John had a greater knowledge of engines. 'He can learn –' he gave a brief reluctant nod of agreement – 'but not with Sam. He can go into Whitby.'

Sarah did not argue. She could get over that opposition without raising her husband's suspicions. She went on. 'Jean has been invited to Gabrielle Harland's birthday party.'

'She's not to go!' snapped Jonas.

'Oh yes, she is.' Sarah's voice strengthened with determination. 'The poor lass is upstairs now crying her eyes out, thinking that what thee did today has spoiled any chance of getting your approval. I'll not have her heart broken.'

Jonas's mind was confused. He loved his daughter deeply. When she was born, he had seen her as a replacement in his affections for his sister, and because of that he had been determined to protect her from the influence of the Harlands.

'I don't want that either,' he replied. 'But I don't want her getting big ideas we can't fulfil.'

'She'll not get those. Our Jean's a sensible lass.'

There was a sharp knock on the door. Jonas opened it. There was no one there. He glanced down at his feet. On the doorstep lay coiled fishing lines. He looked up. Whoever had brought the gift had vanished in the driving rain which still pounded Robin Hood's Bay though the heart of the storm had passed.

'Who is it?' Sarah came to see why Jonas still had the door open in such weather. She saw the fishing lines. 'What . . . ?'

'Sam,' Jonas hissed with venom, realising it could only have been Sam who had brought the lines.

Sarah picked them up. 'Then, be thankful,' she said. 'And get that door closed.'

'He can have them back,' snarled Jonas.

'Don't be a fool,' rapped Sarah. 'Thee's just said that we can't afford to buy more. So how's thee going to earn a living if thee doesn't accept these? He's made a peace offering thee don't deserve.'

'Showing off, more like. Showing he can afford to give them to us.'

'And thee'll accept them.' A hardness had come to Sarah's voice. 'Thee's a family to keep and I'll not be above accepting these lines. If thee doesn't, I will, and the boys can use them. And to keep things right, Jean can thank Sam when she goes to the party.'

'If she goes, she goes without my approval,' snapped Jonas. 'I'll have no more hand-outs from Sam Harland. I'll not be beholden to him after what he did to our Mary.'

Sarah's lips tightened with exasperation but she had won her point. Jonas had not laid down the law by saying Jean must not go.

Jean hurried up the hill towards the Harland house. She was trying to banish the sadness which had filled her when her father had ignored her and had not said how pretty she looked in her party dress.

She had been so proud of the calf-length dress made by her mother from material bought with money saved from the meagre housekeeping allowance, which was dictated by the success of the fishing.

'Thee looks reet bonny,' her mother had commented when she was ready.

The cream dress with tiny blue rosebuds and green leaves suited her complexion. It flared from the hugging waist and matching tie belt. The white Peter Pan collar was edged with scalloped lace, which also added to the lightness of the puff sleeves coming tight above the elbow.

She was sad he had not noticed, but she was going to the party. Excitement had filled the two girls when she had accepted. They would have such fun together.

Pushing her father's disapproval to the back of her mind, Jean let her heart sing with the knowledge that Colin, Gabrielle's brother, would also be there.

Chapter Four

1938

Jean and Gabrielle stepped out of the school door in a state of euphoria. They stopped and let their gaze travel across the scene around them, drawing it into their memories to be stored. Then they looked at each other and their faces broke into joyous grins.

'Free!' Jean whispered with an intensity of feeling that captured Gabrielle, whose eyes widened in sparkling delight as she repeated the word. They flung their arms wide, swirled round and collapsed into each other's arms, laughing.

'Hi, you two! Are you coming?'

They glanced round to see Colin waiting for them.

The two girls linked arms and strode towards him, their steps light with the new-found independence of finishing with school for good.

From the window of her study, Miss Willis, headmistress for twenty years, gave a wry smile as she watched their antics. She knew in their heart of hearts they would miss school, for theirs had been a happy time. They had thrown themselves energetically into the lessons that interested them and tried hard in those that did not. Out-of-class pursuits – netball, hockey and school plays – had equally engaged their enthusiasm. She was pleased that the two girls got on together so well, yet included other friends in their sphere. She was sorry to be losing her star pupils and had to keep a steely control of her feelings when saying goodbye to them, otherwise the dampness in her eyes would have turned to tears. But years of practice at saying goodbye to leavers had brought a determined hold on her sensitivity.

Jean and Gabrielle had held a special place in her mind. They complemented each other and with it came a firm friendship which she knew would make a lasting contribution throughout their lives. Jean was the steady one, a little reserved when out of Gabrielle's company, thorough in her work, meticulous, reliable, level-headed, dependable. Miss Willis had seen Gabrielle's happy-go-lucky nature, inherited from her father, exert a good influence on her friend when Jean's father's bitterness towards Sam Harland might have swamped her. Bright, sharp-witted, adventurous, Gabrielle was at times still a bit of a tomboy. She had her mother's freshness and gaiety with the ability to win friends easily. She and Jean had been near the top in most subjects; Gabrielle had of course excelled at French, having a French mother and visiting her relatives in Paris twice a year.

As she watched them hurry away towards Stakesby Vale, Miss Willis wondered what the future held for them. She shuddered at the thought that they might be swept into the tragedies of war. The policy of appeasement to

Germany and Italy she saw as a prelude to conflict. She hoped she was wrong but her fear deepened when Hitler engineered the Anschluss in March and followed this annexation of Austria by supporting the demands of Germans in Czechoslovakia for autonomy. She wished she had the light-heartedness of the two girls, on whom the rumbling of war had made little impression. To them a rosy future beckoned.

'Feel like us, Colin?' asked Gabrielle brightly as they joined her brother, whose broad grin gave her the answer.

'I do, judging by your actions.' He winked at Jean and flashed an extra smile at her.

Ever since the party two years ago, they had been firm friends. Jean often recalled that day, obliterating the thought of her father's opposition by remembering the happy time she had had. Colin had been particularly attentive. Previously she had been just another of Gabrielle's friends, albeit her special one. A year older, he had always adopted a superior air towards girls, but that day his views had changed. Suddenly he saw Jean in a different light and felt attracted to her. So he had not objected when his father and mother had suggested, after the headmaster's recommendation, that he stay on two more years at school, for it meant that he would share the railway journey to and from Robin Hood's Bay with Jean.

It had helped to deepen the relationship between them and in the past two years their feelings for each other had moved beyond mere friendship. They had wanted to be together more and more and felt as if something was missing when they were apart. They looked forward to sharing

76

talk, discussing each other's views, laughing together and helping each other through their disappointments.

Exactly when they realised they were in love, neither could say. Jean wondered if it was the day when they alone shared the carriage back to Robin Hood's Bay. Gabrielle was sick and had not attended school. It was a Friday, they had little homework and a carefree weekend stretched before them. Their mood was light-hearted but once the train clanked its way out of Whitby station they fell silent. Their cheerful chatter faded, leaving a silent tension in the carriage. Their hands touched. They had done so before but this was different. It was as if a power had leaped between them, bringing a new understanding. Jean shivered but it was a shiver of pure pleasure and with it came a feeling she had never experienced before. Their fingers lingered together. Neither made any attempt to draw them apart and that brought a new bond, which promised much more.

Jean glanced shyly at Colin. A slight frown furrowed his brow as if he was trying to make a decision. His soft brown eyes were clouded as if the contest of thought troubled him. His head was slightly bowed and it had allowed a strand of fair hair to fall across his forehead. She had an urge to smooth it back into place, but hesitated to reach out and do so.

He looked up and met her gaze with a wan smile, embarrassed by the thought that she could read his mind. Jean's heart missed a beat. His lips, perfectly proportioned to the set of his eyes and nose, parted slightly as if he was about to say something which would break the spell. She willed him not to. They closed. He leaned towards her slowly. She did not move. His lips touched hers. They lingered a moment lightly.

Her mind soared as she realised that she had wanted him to do this for some time and now it had happened. Excitement engulfed her with happiness.

Their lips parted. Their eyes held each other. Embarrassed, he blushed and looked away. Her fingers gripped his more tightly.

Her eyes fixed on him. 'Kiss me again,' she whispered.

He looked up, startled by the request. His heart sang with joy that she had not taken offence. He kissed her again, a little longer this time. Then they shuffled back against the seat, cuddling close, holding hands, knowing the rapture of their first kiss had proclaimed a love for each other. They sat in silence in the sheer pleasure of being together.

It was not long before Sarah sensed a change in her daughter and it did not take any probing to know what caused it. She kept her counsel and did not mention it to Jonas, who she knew would be blind to Jean's changing feelings. She prayed for her daughter's happiness and that one day Jonas would see sense, make peace with Sam so that Jean's love would not be affected by his stubborn bitterness born so far in the past.

'Sorry to be leaving?' asked Jean as they headed under the bridge carrying the railway to West Cliff Station and north along the coast to Middlesbrough.

'Yes, in a way, but not in another. I'm glad we're all leaving together.' He gave her a wry smile and she knew what he meant, for she too would miss their journeys together.

'Looking forward to working with your father full time?' she asked.

'Yes,' he replied enthusiastically. 'Starting tomorrow.'

'John always says how good you are with engines.'

'And I hear tell your John's good too,' Gabrielle put in.

'He is that,' agreed Colin. 'A quick learner. A good job your mum got her way. It uncovered a talent and I'm pleased he still comes to the garage in his spare time.'

Jean smiled to herself as she recalled the furore which had broken out when her father had discovered that John was learning about engines from Sam.

The secret had been kept for some time, until one day Jonas had accidentally discovered the truth. Fishing had been completed for the day, a day when John was supposedly in Whitby learning the foibles of engines, and Jonas decided that he would visit Bob Carter for a chat about the old times when there were still several cobles working out of Robin Hood's Bay. On his way home he had realised that the train from Whitby would soon be arriving and with it would come John.

He strolled round to the station and sauntered on to the platform. There was still ten minutes before the train was due and he parked himself on one of the seats provided for waiting passengers. He stretched his legs as he leaned back and took a deep breath of contentment. The air was still, the sun warm, the atmosphere peaceful, and Jonas pushed his worries to the back of his mind. His eldest son, to whom he would pass on his coble and love of his trade, would soon be here.

'Good day, Jonas.' There was a touch of surprise in Will Newton's voice as he approached the seat.

Jonas started. He blinked against the brightness as his eyes focused on the stationmaster. 'Hello, Will.' He pushed himself upright on the seat.

'Long time since I've seen you on the station, Jonas. Going somewhere? If so, you'll want a ticket,' Will reminded him as he pulled his pipe and tobacco pouch from his pocket.

'No, I'm here to meet John.'

'Been to Whitby, has he?' Will fingered the tobacco into the bowl of his pipe.

'Aye, thee knows he always goes on a Tuesday, catches the early train.'

Will glanced up from his pouch and his fingers paused in their action. 'If he's been going to Whitby, he's gone some other way.'

Jonas was startled. He looked doubtful of Will's revelation, yet the stationmaster had no reason to misinform him. 'But he's been going for the best part of a year, learning about engines.'

'Not by train, he hasn't.' The firmness in Will's tone left no doubt in Jonas's mind.

'But there's no other way he could have gone.' Jonas now had a puzzled frown. 'He's talked about the train journey and he's certainly been learning about engines . . .' His voice faded as the possible truth dawned on him. His face darkened with anger. He jumped to his feet and strode past Will, heading for the exit.

Will stared after him in surprise. 'Sorry if I've spoken out of turn,' he called.

'Thee hasn't,' shouted Jonas over his shoulder.

From the determined stride, Will knew Jonas's temper

was near boiling point. There was going to be trouble and Will was glad he wouldn't feel the lash of Lawson's tongue. He shrugged his shoulders and went on charging his pipe while he awaited the arrival of the train from Whitby.

Jonas's lips were set in a grim line as he strode to Harland's Garage. He had been deceived not only by John but by the whole family, for they must all have known that John was learning from Sam instead of in Whitby as Jonas had ordered. What hurt most was the fact that Sarah must have been behind it. She had hoodwinked him, connived with the man he despised.

On such a warm day the garage doors alongside the showroom, just built this year, were wide open. As Jonas passed the petrol pumps, he saw John and Sam with their heads under the raised bonnet of a Morris. Seeing the two of them together stirred his anger even further.

Hearing the sound of approaching footsteps, Sam straightened and glanced round, wiping his hands on an oily rag as he did so. Startled to see Jonas, he tapped John on the shoulder. With a querying look at Sam, John straightened and followed Sam's gaze.

His whole body tensed when he saw his father. His secret was out! How had his father found out? There would be the devil to pay, he could see it in his father's face. He rubbed his blackened hands nervously on the rag he had pulled automatically from the pocket of his overalls.

'Steady, lad,' said Sam quietly, sensing John's apprehension at the coming encounter.

'What the bloody hell is thee doing here? I thought I told thee to learn in Whitby.' Jonas's eyes blazed furiously at his son.

81

John swallowed hard. His mind was racing. He wanted to defy his father, stand up to him, put his own views about going to Whitby, but years of taking his father's word as law held him back.

'Get thee home!' Jonas spat the words with venom.

'See here, Jonas, the lad—'

Jonas turned his fury on Sam. 'Thee keep out of this.'

Sam's eyes smouldered. 'I can't, I'm part of it. I've trained the lad, given him his knowledge of engines. He has a gift when handling them. Can take 'em to pieces and put 'em back blindfold.'

'What bloody good is that?' snarled Jonas. 'All he wanted was to be able to keep the coble's engine right.'

'Aye. And he could do that long ago. He's a quick learner, but he likes engines and asked me to let him keep coming.' There was a touch of admiration for the talent he had nurtured. 'He's as good as Colin here.' Sam nodded towards his own son, who had come from the back of the workshop on hearing the rumpus.

'Out! Out!' Jonas glared at John, ignoring Sam.

'But Dad . . .' John's protest got no further. He saw his father's lips tighten, his eyebrows lower over narrowing eyes. He knew the signs. He looked at Sam. 'I'd better go, Mr Harland. Thanks for what you've taught me.'

'Aye, thee'd better be on your way,' snapped Jonas. 'And never come here again. Thee'll have nothing to do with this family.' His contempt embraced father and son. He swung on his heel and followed John, who had already moved out of the garage.

Sam shook his head sadly as he watched them go. He liked John and recognised his gift with things mechanical.

It had been a pleasure for him to encourage him and teach him what he knew. He was sad that Jonas might stifle a budding talent because of his own bitterness.

Colin's mind was on a different tack, though it still concerned both families. He was wondering how Mr Lawson would react if he knew about that kiss in the train a few days ago.

John quickened his pace. He had determined to have words with his father but he did not want that now. There should be no witnesses to a family disagreement which might flare into an open row. He also hoped to be able to warn his mother before his father arrived. But Jonas kept pace with him, though he was never able to close the few yards between them.

Sarah was startled when the door burst open with such force. She looked up with amazed query from the brass she was polishing. She knew immediately there was trouble when she saw the alarm and concern on her son's face.

'Mum—'

'Thee needn't be saying anything,' snapped Jonas, slamming the door behind him.

Sarah knew immediately that Jonas had found out about John. She took a grip on herself, determined to remain calm in the storm that was coming.

'What the devil does thee mean by letting John go to Harland's when I said he had to go to Whitby?'

Sarah stiffened. Her fingers stopped polishing and her expression hardened. 'Don't speak to me in that tone, Jonas Lawson.' Her lips tightened and her eyes met his demanding gaze without flinching.

His fists clenched in exasperation, the knuckles showing

white. There was an almost uncontrolled fury rising and Sarah recognised it. As he grasped at words, she took the initiative quickly. 'Your bitterness should have been gone long ago. You've let it ruin a special friendship that existed between thee and Sam.'

'*He* did that, and thee knows it,' Jonas spat harshly.

'I know no such thing. Thee wouldn't listen to his explanation.'

'He hadn't one!'

'Oh yes, he had, but thee wouldn't see it. All right, what's done is done. I shielded the children from your bitterness when they were young but now they're older it's affecting them more and more. I don't want that and I won't let it!' The tone of defiance was tinged with challenge.

Jonas read it. This was the first time in their twenty-one-year marriage that they had openly clashed so strongly. He didn't like it but Sarah had been wrong to defy him.

John had moved to his mother's side and laid a comforting hand on her shoulder. It was a gesture not lost on Jonas and he saw it as a sign that the whole family were against him.

He would not have it. His eyebrows tensed above eyes which glowered at his wife. He leaned towards her, hand upon the table. 'Thee shouldn't have done this,' he hissed between clenched teeth. He looked up. His condemning glance sent a shiver down John's spine but he met the look with a determined jut of his jaw. 'Thee went against my wishes—'

'Saved time and money,' John cut in. 'And I should

think you'd be glad of that, the small amount thee makes from your stubbornness to stick to inshore fishing.' The words were out, harsh and fast, almost before he had time to think what he was saying. He swallowed hard as his father straightened.

Jonas's face tightened with shock and anger. The unexpected verbal attack by his son, the first time there had ever been words charged with accusation, struck with a pain as if fish hooks had torn into his flesh. He rose to his full height. John could feel the blow coming but he would not flinch. He met the fury in his father's eyes with a look which dared him to strike.

Jonas drew a deep, trembling breath. He looked down at his wife. 'Is this what thee's brought my children to? Defiance and dissatisfaction?'

'I haven't. But thee has.' Sarah's voice was coldly penetrating.

Jonas shook his head slowly. 'No, it was Sam. Sam!' The last word was spoken with thunder as if to imprint it for ever on the minds of Sarah and John.

Sarah sighed. 'Think what thee will.' A new resonance came into her voice as she faced her husband's wrath. 'But my children will have none of it. If they see friendship extended from the Harlands in spite of thee, then I'll not stop them accepting it.'

'Then on your head be it, Sarah.' Beneath the threat she saw sorrow in his eyes. She knew she had hurt him but she also realised that he knew he had hurt her and regretted it. He turned on his heel and left the house.

Sarah sank against the chair-back. The tension slid from her. She felt as if she had taken a beating. Silent tears

85

flowed and with them came a dread, a cold, empty feeling as if something precious had gone from her life. She wanted to cry out, to bring him back, to hold him tight, to say she was sorry and feel strong, forgiving arms around her soothing away all her cares and putting everything right. But it was too late and she did not know what Jonas's reactions would be.

The door from the kitchen opened and Jean and Martin came in.

'We heard it all, Mum,' said Jean tentatively and added in the way of apology, 'We couldn't help it.'

Sarah gave them a wan smile as she held out her arms to them. 'I'm sorry it's happened,' she sighed.

'But what about Dad?' asked Martin.

'He'll be back,' replied Sarah, drying her tears with her handkerchief. For the sake of her children she must not let them see any more. 'Life may be a bit different, but we must carry on in the same way. Thee lads must go on fishing with him.'

'Will he want me after what I said?' asked John.

'He needs thee both and James, and I ask thee not to let him down.' She looked hard at her two sons and they could not ignore the pleading in her eyes.

'We won't, Mum,' they reassured her.

'What about the garage?' asked John.

'Thee loves engines, doesn't thee?'

'Yes, I do.'

Sarah could not mistake the enthusiasm in his voice. 'Then thee shall continue to go, but it'll have to be whenever thee can fit it in and it must not cross anything your father wants thee to do. Thee have a word with Mr

Harland. I know he thinks highly of your skills so I think he'll help thee all he can.' She glanced at Martin. 'What about thee? Does thee want to go to the garage as well?'

'No, Mum.' Martin shook his head. 'It's the sea for me, but not inshore fishing. That's all but dead, as you know. We just eke out a living. One day I'll be away to the merchantmen.'

'Just as I thought.' Sarah gave a small smile. 'I sensed the sea in thee, always thought it would take thee from me, but I'll not deny thee. Thee'll do well, because thee loves it so much.'

'Thanks, Mum.' Martin bent and kissed her on the forehead.

'And what about my girl?' Sarah turned loving eyes on her daughter, who reminded her so much of herself at the same age.

Jean shrugged her shoulders. 'Don't know.' Her eyes brightened. 'All I ask is that I can go on being friendly with Gabrielle.'

'Of course thee can,' said Sarah firmly. Her voice softened and she looked at Jean with a wry smile as she added, 'And with Colin?'

Jean blushed but said nothing.

Now, as the three friends hastened down Bagdale, passing the elegant houses built by seventeenth- and eighteenth-century merchants and sea captains to escape from the crowded conditions on the east side of the river, Jean smiled to herself at this last recollection. Since then her friendship with Colin had blossomed and deepened into young love. They liked being together, sharing their time and thoughts, happy to walk on the cliffs, stroll on the beach, relax in the sunshine, laugh in the rain.

Often Jean had wondered how her father would react if he had known of her relationship with Colin Harland, but she was careful he did not find out and she drew comfort from her mother's approval.

'You both seem more than happy to be leaving school,' Colin observed, having noted the gaiety in the girls' demeanour.

'We've both got jobs,' announced Gabrielle.

Colin stopped in his tracks. 'You've what?' he gasped.

The girls laughed at the astonishment on his face, and intermingled with the laughter Jean repeated, emphasising each word, 'We've both got jobs.'

'Where?' Colin was still amazed.

'Baker and Turnbull.'

'The wine importers?'

'The same.'

'When did this happen?'

'Miss Willis arranged interviews last week,' explained Gabrielle.

'We just got to know today,' Jean put in, her eyes wide with excitement. 'Gab's ability with French got her a position on the import side.'

'And Jean, coming top with her shorthand and typing, got her the job as Mr Turnbull's second secretary.' Gabrielle knew her brother would be pleased. 'Come on! Stop gawking so or we'll miss the train.'

'Mum and Dad don't know, do they?' Colin asked as they quickened their step.

'No. Didn't want them to be disappointed if I didn't

get it,' explained Gabrielle. 'They'll know as soon as I get home.'

'What about yours, Jean?' he asked.

'They don't know either.'

'How will they take it?'

Jean screwed up her face thoughtfully. 'It'll be a surprise to them both. They've been on about what was I going to do when I left school. I think Mum will approve but Dad's set on me staying at home. Says Mum could do with the help but it's only an excuse to try to get me to stay. He's being overprotective. Thinks the big, bad world out there is going to gobble me up.'

Amusement at this imaginary scene brought laughter to their lips but in Jean's mind there was doubt about facing her father with the news.

The disagreement between him and her mother over John had brought a different atmosphere to the house. Some of the jollity and pleasantries which Jonas had preserved for his family had gone. They were still a family, Sarah was particular to see to that, but Jonas appeared to be less interested in them, keeping himself and his opinions more to himself. This did not preclude outbursts when his ideas were challenged or thwarted. Sarah bore the brunt of these and eventually showed signs of weariness at her husband's outlook, which was marred more and more by the bitterness which had eaten into his mind.

Gabrielle broke into a run when they reached Victoria Square. Jean and Colin were close behind as they raced across Station Square and on to the platform, where the train stood getting up steam for its run to Scarborough.

'Come on, you young 'uns, you'll miss it one of these

89

days,' cajoled the porter, slipping his watch back into the pocket of his black waistcoat. He stooped as if he had the weight of the world on his shoulders and the downturn of his mouth, coupled with his drooping eyelids, created the impression that he was about to cry with the miseries of the day. But the three friends from Robin Hood's Bay knew that was not so. He was a kindly man, ready to hold the train up if he could do so until they arrived, and always had a word for them – a note of wisdom, a snippet of gossip or a bit of Whitby news.

'I won't, Charlie!' Colin laughed.

Charlie closed one eye and inclined his head as if trying to read behind that remark.

'Leaving school today. Start work with my dad.' Colin jumped into the carriage. Charlie held the door for the girls.

'And you two?' he asked, touching the peak of his cap which hung precariously on the back of his head.

'We've left too,' said Gabrielle lightly.

Charlie's face dropped. He had enjoyed seeing these youngsters. They always had a word with him and brightened his day.

Gabrielle tripped into the carriage.

With one foot on the step, Jean paused. 'Don't look so sad, Charlie! Gabrielle and I will still be coming, we've got jobs in Whitby.'

Charlie's down-in-the-mouth look disappeared into a broad smile. 'And my days will be brighter for that.' He swung the carriage door shut with a swish, turned and waved to the guard who had stepped from the guard's van to check that everything was ready for departure. He acknowledged Charlie's signal and, satisfied that all was as it should be, blew his whistle and waved his green flag.

Charlie raised his hand to his young friends as the train gathered momentum. They waved back and then settled down for the short ride to Robin Hood's Bay. Jean and Gabrielle kept wondering how their parents would take their news.

The train rumbled, clanked and hissed to a stop in the pleasant station where flowerbeds and hanging baskets, neatly kept by the porter under the supervisory eye of stationmaster Will Newton, made this one of the most attractive stations along the coast.

'Robin Hood's Bay. Change for Robin Hood's Bay.' Will's voice rang clear. As he watched Jean, Gabrielle and Colin tumble out of the train, he was glad he had seen them through their schooldays. They were always pleasant, with a cheery word for him, occasionally sharing their secrets with him or seeking a bit of knowledge or advice. He had recognised the young love which blossomed between Jean and Colin but kept his counsel and wondered how Jonas would view it if he knew.

'The last time for school. How's it feel to be grown up?' he asked with a twinkle in his eyes.

'Free, Mr Newton, free,' replied Colin, with an enthusiasm which showed that he thought life would now take on a new meaning.

Will saw agreement reflected in the girls' smiles as they posed with an imagined worldly sophistication. 'The world is ours, Mr Newton,' they said, parading around him with a toss of the head.

'I hope it is, but always remember your roots.' He

nodded seriously and then smiled as they set off for the way out, happy laughter on their lips.

Gabrielle glanced back and saw two young people alighting from one of the other carriages. Her footsteps faltered and her eyes fixed on the young man who turned to help a girl to the platform. He was tall, she reckoned a couple of inches over six foot, and held himself erect. His handsome, square face was angled by a firm jaw, which added to the impression of confidence. His thick crop of dark hair, neatly trimmed, had a slight wave which would be the envy of many a straight-haired girl.

Gabrielle wished she was the girl he accompanied but then, as her eyes took her in, relief swept over her. She was so much like him, they must be twins. Gabrielle was startled by the sensation that filled her.

'Hi, Gabs, are you coming?' The shout from Jean broke into her daze and she reluctantly turned to her companions.

'Come on, sis. You in a dream?' said Colin as she joined them.

'Have you seen him?' Her voice was low, scarcely above a whisper but filled with admiration.

Just as Colin and Jean looked beyond her to see the stationmaster talking to the strangers, Mr Newton turned and shouted, 'Jean, Gabrielle, Colin, just a minute.' He started to walk towards them, followed by the new arrivals.

Gabrielle's heart missed a beat. She was going to meet this handsome stranger. Jean glanced at her friend and realised that she had been smitten. When she looked back at the young man she knew why, for she too could sense the attraction.

'This young man and his sister want directing to Clover Road. Thought you might do it on your way home.'

'Sure,' said Colin. 'Be pleased to.'

'Thanks.' The stranger's voice was low, with an attractive timbre.

'Here, let me,' said Colin, reaching out to take one of the cases the young man was carrying.

'We'd better introduce ourselves,' said the newcomer as they all started for the way out. 'I'm Ron Johnson and this is my twin sister, Liz.'

'Colin Harland, sister Gabrielle and Jean Lawson.' Colin made the introductions. Smiles and acknowledgements were exchanged and Colin asked, 'Here on holiday?'

'No,' replied Ron. 'Coming to live here.'

Gabrielle's pulse quickened. This was even better than she had dared anticipate.

Seeing their looks of curiosity, Liz offered an explanation. 'Dad's a teacher, got fed up of being in Middlesbrough, saw a job advertised at the county school in Whitby, applied and got it.'

'He'll be taking old Thunder Joe's job,' said Colin, glancing at the two girls.

'You know the school?' said Liz.

'Just finished for good today,' Jean told them. 'Gabrielle and I are going to work with a firm of wine importers in Whitby.'

'What about you, are you two looking for jobs?' asked Gabrielle.

'I've just finished training as a nurse in Middlesbrough. Now I'm going to the hospital in Whitby,' said Liz.

On this information Gabrielle took their age to be twenty-one.

'I always had an inclination for the sea,' said Ron. 'Guess it comes from my paternal grandfather. He was a ship's captain sailing out of the Tees. So when Dad got this job I wrote to a firm of boat-builders in Whitby. They've taken me on.'

'Then maybe we'll all travel to Whitby together,' said Gabrielle, pleased with the thought of having his company.

'With two girls like you I can't go wrong. Want to be my chaperone, Liz?' Ron's eyes sparkled teasingly.

'As if you'll need one,' his sister returned with a snort of disbelief. Her smile showed a perfect row of white teeth which seemed to add depth to her dark eyes. Her hair was cut short to the nape of her neck and, like her brother's, had a natural wave.

'What about you, Colin? You going to Whitby too?' asked Ron.

'Dad has a garage here; I'm going to work for him. He learned mechanics in the army. He was a fisherman but didn't go back to it after the war, but he still has a coble for his own pleasure. He'll take you out in it.'

Ron's eyes brightened at the prospect. 'Would he?'

'I'll see he does,' Gabrielle put in.

'Thanks. I'll look forward to it.'

Colin stopped, halting the conversation. 'Here we are, Clover Road.'

They were at the end of a row of semidetached, bow-windowed houses which looked out across the red-tiled roofs of the old village.

'Thanks,' said Ron.

'What about a meal?' asked Gabrielle, with some concern that the two new arrivals would have to start getting something ready. 'You're welcome to come home with us.'

'That's nice of you,' replied Liz. 'But Mum and Dad came here three days ago. We stayed with Gran to go to a couple of birthday parties. They'll have something ready for us.'

'If you aren't doing anything on Saturday, why don't you both come to Whitby with us to the pictures?' suggested Jean. She shot a knowing glance at Gabrielle and received a grateful flash in acknowledgement of her ploy.

'That would be nice,' said Liz. 'What's on?'

'*Test Pilot*.'

'Clark Gable, Myrna Loy and Spencer Tracy.' Liz rattled off the names of the stars.

'Real film fan,' commented Ron with a smile of admiration for his sister, and in it Gabrielle read a close bond between them. She knew she would have to win Liz's approval as well as Ron's.

'You've seen it?' asked Jean.

'No,' replied Liz. 'It's been in Middlesbrough but I missed it, so I'll look forward to seeing it.'

As they started down the hill, Gabrielle whispered to Jean, 'Thanks for fixing that.'

When Jean reached the tiny cottage, the table, one end against the window, was set for the family meal and a large black pan, set on the range fire, plopped steadily. Jean thought she would always remember the smell of stew and newly made bread in this cosy room, with its clip rug in front of the black range.

Her mother was filling a kettle ready to hang it on the reckon when she removed the pan from the fire. John and James were sharing the sports pages of the *Yorkshire Post*, no doubt studying the reports on Yorkshire's latest cricket victory, while her father had the news section of the paper. Martin was avidly reading the recent issue of *Picturegoer* and she knew she would have no bother persuading him to go to the pictures on Saturday.

'Hello, lass,' her mother greeted. She put the kettle down on the hearth and straightened to look proudly at her daughter as she hung her light coat on the peg behind the door. The end of schooling – Sarah felt that she had finally lost her little girl. She had experienced some of that when she had realised that Jean's relationship with Colin was more than just friendship, but today the last tenuous connection with girlhood seemed to be severed and her daughter had moved into the adult world. As she watched her, she sensed something more: she was bursting with some news but for some reason was holding back. Could it be good news she was keeping as a surprise, or was it something she could not say in front of her father? Whatever it was, she would wait patiently until Jean told her in her own good time.

'Well, lass, what's it like to think of no more schooling?' Jonas put the question as he eyed her over the edge of his paper. There was no doubt, Jean was growing into a fine young woman, reminding him in many ways of his sister Mary. He hoped that life would treat her more kindly. It would if she kept away from those Harlands, and that would be easier now she had left school.

'All right, Dad,' she replied. 'I suppose I'll miss it for a while.'

'Happen thee will. But there'll be more than enough to keep thee occupied here.'

Jean did not reply and Sarah sensed a tension come to her daughter at the last observation.

'Get thissen washed, lass. The stew's about ready,' said Sarah quickly.

Jean seized the opportunity to go upstairs and discard her school uniform. She washed in the bowl in her bedroom while gathering her thoughts and courage to break the news of her job to her parents. She dressed in a black and white checked skirt and white V-necked blouse and hung a necklace of coloured beads around her neck.

Sitting at the table with their plates of stew and dumplings, Sarah noticed that although Jean was enjoying her meal she was not tucking into the stew with her usual relish. It was one of Jean's favourite dishes and Sarah had prepared it specially for this occasion. But she said nothing, allowing talk of fishing and cricket to flow between the men.

'That was right good,' praised Jonas, sitting back on his chair, his plate finally cleaned of his second helping. 'Something a bit special about it today or maybe I was a mite more hungry.'

'A little more meat gave it that extra flavour,' said Sarah, rising from her chair and starting to clear the table.

Jean helped her mother and on her instructions took a jug of milk, a bowl of sugar and a tin of Lyle's Golden Syrup to the table, where she had already placed six bowls. Sarah took a large oval dish from the oven beside the fire and put it in front of her place at the table. The golden-brown skin heralded rice pudding cooked to perfection. She gave it out and it was only after second helpings all round that she started to gather up the bowls.

'Mum, leave them a minute, I have something to tell you.' There was a timbre of uneasiness in Jean's voice, as if she was reluctant to speak but knew she must.

All eyes turned on her. Her tone told her mother and brothers that what she was about to say would not suit her father, who eyed her suspiciously.

'I've got a job!'

In the stunned silence the atmosphere became charged with foreboding.

'You've what?' Jonas's face was livid. His daughter had gone behind their backs. She knew she was expected to stay at home to help her mother. She had not even asked them. His eyes flashed angrily. 'What's this all about?' he demanded. 'Who's offered thee a job?'

'Baker and Turnbull.'

'The wine importers?'

'Yes. Miss Willis arranged an interview last week.'

'She had no right,' snapped Jonas, his brow narrowing darkly. 'Thee can tell them thee won't be going.'

'But Dad—'

'No buts about it.' Jonas glared at his daughter as if that was the final word.

Sarah saw defiance in Jean's tightening lips and stormy eyes. To try to calm the situation she quickly put in, 'What will thee be doing there?'

'She'll be doing nowt there,' spat Jonas. 'She'll be staying home.'

Jean ignored her father's remark. 'Second secretary to

Mr Turnbull. The shorthand and typing course I did as an extra at school has paid off.'

'Thee did what?' Jonas was taken aback.

'She did it with my approval,' said Sarah firmly.

'Thee didn't think to consult me!'

Jean drew herself up, stiffening her resolve not to give way. 'I knew what your answer would be. You'd say it was a waste of time. Well, it hasn't been.'

'What use is it here? Thee knows your ma wants thee at home.'

'Jonas, think on it.' There was a sharp edge to Sarah's tongue. 'Have I ever said I *wanted* Jean at home? I said it would be nice but that's different. It's thee who's been saying it.'

'No matter, she stays.'

Jean glanced quickly at her mother and read in her expression that she would have her backing, no matter how it hurt her to support her daughter in defiance of her father. 'I'm not giving up the job. I got it on merit and I'm going to keep it.'

At the sight of her rebellious look, Jonas's temper exploded. 'Thee will give it up!' He slammed his hand hard down on the table. The crockery rattled.

'Be sensible, Jonas. Jean would only be whiling away her time here. There's not enough to keep us both busy,' Sarah pointed out, her voice quiet but not lacking forcefulness.

'Thee can have things easier,' rapped Jonas. 'Thee deserves that.'

Sarah was appreciative of his thoughtfulness towards her but she must not weaken in support of her daughter. This was Jean's chance, a chance she herself had longed for but was never able to take. In her day girls were expected to stay at home and marry a local boy, but now things were different. Girls had more opportunity, though they were still expected to stay near home. Their horizons stretched a little way beyond the village and Sarah did not want her daughter to be restricted by old attitudes.

'If thee thinks about it thee'll realise I'd soon be bored to death and Jean would be kicking her heels. If she takes this job in Whitby she'll be able to pay a little towards her keep.' She didn't like bringing financial matters into the reasoning but she thought it might help to settle the situation.

Jonas glared at her but she met his look unflinchingly. 'She stays at home.' His voice was sharp, challenging defiance.

'I'm not giving up this job!' Jean stepped in, accepting the challenge. 'I got it through effort. You ought to be proud of me, Dad. My school results were good and this is a result of hard work. I'll not have it all been for nothing.' Her voice was rising as she saw her father's fury at what he saw as opposition to his wishes and authority, and she realised it was the latter that was making him so stubborn in his attitude. Suddenly she felt a strong urge to throw even more defiance in his face, to hurt him. She felt her love for him had been bruised by his stance and she wanted to hit back. Her voice shook with emotion. 'And thee may as well know that Gabrielle Harland has got a job there too, so we'll be travelling together. And another thing, I'm in love with Colin Harland and he with me!' She sprang from her chair, knocking it over in her haste, and ran from the room.

In the speechless moment that gripped their father,

Martin hurried after his sister. They were close and he felt that she might need his comfort, for he knew that she would be hurting deeply from the self-inflicted wound of defying her father.

John and James quickly left their parents alone together.

Thunderstruck by the turn of events, Jonas looked at his wife. Suddenly he realised how much he needed her support and how much he lacked it.

'Sarah,' he said softly. This was no time for tantrums or harsh words between man and wife. 'Please stop it.'

Sarah shook her head slowly. 'I can't. We shouldn't. I know thee loves her and she loves thee, so don't destroy what there is between thee. Don't break her heart as well.'

Anger flared in his eyes. Condemning words sprang to his lips but by sheer willpower he held them back. As his eyes softened, his face contorted into a mask of sorrowing regret. Why had it all happened? Why had the past influenced the present so terribly? He pressed his eyes with his hands as if he could drive away for ever the memory of the day he carried his beloved sister from the sea. But he could not.

Jonas let out a long sigh. He realised that for the moment he must step back from the situation in which he might lose his daughter's love and respect. 'All right,' he said, his voice low, the words catching in his throat, 'but I hope the Harlands don't do that.'

Chapter Five

1939

'Anyone for fish and chips?' Colin's call was loud to catch the attention of Liz and Martin, who had already started for the station.

It raised some smiles, at the appetite and exuberance of youth, on the faces of other cinema patrons leaving the magical world into which they had escaped for a couple of hours.

'And walk home?' added Jean, seizing on the clear night to have longer with Colin.

The suggestions brought no objections from Gabrielle and Ron nor from Liz and Martin, who turned back to rejoin the others.

It was a perfect night for the five-mile walk. They had done it several times since that first visit as a group of six on the Saturday after Liz and Ron had arrived in Robin Hood's Bay. But tonight was probably the most perfect of them all.

The air was calm and the June sky still held a haunting light to the north. The rising moon splashed Whitby's rooftops with a silvery sheen and created tantalising shadows in the narrow streets.

The six friends bought their fish and chips and headed for the bridge across the river.

Liz and Ron Johnson had fitted into the group easily. It was as if they had all known them for longer than the nine months since they stepped off the train. Liz and Martin had struck up a rapport on that first visit to the pictures, drawn together by a love of the cinema. Since then the friendship had deepened and they found common interests in bird-watching and cricket, being ardent followers of Yorkshire's fortunes.

From the start Ron was captivated by Gabrielle's bubbly nature, her zest for life and the charm which accompanied her good looks, and she revelled in the attention from this handsome young man.

Jean's and Colin's love had deepened. Her mother had told her that she could go on seeing Colin and that her father would not openly object. She figured that he hoped the relationship would die a natural death, but she was determined it would survive. Nor had her father come round to approving her job at Baker and Turnbull. She had settled well and her willing nature and friendliness quickly won her the affections of the staff. Gabrielle soon became an asset to the firm, speeding up dealings with French wine exporters.

Liz was enjoying nursing at Whitby hospital and whenever she had time off she went to Robin Hood's Bay to enjoy home comforts and to see Martin.

The friends crossed the bridge, pausing to admire a moonbeam which danced with the river's movement as it flowed in the gap between the high cliffs to join the sea swirling past the stone piers.

At the end of Bridge Street they turned into Church Street, passing shops and inns in what used to be Whitby's main street when its only dwellings occupied the east bank.

They laughingly made their way to the Church Stairs, so named because one hundred and ninety-nine steps led up the cliff to the parish church of St Mary. Young legs did not seriously notice the steepness of the climb but nevertheless all six were pleased to take a rest on a seat halfway up and there finish their fish and chips. Depositing the greasy papers in a convenient waste bin, they continued their way to the top.

They paused close to the church and looked back over Whitby. The lights shining in the mantle of darkness seemed to convey an air of peace and contentment, of a place settling down for the night satisfied that all was well and life was good.

Jean slipped her arm through Colin's and drew closer to him. The moon enveloped the graveyard in a white shroud. The deathly stillness of an unknown world took over from the twinkling lights which only a moment ago had conveyed hope for the future. Jean shivered and quickened her step. The rest matched her and no one spoke as they hurried across the graveyard.

They came to the path which swung past the gaunt ruins of the once thriving Norman monastery. Jean pressed closer to Colin. Was it true that monks could be heard chanting on certain nights? Did the holy St Hilda still walk an earlier monastery, the scene of the great synod, which had had repercussions throughout the Christian world? Much had gone on up here and Jean loved reading about it as well as exploring the ruins and studying the gravestones, but on a night like this, when the atmosphere seemed charged with the past, she was eager to be away from the stones.

'Scared?' Ron gave a half laugh as he put the question after sensing how the others felt.

'Shut up,' Gabrielle admonished him with a dig in the ribs. The tremor in her voice betrayed her real feelings.

'No more than you,' said Martin, putting on a brave tone, but the tightening of his grip on Liz's hand was more than just a comfort for her.

Colin said nothing but quickened his pace and was glad when they moved beyond the desolate ruins. The brightness in the sky seemed to intensify. The sea shimmered in the moonlight while, far below, the waves swished against the cliffs. The sound was soothing, driving away all the hauntings which had crept into their minds.

'Great picture,' said Martin, returning their thoughts to the cinema.

'Best Western for years,' Liz commented with authority.

'And isn't that John Wayne just something?' Gabrielle exclaimed.

'Better than me?' Ron grinned.

'Well, I can't imagine you riding a stagecoach.'

'True, give me a boat.'

'Not for me,' Colin put in. 'Give me a plane. Wish they'd make another picture like *Test Pilot*. Think I'll join the RAF if there's a war.'

A chill struck at Jean. 'Don't speak like that, Colin, not even in jest.'

'It wasn't a jest. You saw that newsreel tonight. I reckon war's inevitable. What does anyone else say?'

'You could be right,' said Martin.

'But we have the agreement Mr Chamberlain made with the Germans,' said Liz.

Ron gave a derisive laugh. 'A piece of paper. Hitler's taken no notice of agreements and treaties in the past. Look how he's walked into those countries he had no right to, and he's got away with it.'

'But if war does come, we won't be involved personally,' said Gabrielle. 'It'll soon be over. We're too strong for the Germans. They may have a big army but they haven't the planes and a navy like we have.'

'Don't you believe it,' said Ron. 'They've been secretly arming.'

'Ron's right,' agreed Colin. 'War will come and it'll be a long one. We'll all be in it and it'll be the air force for me.'

'Oh, stop talking about it! You'll all be wrong. There won't be a war,' snapped Jean irritably. 'We've had a nice evening so don't spoil it with talk of something that will never happen.'

The sharpness in her voice told the others to be careful, and exchanged glances conveyed an understanding that the subject should be dropped.

It was soon forgotten when the couples drifted away

from each other. They came together again as they approached Robin Hood's Bay, lingered a little longer exchanging last kisses, then separated with promises of another night together next Saturday.

The possibility of war had loomed larger as the year moved into September. It was strongly in the minds of Jean and Martin as they hurried from St Stephen's Church on the first Sunday of the month. People did not linger outside after the service as they usually did, passing the time of day, chatting, discussing the latest church and family news, for they wanted to be home beside their wireless sets by a quarter past eleven when the prime minister was to make an important announcement.

'Do you think there will be a war?' asked Jean of her older brother.

'Looks certain,' he replied.

'You'll have to go?' There was concern in her voice.

'Aye, I will.' He nodded.

'What will you do?'

'Not sure,' he replied. 'I've heard John and James talking about joining the merchant navy.'

'Will you go with them?'

'Shouldn't think so. You know what they are, wouldn't want me along. I'd cramp their style.'

'But it'll be the sea?'

'If I have my way.'

'Navy?'

'Maybe. We'll see. Don't fancy flying like Colin does.'

Jean frowned at the recollection of Colin's enthusiasm for flying. 'He'd have joined the air force before now if his father hadn't persuaded him to wait. Mr Harland didn't disagree with his idea but asked him to wait for his mother's sake.'

'His mother?'

'The talk of war worries her because she still has family in France. So Mr Harland wanted to try to spare her any extra worry over Colin.'

'But if war is declared, Colin will want to go and he'll want to fly.' Martin glanced at his sister. 'How do you feel about it, sis?'

Jean bit her lip and shrugged her shoulders. 'There's nothing I can do about it. Colin wants to be a pilot and he'll get his chance if war comes. I don't like it and I'll miss him terribly but what will be will be.'

There was sympathy in his eyes as he said, 'You love him, sis?'

Jean gave a half laugh. 'I think you all know I do.'

'Dad won't see it because he doesn't want to, you've Mum's support.'

Sarah glanced at her husband sitting to one side of the fire, chewing on the end of his unfilled pipe, staring thoughtfully at the flames. He looked weary, as if he did not want to face another problem. She felt a pang of sorrow for him. Life had not been as kind to him as it might have been, but it was of his own making. Bitterness had marked his face, cramping it with a closed expression.

Sarah, sad-eyed, still weighed down by Jonas's attitude, stirred the fire with a long poker and pushed more sticks under the oven, maintaining the heat for the roasting meat and keeping it hot for the Yorkshire puddings. This was Sunday: there was a family dinner to cook, no matter what went on in the world.

She sat down opposite her husband. 'Another war,' she sighed.

'Looks like it, lass,' he agreed.

'What'll become of us all?' Her voice was drained. 'They'll all have to go.'

'The lads will, nothing more certain, but not Jean,' replied Jonas.

'Maybe even her. She might volunteer for war work.'

'She can get herself a reserved occupation and stay around here.'

Sarah did not pursue the subject. She did not want an argument. She knew there was something of a restless spirit in her daughter. She might seize the chance to throw off the shackles of home and see something of the world beyond Robin Hood's Bay, just as Sarah would have liked to do when she was Jean's age.

'What about thee?' Sarah asked. 'There'll be no more fishing when the boys go.'

Jonas grunted. Without his sons' help he would be forced to give up and look elsewhere for a living. 'Don't know, Sarah love. It's going to be all change for us. I'll have to take the job of some young fella going to war, maybe the coastguard.'

Sarah felt a surge of relief. Jonas was not going to sit back and bemoan his fate. He had been thinking positively and, in that, something of the younger Jonas was resurfacing.

'That's a good idea,' she said brightly.

'Well, let's wait and see what Mr Chamberlain has to say.'

Sarah glanced at the grandfather clock, an heirloom from her mother. Five minutes past eleven.

The door opened and John and James came in. They took off their jackets and hung them on a peg beside the door.

'Want the paper, Dad?' asked John, holding out the *Sunday Express*.

'Not at the moment, thanks. Been far?'

'Just to the coble,' replied James as he pulled a chair from under the table.

'She's all right?' asked Jonas, with a touch of alarm that something might be wrong with his beloved boat.

'Of course,' John reassured him. 'What'll you do with her if war comes?' He pulled a second chair from under the table.

'Have to lay her up. Thee'll all be off to the war.'

'You wouldn't consider selling her?' asked James.

'Selling? Never!' Jonas stiffened. His tone softened as he added, 'Besides, one of thee might want her after the war.'

Neither of his sons made any comment.

Sarah was thankful, seeing the glance exchanged between them. She had known for some time that her two eldest sons wanted to break away, to make their own way in the world and not be tied to a stubborn father's traditional ways. Now they would get that opportunity, when the freedom they yearned for was imposed by a world gone mad. She knew in that glance she had witnessed that they had no intention of returning to inshore fishing even if they came back to Robin Hood's Bay. It might be different for Martin, who wanted to make his life round the village and the bay, but who knew how the war might change him?

The door burst open and Jean and Martin rushed in.

'We aren't too late?' Jean panted as she threw off her coat.

Martin glanced at the clock. 'A couple of minutes to go. Turn up the sound, Dad.'

Jonas reached for the volume knob.

Sam Harland stood in the window of the large lounge with panoramic views of the coast. The wireless was on low. He heard nothing of the programme but he knew the change at a quarter past eleven would immediately focus his attention on what was to come.

His suspicions of a coming war had first been roused in the early part of the previous year, when he had heard that car manufacturers were switching some production to aircraft parts. He had shrewdly looked ahead. Realising that the future of his garage and car business was at risk, he had invested in six lorries, reckoning that transport of supplies would be vital if war came. His supposition seemed to have been well founded when he was able to hire out his vehicles to the quarry firm near Pickering which was supplying stone for the upgrading of old airfields and the construction of new ones in the Vale of York. He had also made it a proviso that he would have the job of maintaining those lorries as well as any others the firm hired. Sam knew that financially he was sound and that there would still be the core of his business on which Colin could build after the war.

But now, with the pointers of the clock nearing the appointed time, with the reality of war so imminent, he wondered about that future. The war was bound to take Colin away, and maybe the boy's interest in flying, which over the past year had developed into something of a passion, would bring unknown dangers.

He wished he could spare Colette all the worries that war would bring. She had settled well in Robin Hood's Bay. He had known he took a risk when he brought her here from the bustle of her sophisticated life in Paris, but the love she had shared with him from the moment of their first meeting had strengthened and had never been in doubt. She lived for him and he found nothing but pleasure in spoiling her. They had a comfortable life and he hoped it would continue that way for her sake.

The talk of war had upset her. She was concerned for her two children, hoping that if war came it would soon be over and that they would not be involved. She was anxious for her relatives and friends still living in Paris. She had tried to persuade her elderly mother to come to England but she had refused, saying that France was her home and no one, not even the Germans, would move her from Colette's brothers and sisters.

Sam knew the worry was eating away at his wife, and she had been ill six months ago. Although she had recovered, she had been left weak. Now she sat pale-faced in an easy chair beside the tiled fireplace where the embers burned low.

Gabrielle, who sat at her mother's knees, holding her

hand, was lost in her thoughts, pondering her future. War was inevitable. What did it hold for her? Her job would be gone, but maybe that was a good thing. She had seen herself getting into a rut, while her spirit cried out for release. She had sensed that her father and mother knew of her yearning for more freedom and she guessed their approval to spread her wings would come in time. There were moments when she felt they saw in Ron Johnson someone with whom she might settle down. They liked him. She liked him too, thought him the handsomest person around and enjoyed his company, but, with her eyes cast beyond Robin Hood's Bay and Whitby, she prevented their relationship from becoming more than friendship. Now, tense with waiting for the change of programme, she wondered what the future held for her.

Colin had no doubt what he would do if Mr Chamberlain announced the country was at war: he would volunteer for flying duties.

In a semidetached house in Clover Road, Tom and Kay Johnson sat in two armchairs with Ron and Liz on the settee, positioned so they formed an arc around the fireplace in the bow-windowed front room. The wireless stood on one side of the fireplace. With its back to one wall stood a china cabinet which held, among sentimental pieces of china, a dinner and tea service in Crown Derby, an heirloom passed to Kay from her grandmother. Apart from three family photographs on one wall the only other two pictures were *Mother and Son*, Liz's favourite, and *The Boyhood of Raleigh*, Ron's favourite because the sailor's pointing finger seemed to be directing him to a future at sea. A small table was positioned in front of the settee and handy to Kay's chair, for she was in the process of pouring out the cocoa, a special treat for Sunday morning. No announcement was going to upset that routine.

Tom would not have dreamed of suggesting they wait, for he saw in the regular pattern of their lives something that would keep Kay's mind away from the coming upheavals. He was glad that they had left Teesside for the job in Whitby. With the steelworks, the shipbuilding yards and the chemical complexes, the whole area around the Tees would be a prime target for German bombers. They would be safer where they were now.

Kay feared that war was inevitable, though deep down she held a slender hope that the prime minister would announce some solution. She had steeled herself that if war came she would have to part with Ron, but she would still have Liz, for her hospital work would keep her here.

She carried on as if everything was normal, but kept an eye on the hands on the clock – with Westminster chimes, a wedding present – as they moved towards eleven fifteen.

'This country is now at war with Germany.'

Sarah switched off the wireless, sighed and said, 'I'll make a cup of tea.'

Jonas stared at the fire. His world was finished. His way of life, his coble, his fishing were of no more use. He set his lips hard. Everything gone because of some little foreign upstart! He took his pipe from his mouth. His grip tightened as his anger rose. The snap of the stem startled him and he looked down at the broken pipe, then

114

tossed it into the fire as if he had accepted that a way of life was over and another would have to take its place.

John and James glanced at each other. Their way was clear – they would join the merchant navy.

Martin picked up the latest issue of *Picturegoer*, not really looking at it as he flicked over the pages, wondering where his future lay.

Jean was left with a confusion of thoughts about what the war would mean to her relationship with Colin.

The prime minister's final words sent a chill through Colette. She stiffened and grasped Gabrielle's hand tightly as if she needed something to stabilise her world. Sam had turned up the volume when Chamberlain had started to speak. He had stood by the set all through the speech and now turned it off. Seeing the tears in his wife's eyes, he knew she was not only concerned about their children but also about her family in France. Sam felt frustrated, unable to alleviate her distress. He came to her, knelt down, put his arm round her and let her weep.

Colin watched it all with mixed thoughts. He wanted to join the RAF more than ever now, but knew if he made the move too soon his mother would be devastated. He would wait a little while, as his father had asked. But he wanted to share his feelings with someone. He caught his sister's eye and inclined his head towards the door. She nodded almost imperceptibly and pushed herself to her feet. This was a time for her parents to be alone.

Kay Johnson turned off the wireless and reached for the cocoa. No one spoke as they watched her pour their second cup. Tom wondered what would become of all the children he had taught. Ron pictured himself on board a destroyer, its bows cleaving through the water in pursuit of enemy shipping. Liz wondered if her nursing would take her away from Whitby to military casualties.

Kay finished pouring, glanced at her family and said in a matter-of-fact tone, 'Well, that's that. We'll just have to get on with our lives, best we can.'

Chapter Six

1940

'Cold morning, Mr Newton,' said Jean cheerily as she came into the station, slapping her gloved hands together. She was muffled into a warm tweed coat, new for the winter, bought from the weekly money she had set aside for this purpose. A pale-blue, woollen scarf, knitted by her mother, was wound round her neck and a red beret perched cheekily on her head. Her galoshes were caked with February snow after her walk up the hill.

'Aye, it is, lass,' replied the stationmaster. 'But we're lucky. I hear tell the snowfalls were heavier further inland.'

'Hope we don't get any more. It gets messy in town.' She eyed Will with curiosity. 'You seem bright this morning in spite of this sharp wind,' she commented.

'Something to celebrate, lass,' he explained, eager to impart his news. 'Remember last year the railway authorities asked me to stay on for a little while when I should have been retiring? Case of seeing how things would be if war came.' Jean nodded. 'Well, yesterday evening they asked me to stay on for the duration of the war.' His smile was full of immense satisfaction.

'I'm delighted, Mr Newton, delighted!' Jean knew how much the railway meant to him. It had been his life and he had not looked forward to retirement. 'You'll be as pleased as my dad getting the job with the coastguard.'

'Aye, I am. How's he getting on?'

'It's given him a new outlook. He'd seen his livelihood gone when war was declared. Seemed to think everything was passing him by. Then he heard the coastguard wanted men to replace the younger ones who were eligible for military service. Applied, got a post in Whitby and felt useful again.'

'I'm glad,' replied Will. 'Heard from John and James?'

'Yes, they've got a ship. Managed to stay together.'

'Good. Now you must excuse me. Got to be ready for the train.'

Jean wandered over to the shelter of the tiny waiting room. She smiled at the two other passengers standing by the fire which Mr Newton had thoughtfully lit on this cold morning, and stood by the window to look out for Gabrielle's arrival.

She hadn't long to wait before she saw her friend hurrying on to the platform. Then a new joy swept through her; Colin was there too. She left the waiting room to greet them.

'You going to Whitby?' she asked Colin.

'Yes.' He held up a bag of tools. 'One of Dad's lorries coming in for maintenance broke down near the Parade last night. Driver, a Whitby man, phoned in. Dad told him to leave the lorry, go home and be back at the lorry when I got there this morning.'

'Good, I'm glad it broke down,' Jean laughed, pleased to have Colin's company.

'All right for some,' moaned Gabrielle, putting on a mock look of disappointment that she had no one to accompany her. 'All I've got is a letter.'

'From Ron?' asked Jean.

'Yes. It was there when I got home yesterday.'

'Still keen?' Jean pressed her curiosity.

'Yes.'

'So what are you going to do about it?'

'He knows I don't want tying down. I'll remind him of that when he comes home, weekend after next.'

'Leave already?' Jean was surprised.

'Just a weekend break in his course. He's wanting to get to something more substantial towards that destroyer he's always dreamed about since there was talk of war.'

'I reckon you think a lot about him, sis.' Colin sounded the wise old man.

'Only as a friend. Not like you two lovebirds.' She gave a twitch of her eyebrows.

Any further discussion about their love lives was halted by the approaching train.

'I'm getting the bus to the Parade,' said Colin as they alighted at Whitby station. 'How about coming for the ride?' His remark was directed at Jean but it was Gabrielle who answered.

She knew Jean would not refuse the suggestion. 'Good idea. I'll come too.' She glanced at her friend. 'You won't want to wait until Colin's fixed the lorry. We can walk back together.'

'But we'd better not both be late,' Jean pointed out, making an attempt to have a few minutes alone with Colin.

'It'll be all right,' replied Gabrielle with surety. 'Old Mr Potter is pretty tolerable; besides, I can get round him.'

Jean knew there would be no putting Gabrielle off. It was true she could work Mr Potter round her little finger. She had been able to do so from the first day they had moved from Baker and Turnbull to the council offices which the younger men were leaving.

'All right, come on,' said Colin, knowing nothing would dissuade his sister once she had her mind set. 'The bus is in.'

They quickened their pace and once outside the station ran to the bus.

Nearing the Parade, Colin spotted the lorry with a man he guessed was the driver standing beside it.

'If this doesn't take long, I'll walk back with you,' he said as the bus pulled to a halt.

With his head under the bonnet, he quickly diagnosed the fault as being dirt in the carburettor.

'Only take a few moments,' he told the girls, who agreed to wait for him.

With nimble fingers he soon had the fault rectified. 'Try it now,' he suggested to the driver, who climbed into the cab. The engine started immediately, and with satisfaction Colin closed the bonnet.

As he secured it, he started. Above the noise of the

engine he heard a distant roar charged with more power. The girls had heard it too, coming from the direction of the sea. Then another unfamiliar sound. For a frozen moment of time, they did not comprehend.

'Machine guns!' The lorry driver's voice was strained with misgiving.

'Good grief!' Colin's eyes widened. The girls stared at him in disbelief and the driver sat transfixed in his cab.

A huge twin-engined aeroplane, rocking unsteadily, smoke trailing from one of its engines, was heading towards the cliffs.

'German!' yelled Colin, recognising the Heinkel from his enthusiastic study of military aeroplanes. 'And Hurricanes!'

Three fighters buzzed around the stricken bomber, two weaving behind while the third remained higher.

The bomber sank. Jean and Gabrielle were paralysed. They were sure it was going to hit the cliffs.

Then, with some supreme effort by the pilot, the bomber lifted. It seemed to hesitate and then it was over them, barely above the house-tops. They saw the pilot quite plainly battling with the controls, trying to keep his plane airborne until it reached open country. There was no mistaking the black cross on its side nor the swastika on the tail.

The war had come to Whitby!

The talk of the phoney war in which nothing of any serious consequence had happened was suddenly erased from Whitby minds. This was the real thing and it was on their doorstep. The two German airmen who had been found on the cliffs near Sandsend the previous October,

121

just over a month after the declaration of war, when their bomber had been shot down in the sea, counted for little after this February day.

'Quick, it's heading for Sneaton Castle!' Colin jumped into the cab, hauling the girls after him.

The driver swung the lorry round sharply and eased it quickly through the gears as he got more power. They raced up Love Lane, swung on to the Guisborough Road and tore past Sneaton Castle.

Colin, straining to keep his eyes on the aircraft, saw it had passed beyond the castle and urged the driver for more speed. He lost sight of the plane but then saw the three fighters circle and guessed it must have crashed.

When Bannial Flat Farm came in sight, they saw the shattered bomber on the snow-covered field. It had torn through a line of telegraph poles and a row of sycamore trees. This had snapped one wing in half but had taken the force out of its momentum, bringing it to a halt a few yards from a pair of cottages.

Colin let out a yell, 'Look at those beauties!' Straining to see the three Hurricanes circling overhead, he was seized by the thrill of having witnessed a German plane brought down. His gaze came back to the wreckage. People were running towards it from the cottages and the farm.

They pulled to a halt near the farm and, as Colin leaped to the ground, he shouted, 'You two stay here! Might be gruesome.' Closely followed by the lorry driver, he raced across the field towards the wreckage.

Colin saw that the body of the plane was intact, though heavily marked by bullet holes where the fighters had found their mark. The front of the aircraft was a mangled

122

mass of twisted metal and its propellers were bent where they had gouged into the ground, leaving behind a trail of uprooted earth mashed in with snow.

A policeman, who had arrived on the scene before them, was standing on the wing leaning into the cockpit. Colin leaped up beside him to see the pilot acknowledging the law after burning some papers.

Several cars had arrived and people were gathering round the wreckage. As the pilot jumped to the ground, the policeman called for someone to keep an eye on him and for others to help him with the two wounded airmen still in the plane.

Both men seemed to be suffering excruciating pains, and one was bleeding profusely from the stomach. The other indicated that he had been hit in the legs and that he could not use them. Before the policeman and his helpers could start their task, there were shouts of dismay and warning from those around the plane.

Colin looked over his shoulder to see that in the confusion the pilot had given his watchers the slip and had fired a cartridge, from the Very pistol he had secreted on his person, into the mangled front of the aircraft in an attempt to destroy it before it could be examined by his enemy.

'Stop that fire!'

'Grab him!'

'Extinguishers!'

'Use the snow!'

Shouts came from all sides. Car owners raced to their cars to grab fire extinguishers or shovels, which they carried in snowy weather.

Seeing what was happening, Jean and Gabrielle snatched

the extinguishers and shovel which were fastened to the back of the lorry's cab. They raced across the field, managing to keep their feet as they slipped and slithered in the snow, and joined the melee around the front of the aircraft. Spray from the extinguishers sloshed across the flames. Shovels were wielded frantically, hurling snow at the front of the plane. The combined efforts saved the aircraft from destruction and the pilot had to watch, helpless to stop his machine falling into enemy hands.

Seeing he had not achieved his objective and was now being carefully watched, he turned his attention to his wounded crew members.

The dorsal gunner, in spite of the fact that his legs were useless, had managed, with the strength in his arms, to extricate himself from the turret and reach his companion, who was screaming with pain. He could do nothing for him and heaved himself out on the wing, where willing hands lowered him to the ground. With the cries of the wounded man still in the aircraft ringing out across the snow, Colin, with several others, tried to help him. Slowly and carefully, realising that each movement sent pain through his whole body, they eased him out of the aircraft.

Concerned for the wounded men, ladies from the farmhouse supervised their removal to their home, where they gave first aid while awaiting the arrival of the ambulance. Meanwhile the body of the observer had been removed from the plane. It lay in the snow until it was taken to the outhouse at the farm.

The action of fighting the fire had kept Jean's mind away from the horrors but once that intense activity was over she saw and heard the bloody side of war. She steeled herself against the thoughts that threatened to overwhelm her – this could happen to Colin; he could be screaming with intense pain, wanting to be released in death, but desperate to cling to life. She turned away, wanting to eradicate the sights and sounds from her mind.

'You all right?' asked Gabrielle, seeing her friend had lost all her colour.

'Yes.' She nodded, her voice hoarse. 'Let's go back to the lorry.'

They had started across the field when Colin came running up. 'Saw you come when the pilot tried to fire the aircraft. You did well, helping to save the plane for examination.' His voice trailed away when he saw that Jean was taking little notice. His excitement over the victory he had witnessed, his enthusiasm for the Hurricanes he had seen in action, waned when he realised that she was upset by what she had seen. He got the signal from Gabrielle to say no more.

Their attention was diverted by an army lorry and an ambulance turning into the farm. They paused to watch. Immediately the army vehicle stopped, an officer was out of the cab and soldiers were jumping from the back. The officer sized up the situation quickly. He issued his orders with precision and two soldiers, armed with rifles, went off to mount guard over the wreckage. The officer went into the farmhouse to emerge a few moments later. He called to two more soldiers, who entered the building. They returned in a matter of moments, escorting the pilot. They wasted no more time but took the prisoner away, his fate an internment camp for the duration of the war, his thoughts on the men he was leaving behind dead and wounded.

The ambulance had barely stopped when all the doors opened. A doctor jumped out of the front. The driver left his seat and joined the orderly and two nurses who emerged from the back of the vehicle, shaken by the fast drive from the hospital.

'Liz!' gasped Gabrielle.

Seeing her friend about to be plunged into the nightmare of shattered bodies, Jean took a resolve. If Liz could cope, then so could she. She must have no more thoughts about the horrors Colin might face. They must be cast out of her mind for ever.

From a distance they watched the hospital crew hurry into the farmhouse.

Liz had been on the wards with Dr Simons when they heard the rattle of machine-gun fire followed by the roar of low-flying planes.

Liz's glance at the doctor was a mixture of query and resolve.

He caught her look and said, 'We might be wanted. Let's be ready.'

She followed him from the ward to the ambulance outside. She liked Dr Simons; he was a kindly, thoughtful man who would stroke his short goatee beard when pondering a patient's symptoms, but was quick on decisions of organisation. In this crisis he hurried through the hospital, summoning an orderly and an experienced nurse to the ambulance and rousing the driver from his cup of tea.

They were ready when they heard the boom of the crash,

followed by a silence punctuated by the sound of weaving fighters with power retarded as if their job was done.

'Let's go,' he called to the driver, whom he had told to have his engine running.

'Where to?'

'We'll soon know when we get away from here.'

The ambulance sped away from the hospital and a glimpse of the circling fighters indicated where the crashed plane must be.

The driver spared nothing for speed and they were soon pulling to a halt at Bannial Flat Farm. Dr Simons saw there were no casualties near the wreckage and realised that if anyone was still alive they must be inside the building. His supposition was confirmed by shouts from some of the people who were still around, awed by the bomber which could have brought destruction to Whitby. He hurried into the house followed by the two nurses, the orderly and the driver, both of whom were trained for emergencies. He weighed up the situation quickly. Two airmen were wrapped in blankets, hugging hot-water bottles, to combat the cold and the shock.

The contorted face of one of the men told him that he was suffering acute pain, whereas the second casualty, although ashen-faced and shaking as he raised a cup of hot tea to his lips, was not in such a critical condition. Dr Simons signalled to the older nurse to look to him while he and Liz went to the first man.

He spoke in English, though not knowing whether the German understood or not. His voice was gentle, offering, by its friendly tone, reassurance that all that could be done would be done. He pulled back the blanket carefully and had to hide the shock he felt when he saw the extent of the man's wounds. He was bleeding profusely from the stomach where the fighter's bullets had torn him apart.

Dr Simons shot Liz, who knelt at the other side of the wounded airman, a quick glance. He saw she had blanched at the sight but had held herself in a firm grip of determination to face whatever came. He found the morphine and, while Liz held the airman's hand to comfort him, made the injection.

'Stay with him,' he said to Liz.

She nodded and rolled the blanket over the German.

As he went to the second casualty, the doctor said to the two orderlies, 'Stretchers.'

They hurried out of the house while he knelt beside the wounded man.

He nodded to him and gave him a reassuring smile. The nurse had rolled back the blanket. She looked at the doctor and said, 'Legs badly shattered.'

The doctor's examination was swift. With the nurse's help, he cut the boots away and put the legs in splints. The left one was broken and was certain to be saved, but the right one was so badly mutilated that he thought it likely that it would have to be amputated.

When he was satisfied that he could do no more on the spot and that the Germans needed hospital treatment as soon as possible, he had the orderlies take the wounded men to the ambulance.

The doctor and the two nurses rode in the ambulance with the two casualties. The airman with the stomach wound cried out in agony and reached out for Liz's hand. When they reached the hospital, he once again reached out as he was taken from the ambulance. Holding his hand, Liz walked beside the stretcher into the hospital, releasing it only when they reached the entrance to the operating theatre. She gave him a gentle, reassuring smile before he disappeared from view.

Sister Wood took over and Liz stood staring at the closed doors for a few moments. Vivid flashes of the man's anguished face, the gaping wound and the oozing blood, whirled in her mind. She hoped she had given him some comfort. She turned slowly, took a grip on her feelings, and went to the ward where she knew they had taken the other German.

From the doorway she saw nurses bustling around his bed, preparing him for the operating theatre. She was not needed. As she turned away, she came face to face with the matron.

'Nurse Johnson, Dr Simons tells me you did well. It has been a harrowing experience for you. If you wish, you may take the rest of the day off.'

'Thank you, Matron, but I would rather stay. I'd like to know what happens to the man in the theatre.'

'Very well, Nurse, but go and make yourself a cup of tea.'

Liz was thankful for that drink. The hot sweetness soothed and calmed when the impact of the ordeal overpowered her. She sank on to a chair, sipping at the liquid, staring unseeingly over the rim of the cup. Her mind in some ways was a blank, insensitive to her own feelings but bringing vividly before her the airman's young face contorted in agony. It swam before her, mingling with his torn body bathed in blood. They faded into the background, leaving only his eyes, blue, with the fire of life burning in them, staring at her, pleading that he be given the chance to live. She felt his touch again, seeking comfort in his torture. She started. All she could feel was the warmth of the cup she cradled in her hands and all she could see was a clinically green-painted wall. She sighed, finished her drink and went back to her duties on the ward she had left during the raid. But it was no longer the same. Her world had been turned upside down.

'Meet you off the train this evening,' called Colin as he left the girls at the end of St Hilda's Terrace where the lorry had dropped them.

Jean and Gabrielle hurried to the council offices.

'Wonder what Mr Potter will have to say,' said Jean.

'About us being late or about what's happened?' Gabrielle gave a little chuckle as she pictured Mr Potter looking at them over the top of his glasses.

Their office was large and high. Five big mahogany tables, each with its own large wicker wastepaper basket poised as if anticipating a deluge of paper, occupied most of the floor space. A wooden upright chair was set at each table except that occupied by Mr Potter. Here he had installed a new swivel chair, his pride and joy, a status symbol showing that he was in charge. He had developed a habit of making a slight swing to and fro when he was talking to one of his staff.

He did this now when Jean and Gabrielle walked in. He watched them slip out of their overcoats and hang them, together with their berets and scarves, on the mahogany coat stand which occupied the corner beside the door.

As they adjusted their skirts and smoothed their blouses, they were aware that he was watching them. When they bent down to remove their galoshes, they exchanged a wink. They straightened and made to go to their tables, the other two being already occupied by their fellow workers.

'Ah, Miss Lawson and Miss Harland, at last you've thought to grace us with your presence.' Still making his sidewards motion with his chair, he leaned against the back, cradling his hands at the top of his waistcoat. With an elaborate gesture, he removed a watch from his waistcoat pocket, glanced at the time and replaced it. 'Well, what have you to say for yourselves?' His small eyes peered over his glasses, darting from one to the other.

Both girls had come to his desk and were standing in front of him, aware of the sniggers from the other clerks, who, while still keeping their heads over their ledgers, had stopped work to listen.

'There's been an air raid, Mr Potter,' said Jean casually.

'I'm well aware that something has been going on,' he replied. He pursed his lips and then, shaking his head, slowly went on, 'But that is no reason why my young ladies should be late. There is work to be done here, no matter what is going on outside.'

'Mr Potter, a German bomber was brought down. It crashed near Bannial Flat Farm,' said Gabrielle, the words pouring out quickly. The tremor in her voice and excitement in her eyes were meant to penetrate Mr Potter's serious nature.

Jean caught Gabrielle's mood and tactics. 'And we were there, Mr Potter. We helped to put out the fire when the pilot tried to destroy the plane.'

At this information the girls saw a light of curiosity in his brown eyes and they guessed he wished he had been there, for they had heard him express regrets that he was just too old to volunteer for the armed forces. They charged quickly into a description of what had happened and diverted his attention from the point that they were late. The fact that they had been there riveted the attention of the other two girls, who left their work and came nearer so that they did not miss one word. They wanted to be able to relate the details to their families and friends with the authority of 'we know someone who was there'.

Exchanging descriptions, emphasised with vivid gesticulations, Jean and Gabrielle held the attention of their small audience for ten minutes. Suddenly Mr Potter stopped his swinging, gave one sharp clap of his hands and straightened up with authority.

'That will do. We've spent enough time over this. There's work to do. So, girls, back to your desks.' Mr Potter always called the tables 'desks', deeming the term more appropriate to an office.

Liz left the ward to dispose of some dressings. Sister Wood was hurrying along the corridor.

'Nurse Johnson.'

'Sister.' Liz waited for her superior, wondering if she had done something wrong, for the sister was a stickler for things to be just right.

'Nurse.' Liz noticed that the sister's voice had taken on a softer tone than the one she usually used. 'I'm sorry to tell you that the German airman you brought in has died on the operating table. There was nothing the surgeons could do.'

Liz felt an emptiness in the pit of her stomach. She stared at the sister, wanting to scream, 'It can't be true. I held his hand.'

'All right, Nurse, get on with your duties.' The sister walked briskly away.

Liz moved slowly along the corridor. For one moment she had seen tenderness in the sister. There had been a brief dropping of the façade of stern regularity. Behind it Liz had glimpsed a sympathetic woman. There was no need for her to have given Liz the news, she would have heard all in good time, but knowing that the airman had wanted Liz there right up to the moment he was taken into the theatre, she realised he would have wanted the nurse to be told this way.

Liz felt dazed. A life gone. A young man who only a few hours ago had taken off from a German airfield, probably laughing and talking with his companions, was dead. Now that made two; the one to whom death came suddenly had not suffered, the other had died only after tormenting agonies. A third lay in a hospital bed needing a desperate fight to save his shattered leg, and the final member of the crew, the lucky one, was a prisoner of war. Their war was over. How futile it all was! Young lives lost or wrecked on the whims of rulers and politicians. The German leaders were to blame for the loss of these airmen just as they would be for the loss of any of our own. And among them could be Ron, Martin and Colin. Their little gang of six could be decimated. A chill gripped her heart. Oh, after what I've seen, she thought, don't let them fly! But she knew that Colin had his heart set on being a pilot and nothing would stop him.

Colin waited impatiently for the evening train to arrive from Whitby. He stamped his feet against the cold and drove his hands deeper into the pockets of his overcoat seeking warmth. His breath, chilled on the cold air, drifted away beneath the dim light of the odd lamp allowed in wartime, provided it was adequately shielded from prying enemy aircraft.

The train was five minutes late. He hoped nothing happened to delay it longer. His concern vanished a couple of minutes later when he heard the distant rumble of the wheels, followed by a whistle.

The train, its carriage blinds pulled down to hide the dimmest of light permitted for travelling, clattered to a halt with a hiss of steam. Doors opened and shut with a dull clump. Shadowy figures hurried along the platform, cleared of snow, towards the WAY OUT sign. Six passed Colin without a glance and disappeared into the darkness. Then he saw Jean and Gabrielle coming towards him.

'Hello! Thanks for coming.' Both girls expressed their gratitude.

They bade good night to Mr Newton as they left the station. Colin produced a torch, suitably blacked out but allowing sufficient light to show the path immediately in front of them when needed.

Colin placed himself between them and they linked their arms through his. They had taken only a few steps when he said, 'I've some news for you.'

There was a fervour in his voice which was not lost on them. They anticipated some exciting pronouncement.

'When I left you this morning, I volunteered for flying duties in the RAF.'

Both girls stopped in mid-stride. Colin was jerked to a halt.

'What!' Gabrielle was the first to gasp.

Jean was speechless. Icy fingers closed on her heart. She was hardly aware of the exchange between brother and sister.

'I'm going to fly. Just like those fighters you saw bring down that German bomber,' Colin elaborated.

'Do Mum and Dad know?' asked his sister.

'Yes.'

'And they approve?'

'Mum shed some tears. I think Dad was proud that I'd volunteered rather than wait for call-up.'

'That's what he did in the last war,' said Gabrielle. 'You sure Mum's all right?'

'Yes, Dad got her to understand and I think in some ways it has lifted a weight off her mind now she knows what I'm doing. The uncertainty was bothering her.'

The words had been only half heard by Jean but suddenly the impact of what Colin had done and what it might mean hit her. 'Oh, no!' The words came as a half moan and then they strengthened as she went on. 'You can't, Colin, you can't! Not after what we saw today. Those Germans. It could happen to you. You mustn't go.'

Colin turned to her. He slipped his arm away from his sister, who tactfully wandered on out of earshot.

He took Jean in his arms. 'I'll have to, sooner or later.'

'Then make it later,' Jean put in quickly.

'It's better if I do what I want to do.'

'But you'll be gone all the sooner. I won't have you here.' The plaintive cry struck at his heart but he knew he had to be firm.

'I'll be back, and you'll like to be seen on the arm of a pilot in air-force blue.' He tried to make light of it.

'But . . .' Jean started, then drew back. She knew he was right. She would be proud of him. She must not spoil his enthusiasm. 'I'm sorry, I shouldn't be a wet blanket. Of course I'm proud of you. It's just . . . after what we saw today.'

'I know, love. I'll be all right. Nothing's going to happen to Colin Harland.' His voice was convincing and then his lips met hers in a kiss which sealed the deep love he had for her. Her response was a kiss that would be with him wherever he was.

Liz woke in a sweat. It wasn't the extra blanket she had managed to scrounge, nor the hot-water bottle, but the nightmare which had haunted her sleeping mind. Mangled metal hung with tortured bodies, spurting blood from gaping wounds, bullets splattering flesh and bone everywhere, faces swirling and turning in torment, mouths wide in soundless screams, hands reaching out, grasping but never able to grip, never finding the comfort they sought, all drove her mind in wild confusion. She sat up in bed, trying to bring order to a mind disturbed by what it had witnessed. Slowly, in the half-world of consciousness, a face appeared, a young face with a flyer's helmet hanging loosely round the neck. The face was unmarked, bore no signs of the horrors of war, and was at peace, the troubles of the world no longer there. Instead there was an aura of tranquillity in the eyes and an expression of thanks for the comfort she had given. Yet she did not recognise the face. It was as if it was an embodiment of all the airmen in the world who might suffer the same fate as the German bomber crew.

Liz started. The face had gone and she was left in a darkened room. She sank back against the pillow with a sigh and groped for her torch. She eased herself out of bed and made her way slowly to the bathroom for a drink of water.

Her steps back to bed were slow, her thoughts dwelling on the illusions which had haunted her, trying to pin some reason on them. She sensed there was a message in them somewhere but it eluded her. She sank into bed, pulled the clothes around her and snuggled down, seeking the soothing warmth. Her mind was active, probing for the meaning behind her dream. Sleep did not come easily and when she did doze off she was no nearer a solution.

When she woke the next morning, it was as if the answer had always been there. She knew the meaning of last night's experience and she knew exactly what she had to do.

She washed and dressed quickly and after breakfast went to the sister's office. Her knock was answered with 'Come in.' Her heart beat a little faster as she opened the door.

Sister Wood looked up from her desk. 'Ah, Nurse Johnson, come in.'

'Thank you, Sister.' Liz closed the door. She licked her lips nervously as she came towards the desk, realising that she was under the close scrutiny of her superior. She liked Sister Wood and knew her strict disciplines were for the nurses' good. She could detect a kind gentleness behind her grey eyes which rarely gave anything away. She had a sympathetic ear but would not condone frivolity nor familiarity.

'Well?' Sister Wood prompted when Liz hesitated.

'Er, Sister, I have a request to make.' Liz paused, trying to read in the sister's face how she would take it.

'Very well, get on with it.'

'I would like to leave, Sister.'

The statement was so sudden and unexpected that for one moment Sister Wood dropped her guard and a fleeting expression of surprise and disappointment crossed her face.

'You want to leave? I think you'd better sit down and explain yourself.'

'Thank you, Sister.' Liz sat down on the wooden chair opposite the desk. She held herself straight, her hands folded together on her lap.

'Has this anything to do with yesterday?' asked the sister.

Liz nodded. 'Yes.'

'I thought it might. But from what I hear and from what I saw when you returned to the hospital with those airmen, you conducted yourself very well indeed. Dr Simons had nothing but praise for you. I am surprised by your request. I thought you were happy with us.'

'Yes, but—' Liz began.

Her superior wouldn't be interrupted. 'And I believed

you to be a dedicated nurse. You have all the qualities, and I think you would have gained promotion in the nursing profession. I must say it makes me sad to think that you want to give it all up after you have shown such promise.'

'Oh, but I don't want to give up nursing,' Liz burst out.

The sister stiffened. 'Then what are you wasting my time for? What is this request all about? You said you wanted to leave.' Her voice had taken on a sterner tone.

'Yes, Sister. I want to leave Whitby, not nursing.'

'Leave Whitby?'

'Yes, Sister. Yesterday's experiences haunted me last night and seemed to tell me something. This morning I realised what it was. I want to be where I am more likely to serve the forces.'

Sister Wood did not speak for a moment but her expression softened. 'And you think that is not in Whitby?'

'Yes, Sister. I think that yesterday was exceptional. That isn't going to happen every day or even every month. In fact, it may never happen again. We are hardly front line.'

'No, but we are essential and I can tell you that there are plans drawn up for us to take wounded men, should the necessity arise.'

'But that will be after they've received initial treatment. I want to be with them before that.'

The sister studied Liz. She saw determination in her eyes and in the set of her face. Liz knew what she wanted, she would get it somehow or other, but it would be easier with her help. She leaned back in her chair. 'Very well, Nur – Elizabeth.'

Liz was taken aback by the use of her Christian name. She had never heard Sister Wood use a nurse's forename before. Her heart fluttered with excitement. She knew she had won.

'Very well.' The sister was going on. 'Had you any particular service in mind?'

'Yes, Sister. Princess Mary's Royal Air Force Nursing Service.'

Sister Wood gave a little nod and allowed a small smile of understanding to touch her lips. 'After the care you showed the German airman, I can understand that. Very well, I'll see what I can do.' She leaned on her desk, signifying that the interview was over.

Liz stood up. 'Thank you, Sister.' She turned and left the room.

The following Friday as Liz came off duty, she received word that Sister Wood wanted to see her. Since Monday she had been wondering what her fate would be. There had been moments when she was buoyed with hopes that her desire would be fulfilled. Other times she despaired, seeing no reason for them to be satisfied. Now her heart beat a little faster as she anticipated the outcome.

'Sit down.' Sister Wood indicated the chair.

Liz looked hard at her face but could glean nothing from it.

Leaning forward on the desk, her hands clasped together, Sister Wood watched Liz settle herself. 'I gave your request careful thought and decided to see what I could do to help. I have a friend, Sister Asher, an experienced nurse who is at Biggin Hill, a fighter station just south of London. She is the first of the Princess Mary's Nursing Service to go there. I told her about you and about what happened last Sunday. Though she has two WAAF nursing orderlies, she has been pressing her superiors in the Nursing Service for an assistant. This phoney war can't last for ever and Sister Asher believes Biggin Hill could be in the front line if there are air raids on England. Then she is going to need more help. She thinks she may have a chance if she can mention a new recruit whom she would like. She said she would see what she could do. She has just rung back and has got her way.'

Liz's heart beat faster. She wanted to jump up and hug Sister Wood.

'The fact that you're a trained nurse helped,' Sister Wood went on, 'but you can't go straight to Biggin Hill. As you probably know, all nurses in Princess Mary's Nursing Service are officers, wear the appropriate braids of WAAF rank, but are referred to as Sister. So in order to qualify for that status you will have to spend some time at Halton Hospital. You have to report there next Friday.' She paused, then added, 'How does that suit you?'

Liz's eyes lit up with delight. Her wish had been granted. 'Oh, fine, Sister, just fine! Thank you so much for what you've done.'

Sister Wood smiled at Liz's excitement. 'Your thanks will be in what you make of it. I strongly recommended you, and both Sister Asher and I have cut through red tape. Don't let us down.'

'I won't, Sister, I won't.'

'Very well, then it's all settled. It's your day off tomorrow, is it not?'

'Yes, Sister.'

'Then I suggest that, since you've come off duty now, you are finished as far as your duties here are concerned.'

'But I'm willing to come in—'

'I knew you would be, but you'll need a few days to prepare and be with your family before you go south.'

'Very well. Thank you, Sister.'

'That's it, then.' Sister Wood relaxed. All artificial barriers were down. She sank back on her chair. 'Elizabeth, I wish you all the luck in the world. You know, in some ways I envy you – young, starting out and maybe going to help young men as you helped those Germans.'

'But I did so little, Sister.'

'You were there with your comfort. Never forget that is one of the greatest assets we nurses have – to be able to offer comfort when needed. People can draw strength from that, maybe even the will to live.'

'Yes, Sister.'

She stood up and Liz took her cue to leave. The sister came from behind the desk. She held out her hand. Liz took it and felt not only warmth but also sentimentality in the grip and she knew that the nurses did not really know Sister Wood. 'Good luck, Elizabeth. Don't forget us.'

'I won't, Sister.' Her words choked.

The sister tightened her lips momentarily, driving away the lump in her throat, then said, 'Matron has been consulted at every stage of this, so don't forget to thank her when you leave.'

'I won't, Sister.' She paused, met the other woman's look of admiration and said, 'Thank you from the bottom of my heart. I'll be a credit to you.'

'I know you will.' Sister Wood swallowed hard.

On impulse, Liz flung her arms round her and hugged her tight. 'Thank you,' she whispered, then turned and fled the office.

She did not see the sister brush a tear away from her eyes before returning to her desk and routine.

Liz was at the station when Jean and Gabrielle arrived for the evening train to Robin Hood's Bay. The train, which had come from Middlesbrough, was already in. Once they were settled in a dimly lit carriage with its blinds drawn, Liz explained the situation and what had caused her to reach this decision.

'Your mum and dad know?' asked Jean.

'No. I have to break the news when I get home.'

'Well, best of luck,' replied Gabrielle. 'It's going to be a blow to them.'

'This is the splitting-up of us six, probably the last time we'll all be together, seeing Ron's on leave. Colin could go any time,' said Jean. 'Tomorrow's Saturday, we should all have a final trip to the pictures together. We must do it.'

'Right. Afternoon performance and a fish-and-chip tea afterwards,' said Gabrielle enthusiastically. 'Your folks won't mind one last time all together?' she added, turning to Liz.

'No, it'll be all right.'

When Jean and Gabrielle left Liz at the end of Clover Road, the two friends commented on Liz's decision.

'She's making a contribution to this war,' said Jean. 'What are we doing? Stuck in the mouldy old council offices. We should be doing something worthwhile.'

'So we should,' agreed Gabrielle. 'It's been on my mind since Colin volunteered.'

'Then why don't we?' A note of enthusiasm had come to Jean's voice.

'Why not?'

They contemplated the opportunity to escape the confines of Robin Hood's Bay.

'Right. Let's say nothing to anyone. Tomorrow you and I will go in on the early train and arrange to meet the others at the cinema.' Jean seized on the chance. 'You tell Colin to see us there and he can tell Ron and Liz when they meet at the train. I'll tell Martin.'

'So, which service?' asked Gabrielle.

'Colin and Liz are getting involved with the air force, so why not us? We'll volunteer for the WAAFs.'

Chapter Seven

1940

'Well, we aren't going to let that spoil our day,' said Gabrielle breezily as she and Jean stepped out of the recruiting office into the pale sunshine.

Jean took her cue from her friend. 'That's right, we aren't. They'll just have to wait until the third of June for us to win the war for them.' The smile disappeared and she looked seriously at Gabrielle. 'You will wait for me, won't you? You'll be nineteen a month before me but you won't join up without me?'

'Of course not, you ninny. We must go together – after all, I've talked you into joining the WAAFs.'

'I don't think I took much persuading when you and Colin are so bent on wearing air-force blue. Wonder when he'll have to go.' Jean still dreaded that day, though in a less emotional way than when Colin broke the news that he had volunteered for flying duties. Now she accepted that everyone had a part to play in ridding Europe of an evil regime which threatened the whole world. Deep down she admired Colin for volunteering. And if she was accepted into the WAAFs when she was nineteen, then maybe she would be posted to the same airfield.

'Let's not say anything to the others about trying to volunteer today,' Jean went on. 'I don't want it to get back to Mum and Dad. He'll try to stop me but when I've signed up on my birthday, he won't be able to do a thing about it.'

Gabrielle readily agreed, for she too did not want to worry her mother.

The two girls spent a pleasant time window-shopping and exploring parts of the old town, until they were due to meet the others off the train from Robin Hood's Bay. They strolled on to the platform from which the thin covering of snow had been swept. Seeing Charlie busy with brush and paste, they sauntered over to see what he was doing.

'Hello, Charlie! They're keeping you busy,' commented Jean.

'Aye, they are that. Replacing all the holiday posters. Shan't need them now. Putting these up instead.' He indicated three which were on the wall.

The girls glanced at the posters, two of which urged people to join up while the third offered advice on what to do in an air raid.

'Will you be joining up?' asked Charlie.

'Not old enough yet,' replied Gabrielle. 'We've got to be nineteen.'

'Maybe then, eh?' He gave them a shrewd appraisal. 'You'd both look smart in uniform.'

146

The conversation was halted when the train's whistle heralded its approach. The two girls said goodbye and walked towards the train, which was slowing down alongside the platform.

They saw Colin's head appear and a huge grin split his face when he spotted them. They could sense an excitement as he vigorously waved what looked like an envelope. The train stopped, the carriage door swung open and Colin was running towards them.

'It's come, it's come,' he shouted. He swept Jean into his arms and whirled her round.

His laughter was infectious. Jean had to laugh with him even though that tiny piece of paper cast a shadow in her mind.

'Has it?' she asked tentatively as he put her down.

'Yes. Letter came after you two had left.' His gaze now embraced his sister, who took pride in linking arms with Ron, looking more handsome than ever in his sailor's uniform. 'I go on Monday.'

'So soon?' Jean felt dejected, but was determined to hide her feelings and not spoil his euphoria. This was something he wanted and had looked forward to; she was not going to cast a gloom over him.

'Yes. Better than hanging about any longer.' He was relieved by knowing exactly what he was doing and when.

'And I've heard too,' put in Martin who, with Liz, had joined the others.

'Monday for you?' asked Gabrielle.

'Yes,' Martin confirmed.

'And with Liz leaving next Friday, this really is the break-up,' said Jean sadly.

147

'Then let's make the most of today,' suggested Colin brightly.

Stars glistened like diamonds and a pale moon hung in a cloudless sky when they alighted from the train at Robin Hood's Bay. The air was sharp and clear and the breeze was hardly noticeable. A peaceful hush hung over the coast. The war seemed a million miles away.

They were in excellent spirits. For the whole day, they had thrust their break-up to the back of their minds and enjoyed each moment. They had had an invigorating walk along the pier, which sharpened their appetites for fish and chips before going to the cinema.

Now, as they left the station, they drifted away in pairs, an unwritten understanding between them.

Jean and Colin, arm in arm, turned off the Bank and passed the nineteenth-century brick houses of the Esplanade. Once they had a view of the sea, they stopped. They did not speak. There was no need. They shared a silence as only two people deeply in love can do. The shimmering path of silvery light across the sea beckoned them to another world where only love mattered. Only the soft lap of the waves far below broke the silence.

Jean did not want these moments to pass. Now Colin was safe beside her. Before long he could be drawn into the world far removed from this peace, a world of horror, of kill or be killed, a world which might take him from her. She shuddered at the thought and snuggled closer to him, reassuring herself that he was really there and that they were sharing these moments of unspoken love.

'Cold?' he asked.

'No.' She gave a little shake of her head. 'But I'm going to miss you terribly,' she said, a tremor in her voice.

He turned her to him, kissed her lightly and said, 'And I'll miss you too.'

'But not as much as you think,' she replied. 'You'll have new places, new people, fresh happenings to occupy your mind. I'll still be in the same old routine here, the familiar all around me, but you won't be here.' The words caught in her throat.

'I'll be back. I'll be coming on leave. But it's too nice a night to be thinking of our parting. Forget that. Treasure these moments so we can carry them with us wherever we are.' He drew her to him and kissed her gently, his lips sending a quiver through her. Then he swept her into an engulfing passion, fierce and unbridled.

For one brief, almost unrecognisable moment, she was startled by the intensity of his kiss, but then she relaxed and let herself be swept along on the tide of sheer joy. Her arms came round his neck and she pressed close to him as she returned his kiss with equal fervour. Her lips trembled and she sensed the hunger in him.

As their lips parted, Colin gasped in a low whisper close to her ear, 'Oh, I love you so much.'

'And I you,' returned Jean.

Still holding her, he eased back so he could look into her face. He saw her love burning brightly, and he also saw adoration and longing. The moonlight caressed her smooth skin with a silvery sheen and played at the wisps of light-brown hair which peeped from beneath her beret. It framed her with a bewitching aura which he found irresistible. His lips found hers again.

With passion flowing between them, he unfastened the buttons of her coat and moved closer to her. Feeling the soft warmth of her body, his fingers moved the buttons on the front of her dress.

She started. 'No, Colin.' Her voice was hoarse. Her hand came to his, protesting and preventing.

'Why not?' he gasped.

'Not here, not now.'

'I'll be gone on Monday. Tomorrow will be so full there'll be no chance.'

She saw that his frustration was touched with annoyance but she met his hurt expression with tenderness.

'Colin, when it happens I want it to be memorable, not some furtive in-the-corner act in the heat of the moment. I want it to be a fulfilment of all the love we feel for each other.'

She saw the haunted look fading from his eyes to be replaced by remorse. Before he could speak, she went on quickly.

'Please don't apologise for trying. I'm flattered that you want me so much, just as I want you, but I want it to be a time we'll remember and in a place which will always be special to us. It would be neither if we gave way now.'

He did not speak but looked into her eyes and saw all the love he was imparting with his tender gaze acknowledged in the way she met that look. He hugged her tight. 'Oh, I love you so. You're right and I'm sor—'

Her fingers pressed on his lips. 'I said, no apologies.' She kissed him and he swept her into his kiss with all the love he felt for her.

When their lips parted, they stood, arms round each

other, in a lover's silence, and absorbed the night around them to remember this time for ever.

Colin stirred. He fished in his pocket and drew out a small box. 'A present for you,' he said quietly, offering it to her.

She took it slowly. Her eyes, touched with surprise and appreciation, met his. 'Colin, you shouldn't.'

'I want you to have something to remember me by,' he said quietly.

'I have our love and memories,' she replied.

'I know, but this will be a reminder. Open it.'

She fumbled in her eagerness but when she raised the lid she stood transfixed, staring at the contents. The moonlight caught the sheen of a silver chain and glistened on the jet pendant which hung from it. Beside it lay a jet brooch shaped and etched as a pilot's wings.

'Oh, Colin, they're beautiful,' she whispered, her words full of appreciation. There were tears in her eyes as she looked up at him. 'I'll wear them always.' Her arms came round his neck and she kissed him in a long and lingering kiss which held all her love for him. 'Please put them on?' she said when their lips parted.

He pinned the brooch carefully to her dress. She handed him the chain and pendant and turned her back to him. He put the chain round her neck and, after a couple of unsuccessful attempts, secured it in place. His hands came to her shoulders and held her still. He took in the delicate scent of Blue Grass which he knew she kept for special occasions. He would remember it always. He pressed his face close to her ear and whispered, 'I love you, Jean. Never forget me.'

151

She twisted round and grasped him tightly. Alarm flicked her voice. 'Forget you? How could I? I love you so much.' She clung to him, never wanting to let him go. 'Can you keep a secret if I let you into one?' she whispered, low as if the night might have ears. She glanced at him and saw curiosity spring into his eyes.

'Of course I can.' Colin made his voice convincing, for his interest had been aroused.

'You must tell no one.'

'Cross my heart.'

'You mustn't even mention it in a letter.'

'I won't.'

'Gabrielle and I intend to volunteer on my nineteenth birthday. We swore we wouldn't breathe a word of this to anyone. I don't want it getting back to Dad. I don't want him to know until I've signed on.'

He saw the earnest plea in her eyes and said, 'I won't tell a soul.'

'Don't even mention it to Gabrielle. She'd think I'd betrayed a confidence.'

'I won't. What service are you thinking of joining?'

'The WAAFs.'

His eyes sparkled with enthusiasm. 'Maybe we'll end up on the same station.'

'Wouldn't that be exciting?' Laughter filled with promise trilled on her lips. She hugged him. 'I love you so.'

Gabrielle and Ron walked from the top of the bank to the path which ran along the edge of the cliffs. Ron slipped his arm round her waist. She snuggled closer and let her arm come round him.

'Know where you'll be going next?'

'Not yet. Posting will be waiting when I get back.'

'You'll let me know?'

'Of course.'

'That's if you want me to write.'

'You know I do.'

'Did Liz's decision surprise you?' she asked.

'No, not at all when she told me about what had happened and how she felt. She's very compassionate and I can see her wanting to be where she thinks she can be of most help.'

The moon sent its beam across a tranquil sea. A slight breeze barely stirred the grass. They stood drinking in the silence until the plaintive cry of a lonely sea bird split the night air.

'Wish the sea was always as smooth as this,' commented Ron.

'You get seasick?'

'This isn't the night to talk about such mundane things.' His voice turned serious as he added, 'What about you and me?'

'Ron . . .' There was a cautionary note in Gabrielle's voice. 'You know how I feel.'

'I know what you've said – you don't want to get into a serious relationship. But that doesn't express how you really feel about me. We've got on so well together, we enjoy each other's company, and I know how I feel about you. I think you may feel the same but won't let yourself admit it.'

'It's true, I like you a lot, maybe I do love you, I just don't know. I don't want to commit myself until I'm sure.

I wouldn't want to tie you down. You might meet someone else.'

'I won't,' Ron broke in with a sharp protest.

Gabrielle gave a small laugh. 'It's all very well to say that on a night like this, moonlight, the stars and a girl in your arms. It's heady stuff and maybe I'll fall.'

'Then why not?'

'They say a sailor has a girl in every port and you're going to sea.' She saw he was going to object and went on quickly. 'We like each other a lot, let's enjoy that and the time we spend together. Don't let's get too serious. There's a war out there waiting to erupt. Who knows where it might take us? So don't let us tie each other down.'

She kissed him and, as his arms squeezed her and he returned her kiss, she knew she had won his agreement.

Liz and Martin's fingers entwined as they left the station. They walked without speaking, just pleased to be in each other's company. They came to Grove Road and Liz stopped.

'Too nice a night to go in yet,' she said.

Martin cocked his eyebrow. 'Like a walk on the beach?' He knew it was a favourite with Liz.

'Let's,' she agreed with enthusiasm.

Hand in hand they left the new buildings on top of the cliff and hurried down the steep roadway towards the beach. The moon cast dark shadows in the narrow streets where the houses and cottages crouched close together as if propping each other up. There was no one about as they hurried down the Bank, along Bridge End and New Road to the Dock and across Wayfoot on to the beach. Martin

154

helped Liz across the slippery scaurs until they came to the sand. They slowed their pace to a stroll and moved across the beach until they came to the water's edge. The small waves seemed to find it an effort to break and run up the sand. They stopped and looked out across the sea shimmering in the moonlight. It filled the bay with a magical aura.

'This is what I'm going to miss,' said Liz, her voice low as if breaking the silence was a sacrilege. Here she found peace and the nightmare horrors of the German plane were laid to rest. She drank in the scene to carry with her through the unknown trials which lay ahead. The future was uncertain but this bay, this sea, this peace would still be here long after the turmoil of war and shattered lives were distant memories.

'So will I,' agreed Martin.

'You're a Bay person,' Liz commented. She had sensed his love of the Yorkshire coast ever since their first walk together, when he had taken her to see the bird life along the cliffs.

'Yes, but who knows what changes this war will bring?'

'You'll never change. You'll come back here.'

'But what to do? There'll be no more inshore fishing.'

'You'll find something. Your heart's here.'

'And you? What will you do?'

'Oh, I'll be back. There'll be nowhere else for me.'

'See you here after the war,' said Martin seriously.

'Shake hands on it.'

Martin smiled and took her hand in a firm grip of resolution. Their eyes met in deep understanding. He kissed her and hand in hand they walked along the beach.

* * *

Jean paused, her right hand on the doorknob. She listened to Colin's footsteps fading as he made his way along the narrow street to the main road to climb the bank to his home. She fingered the pendant which he had fastened around her neck with such tenderness. She must take it off, and the brooch. Her father must not see them. He'd demand an explanation and she could not lie about them, then he would tell her to remove them and never wear them again.

She took hold of the chain to unfasten it at the back of her neck. She stopped. Why should she take them off? Hadn't she promised Colin she would always wear them? So she would. She'd face her father's wrath. She'd stand up to him. She stiffened her spine, lifted her head and walked into the house.

Her father was sitting to one side of the fire reading the paper and her mother sat on the other sewing some buttons on a shirt, a pile of mending on the table beside her. The fire burned cheerily in the grate and a kettle, hanging on the reckon, puffed steam. The scene was cosy and comforting, but soon it would be driven into upheaval.

'Hello, love, had a nice day?' Her mother looked up from her mending.

'Yes, thanks, Mum,' replied Jean, taking off her beret and scarf and slipping out of her coat. As she hung it on her hook beside the door, she noticed that the one used by Martin had nothing on it. He was not home yet. Maybe just as well.

'Like a cup of tea, love?' asked Sarah. 'Kettle's boiling.'

'Oh, yes please. It's a bit parky out there,' she replied, rubbing her hands together, as she turned round.

Sarah, in the act of putting down the shirt she was mending, stopped. She stared at the pendant and brooch. She realised instantly who must have given them to Jean. Questions would be asked and the thought of the impending confrontation chilled her. There was no chance of it being avoided. Jonas couldn't fail to notice them, and, knowing her daughter, she knew she would not lie about them. Sarah realised she might as well meet the dispute head on; besides, Jean would expect her to admire the gifts.

'Those are lovely pieces of jet, love, let me have a look.' Jean came to her mother, who handled the pendant delicately and admired the brooch with approving appraisal. 'They're beautiful, they really are.' She raised her eyes to Jean and saw from her look that her daughter was not going to hold back.

Jonas, lowering his paper to his knees, glanced across at them. 'Let me see.' Jean turned to her father. 'Very nice,' was all he said, but in the pause which followed she knew he was waiting for an explanation of how she had come by them.

'Colin gave them to me.' Seeing her father's face darken at the mention of his name, she went on quickly before he could speak. 'He got his call-up papers today. He leaves on Monday for the air force.'

'And these are a farewell present?' asked Sarah.

'Yes, something to remember him by.'

'Take them off!' Jonas's voice was low but firm and piercing.

'No, Dad, I won't.' Jean's tone was equally firm and there was defiance in her stance as she drew herself upright.

Jonas's eyes blazed. 'Don't thee say no to me. Take

157

them off and tomorrow give them back. I'll have nowt bought with Harland money in this house.'

Fury blazed in Jean's eyes. 'They're mine. I'll not give them back to please a man who's let bitterness eat his heart away.'

Jonas's lips tightened. 'Thee knows nowt about it.'

'She knows the story,' Sarah put in. 'Has done for a long while.'

'Yes, and I know you were wrong.' Jean's voice lashed him like a whip. 'Aunt Mary had things in her own doing. No one else could be blamed.'

Jonas flung his paper aside and leaped to his feet. His body was shaking with anger. He seemed to fill the room with a power which would overwhelm them. For one moment Jean thought that the unlikeliest thing was going to happen. She could feel the blow coming, but she stood unflinching, daring him to do just that. Her mother had sensed the same thing for she was on her feet beside her daughter. There was a warning in her direct, intent gaze – strike our daughter and you strike me.

Jonas glowered at Jean. His anger was at boiling point but he held it back from destroying for ever his relationship which at this moment tottered on the brink of extinction. 'What is Colin to you?' he demanded. 'Thee once said thee loved him.'

'I do.'

Her words sounded a knell in Jonas's mind but he did not heed it. This was the moment when he could turn back, when he could approve of his daughter's relationship with Colin and win back the love she had for him.

'Love? What does thee know of love?' he sneered.

'I know,' she said quietly, with a conviction which shook him.

'Even if thee does, how the hell could thee love a Harland? Thank goodness he's going. Apart, thee'll get him out of your system and come to your senses.' His voice firmed harshly. 'Now, let that be an end to the matter. And don't let me see you wearing that rubbish ever again!'

The cutting edge to his voice, never a mention of Colin, of what he was like, of what he meant to her, and the dismissal of him as if he was nothing hurt Jean and brought tears to her eyes.

'Oh, Dad, how could you?' She shook her head slowly. The tears flowed in spite of her biting hard on her lip. She ran past him, out of the room, up the stairs and flung herself on to her bed and wept into her pillow. For one long moment Sarah stared hard at her husband. The contempt she felt for him threatened to swamp her and she was frightened.

But she had to speak her mind. 'Why, oh, why are you trying to destroy the love that girl has for thee?' Her arms hung wearily by her side as if the weight of her husband's obsessive hatred for the Harlands had at last become too much for her to fight.

'It's not me. She's doing that, associating with Sam's offspring, a man who's a murderer.'

'Rubbish,' snapped Sarah, 'and thee knows it.'

'He drove Mary to the sea.' His intensity heightened. 'Can't thee see it all happening again? I couldn't say anything in front of Jean, it might have put ideas into her head. Colin's off to war, just as his father did. Mary loved

159

Sam just as Jean says she loves this boy. Colin's going out into a big world and could easily find someone else and come home with a wife like his father did. And then what might Jean do? Can't thee see, Sarah, by opposing this relationship now, I could be preventing her heart being torn in two by the shock, just as Mary's was?'

'Jonas, they're grown up. This war has brought them to adulthood sooner than normal. It's in their attitudes to the world and to each other. Give them credit. They'll cope if thee will let them. Give her a chance. Don't break the girl's heart. She loves Colin deeply and, from what I hear and what I've seen, he loves her just as much. Let her wear the mementos. It will break her heart if she can't. I know it would have broken mine if I couldn't have worn that necklace thee gave me when thee went off to war.'

Jonas licked his lips.

Sarah saw a chink in his opposition. She pressed on. 'Don't forget, being apart will let them both see their love in a different light. They may realise that they weren't really meant for each other. If that happens, then all this upset, this fight with Jean, will have been for nothing. You'll have got your way and thee could have had it without all this feuding.'

'Maybe thee's right.' Jonas nodded thoughtfully. 'Besides, Jean will be here.'

Sarah made no comment. She had accepted the fact that one day Jean would fly the nest, and now the war might precipitate this. If Jonas had not seen it, then she was not going to speak of the possibility. Far better to deal with that when the time arose.

'Then make peace with her. Take her a cup of tea and

tell her she can wear them.' Sarah turned to the kettle and filled the teapot. She stood it on the table and let the tea brew while she got a cup and saucer, poured in a drop of milk and added half a teaspoon of sugar. 'And don't forget to say thee's sorry,' she said as she handed him the cup of tea.

'But—' he started.

'No buts. Thee's a stubborn man, Jonas Lawson, but even thee can utter three words if thee's a mind to. Now off with thee.'

Jonas left the room. As she heard his footsteps clumping up the stairs, Sarah sank wearily on to a chair and held her side.

Jonas opened the door of Jean's room tentatively. He peeped round. She was lying face down on the bed, her body racked with sobs. He pushed the door wider, stepped into the room and closed the door behind him. He crossed to the bed and set the cup and saucer on the small table. He sat on the bed and placed a gentle hand on her shoulder.

'Jean, I'm sorry,' he said hoarsely. 'I didn't mean to hurt thee. Thee wear the necklace and brooch whenever thee wishes.'

Jean, who had stiffened at his touch, could hardly believe her ears. She swallowed hard. She turned over, sniffing to try to stop the tears. She looked up at her father through red-rimmed eyes and saw a gentle face so different from the one she had seen downstairs.

'I'm sorry,' he said again.

Jean sprang up and flung her arms round his neck.

'And so am I for what I said.' Tears came again but this time they were tears of joy.

A short while later, her father downstairs again, she heard Martin come in and, after a few minutes, come upstairs. She undressed, put on her nightie and was reading in bed when she heard her mother come to bed. Her father was still downstairs, she could hear the wireless. She slipped out of bed, slung a shawl around her shoulders and tiptoed to her mother's room. She tapped lightly on the door and opened it just in time to see her mother stop rubbing her side.

'Something wrong, Mum?' she asked as she crossed the room. It was a room she had always loved to visit, for, though it was slightly larger than her own, it had a cosy atmosphere. As a little girl she had always felt safe and secure here and it still held that aura.

'Nothing. Maybe a little strain,' Sarah answered brightly but untruthfully. She had experienced a nag off and on for a few weeks but thought lightly of it. There was no need to worry anyone. It would pass. 'Well?' She wanted to divert Jean's attention back to the purpose of her visit.

'Dad said I can wear Colin's presents.' She sat down on the bed beside her mother and took her hand with a loving touch. 'I think you had something to do with it.'

'Maybe I got him to see sense,' replied Sarah, a knowing twinkle in her eyes.

'How?' asked Jean.

'Does it matter? Suffice that he agreed.'

'Does this mean he's going to make it up with Mr Harland?'

'Ah, that's a different matter.' She saw disappointment cross Jean's face. 'Don't thee bother your head about it. Just make the most of what he's agreed.' She turned serious. 'Thee loves Colin?'

'Yes, Mum, oh, so much.' Her body tensed with the thought of him.

'Then I'm happy for thee. But a word of warning, love. This war is going to get much worse and who knows where it will take everyone and what will happen to them? So enjoy your love while thee can, for who knows how it will be tested.' A faraway look had come to Sarah's eyes. Then she started and looked at her daughter. She drank in the silence and Jean sensed she did not want it broken. The moment passed. Sarah smiled, a gentle smile filled with a mother's love. 'And God be with thee, whatever happens.'

The Monday-morning train for Scarborough was on time. Colin, Martin and Ron waited with mixed feelings. They were sorry to be leaving their families and friends but eager to see what the world beyond Robin Hood's Bay had in store for them.

Sam and Colette had words with Colin, Colette offering last-minute advice as a mother would do, ignoring the fact that he was fidgeting to have a few moments with Jean.

Gabrielle had slipped away to have a word with Ron, who was standing with his mother and father.

Liz was chatting to Martin and his mother. Jonas was on duty and had said his farewells earlier in the morning.

As the train rumbled into the station, goodbyes flashed between everyone, kisses were exchanged and good wishes were called.

'You'll be with me wherever I go.' Ron's voice was low as he hugged Gabrielle.

'Don't wait until the end of the war to meet.' Liz smiled at Martin, knowing he would associate her words with the vow on the beach.

'I'll never take them off,' whispered Jean, indicating Colin's gifts as she embraced him.

Carriage doors slammed shut. Mr Newton checked them quickly and signalled to the guard that all was in order. The guard blew his whistle and waved his green flag. The train hissed and chuffed. Its wheels started to turn, slowly at first, then gaining momentum.

'Goodbye!'

'Goodbye!'

'Write!'

'Will do!'

'Take care!'

Then they were out of earshot. The train was moving faster. All they could do was wave. They did so until the train was out of sight. They stood a little longer, thinking they could still see it; then, slowly, they turned away from the tracks.

They glanced at each other. Eyes were dabbed with handkerchiefs. Sam coughed, swallowed hard and took a grip on his emotions as Tom Johnson came to have a word.

'God go with them,' murmured Mrs Johnson.

'Aye,' agreed Sarah. 'And may this war soon be over with them safely back.'

Colette looked round wistfully. 'Only girls left now, and you'll soon be losing Liz, Mrs Johnson.'

'Yes.' The sad look which came to her eyes was mastered

quickly and banished. 'But it's what she wants to do. The war makes them grow up so quickly.'

The three girls had a brief word, then Jean and Gabrielle said goodbye to their parents and waited for the train to Whitby. They would not have to make excuses to Mr Potter, for he had given them permission to see their brothers leave for war.

Chapter Eight

1940

Darling Jean,

I passed my medical and Air Crew Selection Board with flying colours.

Normally we would have been allowed home awaiting posting, but it seems the RAF are needing our services sooner rather than later, so in a few days' time we'll be going on to the next stage of our training. Don't know where yet but I'll write with an address as soon as I get there.

We've been kept busy with medicals, interviews, kitting out, inoculations (some lads in the long queue keeled over at the thought of them!) and drill to smarten us up before we leave here. A few lectures to familiarise us with RAF law and procedure.

I've met some nice lads – four of us have teamed up. Geordie – nickname so there's no need to tell you where he's from – Norman from Brighouse, Tom from Stockton and Eddie from Stoke. Eddie and I were on guard from two until four in the morning with rifles we weren't even shown how to use! Ungodly hours but I kept my spirits up thinking of you.

I miss you so much and long to see you again. You are always with me wherever I am. My three pals said I was a lucky guy when they saw your photograph. There was no need for them to tell me that. I know I am.

I'll always love you.

Take care of yourself, darling,

All my love,

Colin

She read the letter time and time again. It would always be precious.

She wrote back:

16 February 1940

Darling Colin,

Many thanks for your letter which arrived this morning, Friday. I was so pleased to get it and to have an address so that I can write to you. From what you say about moving on, this may be the only one I'll write to this address. Do let me know your new one as soon as you can. It is awful not knowing where you are. I want to know so that I can be in touch with you always.

Liz left today. We were sorry to see her go but it's something she wants to do. Hope it all turns out right for her.

Everyone here is well, except that Mum seems a little bit under the weather. She worries about Dad and your dad. I know it has concerned her all these years but there's nothing she can do.

Gabrielle has heard from Ron. He's on the next stage of his training and seems to be relishing it – though he couldn't say where or what he was doing.

We've heard from John and James. They are still together. They dropped a line between ships. Of course they couldn't say where they had been or where they are going. It's nice they've managed to stay together even when they are moving to another merchantman.

No word from Martin, which is also causing Mum a bit of concern, but I tell her we'd have heard if anything had been the matter.

I think that's the news from here but I can't stop without saying how much I love you. My heart is ever yours and I hold you in my dreams which are continuous even when I am awake.

Take care of yourself. You are very precious. Being apart hurts and I look forward to the day when this war will be over and we can be together always.

My love is only for you.

Jean

PS I'm looking forward to my nineteenth birthday!

Martin's entry into the air force moved swiftly. Once he had been kitted out, inoculated, documented and initiated into air-force procedure and drilled, his posting was speeded up by the fact that he wanted to go into Air-Sea Rescue. This branch of the RAF was being expanded quickly by those who foresaw that there would be need of a service to concentrate on rescuing aircrew who had ditched or baled out over the sea.

9 March 1940

Dearest Liz,

I don't know your address so I am sending this to your home. Hope it soon reaches you. And then I look forward to hearing from you.

I hope you have settled into your new surroundings and that you like them.

Once our preliminary entry into the RAF was through, postings were made and I was one of the first to move. As you will see, I am at Calshot on Southampton Water. I can't say anything about our training here but once it is over we have to wait for a vacancy to occur at one of the ASR bases. From what I hear, there is likely to be a vacancy sooner for a wireless operator so I have volunteered to do that course once I am finished here. So far things are going well and I hope they are for you.

I often think about our walk along the beach that Saturday evening.

You are in my thoughts,

Love,

Martin

'Any letters?' Jean asked as she met Gabrielle on the platform at Robin Hood's Bay.

The May weather was warm. The trees were coming into full foliage. Will Newton took a pride in keeping his railway station spick and span and beautified with flowers in spite of the overshadowing news from the continent. With the German armies having occupied Denmark and Norway and then sweeping through the Low Countries into France, the situation looked ominous for the Allied armies. The British were fighting against overwhelming odds as they fell back towards the coast.

Apart from the thought of what might happen and concern for loved ones involved in the fighting, the news had little direct impact on Robin Hood's Bay. Anti-invasion defences had been placed along the beach and the cliffs, marring the curvilinear sweep of the bay. People were becoming aware of the threat of invasion and the vigilance of the coastguards and the Observer Corps was of some comfort.

'One from Ron. Can't say what he's doing but he seems pleased with the way things are going for him,' said Gabrielle.

'And the rest was personal?' Jean chaffed.

'Of course,' replied Gabrielle with a smile which gave nothing away. 'How about you?'

'Mum and Dad had one from Martin. He's moved to Blackpool, doing a wireless course there. Seems to be enjoying it.'

'Good, but what about you? Have you heard from Colin?'

'Not this week. Last one told me he was halfway through his Initial Training Wing course. Felt he was doing pretty good and was over the frustration of his last posting, where he felt they were just kicking their heels instead of getting on with something important.'

'Will he be getting leave?'

'Doesn't know. He hopes so, when they finish this course, but it will all depend where he has to go to next.'

'Maybe you'll see him before we volunteer. Won't be long now.'

'Happy birthday, love!' Sarah greeted her daughter brightly as she came into the kitchen. She turned from the spluttering bacon in the frying pan on the fire and gave Jean a loving kiss and a hug. 'Saved you a bit of bacon specially for today.'

'Thanks, Mum.'

'Happy birthday, lass,' said her father, straightening from unfastening his shoes, pleased to put on his slippers after his night duty.

'Thanks, Dad.' She gave him a kiss but, knowing what was going to happen before she came home, she felt in her heart that it was a Judas kiss.

He stood up and took a small packet, neatly wrapped in coloured paper, from the mantelpiece. 'Here thee is. A present with our love.'

'Oh, thanks, Dad.' Eyes wide with excitement, she glanced across at her mother, who was smiling in anticipation of her daughter's surprise when she opened her gift. 'Thanks, Mum.' She quickly unfastened the coloured string and peeled off the paper to reveal a small box. She opened it with a sort of reverence and her eyes widened even further when she saw the wristwatch which lay on a piece of mock velvet. 'Oh, Mum, Dad, it's beautiful!' When she looked up, her eyes were damp with joy. 'Thank you so much.' She hugged them both.

'Well, we thought they're going to be hard to get if this war goes on so we'd better get you one now. Your dad picked it up in Whitby before going on duty,' her mother explained.

'But you shouldn't have spent so much,' replied Jean.

'Well, things are a little easier now that your dad's in regular employment. Now sit down, this bacon's about ready.'

Jean sat at the table and Jonas pulled out the chair opposite. He watched her admire the gift, take it out of the box and slip it on her left wrist. She held out her arm for them all to see the watch in place. Its small, round face with clear figures sat neatly on her wrist, the brown leather strap just tight enough to hold it firm.

'It's nothing fancy, lass, plain but attractive,' said her father.

'It's lovely, Dad! Something I'll always have with me to remind me of you both.'

When Jean left the house she felt some remorse. The unexpected nature of the gift had struck at her heart, for she knew when she returned home her news would stun her parents, particularly her father. Her mother would be understanding and accept her decision, but from the hints her father had dropped about her role at home, he would be very much against her leaving.

She feared their old friction would arise again, even though over the past few months he seemed to have mellowed. His acceptance into the coastguards had helped, for he saw in his new job a contribution to the war effort, which he had not wanted to pass him by.

She knew he thought that her close relationship with

Colin had eased since his departure. He only knew of the odd letter for her that arrived at the house, but some she collected from the postman on her way to the station and others arrived when he was in bed after a night shift and her mother secreted them away awaiting her return from work.

As she walked up the Bank, she saw the postman come out of Bloomswell. 'Hello, Mr Chase, anything for me?' she called eagerly and quickened her step so as not to delay him too long.

'Aye, if I remember rightly, there is, miss,' he replied brightly, always pleased to produce what he expected would be a love letter. He fished in the big brown bag which he had slung over one shoulder.

'I'm sorry to be a bother,' Jean apologised.

'No bother at all,' replied Mr Chase breezily. 'Ah, here we are.' A broad smile suffused his ruddy face and his eyes sparkled with delight at giving this young, attractive girl pleasure. 'My word, three for you.' He held them out. 'A special day?'

'Birthday,' she said as she took the letters.

'Then, a happy birthday to you, lass,' he boomed. 'Hope you have a lovely day and that those are from the right folk.'

'Oh, they are, Mr Chase,' she replied with a quick glance at the writing on the envelopes. 'Thanks.'

She started up the Bank and the postman watched her for a few moments, wishing he was young again.

The envelope from Colin had a small bump in one corner. She stopped, opened it carefully and extracted the paper, but nothing came with it. She felt in the envelope and brought out a small object wrapped in tissue paper, which she unfolded. A lump came to her throat and tears dampened her eyes when she saw a small enamelled brooch in white and gold, a replica of a pilot's wings. It lay in her palm expressing Colin's love for her. She kissed it, then slipped it back into the envelope along with the letter. She was dying to read it but she was already behind time and she must not miss her train. Putting the letters carefully into her handbag, she hurried to the station.

The train was already in when she rushed on to the platform. The doors were all closed and Gabrielle was looking anxiously out of one of the carriages.

'Come on, lass, we're holding it up for you.' There was no criticism in Will Newton's voice, just pleasure that his judgement had been right.

'Thanks, Mr Newton,' she gasped as she scrambled through the door which Gabrielle had opened.

As Jean collapsed panting on the seat, Gabrielle slammed the door, Will blew his whistle and with a hoot and a hiss the train started off for Whitby.

'Thought you weren't going to make it,' said Gabrielle. 'If you hadn't, I couldn't wish you a happy birthday.' With a smile she thrust a parcel at her friend.

'Oh, thanks!' Jean returned the smile as she pushed herself upright on the seat and took a deep breath.

She undid the parcel quickly to find an air-force blue, V-necked jumper.

'Oh, it's gorgeous!' gasped Jean. 'Knit it yourself?'

'Yes.'

'Then it's all the more thought about.' Jean was already on her feet peeling off her light coat and cardigan in order to try it on. She slipped it over her head, smoothed it into place and spun round on her toes. 'There, it's perfect! Thanks so much, Gabrielle.'

'I thought it appropriate for today.' She was watching Jean closely. 'You aren't having second thoughts?' she asked when she saw a flicker of doubt brush her friend's face.

'No.' The doubt was gone. 'It's just that I know it's going to hurt Dad. And they gave me this today.' She held out her arm so that Gabrielle could see her watch.

'That's nice. Lucky you!'

'I've something else to show you,' said Jean, excitement returning to her voice as she replaced the jumper with her cardigan and jacket. She fished in her handbag, produced the three letters, and tipped the brooch on to her hand.

Gabrielle's eyes widened at the rich colours. 'Gorgeous,' she said. 'And there's no need to ask who it's from.'

Jean smiled. 'No.'

'What's he say?'

'Haven't read the letters yet. I nearly missed the train as it was.'

'Then you read them. I'll keep quiet.'

Jean sank back against the seat and took Colin's letter from its envelope. She unfolded it and read.

2 June 1940

Darling Jean,

A happy birthday! How I wish I was there to share it with you and give you the best birthday present of them all – my love. The small token of my affection

175

brings that love and whenever you wear it I hope you will feel that I am near.

I had hoped we might get leave after finishing our course but we are still stuck here doing very little, awaiting a posting. Where that will be we do not know but there are all sorts of rumours floating about. This waiting about is frustrating. They might as well let us come on leave but I suppose a posting may come through any day. That day can't come quickly enough for it means we will start flying. But it will also bring the day nearer when I can see you. The longer we stay here, the further off that day will be – and I long for it to come.

I long to hold you in my arms again and tell you how much you mean to me. You are everything. You are there in my dreams and in my waking thoughts.

Until I can kiss you, and beyond, my love is ever there.

Yours till the end of life's story,
Colin

A shiver ran down her spine and for a few moments she sat staring at the final sentence.

'Is my brother all right?' Gabrielle broke the silence between them.

Jean started. 'Oh, yes. He's fine, just fed up of waiting for a posting.'

'And that's all? Aren't you going to tell me more?'

Jean met the teasing twinkle in her friend's eye with a smile. 'That's for my eyes only.'

'Who are the others from?'

'Martin and Liz.' She opened Martin's letter and read aloud.

2 June 1940

Dear Sis,

A very happy birthday! Hope you have a great day. Expect it will be work but no doubt you and Gabrielle will find something to make it memorable.

'We sure will,' Gabrielle broke in. 'Today's the day we change our lives.' Jean made no comment but went on reading:

The course here is going well. I've taken readily to signals and I hope it means I will be assigned all the sooner to a launch. I'm looking forward to that and to getting on the sea again. Wish this course had been on the south coast, we might have got involved in the evacuation that's going on from Dunkirk. There's a magnificent job going on down there. Hope we can get most of our forces out. It's what may follow that worries me, especially with Liz being in the south. Still, what will be will be. Take care of yourself and have a happy birthday.
    Love,
    Martin

Neither girl made any comment. The news over the past few days had been grim. They had listened to the wireless, horrified at the sweeping triumphs of the German army but proud of the rearguard action the British had put up all the way to Dunkirk. And they had marvelled at the miracle that had brought calm seas to the Channel and enabled the valiant little ships to play their part in an evacuation that was almost complete. The next couple of days must see the closure of all escape routes by the Germans, and then – invasion?

Jean opened the other letter and again read it aloud. There would be no secrets in a letter from Liz and Gabrielle would be interested in her news.

1 June 1940

Dear Jean

I had to write and wish you a happy birthday and all the best for the future, wherever that may be.

Sorry I can't be there to share any celebration you and Gabrielle may be planning, but I'm there in spirit and whatever you have, have one for me.

My course is going well but I look forward to finishing and getting to Biggin Hill where I expect to be nearer the action. Will be in touch when I get there.

Love to you, my dear friend, and wherever we all finish up, the memories of our gang of six will always be cherished in my mind, especially your friendship and understanding as Martin's sister. Love to Gabrielle, she is also important to me.

Love,

Liz

Not a word was spoken for a few moments.

'Think Liz and Martin are together? Neither mentions hearing from the other,' Gabrielle asked.

'I think they got close, but I think they have an understanding,' replied Jean.

'You mean like Ron and me?'

'No, different. You think a lot about Ron but you won't commit yourself, not as he wants. You want to leave your options open but I don't think that's the case with Liz and Martin. I think there's a deep feeling between them, almost a serious commitment, but with this war I think they want to go no further. There's a big world out there and who knows what will happen or who they will meet? So they leave their friendship open while remaining very close.'

Gabrielle nodded. 'And you? Doesn't the world out there hold any thoughts that you or Colin may find someone else?'

Jean shook her head. 'No. We love each other too much for that. Doesn't that brooch say it all? My only fear is that the war may take him from me.' There was a catch in her voice and Gabrielle reached out and squeezed her hand.

'Such thoughts are not for birthdays,' she said firmly. 'Colin will be all right.'

Chapter Nine

1940

'We've done it!' Jean and Gabrielle chorused as they rushed into the office.

Mr Potter looked over the top of his glasses, leaned back in his chair, folded his hands across his stomach and beamed at them.

'Well done! I envy you signing on to do your part in the war. I wish I was younger, I'd be out of this office in a flash.'

The two girls started to take off their jackets, ready for the afternoon's work.

'No need for that, girls.' Mr Potter waved a hand to stop them. 'No need to go on working. I know we said you'd leave a week after signing on, but you'll want to have some time to prepare so you may as well start right away. There'll be a week's pay in lieu of notice. And thank you for letting me know your intentions. I kept your secret but it did give me time to line up two married women to take your places as soon as you leave.'

'Thanks, Mr Potter.' They both displayed their appreciation.

He held up his hand in protest. 'No, it's thank *you* for what you've done. I'll miss you. You made this office a much brighter place.' He rose from his chair, came from behind his desk, shook hands with them and wished them well. 'And do come and visit when you get leave. I'll always be interested in your progress.'

'We've the whole afternoon free. Want to go straight home?' asked Gabrielle when they stepped out into the warm June sunshine.

'I'd sooner go home at the normal time,' replied Jean. 'That way I'll only see Dad for a short time before he goes on night duty. And he's going to blow his top when he hears what I've done.'

'Right, let's have a walk along the west cliff and look at the shops on the way,' suggested Gabrielle.

They paused to look in windows in Flowergate and Skinner Street, where displays were not yet showing any marked effects of the war. They came out to the road which ran along the top of the west cliff, walked for a while and then found a seat which gave them a good view across the sea and back across the harbour to the abbey standing high on the east cliff, bleached in the bright sunlight. The sea was calm, the wind sighed but a little.

'Peaceful,' said Jean quietly, as if speaking might bring the horrors of war to shatter it.

'You wouldn't think that there was a war on.'

'No. I wonder where our decision today is going to take us,' said Jean wistfully.

* * *

181

'Had a good day, love?' Sarah asked when Jean came in.

'Yes, thanks, Mum.'

'Pity thee had to work on your birthday.' Sarah set the chip pan on the paraffin stove. The shopkeeper had warned that paraffin would be in short supply and his customers would have to use it carefully, but Sarah had decided that even if she ran out of paraffin she was going to use it today and cook Jean's favourite haddock and chips for her birthday. She had saved a tin of peaches, always a special treat, for this celebratory occasion, and had carefully hoarded some currants and raisins to make Jean a birthday cake. It had baked well in the fireside oven and at this moment nestled out of sight in the pantry.

Jean shrugged her shoulders. 'One of those things.' She was on the point of saying, 'I've finished', but her father looked up from the paper he was reading and asked, 'Watch going well?'

'Oh, yes, Dad. Everyone admired it,' she said proudly.

He smiled benignly, knowing something she did not know. 'Your Ma's got a special treat for thee.'

'I know, fish and chips fried Mum's way.' She glanced at the pans.

'More than that,' said Jonas with a twinkle in his eye.

Jean noticed it. Oh, he could be so nice! They had always had a close relationship. She had realised at a very early age that, being the only girl among three boys, she could weave a special magic and twist him round her little finger. The only mar was whenever any question of her friendship with the Harland children arose. And his objections had become stronger as she had grown up.

She couldn't spoil the meal, so lovingly prepared, by

182

making her announcement now, but she must do it before her father left for work. She couldn't delay for another day since she would have to give a reason for not going to work. She would hide her apprehension about what she had to do, enjoy the meal and reveal her intentions after they had eaten.

'Run and get washed, everything will soon be ready,' said Sarah, turning back to the stove.

Jean seized the opportunity to gather herself together and try to formulate how she would announce her decision.

Once Jean had left the kitchen, Sarah brought the bowl of sliced peaches and the birthday cake to the table. She also produced a plate of home-made jam tarts, the fruit plates and spoons which had been kept out of sight so that nothing was given away prematurely. Satisfied that everything was right, Sarah turned back to the cooker and the scene was one of everyday domesticity when Jean walked in, having put on her best dress, metallic blue, plain at the top, tight at the waist and flaring with small pleats. The wide shoulders ran into tight-fitting sleeves.

She stopped when she saw the table. This was no ordinary meal as she had expected.

'Oh, Mum! This looks lovely. You shouldn't have . . .'

Both Sarah and Jonas were smiling at the surprise on their daughter's face.

'Thee's worth it, love,' said Sarah.

'Aye, thee is.' Jonas nodded his approval.

Tears welled in Jean's eyes, tears of joy and thanks, but her parents were not to know that there were also tears of regret for what she was going to do to them.

* * *

The meal was over and they were savouring a last cup of tea when Jonas said, 'I must be getting ready. No point in having to rush.' He started to rise from his chair.

Jean, dreading the moment which was upon them, swallowed hard and licked her lips. 'Dad, sit down, I have something to tell you.'

He looked askance at the serious expression on her face. He shot his wife a glance but he could see from the way she was looking at her daughter that she did not know what was coming.

'Mum, Dad.' Jean glanced at them in turn. 'Today I volunteered for the WAAFs!'

The silence of disbelief filled the room. Only the measured tick of the clock intruded, seeming to add to the tension.

'Oh, no!' Sarah gasped, not so much because Jean would be leaving, she knew that would come one day, but because of the way Jonas would take it.

'You're not!' Jonas's eyes flared at Jean. He had spoken and there was nothing else to be said about the matter. 'You can get into Whitby tomorrow and withdraw the papers.'

'I can't. It's done.' Jean had determined to stand up to her father, to be resolute and not falter. 'Even if I could, I wouldn't!'

Sarah cringed. Jean's defiance would rattle Jonas. Oh, they got on so well, thought so much of each other but were so alike in many ways that when anything rubbed them up against each other there were fireworks. This time she could sense there would be dire consequences, and she knew, no matter how much she tried, she would be unable to influence the outcome. But she had to put in a word. She sighed and held her side.

'Thee's thought this through carefully?' she asked.

Before Jean could answer, Jonas boomed, 'Whether she has or not, she's not going.'

'I am, Dad, and that's all there is to say.'

He glared at her for trying to put finality on the situation. 'It's not!'

Jean interrupted before he could go on. 'Dad, I'm nineteen—'

'And not old enough to know your own mind,' he cut in.

'You're living in the past, Dad. This war's changed things. There are young men out there, no older than me, fighting for their country. Girls are in the services helping the war effort. I want to be part of it. Colin—'

'Ah, I might have known! So it's Colin Harland who's influenced thee? Those bloody Harlands again!'

Jean straightened. She met his derision. 'No, Dad, he didn't influence me.'

'Maybe not directly. But the glamour of him training for aircrew has rubbed off on thee.' A suspicion had come to his eyes. 'Thee been hearing from him?'

Jean saw no use in denying it. 'Yes, I have. Lots of letters. He loves me. It was natural that he should write. He sent me this for my birthday.' She turned back the small lapel on her dress, unfastened the brooch she had received from Colin that morning and pinned it above her right breast.

Jonas's lips tightened. 'Thee intercepted letters so I wouldn't know.' He glanced at his wife. 'Sarah, did thee have anything to do with this?'

She faced his questioning gaze, matching look for look. 'Yes, I did,' she replied firmly. 'If Jean didn't see the postman on her way to work, and I recognised Colin's writing, I kept those letters out of your sight.' She held up her hand to halt the words which were springing to her husband's lips. 'If thee had known they were writing to each other, life in this house wouldn't have been worth living.'

'Mr and Mrs Harland have no objection to Gabrielle signing on with me today. Why can't you be the same?' Jean demanded.

'So it's Gabrielle, that lass who doesn't know whether she's French or English, who's persuaded thee?'

'She did not persuade me. It's something we both decided individually. But, having decided, she showed true friendship by saying she would wait until my birthday when we could sign on together and hopefully go together when we were called up.'

'Thee knew I wanted thee to stay at home for your mother's sake. She has three sons away in the war – to lose her daughter too—'

'Dad! Don't!' cried Jean. She didn't want to hurt her mother and she realised her father knew it.

Jonas sensed a weakening. There was a little gleam of triumph in his voice as he went on. 'She needs thee, not just for your help around the house but to have something to cling to.'

Jean shot her mother a look pleading for support.

Sarah bit her lip. 'Of course I'd like her here. What mother wouldn't?' There were tears in her eyes. 'But there comes a time when parents have to let their children fly the nest. Give them a blessing and let them go.

Be understanding about it and they love you all the more and they'll come home more often, bringing that love with them because they know that they have your love. That time is maybe now for our daughter.'

'Mum's right,' Jean put in quickly to strengthen her point. 'I'm not going because I love you less. I want to do something worthwhile.'

'And isn't it worthwhile being here with your mother?' snapped Jonas, irritated that his wife had not backed him up.

'Of course it is,' replied Jean.

'Yet thee'll go?'

'Yes.'

Jonas's lips tightened. 'It's those two damned Harlands. They've talked thee into leaving. Probably primed by Sam!'

'Don't talk ridiculous,' snapped Jean, annoyed at her father's unreasonable judgement. She braced herself. 'Dad, I've signed on and I'm going.'

Jonas's eyes narrowed. 'If thee goes, thee need never come back!' His words were cold, leaving no doubt in anyone's mind that he meant what he said. He pushed himself from the table. He took no notice of Sarah's gasp of 'Jonas!' and hurried from the room. He had spoken and that was final.

Sarah stared at the door as it closed behind him. Tears filled her eyes but she bit them back. Oh, why couldn't he be understanding? Why did he still allow the bitterness towards Sam to rule his outlook? She turned to her daughter and saw she was crying.

Jean met her mother's sympathetic gaze. 'Oh, Mum,'

she cried. 'I didn't want to hurt you, nor Dad.' A pleading look came to her eyes. 'But you understand, don't you?'

Sarah gave a wan smile and nodded. 'I do,' she said. 'I was like you once, and this war has brought fresh thinking and new opportunities for girls. I wouldn't have thee miss it.'

'Oh, thanks, Mum!' Jean sprang from her chair and hugged her mother.

'When your father's gone, you can sit down and tell me about it. Let's clear these things away. I'm sorry it spoiled your party.'

'It didn't, Mum. It was a lovely meal and thank you for it.'

They busied themselves clearing the table and putting the food away. They had started to wash up when Jonas returned.

'I'll be off now,' he grunted.

'All right, love, take care,' said Sarah, turning from the sink. She could not let him go without those words of affection. She loved him in spite of his faults but sometimes it was hard when his bitter attitude affected Jean.

He did not acknowledge her tenderness. He reached the door and stopped. He looked back at Jean. 'And thee, young woman, forget about joining the WAAFs. I'll have none of it.'

Defiance sprang to her lips but she felt the slight tap of warning from her mother and withheld it.

Jonas swung out of the door and was gone when Sarah spoke. 'Better not antagonise him any more,' she advised.

Jean smiled. 'Thanks, Mum. I was about to—'

'I know.' Sarah nodded. 'Why do thee think I tapped thee?'

For the next week Jean was on tenterhooks. Her father did not mention the question of her leaving, though she could tell from his attitude that he was still hostile to it and expected her to reverse her decision. Jean wondered if her mother had managed to smooth the situation but she knew that if she had tried she had failed, for when her call-up papers arrived a week later, her father's only words were, 'Thee knows what I said, if thee goes thee need never come back.'

Those words weighed heavily on her heart for the next two days but she drew strength from her mother, who told her, 'I know he's hurt thee but try not to think about it. He'll come round. I'll do my best to make him see reason.'

But she knew what a difficult task her mother had when, on the day of her departure, as she was getting dressed, she heard her mother's raised voice, 'Thee's going off to work without saying goodbye to the lass? Aren't thee going to wish her well?'

'There're no goodbyes to be said. I don't expect her to go, I expect her to be here when I get back.' Jonas's voice boomed through the house.

'Don't be so damned stupid, man! She can't turn back now.' The cold anger in her mother's voice startled Jean. She had never heard it before.

'She can if she wants to but those damned Harlands have influenced her, persuaded her to leave just to get at me.'

'Thee's talking nonsense and thee knows it. Harlands, Harlands, thee's become so obsessed with the name that thee can't see sense.'

'It's thee and Jean that can't see sense,' snarled Jonas. 'Before the Harlands have finished the same thing could happen to Jean as happened to Mary.'

'Rubbish!' lashed Sarah. 'Why keep your head in the past?' Disgust filled her voice. 'Oh, get off to work before she comes down if thee isn't going to say goodbye to her. Let her go without having another argument with thee.'

Jean heard the door bang. She raced down the stairs, ran to the door and jerked it open. She opened her mouth, wanting to make peace with her father, wanting his approval, but the words were never uttered for she heard her mother say sharply, 'Don't, love.' She turned, wanting to protest, but Sarah said, 'It's best not.'

Trusting the wisdom of her mother, Jean closed the door and went to her. She fell on her knees beside the chair on which her mother was sitting, looked hard at her and said, 'I love you so.'

Sarah opened her arms and hugged her daughter tightly, enfolding her into a world of motherly love.

Jean paused at the top of the Bank on her way to the station. She looked back over the red roofs of the old village clinging to the cliffs. Water filled the bay, the sun sparkled on the sea, caressing the white-capped waves with warmth. Shadow and sunlight on the cliffs heightened the contours on the cliff face where it swept to towering Ravenscar, seeming to lend majesty and permanence to a land defying the upheaval of war.

Sarah stood beside her daughter and, without speaking, slipped her hand into hers. She hoped it gave some sort of comfort and reassurance that maybe her father's anger and condemnation would ease with the passage of time. But in the touch Sarah also sought consolation for herself.

Jean's gaze lingered on the scene. She wanted to paint it on her mind to remember every detail of the place she loved, for she knew not when she would see it again. Would she ever return under her father's ban? If she did, and she could not be at the house which was home, would her love for this place be marred for ever? Maybe it would be better to accept the situation and remember things as they were in happier times.

'We must go, love,' her mother said quietly, not really wanting to spoil the bay's magical spell.

Jean nodded and bit her lip to hold back the tears. She turned and hand in hand they walked to the station.

Gabrielle and her parents were already there, and, although the parting was touched with sadness, the two girls experienced the excitement of facing an unknown life together.

'Hello, Colette, Sam,' Sarah acknowledged their greeting.

'Jonas on duty?' asked Sam.

Sarah nodded.

'So this will be your second goodbye,' said Sam, glancing at Jean.

She gave a wan smile and said, 'Yes.'

'Exciting for these two,' said Sarah, wanting to take Jean's mind off her father. 'Wish I was young again.'

'Would you join up as they're doing?' asked Colette

with that lilt of a foreign accent which she had never lost.

'I wouldn't hesitate,' replied Sarah. 'Such a big world out there and they're going to get the opportunity to see some of it. I envy them.'

For a few minutes the conversation carried on brightly until the whistle heralded the approach of the train.

Goodbyes, kisses, and last-minute advice were offered as the train rumbled to a halt. They really did not hear Will Newton calling out the name of the station, nor the clatter of carriage doors as some passengers left the train. Sam opened a door. There were last hugs all round.

'Don't worry, love,' Sarah whispered as she embraced her daughter. 'Think of yourself and enjoy what thee's doing wherever thee are, and always remember me.'

'I could never forget you.' Jean gave her mother a last loving hug, kissed her again and followed Gabrielle into the carriage.

Sam shut the door and the two girls leaned out of the window. With lumps in their throats they forced a smile and knew their parents were doing the same. Jean saw tears in her mother's eyes and her hand reaching out as if she would stop her going but, as their fingers touched, Jean knew her mother was giving her blessing in one final, intimate gesture.

The guard blew his whistle. The train started to move, gaining speed slowly. Everyone waved and shouted their best wishes. Will Newton, further along the platform, gave them his own send-off, which they acknowledged. The figures on the platform got smaller and smaller and then were gone from sight.

* * *

Sarah stood looking even though the train had moved beyond her gaze. In those few moments the growing-up of her little girl flashed through her mind and silently she asked God for his blessings and protection on the young woman she had just let go.

'Come and have a cup of tea with us,' offered Colette.

Sarah hesitated.

'Come on, lass,' urged Sam. 'You'll be going back to an empty house.'

'I have to do it some time, Sam.'

'Aye, but not right away.'

'True. Thanks, I'll enjoy a cup of tea.' Sarah gave a slight smile. 'Wonder what Jonas would say if he knew I was going to have tea with those evil Harlands?' Sam and Colette saw the humour of the situation. Sarah went on, 'I have an appointment at eleven.'

Sam glanced at his watch. 'You have plenty of time to relax over a cup of tea. Don't worry about those two. They're able to look after themselves.'

The surgery clock showed five minutes past eleven when Dr Nichols looked up from the file open on his desk. His serious expression could not disguise the wish that he could do more to help.

He had known Sarah Lawson ever since he had come to the practice twenty-five years ago. He had brought all her children into the world. He had had to treat her only for minor illnesses, but when she had come to him a fortnight ago he had decided that some tests should be made. Sarah was a strong woman but of late he knew that her worries over Jonas had been heightened. He only knew the rudiments of the story but would not pry unless it directly affected his patient. In this case he could see no reason to make a connection.

His light-blue eyes watched Sarah intently as he said, 'I'm afraid it's not good news, Sarah.'

Sarah's features paled. She felt an emptiness in her stomach. Were her worst fears going to be confirmed? She met his gaze and interposed when he hesitated. 'Don't try to gloss over anything, Doctor. Don't hide anything. I want to know the truth.'

Dr Nichols had nothing but admiration for her attitude. He knew she had just seen her daughter off, that her three sons were away and she only had Jonas, who, he realised, could be difficult at times. She held herself straight on the chair.

'Well, Sarah, the tests confirm what we suspected – that you have cancer. And they show that it is much worse than was first thought.'

Sarah dampened her lips. 'Doctor, are thee trying to tell me it's incurable?'

He nodded his head slowly, wishing he did not have to make this announcement. 'I'm afraid I am, Sarah.' He had seen people break down when told this. He had seen them weep uncontrollably. He had heard them utter terrible profanities and curse God, but in Sarah's demeanour he saw the many who accepted it, were prepared to carry on as normal and look ahead by doing what was necessary to put their life in order.

'How long?' There was a catch in her voice.

'Six months, maybe nine.'

'So soon?' The words were a half whisper to herself.

'You could do with Jean at home,' said Dr Nichols sympathetically. 'I know she's just gone, but I could issue a note to say that it is essential for her to be here with you and get her entry into the services deferred.'

Sarah started. 'No, Doctor, no!'

'But—' He started to protest but Sarah cut him short.

'She must not know. I don't want her life upsetting at this time, just when she's embarking on a new one. I don't want anything to destroy the chance she has, a chance I never had, even if it means I shall never see her again.' She paused. 'You see, Jonas said she need never return if she left home to join the WAAFs. I encouraged her to go. I knew what she wanted and I don't want anything to spoil that.'

'And Jonas? Are you going to tell him?'

'No, not yet. If he knew, he might pressure you to do something about getting Jean home. I wouldn't want that. So, Doctor, please, what has been said in this room does not go beyond these walls.'

'You have my word, Sarah. You're a noble mother.'

Chapter Ten

1940

The excitement of starting out on a new life gripped Jean and Gabrielle as the train clattered its way to Scarborough. The train for York was waiting and they quickly settled themselves in the carriage. York station, with its barrel-shaped glass roof and graceful curving track, was a hive of activity. People, many of them in service uniform, were waiting on platforms, enquiring about times, bustling across the footbridge, saying goodbye or seeking some refreshment to while away the time between trains.

A brief enquiry told them that their train, due in five minutes from Newcastle, was on time and would leave from platform eight. They joined the throng of people spread along the platform and, with the arrival of the train, crushed their way on board, only to find the seats were all taken and they would have to stand.

The uncomfortable journey took the edge off some of their excitement, but when they left the train at Kings

Cross their euphoria was heightened. They were in London, the big city, and stood in awe for a few moments once they had passed the barrier. The whole activity almost overwhelmed the two girls, but they soon overcame the feeling of doubt at what they had done and replaced it with the ecstasy of breaking the bonds of home and stepping out into a wide world.

They saw the taxi rank and checked their money. In a strange city, the quickest and safest way was by taxi.

They tentatively approached one of the drivers. 'How much to take us to the Air Ministry?' asked Jean, a little shyly.

The middle-aged man looked them up and down. He noted that they both carried small cases, wore summer dresses with short coats and looked a little bewildered.

'Joining up?' he asked in an accent strange to their ears.

'Yes,' replied Gabrielle.

'First time in London?' There was friendliness in his question.

Jean confirmed this.

'Thought so.' A kindly twinkle sparkled in his eyes. 'Jump in. Won't cost a penny.'

'But—' Gabrielle started to protest.

'You won't get a better offer, so you'd better take it.'

The girls did not wait to be told again and in a matter of moments they were weaving their way through London. The driver kept up a friendly banter, pointing out landmarks to them and enquiring where they had come from.

When they reached the Air Ministry headquarters at Bush House, they offered again to pay the driver but he waved aside their money with a bright smile. 'If I was younger I'd be joining up but I aren't, so say this is just a little of my war effort. Best of luck.' He drove off with their thanks floating after him.

They glanced at each other, took a deep breath and, with an unspoken 'Well, this is it' passing between them, walked into the building.

People were moving everywhere with a purposeful step, except for a sergeant and two lower ranks who were standing behind a long desk answering questions and directing the enquirers to their destinations. Jean thought it looked as though the war was being run from here.

As they approached the desk, they noticed a group of girls in civilian clothes standing in one corner of the lobby, looking a little lost and bewildered by all the activity.

'Looks as though they've just joined, like us,' whispered Gabrielle.

Jean nodded. 'Good job our train was on time – we've arrived with five minutes to spare.' She indicated the clock on the wall behind the desk.

One of the airmen looked up when they reached the desk and before they had time to say anything he said, 'Ah, new recruits,' and then added with a brusque authority, as if he had more important things to attend to, 'Over there,' and waved a hand in the direction of the group of waiting girls.

Jean and Gabrielle wandered over, smiled a little apprehensively at those who met their look, ignored those who glanced at them haughtily, and only half acknowledged those who were looking them up and down, assessing their likely dispositions. Jean was thankful she and Gabrielle were together and she hoped they could stay that way.

The clock moved on to their designated arrival time. Jean saw the sergeant look at it and then, after a glance in their direction, consult the two airmen.

When a few words had passed between them, the sergeant picked up a clipboard to which was attached a sheet of paper. He came from behind the desk and approached the group.

'All right, girls, pay attention. I'm told there's the right number of you reported in, so now I'll check you off individually.' He glanced down at his board. 'Amy Burns.'

'Here.'

The sergeant looked. 'Miss Burns, you're in the air force now.' His voice was understanding. 'So whenever your name is called out, you answer briskly, "Yes, sergeant." Understood?'

'Yes, sergeant,' Amy Burns replied smartly.

'That's better. Now, when your name is called out, you answer as such and then, taking your belongings with you get aboard one of the two lorries waiting outside.'

Jean whispered to Gabrielle, 'Well, he's not the ogre I thought he might be.'

He started down his list. The answers came crisply. The numbers dwindled as the girls left the building one by one.

'Gabrielle Harland.'

'Yes, sergeant.' She picked up her case.

'Myra Hawks.'

'Yes, sergeant.'

Myra, clutching her bag, set off for the door.

Gabrielle hesitated and glanced questioningly at Jean, having expected her name to be called instead of Myra's.

The sergeant glanced up at Gabrielle. 'You, miss, you should be on your way.'

'Yes, sergeant.' She made a tentative step and was on the point of asking about Jean when the sergeant snapped, 'Move! Move!' He smiled as she scurried away and turned back to his board.

Jean was growing apprehensive as the number of girls dwindled. Was her name not there? Was she going somewhere else? Was she to be separated from Gabrielle as soon as they had joined up? Then there were only two of them left.

The sergeant looked up and gave a pleasant grin. 'Don't look so worried, girls. Your names are here, you'll not get left behind.'

Relieved, they both bent to pick up their cases.

'Wait for it. Wait . . . for . . . it.' The sergeant held them up with the tone of his order. 'Kate Simpson.'

'Yes, sergeant.' The girl hurried away.

'And last but not least, Jean Lawson.'

'Yes, sergeant.' Jean caught up with Kate. 'Whew! They had me worried then.'

'Me too.' Kate grinned.

Outside, Gabrielle was waiting beside a covered lorry. The rest of the recruits were already on board, sitting on two benches aligned along the side of the vehicle. The three girls, assisted by the driver, scrambled up the tail-board, which was then raised and fastened.

As soon as the lorry started off, there were speculations about where they were going, but no one knew the final answer, though one of the girls at the back of the wagon blessed with a Cockney accent gave a running commentary on their path through the city. As the lorry started to slow down her final words came as a shock to Jean and Gabrielle: 'Kings Cross. Looks like a train ride for us.'

The tailboard was lowered and they were surprised to see the sergeant awaiting them, for no one had seen him climb in beside the driver.

'All right, gather round,' he called above the chattering. Silence fell on the group. The sergeant surveyed them, then let his eyes rest on Gabrielle. 'You, miss. Gabrielle Harland, isn't it?'

'Yes, sergeant.'

'Couldn't forget a name like that. Never come across it before. Right, you're in charge of this lot. See that they all get to Harrogate.'

'Harrogate?' Gabrielle gaped at him in amazement, as gasps of surprise filtered through the rest.

'That isn't what I told you to say,' rapped the sergeant.

'No, sergeant. I mean, yes, sergeant,' spluttered Gabrielle. 'Sorry, sergeant. But Jean and I have just come down from York. We could have gone straight to Harrogate.'

The sergeant gave a little chuckle. 'What? You'll soon learn, the RAF don't act like that. So you'll just have to have a train ride all the way back. Now, there's a list of these girls, there are your travel warrants, there are two more documents – those and the list have to be handed in at the Majestic Hotel when you get there.' He glanced round the girls gathered around him. 'Don't any of you decide you shouldn't have volunteered and try to skive off. You'll be picked up by the Military Police and you won't like what happens to you then. Transport in Harrogate know what time you should arrive. They'll be there to take you to your hotel.' A buzz went through the group. 'Don't think you're going to be living in the lap of luxury – you'll soon find you aren't.'

So it proved. There was still enough light when they arrived in Harrogate, after a painfully slow journey, to admire the Victorian brick building from the outside. It had a solidity about it that was very English. When they went inside they could appreciate the refinements in the beautiful woodwork, the high ceilings and the elegant staircases, even though the hotel held only austere, functional RAF furniture.

Weary from their journey, they were pleased to be greeted by a sergeant and two corporals. Soon they were wading into enormous helpings of mince, potatoes and cabbage, followed by a treacle sponge and custard. Slapped on the plate, simply served and washed down with a mug of hot, sweet tea, it was hardly appropriate to the magnificent dining room, but they all felt better for it, even though one or two had a few moans and groans.

While eating, they learned that a WAAF sergeant would see them all in the hall after the meal, when they would be allocated to their rooms, and that the next day they would be kitted out and start induction into RAF ways and what WAAFs should and should not do.

When the allocation of beds was made, Jean was pleased that she and Gabrielle were together. Of the other three, two had joined up together. The third occupant of the room was Kate Simpson and, since she and Jean had already spoken, she automatically took to them when the other couple did not appear to want to extend the hand of friendship.

When a tired Jean climbed into bed, she expected sleep to come quickly but it eluded her for some time. The unfamiliar surroundings and the fact that she was sharing a room with strangers were causes and she could not help worrying about Colin.

She had had frequent letters while he was waiting a posting to Elementary Flying School, but these had ceased after her birthday and she had been left wondering where he was. She hoped she would hear soon and that it would bring the news that he was somewhere within easy distance so that they could meet now she had broken the ties with Robin Hood's Bay.

She would have realised how impossible that was had she known that at that moment Colin was on board the Canadian Pacific Railway heading west.

Colin looked out of the window at the monotonous landscape of flat prairie. He had to admit that this was ideal flying country and the British government had been wise in coming to an agreement with the Canadian government to establish airfields across Canada for the training of aircrew. For the most part good weather in a land away from the war, where aircrew could be trained unmolested by the enemy, made ideal conditions. He was looking forward to his first flight – the next step in a life which was becoming something of an adventure.

Once the waiting for a posting was over, he had been sent by train to the Clyde, where they boarded the magnificent liner *Aquitania*, converted to a troop ship, and then made the dash, unescorted, across the Atlantic to Halifax, Nova Scotia. A few more days were spent waiting at a holding unit at Moncton, New Brunswick, where he and his pals enjoyed life without the austerities of war. He had faithfully kept a diary, unofficially, of all that happened to him and his thoughts about it. He wanted to share his life with Jean and had figured that this was the way he could do it. Now he would soon experience flying.

Jean, excitement in her eyes, turned to Gabrielle after collecting their mail. 'One from Colin. He sent it to your home to be forwarded. He's in Canada! Look at the stamp.' He was so far away! When would she see him again? She slit the aerogram open and read:

June 1940

Darling Jean,

This will no doubt come as a surprise to you. Yes, I am in Canada to continue my training. It is all very exciting. We are only in a holding unit. It shouldn't be long before we are posted. I'll let you know my address as soon as possible. I'm longing to have a letter from you to hear all your news and to know where you are and if you and Gabrielle were able to stay together.

I think of you often and long to have you near, to hold you in my arms and tell you how much I love you. You are everything to me. A safe future with you, able to please ourselves what we do, makes this war seem worthwhile. The time cannot go quickly enough for my training to be over and to be back in England so that we can meet and share some time together.

Love to Gabrielle if you are still with her – but just

a tiny bit because you must keep practically all of it for yourself.

See you soon, in the meantime I live on memories. Until we are together again, remember I love you and always will.

Colin

She passed the little news there was to Gabrielle and gave her Colin's love.

'Lucky guy,' Gabrielle commented, 'being posted to Canada for his training. Expect he'll be living on the fat of the land. And no blackout.'

But that wasn't something Jean thought about. She said, 'Hope I get his address soon, so I can write to him.'

That address came ten days later. It was written the day after Colin arrived at the Elementary Flying Training School at Bowden, Alberta.

After the settling-in period, during which they had received lectures on the Canadians, their views and attitude to the war, and been told what was expected of them and what form their training would take, each pupil was allocated an instructor. Colin found himself under the tutelage of Flight Lieutenant Kershaw, a quiet-spoken man whose grey eyes, although at first seemingly listless, were sharp and missed nothing. His voice was soft, encouraging confidence. He could admonish or criticise without hurting or upsetting but he would stand no nonsense. As the officer in charge of A Flight he had allocated the pupils to the instructors under his jurisdiction and had chosen this new arrival for himself, for he was interested to see if his capability in the air equalled his ground report, which was outstanding.

He sensed the enthusiasm and excitement in Colin as they walked out to the Tiger Moth.

'First time in the air, Harland?'

'Yes, sir.'

'Looking forward to it?'

'Yes, sir.' There was no mistaking the feeling of sheer joy at achieving something he had set his heart on.

'Right, we'll soon see how you like it.'

Reaching the tiny biplane, he showed Colin round it and introduced him to the two civilian groundcrew who were waiting to swing the propeller and remove the chocks.

'You've been shown how to fix a parachute?'

'Yes, sir.'

When that was done, Colin felt ungainly with the pack flapping against his legs as he clambered into the front seat. He settled himself with the pack acting as a seat, strapped himself in and, with excitement, waited for his instructor. With all checks carried out and the engine running, Flight Lieutenant Kershaw waved for the chocks to be removed. Once the groundcrew had done so and were clear of the aeroplane, he taxied across the grass field and turned into the wind for takeoff.

The officer opened the throttle slowly and the Tiger Moth began to roll forwards. They were on their way. Exhilaration surged through Colin. His eyes, fixed ahead, saw the distant hedge coming nearer and nearer, faster and faster. When were they going to take off? He glanced over the side of the open cockpit and saw space between them and the ground. They were airborne and he hadn't realised it. He hoped all his takeoffs would be as smooth – he would certainly remember this one.

They started to climb and Colin saw the objects on the ground get smaller and smaller with the increasing height. He was flying. He felt free in the wide open space which stretched as far as he could see.

He had escaped from earth and his heart delighted in the new sensation. The air was clear and the distant Rockies stood out sharp against a blue sky. This was the way to view the world. He knew then that his new-found home would always pull at his heartstrings. He wished Jean was sharing the joy of flight with him. He would always fly, even in peacetime, of that he was certain, and then he could share this wonderful world of flying with her.

He never lost his enthusiasm, which mounted even more as he learned how to do sharper manoeuvres, pull the aircraft out of a spin and perform a quick emergency landing.

Two weeks later Flight Lieutenant Kershaw put Colin through all that he had learned. He praised his smooth landing and, when he had brought the aircraft to its allotted site, he shouted to Colin to leave the engine running. Colin started to unfasten his straps when the officer called, 'Stay there.' Colin, wondering what was happening, was surprised when the Flight Lieutenant was on the wing. He leaned towards Colin and yelled, 'Take her up. Nothing fancy, just once round the circuit and land.' He gave him a good-luck tap on the shoulder and jumped to the ground.

For a brief moment Colin felt an emptiness in the pit of his stomach. He was to fly alone. Then he thrust the feeling aside. Wasn't this what he'd come for? Wasn't this what he wanted to do?

He glanced around, saw that everyone was clear of the plane, and taxied to the takeoff point. He felt his hands clammy, rubbed them on his sleeve, settled himself and then went through the routine checks. Satisfied, he opened the throttle. With an increasing roar, the Tiger Moth hurtled across the grass. Gently Colin eased her off the ground. He was away, he had left the ground behind, he was flying. The temptation to fly off and enjoy the sense of space was strong but he knew that would put paid to his flying career. He flew round the circuit, enjoying the few minutes in the air alone. He made a good landing and taxied to the crew hut, where he knew Flight Lieutenant Kershaw had been watching him. He closed the engine down, climbed out of the cockpit, overjoyed that he had flown solo. There would never be another day like this. He felt on top of the world. His face was broad with smiles as he walked to his instructor.

'Well done, Harland, nice takeoff. Your approach for landing was a little high.'

'Thought so, sir. I had to stick the nose down a little.'

'Right. Watch it next time. This afternoon you'll do a few more circuits and bumps solo and then we'll do some more airwork together over the next week or two and I'll tell you when you can do the more complicated manoeuvres on your own. A word of warning – do not attempt anything unless I have told you.'

'Yes, sir.'

'The temptation to do so will be strong when you're on your own and out of sight of the airfield. But don't be tempted. If you are, you'll be out of aircrew as fast as your legs can take you and in your case the air force will lose a promising pilot.'

During the succeeding days Colin had to force himself to hold back. Alone in the sky, he felt the temptation to see what the aircraft could do and to test his own ability. Pupils would come back bragging to their fellow pupils about the low flying they had done solo, but Colin would not defy instructions. He was determined to be the fighter pilot he had set his heart on.

During July and August, letters frequently crossed the Atlantic between Harrogate and Bowden in both directions. Jean buoyed Colin's resolution to succeed, for he wanted her to be proud of him. His letters comforted her in the dreary rounds of drill, learning to salute properly, barrack-room cleaning, skivvying, cookhouse duty and the other menial jobs which were passed off as part of training.

Although there were plenty of moans and groans, the heterogeneous group of girls had to admit that they had become a disciplined, efficient company who had learned not only to cooperate with girls from differing backgrounds but had learned much about themselves and their capabilities.

Jean and Gabrielle had soon come to accept rules and regulations though some regarded them as there to be broken. The two friends, with an eye to the future, kept in line, determined to prove themselves, for they realised that through all this early training their aptitude and ability to cope were being assessed.

It was with some satisfaction that at the end of their stay in Harrogate they were both assigned to Special Duties. They did not know what that meant but they knew they would be not trained as cooks, transport drivers, clerks or any of the ordinary trades open to the WAAFs.

They were kept waiting for a few days before they knew where they were going. Of the fourteen girls singled out for Special Duties, twelve were informed that they would be told what their training would be when they arrived at their destination. Jean and Gabrielle said good-bye to them not knowing their own fate.

Two days later they were surprised to be called to a special interview. Wondering what it was all about, they duly presented themselves at the commanding officer's office. Jean was the first to be called. Her nerves tightened when she saw three high-ranking WAAF officers sitting behind a table facing a single wooden chair.

In spite of her racing mind wondering what she had done wrong, she coolly made a smart salute, which was acknowledged by her commanding officer.

'Aircraftwoman Lawson, do sit down.' The CO smiled pleasantly and Jean thought that this might not be a disciplinary hearing. It surely couldn't be, with a wing officer and a squadron officer also present.

During the next half-hour she was subjected to an interview which resembled a general chat but was laced with pertinent questions. They searched her aptitude, knowledge, powers of interpretation, her manner and ability to get on with people, her skill at presenting facts and at eliciting information from others.

The interview finished when her CO said, 'I think we

have all we want.' She glanced at her fellow officers, who nodded their agreement, and then looked at Jean with a smile. 'Thank you very much, Aircraftwoman Lawson. We would like you to wait outside. Say nothing to Aircraftwoman Harland except to send her in.'

'Yes, ma'am.' Jean stood up, stepped to one side of the chair, saluted smartly, turned sharply and strode from the room.

When she stepped into the corridor, Gabrielle looked enquiringly at her.

'You're to go in,' said Jean.

'What's it all about?' whispered Gabrielle, wanting some hint at how she should conduct herself.

'Don't know,' replied Jean with a shrug of her shoulders.

'You were a hell of a time.'

'No doubt you will be. Now get going.'

Gabrielle pulled at her tunic, pushed her shoulders back, knocked at the door and walked into the room in answer to the call of 'Come in'.

Half an hour later she reappeared, closing the door behind her. Jean looked askance at her.

'Whew!' she gasped and flopped on to a chair beside Jean. 'That was some interview.'

'What happens now?'

'I was told to wait with you.'

'Any clues to what it's all about?'

'No. But I bet you didn't have ten minutes' interview in French.'

'French? What's that got to do with it?'

'Don't know. It just arose out of the blue. They seemed

211

surprised when I could speak French and then no doubt the old dears wanted to show off their ability. Mind you, they were good, especially one of them, spoke it like a native of the Paris area.'

'Like you.'

Gabrielle smiled. 'Yes. It was a bit of fun.'

Conversation was halted when the door opened and a WAAF corporal appeared and said, 'You're to come in now.'

The corporal closed the door after them and then went into an adjoining room, where Jean reckoned the second chair must have come from.

They both came smartly to attention and saluted as one, then sat down when indicated to do so by their CO.

She eyed them both for a moment, then said, 'Wing Officer Laing has something to say to you.' She indicated the officer on her right.

Both girls had received searching questions from the wing officer and now they wondered what else she could ask them, but more questions were not forthcoming. She adopted a less formal attitude by leaning forward with her arms resting on the table but she still retained an air of authority which would preclude familiarity with the lower ranks. The hint of sternness in her face was softened by the intensity of the blue of her eyes. Jean and Gabrielle got the impression that she was still studying them for flaws even as she spoke.

'I am in charge of expanding the role of the WAAFs in the Intelligence Section of the RAF. The higher authorities are particularly keen on this and I have persuaded them that we have an important role to play beyond

Command and Group Headquarters. I believe that we as women would fit the role at station level admirably, especially in Bomber Command, where we could be more than assimilators of information regarding targets, enemy fighter and anti-aircraft positions, et cetera. I believe that we can play a vital part in the interrogation of aircrews after raids. Their information can be of the utmost importance and I believe tired crews, who may have been through terrible horrors, would feel more relaxed and give much more if they were debriefed by a woman. The course for such a role for WAAFs is being set up at the present but the venue and the make-up of the course have not been determined yet. But when that day comes I want a full complement of girls ready to move in. That was one purpose of these interviews. We think that you both would be suitable for the course.' She paused and in the brief moment glanced at both girls, making a final assessment before she said, 'Would such a role be of interest to you?'

'Yes, ma'am,' they both answered briskly.

'Good.' She smiled and leaned back in her chair, satisfied that she had two keen recruits.

Both Jean's and Gabrielle's thoughts were racing. This was a better prospect than they had expected and they were visualising all sorts of possibilities when their thoughts were jerked back to the present by the voice of their commanding officer.

'Squadron Officer Nesbit has something to say.' She glanced at the officer on her left.

Her round face and plump figure gave her a motherly look but both girls knew from her questioning that she was not to be taken for granted. Whatever she was in charge of would be run with efficiency and discipline.

'Wing Officer Laing is satisfied that you would work well in Intelligence and I agree with her. Now, we were also interviewing you with something else in mind. The position you would hold on a bomber station would mean that you would have to be commissioned. So this interview was also to see if you were officer material. From what we have seen and from your reports,' – she tapped the folders on the table – 'we are satisfied that you are.'

Both girls felt a surge of excitement. This was more than they had dreamed about. Commissioned! Officers! They were glad they had chosen the WAAF.

'As the Intelligence course isn't ready yet, we propose that, if you are interested, you go immediately to the WAAF Officers' School of which I am in charge.' She looked enquiringly at each in turn and received a 'Very interested, thank you, ma'am'.

'Good. I'm sure you will do well.'

'Continue in the way you have shaped here and you will be a credit to the WAAF and I'm sure you will find Intelligence work satisfying.' Their CO smiled warmly. 'I wish you both the best of luck.'

'Thank you, ma'am.' Knowing the interview was finished, they both stood up, whipped up a smart salute, turned and marched from the office.

As soon as the door closed behind them, they relaxed. 'Whoopee!' They both gave a whispered shout and with laughter on their lips flung their arms round one another.

* * *

Inside the room, Wing Officer Laing glanced pensively at a sheet of paper on which she had made some notes during Gabrielle's interview. She tapped her lips thoughtfully and then said, as she handed the paper to Squadron Officer Nesbit, 'Put that in Harland's file. It may be worth remembering she speaks French.'

The July day was bright. A good day to be going to a new posting, thought Liz as the train rumbled to a halt close to the buffers at the end of the platform. Doors opened the full length of the train and passengers swarmed out in hurried steps towards the exit. Civilians were outnumbered by men and women in uniform, soldiers struggling with kitbag and rifle, sailors with distinctive white collars complementing their jaunty hats, airmen with greatcoats hiding the evidence that they were fliers or ground staff. The whole station bustled with activity, people leaving trains, seeking trains, enquiring about directions for their onward journey, or anticipating a cup of tea while they waited.

Liz, carrying a small case, emerged from her carriage and was swept into the movement towards the barrier where the crowd funnelled out past two elderly ticket collectors.

She reached the barrier and slowed with the queue handing in their tickets. Then she was through, a little bewildered as people criss-crossed the concourse, all seeming to know where they wanted to be and how to get there. She knew her destination but how was she to reach it? She stopped and looked around for an enquiry office.

Through the crowd flowing around her, she caught a glimpse of a WAAF. She held a board in front of her and Liz was startled to see written on it: 'Sister Johnson'.

She felt a little pride. Sister! She had passed her course at Halton Hospital with a good report and was now entitled to be addressed as Sister. She glanced at the pale-blue bands, which signified the rank of flight officer, on the sleeves of her well-fitting uniform. She felt pleased with her achievement and was sure Sister Wood, back in Whitby, would be proud of her.

She went towards the WAAF. 'I'm Sister Johnson,' she said.

The young woman saluted smartly and said, 'ACW Beryl Hapton, ma'am. Hope you've had a good journey. May I take your case?'

'Thanks,' replied Liz, handing it over. 'Journey was all right but the train was crowded.'

They started to walk towards the exit. 'Always are these days. I've a car waiting, ma'am.'

'I didn't expect to be met,' Liz said gratefully. 'I was just wondering where I had to go.'

'Sister Asher fixed the transport, ma'am.' ACW Hapton led the way to a Hillman saloon, drab in its camouflage paint, and was soon skilfully manoeuvring the car out of London.

The hour's drive passed pleasantly. The road climbed and twisted up the North Downs. They passed Keston and came to a ridge overlooking rolling country dotted with woods. After the congestion of London there was a sense of freedom over the Weald of Kent.

'Leaves Green,' said Beryl when they reached a group of houses strung along the roadside. 'Soon be there. Village of Biggin Hill, bigger than Leaves but not very big, is beyond the aerodrome, one of the top airfields in Fighter

Command.' There was a sense of pride in her voice. 'Though there won't be an aeroplane in sight.' She chuckled at the puzzled expression which had come to Liz with this contradiction. 'Two squadrons moved out to allow constructors to have freedom to lay a concrete runway and make deep air-raid shelters. But they'll be back.'

After a brief stop at the guardroom, ACW Hapton drove Liz to the sick quarters. Liz thanked her, went inside and knocked on a door marked 'Sister D. Asher'. She opened the door on the command 'Come in' and came smartly to attention to salute the tall woman, one rank higher than herself, who was sitting behind a desk.

'Sister Johnson, ma'am.'

'Ah. Pleased to have you with us, Sister.' She smiled, came from behind her desk and extended a welcoming hand.

Liz felt a warm, firm grip. Sister Asher held herself erect, giving her an aura of command, making the insignia of rank unnecessary. Her face was long and thin but severity was dismissed with a kindly turn of the mouth and bright, friendly, understanding eyes.

'Do sit down. Elizabeth, isn't it?' She returned to her seat behind the desk.

'Yes. Most people call me Liz.'

'Right. I'm Dorothy. We have two ACW nursing orderlies, to them we're Sister. You come with a glowing report from Sister Wood in Whitby and I'm informed that you did excellently at Halton. I'm sure you'll live up to your reputation and enhance the status of our service as we are just establishing ourselves here.'

'I look forward to doing so,' replied Liz confidently.

'Good. I'm sure, when you get settled and enter into the spirit of the station, you'll enjoy life here.' She leaned back in her chair, her eyes still fixed firmly on Liz. She had made her assessment even though Liz had spoken little. She didn't need many words to make a judgement; she based it on what she saw in the way a girl held herself, the neatness of her dress, but most of all her face and eyes. 'I think you'll do very well. Now, tell me about Sister Wood. How is she?'

For ten minutes they chatted about her, about nursing in Whitby and Liz's time at Halton.

Sister Asher rose from her seat. 'Now I'll show you to your quarters. Boyfriend?'

'Well . . .' Liz drew the word out.

'That means yes but not sure whether it's serious or not.'

Liz nodded. 'We have an understanding.'

'I've heard that before.' Dorothy smiled.

'No, we have. We aren't tied but . . .'

'You think a lot of each other.'

'Yes.'

'Well, remember that. Here we females are outnumbered. You're pretty, you'll catch many an eye and they'll be gunning for you. Life can be a bit heady, especially when the pilots return. The fighter boys think they can sweep you off your feet.' Dorothy laughed. 'I'm painting a picture of a lot of lecherous men. Maybe they are to some extent but the majority will respect a girl. They talk of their prowess with women, especially among themselves, but most of it's hot air. What's your boy do?'

'He's in Air-Sea Rescue.'

'Likes the sea?'

'Yes.'

Liz was pleased with her room for it afforded her a view across the airfield.

The tension throughout the RAF fighter stations was typified by Biggin Hill. When the squadrons returned, Liz saw the pilots were living on a knife edge of anticipation. Every member of the station was keyed up for the unknown fury which might be leashed upon them any day. All ranks made light of the tension, especially the men who might have to take to the air at any moment to try to repel the enemy. No one knew what form it would take but with the Germans only a short distance away across the Channel, with airfields available to them within easy range of British targets, it was expected that bombers would be launched against the country.

Spasmodic attacks and nuisance raids against shipping and on targets as widespread as Aberdeen, Liverpool and the Thames estuary had taken place. The Biggin Hill squadrons were active but were engaged in nothing of major significance. A sense of the lull before the storm pervaded the atmosphere. Even Liz felt it and though there was little in the way of medical treatment to be carried out, except for normal complaints, she kept busy.

The pilots were friendly, ever ready to chat up a pretty young nurse, and she was flattered by their attention. Dorothy informed her who would try to take liberties and who just wanted female company. She warned her not to become too attached to any of them for it could mean a broken heart.

Then one day, after a fierce engagement protecting a convoy in the Channel, a young pilot officer was brought into sick quarters rushed by ambulance from his Hurricane after he had made a successful landing and taxied his plane to its standing. He had leg wounds and had to be helped from the cockpit.

He was stretchered into the hospital, where the medical officer, Sister Asher, Beryl and Liz were waiting to give him every attention.

As the doctor examined his wounds, the pilot said with a cheery smile, 'Fix me up quick, doc. I don't want to miss the big show which must come soon.'

'Pilot Officer Alec Crooks of 32 Squadron, isn't it?' said the medical officer.

This brought a surprised look to the young man's face. 'My reputation as bad as that?' he quipped with a wink at Liz.

'Make it my duty to be able to recognise all you pilots,' replied the doctor. 'Just been promoted, haven't you?' He straightened from the examination. 'Well, young man, nothing serious there. A couple of bullets to come out. They'll be no trouble. You're lucky they haven't done any serious damage.'

'Okay, doc, get on with it. The sooner they're out, the sooner I'm back in the air.'

Liz was astonished not only at the light-heartedness of someone who had been so near death, but also at how young he looked, little more than a schoolboy, bearing the brunt of fierce combat on his shoulders as lightly as if it might all be a game.

But as she attended him through his post-operative

period and convalescence, she realised that beneath his happy-go-lucky nature there was a serious side and that deep down he looked upon his flying with a sober responsibility. He was still only nineteen, so occasionally something of the boy came out, but there was no youth; this war had plunged him from boyhood straight into manhood.

His features could break out into a Puck's smile at any moment, for he could see humour in everything. But he could also be serious, especially when talking about aeroplanes, particularly his Hurricane which he spoke of with a tender, loving admiration. His unruly, fair hair added to his nonchalant aura but it was his deep-blue eyes that held the attention and compelled people to meet his gaze. He was a talker, ever ready with a joke and a quip, and as she nursed him, Liz enjoyed his banter.

'Come dancing tonight, Liz?' he said the first day she helped him walk a few steps in the ward.

'Oh, sure,' she replied with a grin. 'We'll really make the floor rock.'

'You do dance, then?' he asked.

'Yes.'

'Right, first opportunity, you and me?' He looked at her expectantly.

She was going to say no but she liked him and he obviously found some pleasure in her company for there was always a ready smile for her.

'All right.'

His eyes brightened. 'Don't forget. Promise?'

'Promise.'

He reminded her of that a week later when he left the

221

hospital, and added, 'Take care, Liz. Jerry will try to knock us out by bombing our airfields.'

Liz glanced round. They were alone. She kissed him quickly on the cheek. 'You too.'

He grinned and touched his cheek where she had kissed him. 'See you.' He winked and walked away.

She watched him for a few moments, little knowing how prophetic his words would soon become.

On Monday 12 August, Pilot Officer Crooks was on his way to the mess at seven thirty when the Merlin engines of the Spitfires of 610 Squadron shattered the silence of expectancy which had hung over the station. He stopped. Takeoffs always thrilled him.

610 had been on dawn readiness and Alec knew that a few minutes ago the shout of 'Scramble', after a telephone call to the squadron's hut, would have sent twelve pilots racing to their Spitfires.

As he watched the whole squadron becoming airborne within three and a half minutes, Alec nodded his approval. 'Lucky buggers,' he muttered as they rose through the thin mist and climbed quickly to attain their allotted height. He envied them the action.

Even as they headed for the coast, the Tannoys throughout Biggin Hill were calling 32 Squadron to readiness. Something big must be developing.

Although there was still much activity on the airfield, it was carried out with a touch of anxiety for everyone's minds were on their pilots, hoping that they would all return safely.

Less than an hour later specks appeared in the distance,

accompanied by the throb of engines which were recognised as Merlins. The distant aircraft enlarged to become Spitfires as they came nearer and nearer. One by one they returned, circuiting the airfield to land and taxi to their dispersal point. Anxious eyes were turned to watch and count. One, two . . . five . . . seven . . . still they came, raising hopes that all were going to come back. The airfield was alive with the sound of taxiing aircraft. Ten . . . eleven . . . Eyes pierced the sky, searching, searching. The sounds of the aircraft died away, leaving a heavy atmosphere hanging like a pall over the aerodrome. One missing.

Alec was anxious. He had listened intently to the landing aircraft, picking out the low, moaning whistle coming from the guns, created by the wind in the exposed muzzles. Their thin covers had been broken. They had been fired. There had been combats.

The pilots reported intense activity over the Channel, so much so that more was expected later in the day. The intelligence officer took their reports, vital for the group to assess the operations of all the squadrons in its command. He learned that the missing pilot had been seen to bale out over the Channel, but whether he had survived was another question. Tension gripped the station until a telephone call came to say that the pilot was safe and in hospital in Dover. The news, bringing delight to everyone, swept through the station like a prairie fire.

The station settled down to an uneasy peace, further disturbed when reports filtered through that the Luftwaffe had done well. Apart from the convoys in the

Channel, carrying vital supplies to the beleaguered island, radiolocation stations vital to the defence system had been put out of action and Portsmouth had suffered a heavy raid. No one held the illusion that that was the end for the day. They seemed to be sitting on the edge of a volcano which was about to erupt.

Pilots of 32 Squadron tried to relax. Some played cards, some slept, others read: young men seemingly not at war but ready for it in their flying boots and Mae Wests – the life-saving jackets, should they come down in the sea.

At two thirty the phone rang in 32 Squadron's hut. The duty orderly answered it in the tiny room next to the pilot's crew room. He stiffened, acknowledged the call and, before he had even replaced the telephone, poked his head round the door and yelled, 'Squadron, scramble! Dover 10,000 feet!'

The room burst into life. Pilots scrambled to their feet, flung down their cards, cursed their luck that Jerry should deny a win, or dropped a book, forgetting what had been read.

They rushed out into the sunshine, racing for their Hurricanes. Helped by one of the ground crew, Alec got into his parachute, which he always kept ready on the wing of his aircraft, clambered on to the wing and into the cockpit. In a matter of moments he was taxiing quickly across the airfield with other Hurricanes buzzing for takeoff.

His squadron leader was first away, with Alec close behind. He was barely clear of the ground when he heard the officer's voice over the radio transmitter, 'Foxtrot Blue Leader calling Sapper. Airborne.'

'Hello, Foxtrot Blue Leader. Loud and clear. Patrol

Dover–Hawkinge. 10,000 feet,' came the reply from the controller.

'Message received and understood.'

Following his leader's adjustment of speed and rate of climb, Alec saw the rest of the squadron closing in and taking up their positions. They carried out their patrol without seeing an enemy aircraft. They returned to base and refuelled and were in the air again at four fifty. They continued their patrol and with only five minutes to go before they should return to base, they were resigned to another day of no action.

Then: 'Foxtrot Blue Leader. Here they come. One o'clock. 12,000 feet.'

Alec saw his leader already turning and climbing. He followed suit and drew a gasp of breath. 'Hell, what a swarm!'

The sky looked black with planes. A dark, moving mass of Dornier 215 bombers with Messerschmitt 109 fighters fussing about in protection.

'Must be nearly a hundred,' muttered Alec to himself. 'And only twelve of us,' he added ruefully. He licked his lips. The distance was closing rapidly. The Hurricanes were in full boost. He switched his reflector sight on and turned his gun rings to fire.

'Tally ho!' The leader's signal for attack.

The Hurricanes were in among the enemy, spitting and harrying. The air vibrated with the blast of gunfire and the whining sound of engines stretched to the limit. Alec, beads of sweat across his forehead, whipped his plane round after raking a bomber with gunfire. What happened to it he did not see, for as he broke away he fastened on

225

to a Messerschmitt 109. The German twisted, trying to shake off his pursuer, but Alec, mouth set in a determined line, clung to his tail, pushing his Hurricane to get within firing distance. The gap closed. Alec's intense gaze judged the range. Then his thumb pressed the gun button. Eight synchronised Brownings fired smoothly. He gave a sharp burst. The German dived steeply. Alec followed. The air screamed with the torturous plunge. He touched the gun button again, and saw his bullets rip into the German plane. Smoke started to pour from it. Its dive became steeper. He saw the canopy slide back and a figure scramble out. Alec hauled his aircraft out of the dive and climbed away to starboard. A glance back and he saw the Me-109 diving headlong for the sea and, way above, a white dome of silk floated in the sky. Here was peace. The rattle of war seemed far away.

Alec searched the sky. He was not near enough to re-engage in combat for his fuel was running low, so he turned his Hurricane for home. The bombers had been so numerous that some of them must have got through to their targets but at least the squadron had split them, eliminating some of them for ever, sending others scurrying back to their bases to lick their wounds, and forcing many to drop their bombs indiscriminately. He felt they could be satisfied with a job well done.

As he headed inland he spotted three Hurricanes forming up on their leader. He turned to join them. With petrol low they knew they would not reach Biggin Hill so they turned to Hawkinge. As they approached the airfield, Alec gasped at the sight of the destruction. Hangars and buildings were smoking ruins and the field was pockmarked with craters. They must go elsewhere, but it couldn't be far. Then he heard over the radio the Hawkinge controller informing them that Manston and Lympne were in as bad a state.

His own leader cut in, 'Hello, Sparrow Control. This is Foxtrot Blue Leader calling. Sorry, but we must pancake.'

'Hello, Foxtrot Blue Leader. Request understood. Bit of trouble here, but permission to pancake granted. Take care.'

'Hello, Sparrow, Foxtrot Blue Leader here. Message received and understood. Thanks.'

One by one the Hurricanes came in to land. Ground-crews held their breath. Those on the firetenders and ambulances were ready to head for another disaster. There were too many craters, too many unexploded bombs. But every Hurricane touched down lightly, its pilot having quickly assessed the best place to land. They weaved their way between the craters and as soon as they had reached the dispersal point, the groundcrews went into action, refuelling and rearming.

In the middle of it, with the pilots anxious to get airborne again, came the ominous drone of steadily approaching aircraft. Eyes turned in the direction of the sound.

'Bloody Jerries!' someone yelled.

Everywhere there were pounding feet as they raced for shelters. The attack was sharp. The bombers were suddenly there and then gone, their loads screaming down on an unprotected airfield. The air filled with a cacophony of crashing sounds and then just as quickly silence settled over the field.

Anxious pilots emerged from the shelters and ran to

their Hurricanes. Swift inspection brought relief; somehow they had survived the bombing. The groundcrews needed no cajoling to get their work on the planes finished.

Alec looked around at the destruction. Ambulances and medical orderlies were busy attending to the wounded. Some, with bandages round their heads, walked to sick quarters; others, with broken limbs, were stretchered to the ambulances. His lips tightened as his light-heartedness suffered a blow. This could happen at Biggin Hill. Liz could be caught up in similar devastation. She could be a victim!

Chapter Eleven

1940

Six days later the sirens sounded throughout the Kent countryside. No one was surprised. Over the last six days they had sounded regularly and more frequently than ever. The Luftwaffe had been on a determined course to knock out the British airfields as well as keeping up a continual attack on coastal towns.

32 Squadron had been constantly called to challenge the bombers and each day Liz waited anxiously, a strange numb feeling gripping her even though she went about her duties alert, fastidiously attending any casualties among the pilots. Whenever she heard returning planes, she watched for Alec's Hurricane, and every time she saw it an immense pressure lifted from her.

The siren's wail indicated that today would be another such, or would it? She knew other airfields had suffered badly from the bombing. Would it be Biggin Hill's turn today?

The roar of an aircraft's engine starting up was joined quickly by others until the whole field reverberated with a deafening crescendo. It rose and fell as pilots, satisfied that all was well, taxied out for takeoff. Within a matter of minutes all Biggin Hill planes were in the sky, climbing into position to defend the airfield from the bombers which had been plotted as heading in its direction.

Liz looked skywards and prayed that Alec would return safely. Her mind was jerked back to the danger for those on the ground when the Tannoys vibrated with the sound of the station's warning alarm. It was followed immediately by the commanding officer's order for all personnel, except those on essential services, to take to the shelters because it appeared that the airfield was about to be attacked.

There was no panic. Airmen and airwomen just moved a little faster to take cover, leaving their jobs half done. The inevitable was about to happen. Everyone had known it must come some day: reports had filtered through about attacks on other airfields. Now it was Biggin Hill's turn.

Sister Asher never insisted that her nurses go to the shelter. She herself always stood by in case of emergency, and was pleased when her staff chose to do the same. She had had one of the small rooms in the sick wing sand-bagged for protection, leaving one window to give a view of the airfield, and an extra telephone had been installed so that they were on instant call if necessary. The two sisters and their nursing orderlies hurried to that room and for a moment stood looking out of the window.

'My God, look at them!' gasped Sister Asher when she saw the swarm of bombers, escorted by fighters, heading from the south.

Hurricanes and Spitfires tore towards them, ready to do battle. The menacing drone of the bombers was broken by the whine of buzzing fighters, determined to defend their precious airfield. Suddenly there seemed to be planes everywhere. Fighters against bombers, fighters against fighters, each bent on coming out of battle triumphant. The staccato chatter of machine-gun fire cut through the noise of whirling aircraft.

The nurses gazed transfixed at the battle, which ranged nearer and nearer. They saw a couple of bombers develop smoke trails and turn out of the stream, one suddenly going into a vertical dive to explode and leave a plume of smoke rising from the ground. Still the bombers came on, their formation less orderly, but with a dogged threat that chilled the heart. They realised that, with the British fighters outnumbered, some of the bombers were bound to get through.

The planes came on. Bombs started falling.

'Here they come!' Sister Asher and her nurses dropped to the floor and flattened themselves under the heavy table.

The first crump sounded far away, but then the explosions sounded louder and louder, getting nearer and nearer. The earth reverberated, the building shook. The blast seemed to flood into the room and they felt as if their limbs were being torn from them, but the building stood up to the shaking and pounding. More bombs fell on the airfield, sending geysers of soil and concrete erupting in destructive patterns.

The explosive sounds died and the noise of weaving aircraft drifted away. The silence which settled over Biggin

Hill was eerie. The quietness was charged with tension, waiting for someone to break it.

'Come on, girls!' Sister Asher scrambled from under the table and was out of the door, closely followed by Liz and the orderlies.

They took in the scene with a quick glance. Men and women were emerging from the shelters. Some, dazed by the attack, stared around them. Others supported wounded comrades, looking for help. More, aware that their pilots would soon be returning, were hurrying to see what could be done to make the landings safe. Among them a WAAF, carrying red flags, was already marking the positions of unexploded bombs at great danger to herself.

'MT Section?' called Liz as they ran across the airfield.

They saw the area had received a direct hit and was now a heap of rubble and twisted metal.

'That would be empty of personnel,' yelled Sister Asher. 'Liz, take that shelter.' She indicated one which had received a near miss and from which the occupants were struggling to get out with the help of some airmen who had already reached them.

Liz, with one of the orderlies, went speedily into action alongside the airmen who were digging frantically at the upheaval of earth and brick in response to cries for help from those buried alive. Liz and her WAAF orderly examined, made assessments quickly, tended wounds and relieved pain. Liz ordered walking wounded to head for the sick quarters and directed airmen to place those who needed stretchers as comfortably as possible on the grass to await the arrival of the ambulance. She gave comfort and reassurance and no one questioned her authority or skill.

She kept hidden the emotions which stirred in her at the sight of shattered limbs, gaping wounds, blood that would not be staunched, and the two WAAFs beyond her help.

When everyone had been seen to and the ambulance had taken away the last of the stretcher cases, Liz allowed herself to relax. She sank back against a pile of rubble and gazed wearily across the airfield. It was only then that her mind turned to Alec. Ammunition spent, returning planes had been taxiing carefully among the craters and unexploded bombs, to be taken over by the groundcrews, who lost no time in rearming them and making them airworthy. Who knew how soon they might be called into the air again?

She watched two planes, which had pursued the bombers across the Channel, circle the airfield and come in to land. Relief swept over her when she recognised one as Alec's. She watched him land, then pushed herself to her feet and walked towards his dispersal point. She was there when he jumped out of his plane.

'Hi there!' He winked. 'Had fun?'

'She sure did, sir,' put in one of the groundcrew. 'She was a marvel. One of the shelters got badly damaged. I was there. There's more than one will owe their lives to her.'

Embarrassed, Liz brushed his praise aside. Later, having heard from other sources about what she had done, Alec brought it up that evening as they walked to the camp cinema. But she would not even talk about it and he respected her wishes. After the traumas of the day, she was glad to be with him, for she drew reassurance and comfort from his effervescent outlook and belief that nothing could happen to him.

'I'm indestructible. Jerry doesn't know how to kill me,' he said with a confident laugh.

It came as a blow to her when ten days later 32 Squadron moved to Acklington in Northumberland. It had seen tremendous action and the powers that be deemed it wise to take it out of the most active area for a while for a comparative rest. There was less likelihood of concentrated activity by the enemy in the north.

Before they left, Liz helped him celebrate the award of a Distinguished Flying Medal gained before his promotion. She was there to wave him off and watched with mixed feelings as his Hurricane took to the air and formed up with the squadron to head north.

His promise to write had reminded her of the letters she received once a week from Martin. He was now a member of an Air-Sea Rescue working out of Blyth on the Northumberland coast. Occasionally his letters verged on the point of professing love for her but then drew back as if remembering their understanding.

As she watched the Hurricanes leave, she wondered if she was in love with Alec. She felt admiration and sympathy for him, and was drawn by those wings on his breast. At any rate, with the Hurricanes mere specks in the sky, she knew she would miss Alec.

The same day 79 Squadron returned to Biggin Hill from Acklington to join 610 Squadron. They were in action daily. Shortly before noon on 30 August they broke up what appeared to be an attempted raid on their airfield claiming ten victories between them. The bombers that got through were so harried that their bombs fell wide of the airfield; unfortunately they caused casualties in the nearby village instead.

The day continued with battles over southern England and 610 Squadron were in action far from base when at six o'clock a small formation of bombers heading for the Thames estuary turned quickly and came in low to Biggin Hill with 1,000-pounders. The surprise was complete to an airfield reflecting on the day's successes. The bombers were bearing down on the airfield even as the warnings of a raid went out.

Men and women coming from their messes dashed for shelter. Those on essential duty ran to their posts. Ground-crews raced to the Spitfires of 79 Squadron, making desperate attempts to assist the pilots to get airborne.

Liz was on her way to sick quarters when she saw the bombers winging low towards them. She started to run. Her heart pounded faster. She must get to their shelter, it seemed imperative that it had to be theirs. Just ahead of her, an officer was also racing for protection. The roar of engines shattered her ears. She glanced over her shoulder and saw the bombers hurtling towards them. As they ran past a stationary lorry, she threw herself at the officer, dragging him to the ground behind the vehicle.

Machine-gun bullets, with an unnerving clatter, channelled a path where they had been running. Tarmac splattered over them as they cradled their heads in their arms. The immediate noise faded, leaving only the roar of aero engines amid the thumps and blasts of exploding bombs, the pounding of anti-aircraft fire and the chatter of machine guns.

They looked at each other.

'Thanks' was all he said, but there was real gratitude in his tone.

'Come on,' Liz cried, ignoring her torn stockings, dirt-marked uniform and scraped shoes as she pushed herself to her feet. She grabbed his hand, hauled him upright and they both ran. They tumbled through the door of the sick quarters and into the shelter room. With bombs still exploding, they flung themselves on to the floor beside Sister Asher and the orderlies.

'Thank goodness you're safe!' The worry left Sister Asher's face.

Looking at him again Liz realised that she knew this officer. 'Squadron Leader Davey of 32 Squadron?' she said tentatively.

'Yes.' He smiled. 'And still alive, thanks to you.'

Liz frowned and shook her head. She wanted no fuss, but Sister Asher seized on the remark and insisted on the story. She was proud of her nurse.

'Expect you're wondering what I'm doing back here, having just left,' the squadron leader said. 'Had some business to see to with my counterpart in 79. My Hurricane hadn't been refuelled, otherwise I'd have been up there.' There was disappointment in his voice.

'Pilot Officer Crooks all right?' asked Liz.

'Fine,' came the reply. 'Any message for him?'

'Just say Liz wishes him well.'

Squadron Leader Davey nodded, thinking he would tell Pilot Officer Crooks a little more about her. 'Things are quieting down,' he added, using his interpretation of the outside sounds. He stood up and the nurses did likewise.

Leaving the sick quarters, they were shocked by the sight that met them. Devastation was everywhere. Workshops, cookhouses and the NAAFI canteen were heaps of rubble. Two aircraft were ablaze, transport was all but destroyed and the barracks were severely damaged. One hangar and all its equipment was no more.

They were strangely aware of the beautiful summer evening with birds singing. The air was still and an unusual silence hung over the airfield, which only a few moments ago had resonated with the crunch of bombs and the roar of explosions.

Then the field burst into action. People were running to help those who had suffered.

Liz reached the nearest shelter. Her mind was thrown into confusion by the horror of the carnage that had been wrought by the near-direct hit. Bodies were twisted in lifeless poses. Airmen were already digging to reach the cries of those still buried. One young airman, little more than a boy, shovelled back some earth, then staggered away and was violently sick. Squadron Leader Davey grabbed his spade, turned to carry on the work and recoiled at the sight of the horribly mangled face which stared at him. He swallowed hard, and started to dig.

Ambulances were darting about the airfield, stretcher orderlies were kept busy and the doctors and nurses knew no respite in their attendance on the wounded and maimed. Liz tried to shut out the horrors and nightmares which she witnessed. She worked tirelessly, bringing relief and comfort to many. She heard snatches of what it was like around the airfield. Engineers were working frantically to get the gas, electricity and water functioning as

237

quickly as possible. Telephone engineers were racing to get Biggin Hill's vital contact with 11 Group Headquarters re-established. Craters across the airfield were being refilled so that it could welcome back its planes, which had been diverted elsewhere, and become operational again as quickly as possible.

Having once returned to sick quarters, now full, the nurses were kept occupied without noticing the darkness and the dawn.

When all had been done that could be done for their patients, one of the WAAF orderlies made a pot of tea. Liz took hers outside and stood against the door, gazing over the airfield. The sky was clear and lightening slowly from the east. Soon the sun would peep above the horizon and add its heat to what was already a warm morning. The silence was almost penetrating with its peace. The war in these still moments could be far away and yet the silhouettes of mangled buildings and shattered aircraft were a reminder that this had been a battlefield. She sighed and sipped her tea. With the activity and tension gone, she suddenly felt weary. She could feel her face drain, and a great fist seemed to be pressing her down and down, threatening to bury her by forcing her deep into the earth. As she slid slowly to the ground the cup fell from her grasp to spill its contents across the grass.

Liz stirred. Her eyes flickered open. Ouch, the light was bright! She shut them again, then opened them slowly. Where was she? Sheets? Bed? Why? What had happened? She recalled watching the still dawn over the shattered airfield, then nothing. She frowned. Her senses sharpened.

238

She looked around and recognised the small room where two beds were kept exclusively for nurses so they could snatch some rest if exceptional duty kept them on call.

The door opened and Sister Asher looked in. 'Ah, you're awake.'

'Sorry, Sister. Foolish thing to faint.' Liz blushed.

'Nonsense. It's happened to us all,' replied Dorothy. 'You stay there for twenty-four hours,' she added with a firm voice.

Knowing she would not tolerate any objection, Liz sank back on the pillows.

She was woken about noon by the drone of approaching aircraft. Bombers! She had recognised the engine sound, so different from fighters. She sat up. Bed was no place for an able-bodied person. She dressed quickly and found Sister Asher and the medical orderlies in the wards.

'I might be needed,' she said firmly before the sister could scold her for being up. 'I don't hear any machine-gun fire,' she added with some apprehension.

'Number 610 Squadron left for Acklington before the alarm. 72, who're replacing them, haven't arrived. That left 79 and they were dispatched to meet raiders over Dover.'

'So we are almost defenceless?'

The sister nodded grimly.

But their worst fears did not come true. The Dornier 215s dropped their bombs from 12,000 feet, many missing their target, and those that hit damaged only the runways. Every available person was set to fill in the craters and by teatime one runway was ready to receive the incoming aircraft.

Determined to knock out Biggin Hill, the Germans

made five raids in forty-eight hours. Although the field was kept operational, the buildings were demolished to rubble. Accommodation, water and communications were essential and not a moment was lost in trying to restore them. Casualties were heavy and the nursing staff were plunged into the horrors of mutilation, wounds and death, but no one flinched at the ordeal. In their minds they prayed for the time when the raids would stop, if ever they would.

By the end of the first week in September, the RAF in southeast England were breathing a little easier as the huge daylight raids by the Luftwaffe petered out. The bombers were switched to attacks on London, leaving only sporadic but annoying raids on the airfields.

On 8 September, 92 Squadron joined 72 Squadron, replacing 79. The new pilots had their own jazz band and loved partying. They had an eye for the girls and many a WAAF was swept up into their enjoyment of life. But no matter how hard they played, they were always ready for combat and their proficiency in the air was second to none.

Things began to settle down at Biggin Hill as services were restored and personnel were rehoused and re-equipped. The WAAFs were billeted in the Cedars, a large house in nearby Keston, while the squadrons lived in two nearby country houses; the station commander had deemed it wise to separate them in case a direct hit should wipe out his entire fighting force.

The pilots were in constant action. Liz was swept up into 92's euphoria at their triumphs, mourned briefly at their losses and adopted their today's-for-the-living attitude. She partied with them frequently, and accompanied

240

them on expeditions to the White Hart in Brasted, an attractive pub with low ceilings, polished brass and timbered beams, where the genial host and his wife made them welcome in escaping for a short while the traumas of their unnatural lives. Liz was friendly with them all, known to be good fun and nice to be with. They knew just how far they could go with her and respected her all the more because of that.

She did not realise it but after all the bombing, dealing with maimed and dead, dancing with her arms round a pilot who next day was blown from the sky, she was beginning to live on her nerves and it was taking its toll.

Sister Asher watched her nurses carefully. Seeing what was happening to Liz, she sent for her.

'Liz, I'm sending you on ten days' leave.'

'But, Dorothy, I—'

'I knew you would object,' Sister Asher cut in, 'but it's essential for your own good and for the good of my unit here. You've had a trying time since you arrived. There was the newness of a strange place, of unfamiliar surroundings, and the bombing. You've seen pilots go to do battle and some not return. You've seen ground personnel, including WAAFs, killed and Biggin Hill devastated. It's inevitable that we feel these losses and we make it hard on ourselves by having to keep our emotions under control. You've shown exceptional courage and devotion to duty and outstanding bravery when you saved Squadron Leader Davey's life. The strain has been mounting on you all. I intend to see my nurses get some leave and you're the first. The change and a mother's care for a few days will do you the world of good.'

'I appreciate your thought, but I feel I would be letting the team down if I go now.'

'You might be letting it down if you stayed and cracked up under the strain. You should try to see it that way because here's your pass dated for tomorrow.' Sister Asher pushed a document across her desk.

Liz knew no amount of pleading would make Dorothy change her mind. Much as she wanted to stay where the action was, she had to admit that Sister Asher was right and she was pleased to be going home for a few days.

Liz walked by the sea. The air was still. The sun shone from a deep-blue sky frilled with white clouds. Small waves broke and ran hissing up the beach. She breathed deeply, enjoying the tingle in her lungs. It was good to be here, enjoying the peace of Robin Hood's Bay and being spoiled by her mother. She felt much better and the nightmare of Biggin Hill had retreated from her mind. This was her favourite place along the shore and she shut out the marring marks of metal and concrete defences, trying to see it as it was when she first walked here with Martin. She hoped she would find it just the same after the war.

But will life ever be the same? she mused. What will the future hold?

She started. The drone of planes, which she recognised as fighters, came to her from over the sea, spoiling her illusionary tranquillity. Way out over the sea she saw two Hurricanes heading north and wondered if one could be Alec on his way to Acklington. Whoever they were, she wished the pilots well.

She had had a letter from Alec in which he hoped she

was safe from all the bombing he had heard Biggin Hill had been subjected to. He felt frustrated that he was not there to give the 'bloody Germans hell' and see she was all right. He hoped that when the squadron returned to Biggin Hill she would still be there and they could renew their friendship, for he had found consolation and peace from the horrors of battle in just being with her.

She wondered about him as she watched the Hurricanes become smaller and smaller and finally disappear from view, with only the sound of their engines as a reminder of their passage. That too faded, leaving the swish of the waves to break the silence. She liked Alec and she had missed his effervescent personality, especially after the bombing raids. She had always been buoyed up by his light-heartedness and there had been moments of depression when she had yearned for it. As she gazed across the sea, she wondered if she really was falling in love with him.

She kicked the sand. It sprayed before her, breaking the image of Alec in her mind and replacing it with Martin. This had been their special walk and she recalled the night before they parted and the vow they had made to meet here after the war. She wondered what he was doing now.

The engine of the Hurricane faltered, picked up and faltered again. Pilot Officer Alec Crooks glanced anxiously at his instruments. They were going wild, pointers spinning. The engine spluttered again and puffs of black smoke sent alarm bells ringing in his mind. The burst of machine-gun fire from the German bomber, which they had downed before it could press home its attack on the North Sea convoy, must have inflicted some damage which was only now becoming apparent. He looked round quickly, summing up the situation. Though the coast was in sight, they still had some way to go to base. He glanced down at the sea: 500 feet. He looked across at his companion, flying close on his starboard, and saw the concerned look Tubby Briggs gave him as he gesticulated towards the sea. Bale out or ditch? The smoke was getting worse. Decision – quick.

Alec put the nose of the Hurricane down. He made a quick examination of the sea. It was fairly smooth. With any luck he should make a reasonable landing. Then he must be out quickly.

He kept his descent steady without delaying it. He saw Tubby had started to circle and knew that he would already be calling up base on the radiotelephone, informing them of the situation and of their position.

Smoke was pouring out of the engine. Had he judged wrongly? Should he have baled out? Not fire! Please God, not fire! The one thing Alec dreaded most was being burned, but his mind had shut the possibility out until now. The sea, where was it? He strained to see beyond the smoke. There! Only a few more feet. Thank God! Alec pulled back the canopy.

He braced himself against the impact. The plane hit and shuddered through its entire frame. It bounced, struck again and skidded across the water, its nose ploughing through the waves, sending water spraying high. Alec held steady. Tempting as it was, he must not move too soon. The Hurricane settled nose down. Now! He released his harness and parachute and scrambled out of the cockpit as the plane began to sink. Water sloshed around his

244

legs as he got on to the wing. Then he was in the water, his Mae West keeping him afloat.

He shivered with the shock of the cold water, and was thankful that he had chosen to fly today in his fleece-lined leather jacket. He glanced skywards. Tubby was still circling, keeping him company. But for how long? Three minutes later the Hurricane banked and swooped across the waves. Tubby waggled his wings and gave a thumbs-up sign, which reassured Alec that he had done all he could to speed his friend's rescue. Alec watched with mixed feelings as the Hurricane climbed away and headed for home.

With the sound of its engine fading into silence, Alec felt insignificant. He was a mere speck on a vast sea. How could anyone hope to find him? The immense size of the ocean was overwhelming, and he was helpless in the undulating waves. After some time his mind began to mock him, telling him this was the end, an inglorious finish, sapping at his will to live. He started, driving the disabling thoughts from his mind. There was a chance. He had known pilots who had ditched in the Channel and had been picked up by the Air-Sea Rescue, so why not him? But he must fight to stay alive, concentrate on the thought of being rescued – after all, he was lucky. Tubby would have reported where he had ditched. But a huge expanse of sea surrounded him, the waves would try to hide him. Stop! His mind screamed at him. Think of Liz. She hadn't gone under in the tremendous blitz on Biggin Hill. He wouldn't give up. He must see her again.

The moment Tubby Briggs saw that Alec was in trouble, he sent out his SOS call to Acklington, giving their position. Immediately the CO of 32 Squadron ordered two Hurricanes to patrol the area. Word was sent straight away to Group Headquarters in Newcastle, who in a few seconds had alerted Area Combined Headquarters, from where Coastal Command, the navy and Air-Sea Rescue were informed.

The Hurricanes were first away, anxious to locate their comrade. They were over the sea when the first directions from base, calculated from the continuous information supplied by Tubby, were received. They altered course accordingly and started their search.

Within a few minutes of their takeoff, a Hudson of Coastal Command with rescue gear on board took off from Thornaby.

At the same time the alarm was raised in Blyth and the crew of Rescue Launch 124 raced to their stations. Even as the last man leaped on board, the engine was started and ropes were cast off. The launch speeded out of the harbour. Martin was at his wireless set receiving the latest information and passing it on to the flying officer in charge of the boat. Every man knew his job without instructions. Aircraftmen manning the two gun turrets scanned the sky, the two fitters were at the engines and the two wireless operators at their sets. The rest of the twelve-man crew were ranged around the deck on lookout. A pilot with no dinghy wanted to be out of the water as soon as possible. The sergeant coxswain at the wheel increased the speed to 24 knots, sending the launch cleaving through the sea, its bow set high, its Air-Sea Rescue flag taut at the masthead.

* * *

Alec searched the sky. Nothing. Maybe he was destined not to be rescued and would instead end up with the sea for his grave. The feeling of despair was hard to combat with the waves pushing him like a doll. He must fight. He started talking.

'Liz, we had some good times together. Knowing you would be there when I got back helped me to survive those battles in the air. You kept me alert, determined and cautious. Talking to you now brings back memories of the happy times together. At least they were happy for me and I hope they were for you. Now, in this predicament, I can see that my feelings were maybe more than friendship, but I suspect that you were not ready for a deeper relationship. Maybe if I survive this one . . .'

His words faded. He inclined his head, sharpening his hearing.

Aero engines? Wishful thinking? Silence. The sea mocking him. He cursed it. A sound? Yes, there it was again: a far-off drone. Excitement coursed through him. The noise grew louder and louder. Two Hurricanes. Alec let go a whoop of joy. 'Good old Tubby!'

They were way over to his right. 'This way! This way!' his mind screamed. 'Over here!' He waved frantically as they proceeded on their course. They were past, going on and on. The noise of their engines, which a moment ago had filled him with hope, now sang a song of doom. He sank back on his Mae West, overcome with disappointment and despair. Tears started to fill his eyes.

The Hurricanes were almost out of earshot when he noted a slight change in their engines. They were turning. Coming back? He straightened, searching the sky. The sound was louder, coming nearer. He saw them. They had swung closer to him. He waved and waved and waved. They must see him. They must! They zoomed past to his left.

'I'm here, you buggers, I'm here!' he screamed. The words froze on his lips. One of them had swept into a sharp turn and the other followed a few moments later. They came round in a huge sweeping arc, line astern, levelled and came straight over him, waggling their wings. They had seen him! His feelings were ecstatic. Tears of joy flowed down his cheeks. He was saved.

The leading Hurricane continued to circle him at low level while the other climbed higher to circle, both marking his position for rescue.

He watched them, willing them to stay, a sign of hope to him. Then he heard a different note coming from the sky and a few moments later saw a Hudson approaching. He watched it start to turn; once it had completed a full circle, the fighters tipped their wings and headed for home, knowing the greater flying time of the bigger aircraft would keep it on station longer than they could have stayed.

Alec kept his eyes on the new arrival, expecting a dinghy and supplies to be dropped, but after it had circled him three times he began to wonder what was happening. 'Hurry up, you bastards! It's bloody cold in here.'

Then, with the coming of a new sound, he knew why the Hudson crew had not dropped supplies. A high-powered engine was storming in his direction. It could only mean a launch and the Hudson crew must have been informed.

The Hudson tightened its circle to indicate his position for the launch. It came in sight, nearer and nearer. Men waving. They had seen him. The Hudson did one more circuit, swooped low and flew off in the direction of its base.

The launch slowed and manoeuvred close to him with the utmost care. He admired the skill of these airmen-sailors as they stopped beside him. Two were already over the side, hanging on to the ratlines which had been dropped from the deck. They reached out for him and willing hands grabbed his raised arms. They lifted him until his feet could feel the ropes. He pushed as they hauled him up and passed him to two more airmen, who tumbled him on to the deck.

Martin Lawson had left the second wireless operator to pass the news of the successful rescue to headquarters and then to base. He now stood over Alec, who was propping himself against the hatch. 'Here, get this down you,' he said pleasantly, handing the flier a glass of rum. 'Do you good,' he added with a wink.

He hurried away as the pilot was taken below decks. When he came to the cabin a few moments later with a mug of steaming coffee, the pilot's wet clothes had been exchanged for dry ones, including a warm jersey and thick socks.

'Thanks,' said Alec, cradling his hands round the mug. It was good to feel the warmth, especially when it chased the rum into his stomach.

The launch was already heading for Blyth. The flying officer had elicited the essential information from Alec, seen that he was comfortable and well cared for before returning to the deck.

Martin sat down beside Alec. 'From Acklington, I believe?'

'Yes. I'm thankful I'll see it again, thanks to you and the rest of the crew.'

'All in a day's work.' Martin grinned. 'This was an easy one, thanks to the pilot you were flying with. Passed information which was accurate. You'd drifted a bit but not too much. Thank goodness there wasn't a heavy sea running.'

Grateful to be alive, Alec began to relax and talk to his rescuer. 'Where you from?' he asked after a while.

'Little place down the Yorkshire coast, Robin Hood's Bay. Don't suppose you've ever heard of it,' answered Martin.

'Robin Hood's Bay! Of course I have. Met a girl from there when I was stationed at Biggin Hill. A nurse. Great kid! Pretty, good dancer, likes the flicks.' He didn't notice Martin stiffen at this information. 'You might know her, Liz Johnson.'

Martin hesitated thoughtfully. This pilot had obviously seen a lot of Liz. Maybe there was more to their relationship, and he would not want to mess it up for Liz by admitting to a deep friendship. 'Only slightly.'

'Brave girl, too. We'd left Biggin Hill before the first big raid by the Jerries but our squadron leader was there. She saved his life and then did sterling work after the raid. Biggin has received a heavy pasting since then, pretty bad from the news that's filtered through to Acklington. Hope she is all right and hope she's still there when I return.'

'Know when that will be?' asked Martin, steering the talk away from Liz. He had heard enough to know this flier thought a lot about her and he wondered if that feeling was reciprocated by Liz.

'No, but it can't be soon enough for me. Acklington's a picnic after Biggin.'

'What, and you just fished out of the drink?'

Alec laughed. 'I see what you mean, but the action's all in the south and once you've been in it you want to be there. You feel as if you're letting the rest of the fighter boys down 'cos you're on a cushy number.'

'Must get back to my wireless,' said Martin, rising to his feet. 'Best of luck and take care.'

'And you,' Alec turned with a wink. 'And thanks for saving me.'

Martin frowned at the deep pang of jealousy which hit him. Was it a sign that he loved Liz more than he had admitted?

Liz had been back at Biggin Hill for five days and got quickly into the swing of station life once again. Sister Asher saw that the leave had done her the world of good. Her features were less drawn and there was colour back in her cheeks, but what pleased her most of all was that the serenity she had first admired in Liz had returned.

92 Squadron gave her a warm welcome and, though she was sad to see some familiar faces no longer there, she drove that from her mind and got on with life. She knew those pilots would not want her to mourn for them.

Invited to tea with two of the pilots, she was enjoying their chat, pleased to be able to bring to them some reassurance of what, for an hour or so, seemed a normal life with pleasant female company, when the door to the anteroom opened.

'Ah, a new bod,' exclaimed one of the pilots, seeing a stranger sporting wings and a DFM.

Liz looked round and her eyes widened with surprise. 'Alec!' she gasped, jumped to her feet and hugged him tightly. 'What on earth?'

'Can't do without me here,' he said grinning. He stood back and, still holding her hands, looked her up and down. 'Still the same old Liz.' He winked. 'It's good to see you.'

'And you.' There was genuine pleasure in her eyes. 'You've joined 92?'

'Yes. Come to show them how it's done.' His attitude was infectious and the two pilots took no offence. Their exchanged glances was one of 'This one will fit in'.

Liz made the introductions and explained how she knew Pilot Officer Alec Crooks.

When it came time for her to leave, Alec said he would walk with her to the sick quarters and catch up on the latest news.

She showed concern when he told her about ditching in the North Sea. 'You could have been drowned!'

'Couple of Hurricanes from base spotted me. Air-Sea Rescue were already on their way so it was a fairly speedy rescue. I was lucky,' he explained. 'Oh, by the way, one of the wireless operators on the launch was from Robin Hood's Bay. I mentioned you but he said he knew you only slightly.'

Liz's mind raced. It must be Martin. He had to be the only wireless operator from Robin Hood's Bay on Air-Sea

252

Rescue, stationed at Blyth. About to disclose that she knew him, Liz drew back. Martin's denial had stunned her. Why had he done it? She was disappointed. She would have liked to have been acknowledged.

'Did you get his name?' she asked casually.

'No. You know how it is with these things. Should have done. Sorry.'

Liz shrugged her shoulders. 'Doesn't really matter.'

Two days later, with Martin's denial still preying on her mind, she picked up a pen to write to him. She was going to challenge him about the rebuff but as the words began to flow she thought better of it. She was taking him to task like an upset sweetheart. They had never pretended to mean that much to each other. Maybe Martin had someone else. Instead she wrote:

27 September 1940

Dear Martin,

I hear that you have been partially responsible for the rescue of a fighter pilot I know, and looked after him on board your launch.

He has returned to Biggin Hill and I got the story from him. He made light of his experience but I know if it hadn't been for you and the rest of your crew he could easily have perished.

I am *so* proud of you and just had to write to thank you.

In fact, our gang of six seem to be doing all right. Jean and Gabrielle should soon gain their commissions, Ron is somewhere at sea on a destroyer as he always wanted, and Colin, as you probably know from

Jean, is progressing well and hoping that the Canadian winter isn't too severe to hold up his training.

Take care of yourself.

Liz paused, reread what she had written, looked thoughtful for a moment and then added:

Sorry meeting seems impossible – leaves never coincide, and being at the opposite ends of the country doesn't help. Still, there's always the beach at RHB after the war.

Affectionately

Liz

Martin slit the envelope open. He had recognised Liz's writing.

Several times he had found himself embroiled in jealousy since pulling that pilot out of the sea. He had started to write to Liz to tell her how he felt, but he always drew back. He did not want to complicate things for her. If she was taken with this pilot, could he blame her? He seemed a nice enough chap and wasn't there a certain glamour about a fighter pilot?

Now he wondered what she had to say. His eyes scanned the letter quickly. 'Damn,' he hissed to himself. The pilot was back at Biggin Hill. They would be together again. He pulled himself up. If that was what she wanted, then so be it. But what could he read into the reference to the beach at Robin Hood's Bay?

Chapter Twelve

1940

22 October 1940

My dearest girl,

I am so pleased that you passed your course successfully and have got your commission. I am very proud of you and see in you something of what I would have liked to have been and that gives me great pleasure.

The only sadness is that your father does not acknowledge your achievements. He hears them for I read your letters aloud and he wouldn't dare get up and leave when I start to do so. I suspect that he wouldn't want to because I believe he really wants to know what you are doing. He makes no comment and I can see that he is still seething that you defied him. I know he still believes that the Harlands are to blame for tempting you away. I know that is nonsense but he won't see it.

I have no message from him to you. He sends none.

I would dearly love to see you but I would not advise you to come home when you get a leave. Your father's opposition would spoil the leave for you as well as upsetting me. So I will wait patiently until things are better.

John and James were torpedoed in the Atlantic but fortunately were picked up by an escorting destroyer. They were none the worse for their ordeal. They managed forty-eight hours at home and will be back at sea again now, I expect.

We hear from Martin once a fortnight. He seems to be well but says little about what he is doing except that he is happy in Air-Sea Rescue.

I wonder if you have heard the wonderful news about Liz? I saw her mother yesterday and they had just received word that Liz has been awarded the Military Medal for saving a squadron leader's life and doing exceptional work during severe attacks on the airfield where she is stationed. She was home on leave in September. I could see she had been under some strain but she looked much better when she went back.

I am pleased that you are hearing from Colin and glad to know that all is well with him. I wonder when he expects to be back in England.

Take care of yourself, love. I hope you and Gabrielle can stay together when you have finished this new course.

Love,
Mum

Jean's reactions changed as she read the letter. It was always a joy to receive one from her mother, but there was never any sign of reconciliation from her father. Today, however, that sadness changed to euphoric excitement when she saw the news about Liz. She and Gabrielle immediately sent a congratulatory letter to her.

The personnel at Biggin Hill were proud of their nurse, none more so than 92 Squadron, who insisted on a party though Liz was wanting to play the award down. Alec was especially proud of her and suggested taking her to London to buy her a present.

Liz was a little apprehensive about the outing, fearing that he might have his mind set on a ring. Having settled her in a restaurant, he escaped for a few minutes and returned to present her with a marcasite brooch in the shape of pilot's wings.

'It's beautiful, Alec, but you shouldn't.'

'Why not? What's money? I might not need any tomorrow.'

Liz frowned. 'Don't talk like that! You used to say you were indestructible.'

'So I am,' he said breezily with a broad grin. 'Even so, what's money for but to be spent? So why not on you, especially on this occasion?'

Alec was watching her with intense eyes. For one moment Liz thought he was going to propose and put in quickly, 'I hope by that you mean my award?'

'Of course. What else?' He grinned broadly. 'Did you think I was going to propose?' He tapped the side of his nose. 'Ah,' he went on, 'Alec's a wise old bird. I don't think you're ready for a proposal. I think that there's someone else.'

Liz met his searching gaze. 'I don't know, Alec. There might be, there might not. I'm not sure.'

'More fool him for not grabbing you while he can. Boy from back home?'

She nodded. She was almost on the point of saying that he had met him but she held back.

'But nothing definite?'

'No.'

'But you think a lot about him?'

'We get on well.'

'That's not love.'

'No, I agree. But is yours? We're two people swept together in war. We find escape in each other's company from the horrors. I like you a lot, I like being with you but I don't know whether there's a love there which could survive in peacetime.' Her voice became even more serious. 'You've changed since joining this squadron.'

'And you don't like what you see?'

'Oh, no, it's not that. There's still much of the old Alec in you, that fun person with a zest for life, but I think 92 have put into you a restlessness which will never be curbed even after the war.'

'And you couldn't live with it?'

'I don't think so.'

'Then we shall just have to wait and see what happens. But I hope we can still go on seeing each other. You're good for me, Liz, and I'd lose out in the air if I thought you weren't there for me to come back to.'

'Of course I'll be there.' She reached out and touched his hand across the table. If she brought some calmness to his mind, then she was happy. She glanced at the brooch.

'Maybe you should take this back. I don't want you to think that it can be a sign that—'

'It wasn't bought for that purpose,' he broke in quickly. 'But out of admiration for you and a reminder of these days together at Biggin Hill.'

'Any news of Colin coming home?' asked Gabrielle, knowing that the letter Jean had just read had come from Canada.

'No,' replied Jean. 'He says it looks as if it will be early-ish in the new year, depending on how the winter weather affects the flying. I'd hoped he might be home for Christmas.'

Gabrielle eyed her friend. 'And what would you have done if he had been? Would you have gone home?'

'No. Mum still thinks it wouldn't be wise. But Colin and I would have managed to be together somehow for part of his leave.'

'What will you do? You could come home with me, but . . .'

Jean gave a little laugh. 'Exactly,' she said, reading Gabrielle's unspoken thoughts. 'Can you imagine Dad if he knew I was spending my leave with the Harlands in Robin Hood's Bay? I'll be all right. Liz will only have a forty-eight-hour pass over Christmas, and she's suggested that we spend that time together in London. I'll do that. Then I'll see if I can report to my new station a few days earlier. But I'm flexible – an alternative might crop up while I'm in London.'

Gabrielle nodded understandingly. 'Seems a good idea. I'm glad that you and Liz can get together. I'd hate to think of you on your own. Wonder where we'll get posted. I'm afraid it won't be together.'

'Let's hope we're not too far apart. If we get to the same bomber group it might be easy to meet.'

The night before the course was officially finishing, Jean wrote to her mother:

22 December 1940

Dearest Mum,

Our course finishes tomorrow. We have had our results and both Gabrielle and I have passed, finishing in the top ten, so we are quite pleased.

We are getting some leave. I am sorry you think it wisest if I don't come home, but I will take your advice. I'll miss you at Christmas. It was always such a happy family affair and I have treasured memories of those days. I suppose it will never be the same again. This war has spoiled that. It has broken the family up and who knows where we will be or what our attitudes will be when it is all over. But we will make the best of it and I look forward to our reunion, whenever that may be.

Don't worry about what I will do over the Christmas period. I am meeting Liz in London for a few days and then in all probability I will report to my new unit sooner than I need and get settled in. I don't know where that will be until tomorrow. Gabrielle will be able to tell you. She is coming home on leave and I am asking her to bring this letter to you.

Tomorrow Gabrielle and I will probably be posted to different stations. We are hoping that they will not be far apart. I will miss her. She has been a great companion. Good fun to be with yet confident and serious. But don't worry about me. Your little girl has really grown up. I can look after myself. Life in the WAAFs so far has been interesting, an experience I'm glad I was able to take, and I anticipate, after this course, life will continue to be so.

Give my love to Dad. Tell him I often think of him. A very happy Christmas to you both. I will miss you. Love,

Jean

She read the letter through, folded it and made the crease with a deliberate stroke. She pushed the paper slowly into the envelope, which she had already addressed, and sealed it, her thoughts dwelling all the while on her mother.

The following morning the postings were issued and Jean found that she was to report to RAF Waddington, a bomber station in 5 Group, situated in Lincolnshire.

At the end of the list one name remained unallocated, that of Gabrielle Harland. Jean looked askance at her as she whispered, 'What about you?'

Gabrielle gave a little shake of her head and a slight shrug of her shoulders.

The officer in charge of the postings was speaking again. 'Section Officer Harland, you are to report back here on January second. You will have eleven days, the rest have seven, reporting to your new postings on Monday the thirtieth.'

Excited girls left the room, chattering about their

postings. Only Gabrielle and Jean were puzzled. They speculated, but could find no reason why Gabrielle had not received a posting.

'I'll let you know as soon as I come back,' Gabrielle promised.

'You must. We just have to keep in touch.'

'We will,' Gabrielle reassured Jean. 'Now, let's find a map and see exactly where Waddington is.'

They soon located it about five miles south of Lincoln.

'Provided the station is all right, that's not a bad posting, so close to a town.'

Gabrielle jumped down from the carriage with a light step. The air was sharp. The overnight hoarfrost still clung to the trees and hedgerows, bringing a Christmas look to Robin Hood's Bay. Clouds threatened from the north but there had been no talk of a white Christmas.

'Miss Gabrielle! Lovely to see you again.' The station-master's face broadened into a welcoming smile.

'And you, Mr Newton. It's good to be home.'

All further conversation between them was stopped by the shout of 'Gabrielle!'

Turning to see her mother and father bustling on to the platform, she dropped her case and rushed to them. 'Mum!' She flung herself into the outstretched arms and they hugged each other with undisguised pleasure. She turned to her father and held out an arm into which he came with his love.

'Let's look at thee, lass.'

She stood back and did a little twirl in front of them. There was admiration in their eyes when she faced them again.

'Thee looks right smart,' said Sam with a slight nod of approval.

'We are so proud of you,' said Colette. 'You've done well.' She held out her hand and mother and daughter started towards the exit.

Will Newton handed Gabrielle's case to Sam, commenting, 'A right fine lass, Sam. Looks well in uniform.'

'Aye, she does that,' agreed Sam with pride.

He hurried after his wife and daughter and caught them up just in time to hear Colette say, 'How's Jean? It's a pity she isn't with you. I think she ought to have come.'

Gabrielle stopped, puzzled by the serious note of criticism in her mother's voice.

'What do you mean, Mum? Jean didn't come because her mother has been telling her not to. She feared the trouble there would be with her father if she did after he had told her never to come home again.'

Colette cocked an eyebrow and shot Sam a glance before looking back at her daughter. 'Jean doesn't know her mother's ill?'

'Ill? No.' There was no disguising that Gabrielle's surprise was genuine. 'Jean's heard regularly from her mother but she has never mentioned being ill.' She paused momentarily, then added thoughtfully. 'In every letter Mrs Lawson was adamant about Jean not coming home, always blaming it on Mr Lawson's attitude. I'll bet it was also because she didn't want Jean to know about her illness. I don't think I'll see her after my leave, she's being posted to Waddington and I don't know where I'm going, but I'll be able to get her address and I'll let her know.'

'I'm afraid it'll be too late,' said Colette.

Gabrielle stared at her. If she read the meaning behind those words correctly, it chilled her. 'You mean . . . ?' Her words trailed away.

'Yes, love. I'm afraid Sarah is dying.' Her father's voice was low as if that would lessen the impact.

'Oh, my God!' Her thoughts were filled with the terrible shock this was going to be to Jean, who adored her mother and enjoyed her letters with the deepest enthusiasm for the one link with home.

'Can thee get in touch with her right away?' asked Sam.

Gabrielle looked troubled. 'No, I don't know where she is except that she's somewhere in London. She went on leave today. She and Liz are spending Christmas together. Don't know what Jean is going to do after that.'

'And there's nowhere you can write to her?' Colette added, 'But that wouldn't be any use, a letter could be too late.'

Gabrielle tightened her lips with frustration at the hopelessness of the situation.

'Come on, love. There's nothing thee can do at the moment.' Sam knew his words were of no comfort to a daughter who wanted to spare her dearest friend the shock of her mother's death. 'Jonas will surely write to her.'

'I doubt it, Dad. He's never been in touch with Jean, never even sent a message in her mum's letters. John and James are away at sea so they won't know. Martin is the only one who could tell her, but he won't have Jean's new address until she contacts him.' She gave a sigh of despair. 'I can't let Jean receive the news in cold, bleak words on paper among people she does not know, with no one to turn to. I've got four more days' leave than she has. If you don't mind, I'll go back a couple of days early and go via Waddington to tell her. It's near Lincoln so I can find somewhere to stay if I can't get a bed at the base. I'll be there if she needs me.'

Although she would have liked to keep her daughter as long as possible, Colette saw the true friendship in Gabrielle's gesture and admired her for it. Sam was pleased that the younger generation bore no ill will towards each other because of Jonas's bitterness.

They had reached the house and as she stepped inside Gabrielle felt the warmth envelop her. Home! She revelled in the comfort and the feeling of being secure and safe for the time being.

'I have a meal all ready for later on, but we'll have a cup of tea and a piece of cake now,' said Colette as they slipped out of their coats.

'That will be nice,' said Gabrielle. 'Then I'd better go and see Mrs Lawson. I have a letter from Jean for her and after what you've told me it will be better if I get it to her today.'

'Want me to go with thee?' said Sam. 'Jonas will be at home.'

'No, Dad. Thanks, but it'll be better if I'm alone.'

'Thee thinks he'll let a Harland into his house?'

'He won't stop me.'

Sam thought his daughter was right when he heard the cold determination in her voice and sensed the no-nonsense attitude of an officer's training, epitomised outwardly in the authority and set of the uniform. He was pleased with what he saw. His daughter had turned into a fine young woman.

* * *

Gabrielle rapped on the door of the Lawson cottage. She received a shock when the door opened and she saw a man whose shoulders drooped as if the world weighed heavily on him. His face was drawn in lines of despair, and exhaustion stared from the dark eye sockets. This was far from the Jonas Lawson she remembered.

'Good day, Mr Lawson. I'd like to see Mrs Lawson,' she said with a friendly tone.

She saw Jonas staring at her with a puzzled frown as if trying to jolt his mind into recognition. His eyes widened with surprise before clouding with suspicion. 'Miss Gabrielle Harland, isn't it?' As the name of Harland came from his lips, Jonas straightened. He drew his shoulders back and tensed his body in defiance. No Harland should see him bowed down under trouble, not even with death stalking close by.

'It is. I'm pleased to see you, Mr Lawson.'

'Well, I'm not pleased to see thee. Thee ain't welcome here.'

Gabrielle jutted her chin defiantly. 'I've done you no wrong, Mr Lawson.'

'Thee and thy brother tempted my daughter away when she should have been here helping her mother.'

'We did no such thing. Jean had a free will. It was what she chose to do. If anyone was responsible, it was you, creating the atmosphere you did by living with an incident in the past that's best forgotten.'

Jonas's lips tightened. 'Thee'll not speak to me like that, young woman.'

'If the truth hurts . . . but enough, I'm not here to hark on the past, I'm here to see Mrs Lawson because I have a letter from Jean for her.'

'Then give it to me.'

'No,' snapped Gabrielle. 'I promised I would deliver it personally.'

'Then thee can't keep thy promise.'

'You'd deny your wife a letter from her daughter?' she snapped in disgust. 'Even if it might be the last? Have you no interest in Jean?'

'She left against my wishes. I wanted her here to help her mother.'

'Mrs Lawson wasn't ill then.'

'Maybe not. Maybe she would never have been ill if Jean had stayed.'

Gabrielle was shocked that he should lay the blame for his wife's illness on Jean. From what her mother and father had told her, Mrs Harland had kept the real nature of her illness from Jonas until recently.

'That's not true and you know it,' stormed Gabrielle, her eyes blazing with fury. 'Now, I want to see Mrs Lawson.'

Before he could reply, a weak voice finding some strength called from upstairs. 'Who is it, Jonas? Is it Jean?'

He half turned to reply. In that moment, with his attention elsewhere, Gabrielle seized her chance. She squirmed past him and before he realised it she was mounting the stairs two at a time. Reaching the small landing, she saw a door ajar and heard a low call filled with a desperate hope, 'Jean?'

Gabrielle pushed the door wide and stepped quickly into the room. A pale, emaciated face lay on a white pillow. The grey hair spilled across it, forming a halo and emphasising the drawn lines of suffering. The eyes were sunken but when they focused on Gabrielle as she stepped towards the bed, they found a new life, one which sparkled with recognition and joy.

'Jean! Oh, I'm so glad thee's come.' The voice trembled but there was a new mustering of strength in it. Sarah held out her arms. There was happiness on her face.

Gabrielle was about to tell her who she was and that she only had a letter from Jean when she drew back. Why spoil this dying woman's happiness? Why shatter her illusion? What did it matter if Sarah thought she was Jean? There was nothing wrong in it if it brought some comfort to her. Gabrielle moved forwards and leaned on the bed to let Sarah take her in her arms. She felt those thin, bony arms come around her with a motherly love. Gabrielle embraced her. Sarah shook with joy.

'Oh, love, it's good to see thee.'

'Mum, I love you.' Gabrielle realised Mrs Lawson would not see through her pretence. It was Jean she held and it was Jean's voice she was hearing.

'That's all that matters to me,' said Sarah. 'And remember thee always has my love, wherever thee are. Thee marry Colin, thee'll be happy with him. Thee has my blessing.'

'Thanks, Mum. That means a lot to me.' Gabrielle raised her head and kissed Sarah on the cheek. She saw tears of happiness running down the frail cheeks and hers flowed too.

She heard footsteps on the stairs and tensed herself for the fury which would burst upon them. The steps stopped at the door.

'See, Jonas, Jean's come.'

Dread came with a cold pressure on Gabrielle's chest. What would Jonas do? Surely he couldn't shatter his wife's belief that she held her daughter? Gabrielle waited on a knife edge.

'Yes, Sarah, I see.' The words, soft and gentle, floated across the room.

Gabrielle closed her eyes with relief.

'That's all that matters.' Sarah gave a contented sigh. She turned her head, smiled at Gabrielle and kissed her forehead. 'Take care of yourself, my darling girl. Thank you for the happiness you have given me.'

She sank on the pillow. Gabrielle felt her arms go slack. 'Oh, no!' The cry came involuntarily as if it could arrest death.

Jonas was across the room and on his knees beside the bed, taking his wife from Gabrielle's arms and holding her to him, silent tears streaming down his cheeks.

Gabrielle rose slowly to her feet, placed a brief comforting hand on Jonas's shoulder, then turned and walked slowly from the room.

As she climbed the hill, her hand closed round the letter in her greatcoat pocket. There had been no need for it.

Chapter Thirteen

1940

Jean hurried along the platform at Paddington. She felt light-hearted. She had shrugged off her two regrets; that she was not going home and that Gabrielle was not with her. But she was meeting Liz, and she was looking forward to that.

Jean peered past the people streaming through the barrier ahead of her. Seeing her friend, she waved and gave a broad smile of pleasure.

'Good to see you, Liz,' she said as they hugged each other. 'And congrats on your medal.'

'Thanks. I've got us booked into the WAAF Junior Officers' Club near Trafalgar Square. I suggest we go straight there and then plan what we're going to do.'

'Good. I'm in your hands. I don't know London, so I'll leave everything to you.'

'Let's see if we can find a taxi first. They're at a premium.'

They left the station and twenty minutes later managed to share a taxi with a couple of army officers who wanted to get to Trafalgar Square.

Once they had checked into the club, they settled down for a good chat over tea at the Lyons Corner House in the Strand.

'Looking forward to your posting?' asked Liz.

'Very much. You get tired of training when you hear of people such as yourself, doing something more positive. Was it bad, Liz?'

'Yes, but it's surprising how resilient people are. The worst part is the waiting to see if all the pilots are coming back. The time gets longer. And then you know someone isn't going to show up. You wonder if they have landed away, baled out or if you'll never see them again.' She eyed Jean seriously. 'You'll experience that once you get to a bomber station. No matter how much you try, you can't stand aloof from what is happening around you. You become part of the squadron, and its triumphs and losses affect you. You could be shattered by it if you didn't remind yourself that you have a job to do and life must go on.'

'You're among the glamour boys of the air force right now. Haven't you been swept off your feet?'

Liz hesitated. Was Jean fishing for her brother's sake?

Jean appeared to read her thoughts and added, 'Sorry, Liz. I'm not prying.'

Liz smiled. 'It's all right.' She paused. 'Of course I'm involved. They're a breezy, devil-may-care lot, especially 92 Squadron. Lots of parties, living it up, and inevitably you get swept up into their lives. They like a pretty face and they find escape and some comfort in feminine company.' She gave a half-smile with a look as if she was recalling some particular memory. 'You could fall in love over and over again, but then you realise it might only be the euphoria of the moment and that the glamour of the situation is playing a strong part. So you hold back, knowing that love must have a stronger base. Oh, deep loves do develop and bloom, I've seen them.'

'But not for you?'

'Martin? You're wondering about me and Martin?'

'It crossed my mind as you were talking. You seemed to be close back home.'

'We were. Still are. But the war has given us other experiences. It can widen the gap.'

'Absence can make the heart grow fonder,' Jean reminded her.

'Like you and Colin?'

'It does for me and, from his letters, I should say it does for him.'

Liz gave her an understanding smile. 'But the love between you was different, right from the start. Martin and I weren't as committed as you two were.'

'You've found someone else? One of these pilots?'

'At one time I thought maybe I had, but I wasn't sure. He flew with 32 Squadron. They were sent to Acklington in Northumberland but he has been transferred to 92 Squadron and so is back at Biggin Hill.'

'And?' prompted Jean when Liz hesitated.

'He'll be restless all his life, never settling, and that's not for me. I realised that when I was in Robin Hood's Bay on leave. He knows that but he likes my company and more often than not we're just part of squadron parties. A good time with all.'

'And Martin?'

Liz gave a shrug of her shoulders. 'I'm not sure of the situation. We respect each other's wishes not to get too serious until we see what happens during the war. But I think Martin may have other thoughts, maybe even has someone else.' She looked enquiringly at Jean. 'Has he said anything to you?'

'About someone else? No. What makes you think he has?'

Liz told her about Alec's ditching and being rescued by Martin's crew and how Martin had claimed he only knew her slightly.

Jean frowned at this. It was unlike Martin. He would have declared his interest if he had had strong feelings for Liz. Maybe seeing a new life had changed his attitude. Jean had always seen him as a home-bird, and Liz's declared love for Robin Hood's Bay made them seem an ideal couple. But they had this understanding and that was their affair.

'When Alec told you about meeting Martin, did you tell him you knew him well?'

'No. There seemed no point when Martin had denied me.'

'And you thought Martin had someone else and you'd respect the pact you'd made?'

'Yes.'

'Didn't it occur to you that he might have thought the same, that Alec might have sung your praises and given Martin the impression that there was something between you and Alec? Write to Martin and ask him?'

'That might be committing ourselves. It might be pushing him to make the situation serious,' Liz objected.

'And you don't want to be? You want it to remain as it was?'

'Oh, I'm not sure.' She screwed up her face with doubt.

'Still carry something for Alec?'

'No. Just good friends now.'

'But you think that, having almost fallen for him, there could be some other pilot come along and sweep you off your feet?'

'Who knows?'

'Then leave things as they are,' advised Jean. 'But let Martin see from your letters that there's nothing between you and Alec, even if you don't mention it directly. Gentle hints that all is well in your feelings towards Martin should do it, and leave you both with a better understanding.'

Liz looked thoughtful, then nodded her head slowly in agreement. She brightened visibly and said, 'It's been good having this talk.'

Jean laughed. 'I've done nothing.'

'Oh yes, you have,' said Liz appreciatively. 'Now, the rest of your leave.' She quickly outlined some things she had in mind and then added as an afterthought, 'You'll have another four days' leave after that. I have to be back on the morning of the twenty-sixth. What are you going to do?'

'Don't know. Haven't made any plans. Probably go to Waddington.'

'Oh, you can't do that! For one thing, they won't be expecting you.'

274

'I know. I don't really fancy arriving early.'

'Then why not come back with me?' said Liz enthusiastically. 'The White Hart in Brasted is the local, which 92 have adopted as their own. Bill Haylock and his wife Helen run the Hart. Charming couple who have taken the pilots to their hearts and anyone from Biggin Hill, for that matter. I'm sure you'd be comfortable there and they'd make you most welcome.'

'Well . . .' Jean hesitated.

'Oh, come on,' urged Liz. 'You've nothing else to do. Come and meet some of the pilots.'

Jean brightened. The uncertainty of the rest of her leave was solved. 'Why not? Right, I will.'

'Looks a charming place,' Jean commented as they entered the White Hart.

'It is,' replied Liz. She glanced into the bar. 'Ah, Bill's in here.'

Jean saw Christmas decorations brightening a cosy room in which a fire burned cheerily in a wide grate. A Christmas tree stood in one corner, its baubles reflecting the ceiling lights. The bar and all the tables shone, and thick, flowered curtains added to the comfortable atmosphere.

The man behind the bar, glass and cloth in his hands, turned on hearing the door open. His eyes brightened in recognition. 'Ah, Liz, good to see you. Enjoy your leave?'

'Yes, thanks, Bill,' she replied with an equally friendly smile. 'I want you to meet a friend of mine, Jean Lawson.'

Bill put down the cloth and glass and extended his hand across the bar. 'Pleased to know you, miss.' His broad hand gripped firmly and he smiled a welcoming smile. His eyes were bright, assessing but encouraging a return of friendship if he deemed the person worthy of his. Jean judged him to be nearly sixty years old, without the paunch that might be associated with a landlord. His cheeks were round and rosy, seeming appropriate to his surroundings.

'Bill, Jean has four more days' leave. She's on her own. I persuaded her to spend them here. Can you put her up?'

'Of course,' he replied without hesitation. He looked at Jean. 'Anything for an RAF uniform. You're most welcome for as long as you like.' He turned to a door at the back of the bar, pushed it open, stuck his head round and called, 'Helen!'

While he was doing so, a quick whispered exchange took place between the two girls.

'He approves of you,' said Liz.

Jean smiled. 'Thought he was weighing me up.'

Bill came back to the bar and almost immediately a woman of about the same age appeared.

'Helen, love. Meet Jean Lawson, friend of Liz. She still has some leave. I've said she can spend it here.'

'Very well.' She gave Jean a smile which tugged at her heartstrings. Oh, it was so like her mother's! She shook Jean's hand firmly but with a touch that spoke of a gentle person. She was shorter than her husband by six inches and rounder, not fat but comfortable, a person Jean felt would be cuddlesome in a motherly way. In her grey eyes and soft voice was a deep sincerity and respect for anyone who came up to the judgement she made. 'You're most welcome, my love. We'll make you comfortable, and please treat the White Hart as your home.' She

276

sensed that there was disappointment or even tragedy in this girl's life, otherwise why hadn't she gone home for Christmas?

'Thank you so much, Mr and Mrs Haylock. I'm most grateful.'

'Ah, now for a start, miss, it's Helen and Bill.' Mrs Haylock glanced at Liz. 'What would our young pilots think if they heard Jean addressing us as Mr and Mrs? They'd think we'd gone very formal and were trying to spike their parties.' She looked back at Jean. 'Oh, miss, you'll like "our boys"! Boisterous but gentlemen, they know their place.'

'I'm looking forward to meeting them,' said Jean. 'And if you're Helen and Bill, I'm Jean.'

'We'll put her in room two, Bill.'

He looked at Jean. 'Most comfortable bed in the place,' he said. 'I'll light a fire for you.'

'Oh, please don't go to a lot of trouble,' Jean protested.

'It's no trouble, especially for someone in that uniform,' Bill replied. He was about to go when the squeal of tyres stopped him. They heard the doors bang and footsteps hurry into the inn. The door into the bar burst open and two young RAF officers strode in.

'Hi! It's a great day for drinking,' called the tall flying officer, tossing his hat on the bar.

'Sure is,' his companion agreed with a wide, boyish grin.

'Not yet, it isn't,' replied Bill with a glance at the grandfather clock, which stood at one end of the bar. 'Quarter of an hour to opening time.'

The young pilot officer strode over to the clock, opened

277

the glass face and moved the pointers on a quarter of an hour. 'Now it is,' he said with a flourish.

'You'll get me locked up.' The protest was made as Bill picked up a glass and started to draw the beer.

'Liz, you just back off leave and starting to booze already?' There was jocular admonishment in the flying officer's voice.

'No, I'm not here for a drink. Just seeing if Helen and Bill could put my friend up for the rest of her leave.'

'And Helen and Bill must not refuse this lovely girl, or else they'll have all of 92 wanting to know why.' He bowed to Jean and held out his hand. 'Flying Officer Clive Munson at your service, ma'am, but you may call me "C", everybody else does, or if they're scrounging, it's "Muny". Then I beat a hasty retreat.'

There was a teasing twinkle in his blue eyes. Jean noticed a Distinguished Flying Cross and bar beneath his wings and knew that here was a brave man whose outward show of insouciance concealed a deadly serious side. His thin face was pale and bore the lines of a strain not admitted.

He turned to Liz. 'If you're on duty, you want a lift to base. Come on.' He grabbed her hand, swept his hat off the bar and, dragging her after him, headed for the door.

'See you later, Jean,' Liz called over her shoulder, a 'sorry I can't help it' look in her eyes.

'Save my pint, Bill! Don't let that bastard Dave have it,' shouted Clive.

Bill shook his head with a smile as he glanced at the closing door.

'Don't mind them, Jean. Life's like that when they're

278

around,' said Helen. 'But they're a grand lot. Don't know where we'd be without them.' She glanced at Dave. 'And don't you go getting big-headed at that.'

Dave slid up to the bar, leaned across it quickly and gave Helen a kiss on the cheek. 'Now would I be doing that?'

'Ah, away with you,' said Helen, flapping her hands at him indignantly. Though she liked the fuss 'her pilots' made of her, she knew they would not enjoy it half as much if she didn't make some sort of protest at their fussing. The sound of the car roaring away raised a comment from her, accompanied by a shake of the head. 'I don't know where you pilots scrounge your petrol to be running around as you do.'

'That's a well-kept secret, Helen,' said Dave, tapping the side of his nose. 'Now, are you going to introduce me to your guest?' he asked with a wink at Jean.

'If you want it formally, unlike your brash companion, yes. Jean Lawson, Dave Pitman, another from 92.'

'Pleased to meet you.' Dave held out his hand.

Jean took it and sensed a little nervousness in it. She smiled her greeting.

'Will you join me in a drink?' he offered.

'Well, I've only just arrived.'

'You have time,' Helen put in. 'I'll pop up and see everything's ready and Bill will light the fire. And then I'll see about some lunch for you.'

'Thanks, Helen. You're most kind.' Jean turned to Dave. 'A gin and tonic, if you don't mind?'

'Bill?' said Dave.

'Coming right up.'

'Thanks.' Dave took his beer and escorted Jean to one of the tables and then returned for the gin and tonic.

Jean watched him as he did so. So young, same age as Colin. Was this how Colin would look? Smart in his uniform, attractive. Wings waiting for a DFC to be sewn underneath them. He was taller than Colin and thinner. His fair hair was neatly cut and heightened his narrow face.

'How long have you been with the squadron?' she asked.

'A couple of weeks. Obviously C's got a lot more time in than I have, so you're wondering how we . . . Knew him at school. He joined up from school. I went into banking but left to join the RAF, so I was behind him. When I turned up to join 92, he sort of took me under his wing. Great chap, taught me a lot.'

Behind the confident voice, Jean detected a slight lack of belief in his own ability. Maybe that wasn't such a bad thing, it might make him more cautious in the air, unless it had the opposite . . . She dismissed the disturbing thought to answer his question.

'What about you? Are you posted to the Bump?'

'The Bump?'

'Nickname for Biggin Hill – we're on a hill.'

'Oh. No, I'm going to Waddington in Lincolnshire, bomber station. Intelligence Officer.'

Dave raised his eyebrows. 'Brainy type,' he said with a teasing grin. 'Hope you enjoy it,' he added more seriously.

'Hope so, I'm looking forward to it.'

Ten minutes later Helen announced the room was ready.

'See you later, and thanks for the drink,' said Jean as she rose to follow Helen.

'Look forward to that,' replied Dave, getting to his feet.

Jean found a fire crackling in the small grate in the low-ceilinged bedroom. The bed faced the window, to one side of which there was a neat dressing table. A chest of drawers backed on to one wall. A small table with a lamp stood beside the bed.

'Did you make that?' she asked, indicating the patch-work quilt.

'Yes,' replied Helen, pleased that the quilt had been noticed.

'It's beautiful. Reminds me of the one on my bed at home. My mother made it. I suppose it was so familiar that I never appreciated it, but now, away from home, living WAAF-style, and seeing this one . . .' A wistful look had come into Jean's eyes.

Helen noticed it, wondered but said nothing. It was no good opening old wounds if there were any. But she resolved to give this girl all the home comforts and spoiling she could.

'Bathroom's just down the corridor. If there's anything you want, just ask. You're very welcome.'

'Thanks, Helen, you're so kind.'

Helen paused at the door. 'There'll be some lunch in half an hour.'

Jean unpacked her few belongings, washed and, feeling fresher and contented, tried the bed. She would revel in the soft feathers that night. She took a few minutes to relax in the wing chair positioned so that she could get a glimpse of the Kent countryside from the window. The sound of aircraft flying low brought her to her feet and

281

she saw Spitfires coming in to land. Wondering if all of them were returning, she felt numb in her stomach. She started. She had only had contact with two pilots for a few moments and already she was experiencing concern. She must take a firmer grip on her feelings.

When she returned to the bar, Dave was still sitting in the same place. Half a dozen middle-aged men, whom she judged to be locals, lined the bar and cast her approving looks as she crossed the room to join Dave.

'C not back yet?' she asked.

'No,' he replied. 'It's a wonder he's keeping a pint waiting.'

Ten minutes later they heard a car engine change its tune as its driver moved down through the gears.

'C. I'd know his driving anywhere,' remarked Dave.

He was right, for a few moments later the door to the bar swung open and Clive swept in, followed by another flying officer.

'There you are! What did I tell you? Prettiest popsie you've ever seen,' said C with an infectious enthusiasm.

Jean blushed a little as she came under the newcomer's appraising gaze, which revealed agreement with C's assessment.

'Saw the squadron returning so just had to wait for Scotty so I could introduce him to our charming surprise,' said Clive, explaining his late return. He turned to the bar and called for drinks.

Scotty did not wait for a formal introduction. 'Hello, I'm Alastair Lewis, but always known as Scotty.' His dark eyes drew attention, he was good-looking and knew it.

'Hello to you.' Jean smiled. 'Jean Lawson,' she added

as if trying to break the spell which had immediately spanned the gap between them. She was so aware of his charged presence as he sat down beside her that it sent alarm bells ringing in her mind.

The lines of his mouth bore the slightest of smiles which she felt certain would never leave them. His thick, dark hair was brushed back in a tantalising curve around his ears, mellowing his strong, determined jaw and straight nose. The perfectly set eyes were serious, yet laughter was not far below the surface. She imagined him in total earnest once he was in the air, yet away from his Spitfire he could throw it off and bubble with life. His ability was evidenced in the same decorations as Clive, but she realised even in this short meeting that they would be two different personalities in their aircraft. Some of C's easy-going nature would come through, whereas Scotty, at one with his Spitfire, would become a deadly fighting machine. She gave a little shudder at the thought but was immersed in his charm.

'Posted to Biggin?' he asked.

'No, I'm on leave. A friend of Liz Johnson.'

'Ah, our brave and gorgeous nurse.'

The soft Scottish lilt to his voice sent shivers down Jean's spine.

'We spent Christmas in London. She persuaded me to come here for the rest of my leave.'

'Good for her. Our gain, even if it is only brief. When will you break our hearts by leaving us?'

'Monday the thirtieth. But I hope I won't break any hearts.' She gave a small laugh of amusement.

Scotty gave a slight knowing shake of his head. 'Oh,

283

but you will. You've captured mine already.' He held her with his gaze, defying her to look away.

She was flattered that she had had an effect on this man who she felt certain could draw any girl to him like a moth to a flame.

'Hey, don't monopolise the girl,' cried Clive, bringing the drinks to the table. 'What are you thinking of, Dave? Don't let Scotty get his claws into her.'

The spell was broken. Jean felt relief, yet she wanted the magic to go on. So, though she made mild protests when invited to a party in the mess that evening, she was pleased that the three pilots would not take no for an answer.

At seven that evening she heard a car draw up outside and hurried from her room, expecting to find Clive waiting for her. Instead she found Scotty in the bar.

His eyes lit with amusement when he saw the shocked surprise on her face.

'Expect old C?' he asked, his mouth twitching with a smile.

'Well, yes.'

'Disappointed?' It was said probingly, demanding a serious answer.

'No.'

'Good, then let's away.' He took her by the arm.

'Jean, here's a key,' called Bill.

'Thanks, but I won't need it.'

Bill smiled. 'I know these fighter types when they get a party going. Take it, miss, I think you'll need it.'

'She sure will. Thanks, Bill.' Scotty took the key and swept her out of the door.

The night was frosty. Stars pricked the dark canopy of the heavens and the countryside held a magical stillness. Jean wished it hadn't, wished it had been raining hard instead, for she sensed what was going to happen and felt helpless to resist it.

They reached the car. Scotty paused in opening the door. They were close. His hand came to Jean's arm and drew her nearer. She did not hold back.

'Jean,' he whispered. 'I love you.'

She looked up at him. 'You can't. You've only just met me.'

'I knew the moment I walked into the White Hart earlier today. In fact, I sensed something was going to happen to me when old C waited for me to return.'

'Please, Scotty, don't . . .' There was a catch in Jean's voice.

'But you felt it too.'

'I was attracted to you. I liked you.'

'Well, then.'

'It's not the same as loving.'

'It's halfway there.' A slight trill came into his seriousness. 'And it will be all the way before you leave.'

'No, Scotty.' The words faded as he kissed her and she was swept into his embrace without any further protest.

When their lips parted, she said, 'I think we'd better go.' A troubled frown furrowed her brow and he knew not to press the matter. He opened the door and she climbed into the car.

With only the narrow slits in the blackout masks on the headlights to give the minimum of light, Scotty drove steadily, thankful of the glow from the heavens.

285

Jean, lost in her troubled thoughts, did not speak. She could not deny that she was attracted to this handsome pilot, but there was Colin and the undying love they had declared for each other. Was she merely being dazzled by the glamour of a fighter station and the live-for-today attitude of its pilots?

They could hear the lilting notes of 'The Anniversary Waltz' coming from a piano as they stepped out of the car. Jean shivered and started a brisk step towards the mess as if to get out of the cold quickly. She did not want to give Scotty a chance to express his feelings again.

They shed their greatcoats and, as Scotty escorted her towards the double doors open wide on the right, he indicated the door on the opposite side of the hall. 'The dining room. Set out for a buffet meal.'

The piano still played above the noise of the chatter. The carpet had been removed from the centre of the floor, exposing polished beechwood, ideal for dancing. A flight lieutenant with flaming red hair ran long fingers over the keys of a grand piano standing in one corner of the room. A double bass, close to a set of drums, leaned against the wall and a saxophone and a trombone lay on a table beside the piano. Several couples were dancing, others with drinks in their hands stood in groups, and there was movement through a door at the opposite side of the room.

'The bar,' said Scotty. 'Fancy a drink?'

Before Jean could reply, Liz, with Alec beside her, crossed the room and greeted them with a smile. 'Scotty doesn't hang about when there's a pretty girl around.'

Scotty twitched the corner of his mouth, but there seemed an earnest depth to his eyes. 'Ah, Liz, this time it's serious.'

Liz shot Jean a sharp glance and was troubled when she saw a touch of distress cross her face.

She introduced Alec, who immediately suggested a dance to Jean. They moved smoothly into the waltz and Alec's chatter flowed with exuberance. They had circled the floor three times when he said quietly, 'You've captured Scotty's heart all right.'

Alarmed at the observation, Jean cast him an enquiring look.

'He's dancing with Liz, he's keeping up a polite conversation as Scotty would, but he keeps glancing at you with eyes that say "she's mine, keep off." '

'You must be imagining it just because he brought me here tonight.'

Alec gave a little laugh. 'No, it's not that. I know Scotty. He meant what he said to Liz.' He saw the conversation was troubling Jean. 'But forget it. I can tell you can handle it. You're here to enjoy yourself tonight.' They were close to the piano. Alec turned his head and called, 'Liven it up, Rusty.'

The flight lieutenant looked up, grinned at Alec and went smoothly into a swinging tempo with 'Oh! Johnny'. The bass player drifted over and began plucking at the strings. The rhythm of the drums sent a throb through the room. A few moments later the mellow sound of the saxophone joined in and then the trombone. The party was now really under way and soon the room was rocking to the music. Drink flowed and Jean began to wonder if any of these men would be fit to fly in the morning but, when she looked back, she could not remember seeing any of them drunk. She realised that they knew their capacities so as not to impair their reactions in the air. Everyone marvelled at the extent of the buffet the cooks had managed to prepare but knew better than to ask where the extra luxuries to make this a memorable spread had come from.

Jean pushed her thoughts about Scotty from her mind. This was an occasion to enjoy untroubled by any worry. These men were not disturbed by what tomorrow might bring so why should she be? She danced with an abandoned joy, she enjoyed her food and interspersed her three gin and tonics with orange squash, knowing that three was her limit. And when the singing started she sang along with everyone, laughed at the ribaldry of the squadron's versions, and had some regrets when the party was closing down.

Scotty got their coats and a few minutes later was driving to Brasted. He pulled up outside the White Hart and cut the engine. He turned towards Jean, his arm sliding across the back of her seat.

'Thanks for a lovely evening, Scotty. It was great fun.'

'Glad you enjoyed it. They're a great bunch. Jean . . .' His voice had gone quiet, his eyes took on a misty look as they became serious.

'Scotty, don't.' Jean rushed her words to interrupt him before he could say any more. 'Please don't say what you said when you picked me up.'

'Why not? It's true. I realised it even more tonight.'

'But the time has been so short.'

'What is time? Time is nothing when you love.'

'Oh, Scotty.' There was a catch in her voice. 'But I don't feel the same way about you.'

'When our eyes first met I know you felt something.'

'But that's not sufficient.'

'It will grow.' His urgent note faltered as a devastating thought he had not considered struck him. 'There's someone else?'

Jean hesitated, damping her lips. She nodded. 'Yes, there is.'

'Back home?'

'Yes, but he's in Canada now.'

'Doing what?'

'Training to be a pilot. Colin set his heart on fighters.'

'Good for him.' He gave a half-smile. 'But he's far away so I'll take my chance.' He leaned forward and kissed her.

Her lips trembled to his touch. They parted for the briefest moment, then kissed again, prolonging their intimacy. Her mind whirled. She should stop this now. She should go. But she couldn't. The magnetism of this man held her. She must break it. She must! She drew back suddenly, twisted round and was out of the car before he could stop her. She ran to the door of the White Hart, fishing for the key in her pocket, and pushed it into the lock.

'I'll see you tomorrow, seven o'clock, dinner.' Scotty's voice carried on the sharp air.

Jean half turned. 'No!' was on her lips but the word would not come. Besides, Scotty was already away with a roar which wouldn't take no for an answer.

Jean stood a moment, her thoughts confused, then she went inside.

* * *

Off duty the following morning, Liz came to the White Hart and the two girls enjoyed a walk in the frosty countryside.

Still perplexed by her attitude to Scotty, Jean sought Liz's advice.

'You have to be firm and say there's no hope because of Colin.'

'I don't want to hurt him. He's too nice for that.'

'Then tell him to stand back a bit, don't rush things and see how feelings run once you've left. You're going to Waddington and things could die a natural death once you're away from here. You'll both probably see things in a different perspective.'

It was with this advice in mind that Jean waited for Scotty that evening.

He picked her up at seven and took her to a country inn five miles away.

'They know me here,' he told her. 'They'll have a meal for us, it may be fairly basic but it's cosy.'

So it proved. Jean enjoyed the home-made soup followed by a steak-and-kidney pie and bread and butter pudding. They savoured a bottle of wine and lingered over a brandy after the meal.

It was only then that Scotty approached the subject of themselves, but before he said too much, Jean interrupted him.

'Scotty, I'm flattered that you think so highly of me. I don't deserve it. I like you a lot. I told you about Colin and I believe that is where my heart still is, but who knows? Canada may have changed him, other things may have done so too. But I'm not prepared to jeopardise the love that still seems to be between us.' He started to speak but she reached out and silenced him with a gentle touch on the lips. 'Scotty, let's go no further than we have. Let's enjoy each other's company in the short while I have left here and let the future take care of itself.'

He met the pleading sincerity in her eyes and also saw there a hope that he would understand.

'If that's the way you want it. But remember, I'm hopelessly in love with you and if there's half a chance that the relationship between you and Colin has changed when he returns, then I'll be there.' He gave a wan smile and winked at her. 'You're a grand girl and whatever happens, I'll always remember you.'

'And I you. There'll always be a special place in my heart for you and I'll always have happy memories of my leave with a brave Spitfire pilot from Biggin Hill.'

When they kissed good night, Jean asked, 'See you tomorrow?'

'Oh, damn, I almost forgot. I shan't be able to make it tomorrow. Patrol midday and the wing CO wants all pilots confined to camp after that. Probably some special duty coming up Saturday morning. I'll try and make it for three o'clock Sunday afternoon and then we'll have the rest of the day together before you leave for the bomber boys on Monday.'

Jean nodded. 'Till Sunday, I'll miss you. Take care.' She watched him drive away and then turned and walked slowly into the White Hart.

Jean toyed with her gin and tonic in the bar at the White Hart. The locals had all gone after their lunchtime drinks and she was alone except for Bill behind the bar.

He had let his conversation run dry when he saw she was in a contemplative mood. He would be sorry to see her go tomorrow. She was a pleasant and attractive girl and had fitted in well with the fighter pilots, especially with Scotty, a nice young man. Always a good mixer, he knew his manners and when to draw the line. Bill reckoned they would be good together; a pity she was leaving.

Jean glanced at her watch, the present from her mother and father. Three o'clock. He should be coming soon. She had heard the planes go out and come back. She sipped her gin, her ears tuned to catching the sound of a car.

Three fifteen. Something was holding him up. Maybe an extra-long debriefing.

Three twenty. A car. Nearer. This must be him. She heard the roar as it swung into the car park. Then silence.

She watched the door eagerly, then pulled herself up. She was acting like a love-sick schoolgirl anticipating a meeting with her boyfriend.

Footsteps. The door opened. Flying Officer Munson walked in. The door swung shut behind him. Jean looked askance at him.

He glanced at Bill. 'Pint please, Bill.'

Bill nodded. Something was wrong, he sensed it.

Jean felt it too.

'Hello, Jean.' Clive sat down with a sigh and dropped his hat on the table.

'Hello, C.'

He looked at her and met her questioning gaze. 'I'm sorry, Jean. Scotty won't be coming.'

'He's hurt! Badly?' Alarm grasped her.

'I'm afraid he won't be coming ever.'

'Oh, no!' Her stricken cry came in a long-drawn-out whisper. She closed her eyes. She felt C take her hand, an unusual gesture for him, but she found it so comforting. When she opened her eyes they were filled with tears.

'I didn't know him long, but I liked him.'

Grim-faced, Clive nodded. 'I know. Everybody did.'

'What happened?' When he hesitated, she pressed him. 'I want to know.'

'We were patrolling over Dover when we saw German bombers escorted by fighters. The action was fast and furious but we seemed to have come out of it well. The bombers scattered and the fighters chose the role to keep guard over them. Dave Pitman went after them, ignoring the call to re-form. I saw Scotty had spotted the danger when two Jerries came out of the sun at Dave. Scotty went after them and downed them both. He closed on Dave to turn him back. Whether Dave mistook him for another German and panicked we'll never know, but in what appeared to be a manoeuvre of escape he turned the wrong way and too sharply and collided with Scotty. They both plummeted to the ground. No one baled out.'

Jean sat there numb. Her grip on C's hand tightened as he told the story. It was as if she was clinging on to her sanity. Scotty gone! It just couldn't be true. She looked at C to find some hope but there was none.

She sensed someone slide on to the seat beside her and felt an arm come round her shoulders. She turned her head and saw sympathy and understanding in Liz's eyes.

'I had to come,' Liz whispered. She gave her friend a reassuring hug.

'Thanks,' replied Jean. She looked in amazement. The

293

bar was full of 92 Squadron pilots. She had been unaware of their arrival. Releasing her grip on C, she sniffed and held back her tears. She must not be seen to break down.

The atmosphere was gloomy, with no chatter. The only sound was of Bill and Helen drawing pints, and they seemed to do it with less noise than usual.

C picked up his pint, as yet untouched. He stood up when he saw that all the pilots had been served and said solemnly, 'Pilots of 92.' He raised his glass.

'Here's a toast to the dead already,
Three cheers for the next man to go!'

The pilots repeated it with a roar and drank. Soon the squadron was back to normal. Each would mourn the loss in their own way but no one would show it. The gap in the squadron created by the two deaths would be filled by pilots who had never known Scotty or Dave. That was life.

Jean looked round. They were all now behaving as if nothing had happened. She wanted to scream at them to stop.

Liz sensed the rising belligerence in her friend. She held her tightly. 'Steady, Jean. This is their way of paying their respects to those who have gone.'

Jean nodded and swallowed hard. She drained her drink and gave Liz a wan smile. 'I'm all right now.'

Someone slid two gin and tonics in front of them. Who, they never knew, but they appreciated the gesture.

The next morning Liz got time off to accompany Jean to London, where she would catch the train north from

Kings Cross. They found a compartment and then waited on the platform.

'Thanks for this leave, Liz.'

'I'm sorry there was sadness to it.'

Jean shrugged her shoulders. 'One of those things. I'll try to remember only the nice things about it all.'

'Good for you.' She smiled encouragingly. 'And remember, you're going to an operational airfield. Don't get emotionally involved with any of the bomber boys. They fly with death on their wings too.'

'I won't.'

The moment came for leaving. They hugged each other and said goodbye. They waved as the train left the station, then Jean sank back on her seat with a sigh. Wasn't she already involved? Colin could . . . She shuddered.

Chapter Fourteen

1940–41

It was mid-afternoon when Jean reported at Waddington guardroom and was escorted to the WAAF Admin Office.

'Pleased to have you with us. I'm Wendy Carter.' The slim, petite officer came from behind her desk to meet her. She had a firm, purposeful grip and a pleasant, welcoming smile. Her eyes were bright and alert.

Jean sensed they would get on well.

'Had a pleasant leave?' asked Wendy, indicating a seat.

'Yes, thank you, ma'am.' Jean sat down when Wendy had resumed her seat.

'I'll take you to the WAAF officers' quarters in a few minutes. Your room is ready. I hope you settle and enjoy it here. Just one word. You won't have had experience of an operational station and it is so very different from those that are not. Here you are in close proximity with men who are risking their lives. Inevitably some do not return, others are badly wounded, you may witness horrifying crashes.

You must try to stand aside from these, not let them upset you. In time you will cope and realise that no matter what happens, life has to go on.'

Jean nodded and said nothing about her experiences at Biggin Hill. She felt she was already hardened to squadron life.

'Find your own way of dealing with such things and I'm sure you'll be all right. It's a good life here at Waddington. You'll like it.'

'I'm sure I shall. I've been looking forward to coming ever since I knew the posting.'

'Good. I can't say how pleased we are to have another WAAF officer with us. There's myself and Section Officer Sally Burnet, my assistant, and four other WAAF officers in various capacities around the station. And of course our WAAF CO, Squadron Officer Turner. A bit older than any of us, looks formidable, but she's not a bad sort, bit of a stickler for discipline among the WAAFs. I suppose that's only to be expected when you've got more and more girls filling roles which used to be exclusively for men and they find themselves among the glamour of serving aircrew. Any questions?'

'No, I don't think so, ma'am. I'll pick things up as I go along.'

'Good.' Wendy rose from her chair and Jean did likewise. 'I'll show you to your room and then we'll go to the mess for some tea.'

Jean appreciated the trouble Wendy was taking to make her feel welcome.

As they walked to the WAAF quarters, Wendy told her, 'You've arrived at the right time – New Year's Eve tomorrow. Very unlikely there'll be any flying and there's sure to be a party in the mess.'

Reaching the WAAF officers' quarters, a red-brick building, erected before the war, Wendy led the way to the room which bore the name Assistant Section Officer Lawson on a small card on the door.

'Settle in. I'll be back in ten minutes and we'll go to the mess,' she said with a smile.

Jean looked round the room. It was spartan but comfortable as far as RAF furniture went. Beside the bed was a small table on which stood a lamp. A slightly larger table stood near the window and was flanked on one side by a small wardrobe. She had two chairs, one wooden with an upright back, the other an easy chair offering a little relaxation. A washbasin occupied one corner and she guessed the bathroom facilities were along the corridor. She could be quite comfortable here and was glad that Waddington turned out to be what was known as a 'permanent station' instead of one of the new airfields which were being quickly constructed and where the quarters were likely to be a Nissen hut or the dormitory type.

Jean was preparing to tidy herself after the journey when there was a knock on the door, which opened at her call of 'Come in'.

'Good afternoon, ma'am. I heard you arrive. Thought I would make myself known. Aircraftwoman Brenda Rowe, batwoman for this corridor.'

Jean saw a short, plump girl of about her own age, who smiled tentatively as if wondering what sort of reception she would get from a newly appointed officer.

'Come in. I'm pleased to meet you.' Jean put her at ease with a friendly tone and reassuring smile.

'Thank you, ma'am.'

Jean could sense relief from the girl, though she still remained on the shy side. 'I'm sure we'll get along famously. Anything I should know?'

Brenda's large dark eyes showed surprise that an officer should be asking her, but it eliminated any tension she had left.

Jean noticed it and was pleased with her first attempt at relating to other ranks.

'No, I don't think so, ma'am. It's a friendly station. If there's anything you want or would like me to do specially, please ask. And if ever you feel like a cup of tea, just give me the nod.'

'Thanks, Brenda. I will.' Jean knew it made sense not to enquire how she managed that; batwomen had their ways of getting supplies.

Brenda paused when she reached the door. 'I hope you will be happy here, ma'am.'

'Thanks,' called Jean as the door closed.

Tea in the mess was a free and easy affair in the anteroom. Wendy introduced Jean to the CO, a full-bosomed woman of about fifty. She presented the formidable air described by Wendy, but behind the exterior lay a heart of gold. She demanded in return loyalty and etiquette in upholding the good name the WAAFs had established on the station.

Among the others Jean was introduced to was Flight Lieutenant George Sugden, in charge of the Intelligence Section.

'Delighted to have you.' He smiled benevolently, making no disguise of his pleasure at having a pretty young woman assigned to his section. Apart from easing his workload, it would help to have a WAAF officer when the rest of his staff consisted of three aircraftwomen. Besides, this one reminded him of his own daughter, who was serving in the Wrens.

'Pleased to be here,' replied Jean. She liked the look of this ruddy-faced man. His ample figure gave him an air of steady reliability and Jean felt sure he would be meticulous in running his department. She hoped she could live up to his demands.

The next day she familiarised herself with the station, especially the conclave of huts which housed the briefing room, locker room, parachute room, offices for each aircrew category and those for A flight and B flight. She noted the squadron commander's office and that of his adjutant. Close by was the control tower with its operations room, the nerve centre from which returning bombers would get their first contact with home. From here they would be talked down safely by the WAAFs on duty, supervised by the flying control officer.

When she called at the Intelligence Section, George introduced her to the WAAFs, then took her to a small room which he had allocated as her office.

'Sorry it's so sparsely furnished,' he apologised, eyeing the RAF-issue desk, filing cabinet, table and two chairs.

'It'll be fine, thanks,' said Jean.

'I managed to wangle another typewriter when I heard you were coming. Clare will do your typing.' He saw her eyeing his pilot's wings. 'First World War,' he explained. 'When this lot started, I wanted to do something positive. Volunteered right away. Knew they wouldn't let me fly so came into Intelligence. Thankfully I was posted to an operational station.'

She could see that this man wished he was twenty years younger so that he could fly alongside the men he was serving. She realised that, knowing what it was like to fly in combat, even though his time was so different from theirs, he would serve them beyond his duty and would expect it of her. She made a vow not to let him down.

He explained the way he ran his section. 'Now, as you probably know, there are two squadrons here, 44 and 207, both flying Hampden bombers. I suggest that, while we're both responsible to serve both squadrons, you take on 44 as your special baby and I'll have 207. Before a raid I suggest we make ourselves available for our particular squadron and that we both attend the main briefing. There I will give out any relevant information and you can take a turn once you're familiar with the proceedings.' He gave a wry smile and added, 'And I'll tell you what, the aircrews would rather have you standing up there than me.'

'I hope I'll do as well as you,' remarked Jean.

'Of course you will. There's nothing to worry about,' he reassured her. 'We're dealing with facts and figures, passing on the latest information, sent to us from Group Headquarters. It comes in no logical order, so we assemble it as we wish. There is a certain amount of interpretation, but that comes mainly after the crews have returned from a raid. We will be at debriefing, which can be any time depending on the length of the operation, so

301

I'm afraid sleep can be disrupted. You'll have been trained in debriefing procedures and you'll find by practice what are the important things to look out for. The crews are more likely to chat to you, instead of an old codger like me, so you'll probably get more out of them.'

'I'll do my best.'

'I know you will. Now, I think that's enough shop for the day. There are no operations scheduled for tonight – didn't expect there would be, New Year's Eve. There'll be a party in the mess. You'll be there?'

'Wouldn't miss it,' Jean said with a grin.

The party went with a swing. Jean was swept into the gaiety and found that as a newcomer and female she received a great deal of attention. She loved it and showed interest in everyone.

Although she was reminded of the recent party at Biggin Hill, with sad memories of Scotty, she pushed them to the recesses of her mind. Scotty would not want her to mourn. Many of these men around her were risking their lives just as he had. How many of them would see the next New Year's Eve? She hoped that thought was far from their minds as they drank, sang, danced, cracked raucous jokes and did outlandish party tricks, each trying to outdo the other.

Looking round, Jean saw it would be easy to fall for some of them, but after Scotty she had sworn never to let herself become involved with anyone else, except Colin.

When midnight struck and there were kisses all round, she thought of Colin and was pleased time had moved into the year when he would be home. In spite of the revelry around her she felt a touch of sadness that they were separated and experienced deep desire to have him there, his arms around her, their lips close, and a future – unknown, challenging – to face together. She prayed he would be home soon. But it was not news of him that shattered her on New Year's Day.

It was two o'clock when the phone rang in Jean's office and she was informed that Assistant Section Officer Harland wished to see her.

Excitement gripped her. Gabrielle here! Posted to Waddington? They'd be together again.

'Please, could someone show her to the officers' mess? I'll be there in a few minutes,' she requested.

As she hurried to the mess, after informing George why she was leaving the office, her mind started to sort things out. Gabrielle wasn't due to finish her leave until tomorrow and she had to report back to the training school for her posting. Maybe she had received notification at home to report to Waddington. But George hadn't said anything about someone else joining them. She was puzzled. Why was she here?

She hurried into the mess to find Gabrielle sitting in the anteroom.

'Gabrielle!' Her eyes were wide with excitement as she asked, 'You posted here?'

As they hugged each other in joyful reunion, Gabrielle said, 'I'm afraid not.'

In spite of the genuine pleasure in their contact, Jean sensed a certain tension in her friend and, as she stepped back, she saw a pained seriousness marring her features.

303

'Then what brings you here?'

'Shall we sit down?'

They perched on the edge of a big settee facing each other.

Jean, worried by a premonition that something was wrong, waited for her friend to speak.

Gabrielle's lips tightened momentarily. 'I don't know how to begin.' She made a slight, thoughtful pause, then fished an envelope from her pocket. 'This wasn't needed,' she said quietly.

Jean took the envelope, stared at her own writing, and saw that it was unopened. She looked up slowly to Gabrielle. 'Wasn't needed? What do you mean? You didn't deliver it?'

'Your mother died the day I got home.'

The statement stunned Jean. She stared uncomprehendingly at Gabrielle. 'Dead? She can't be!' The words came as a natural protest.

Gabrielle reached out and took her friend's hand in hers. 'I'm afraid it's true. I was there.'

Jean's mind reeled as the realisation of what had happened impinged on her mind. Her whole body seemed to fold and her cry came as a long-drawn-out moan. 'Oh, no!' The words choked in her throat. Her face screwed up with horror at the truth, and tears started to flow. She collapsed into Gabrielle's arms. Gabrielle let her cry while keeping a comforting arm around her.

She cried the acute pain out of her and, as she straightened, fishing for a handkerchief, she was left with a dull ache and a hollow sense of loss. She dabbed her eyes and straightened her tunic. 'Tell me about it.' When she saw

304

Gabrielle hesitate, she added, 'I want to know everything.' It was as if she had pulled on a determined cloak of resilience. Gabrielle saw that she would cope with whatever she had to tell her.

She told her story and Jean listened without interrupting. 'I hadn't the heart to tell your mum that I wasn't you,' Gabrielle concluded. 'I hope I did the right thing.'

'Of course you did. If it allowed her to die happy then I am pleased you pretended to be me.' She ran her tongue across her lips. 'Why didn't Mum tell me she was ill?'

'I don't know,' Gabrielle said slowly.

Jean looked thoughtful. 'She kept telling me that it would be better if I didn't go home because of Dad's attitude.' She sniffed back the tears which threatened again. 'That may be so, but I'm beginning to think she did not want me to see how ill she was. She wanted me to remember her as I knew her.'

'I think you're near the truth,' agreed Gabrielle.

'And Dad? How was he?'

'Shattered. A lonely man. He had no family around him at the funeral until Martin arrived halfway through the service at the grave.'

'Dad could have had me,' whispered Jean with regret. 'But I never had a word from him. He hasn't even written to tell me she died. There would be letters from our training days, there would be an address and if he'd written there, it would have been sent here.' She shook her head slowly. 'Obviously, he wants nothing to do with me.' She looked askance at her friend. 'And why didn't Martin let me know? My favourite brother could have written.'

305

'He explained that he had gone to spend Christmas with one of his mates. Then they were at sea the day after Boxing Day. He only got your father's letter when he got back. Just made it to the funeral and had to return the same day. I just got a few words with him on the way to the station. He said he would write to you straight away but I persuaded him to wait until after I had seen you – better for you to hear it from me than from a letter.'

Jean nodded her understanding. 'Thanks for being there for Martin and thanks for coming to tell me. I know you've sacrificed some of your leave. I appreciate it very much. You're a true friend, Gabrielle.'

'What about tonight? Would you like to be together? We could find a hotel in Lincoln.'

'I'll be all right,' said Jean firmly, determined not to give way again under the strain of her loss. 'Look, let's see if we can get you fixed up here.'

'Think we might? We're only assistant section officers and fairly new ones at that.'

Flight Officer Wendy Carter gave them a sympathetic ear and fixed it so that Gabrielle could stay the night.

Martin's letter arrived the following morning.

Dear Sis,

I really don't know what to say. I'll miss Mum and I know you will. Though she loved us all, I think you, being the only girl, were her favourite.

I am sorry you weren't at the funeral but I understand that you did not know that Mum had died. Dad should have let you know. It came as a shock to me because he hadn't told me she was ill.

Gabrielle told me the story of being with Mum. I'm glad she saw her, as I know you will be.

Dad's a lonely man. I'm pleased I was there for him, if only briefly. He'll miss Mum – they were close. His obsession with the Harlands sometimes threatened their relationship, but it survived and they still meant a lot to each other.

I wish he could see that he is missing out by not acknowledging your love for Colin and accepting your wish to join the WAAFs.

We must meet some time.

I will always be here if you need me.

Take care of yourself.

Love,

Martin

When Jean and Gabrielle said goodbye, they still did not know where Gabrielle was being posted.

When Gabrielle reached Windermere, she found a message instructing her to report to the commanding officer the next morning at ten o'clock.

She was full of curiosity when she walked into her office, saluted smartly and sat down when her CO indicated she should do so. Everyone else's posting had been straightforward. Why was hers so different?

'You are no doubt wondering why you had to come back here after your leave. Yours is a very special posting and, before I reveal it, I want you to understand that I'm the only one on the station to know it, but even I do not know what will follow immediately you report.'

Gabrielle's interest intensified. Why the mystery?

'Another thing I must tell you, and no doubt it will be drummed into you more and more. There is the utmost secrecy about your posting. You must tell no one, not even your family or your closest friend where you are or what you are doing.' She saw questions forming on Gabrielle's lips but raised a hand to stop them. 'As far as they're concerned, you are staying here as an instructor. Subsequently, if there is any change, you will be told. All your letters should be addressed to you here and will be forwarded to you, maybe not directly but they will reach you. Those you write must come here to be posted so that it will appear you are here.'

The CO paused and Gabrielle shot a question in quickly. 'Can't you give me any indication what this is all about? It sounds so mysterious.'

'I'm sorry, Harland, I can't. I know very little about it myself and even if I did I wouldn't. Now, your instructions.' She passed an envelope over the desk. 'There's your railway pass for the afternoon train to London. When you go through the barrier you will see a bowler-hatted man in a raincoat carrying a furled umbrella. He will have a briefcase and be wearing two odd gloves – a black one and a brown one. Walk past him and head for the taxi rank. He will just beat you to it, but when a taxi arrives he will offer to share it with you. Accept his offer.'

'And?' prompted Gabrielle when the CO stopped.

The officer gave a half-amused laugh. 'I know no more.'

'But ma'am—'

'Ours is not to reason why.'

* * *

Gabrielle stepped off the train, hoping that she would soon have some answers to the questions going round in her head.

As she neared the barrier she noticed a man fitting the description she had been given, idly watching the passengers jostling past the ticket collector. Bowler hat, briefcase, furled umbrella. His gloves! She could see only one hand: a brown glove. The other was behind his back. Could this be the person? Her gaze swept quickly across the concourse beyond the barrier. There were three other men similarly dressed dotted across the space. She began to panic. Which one? What if she chose to pass the wrong one? What if there was no contact? What would she do? She had no idea where she was supposed to be going.

She was nearing the barrier. Some of her tension eased. Two of the men were not wearing gloves. Still undecided which direction to take, she was through the barrier. She saw the first man turn and start to stroll away. The hand behind his back held a black glove! Relief swept over her. This was her man. She quickened her pace slightly and overtook him, only to have him pass her just short of the taxi rank.

The queue shortened. A taxi swept in. The man opened the door, calling to the driver as he did so, 'Mortimer Street, please.' He started to get into the taxi, then paused and turned to Gabrielle. 'Would you like to share if you're going my way?' His invitation was neither gushing nor offputting and was delivered with what she would call an upper-crust accent.

'Thank you. Mortimer Street will suit me. Very near where I want to be.'

The man, whom, on closer inspection, she judged to be in his late forties, was pleasantly conversational about everyday matters. He gave nothing away about himself and asked no questions of her, though she felt she was under his close scrutiny. Gabrielle could learn nothing from his demeanour and wondered what would happen when they reached Mortimer Street.

The taxi swung round the corner and started to slow.

'Whereabouts, guv?' the driver called over his shoulder.

'By that second lamppost, please. Will that be all right for you?' he added, glancing at Gabrielle.

'Yes, thank you,' she replied.

When they alighted from the vehicle, the man, in spite of her protests, insisted on paying the fare. 'You've been pleasant company,' he said. 'It's cost no more giving you a lift.'

The taxi pulled away. The man glanced up and down the street, then said, 'This way.' He turned to his right and set off at a brisk pace. Gabrielle fell in beside him. There were a hundred questions she wanted to ask, but she knew better than to put them; besides, she knew she would get no answers.

Twenty yards along the street they entered a house and went straight to a room on the left. They were greeted by a man, whose appearance showed he liked good living. He was well dressed in a dark-grey suit and wore what Gabrielle guessed was some regimental tie. His hair, greying at the temples, gave him a distinguished look.

'Ah, Jenkins, you found our little lady.' He gave a chuckle. 'Or rather, she found you.'

'She behaved impeccably, sir. Exactly as she was told, and was sharp enough to play along.'

'Splendid.' He smiled warmly at Gabrielle. 'It's a pleasure to meet you, Miss Harland.' She noticed he did not use her service rank. 'May I call you Gabrielle?'

'Of course,' she replied, her curiosity rising even further.

He indicated an easy chair for her and came to another, set at an angle to it. As they sat down she was aware that Jenkins was no longer with them.

'No doubt you have a lot of questions to ask, but wait until I have told you more. First, I must emphasise that whatever is said goes no further than these four walls. I must have your solemn oath that you will never divulge what happens from now on.' He paused.

She hesitated. What was she getting into?

'Well, my dear, have I your promise?' he added.

'Er, yes, of course. Nothing will ever be mentioned.'

'Not even to your family, your boyfriends, or anyone else who is close to you?'

'Not even them,' she replied firmly.

'Good.' He sank back in his chair and eyed her shrewdly. 'Now I can introduce myself: Brigadier Irwin. I'm in charge of the recruiting section of an organisation you will never have heard of. It is top secret.'

Gabrielle's interest deepened.

'You have been under close scrutiny since you were interviewed regarding a commission. You may remember that interview?'

'Indeed I do, sir,' Gabrielle answered and then added in French, 'The three high-ranking officers were interested when I happened to say that I spoke French. In fact, from then on a lot of the interview was in French. Is that why I am here?'

311

The brigadier smiled and replied in French, 'It is. You're sharp. One of those officers is always on the lookout for people who she thinks might be useful in a new organisation.' He reverted to English. 'In July last year, after the fall of France, the prime minister instructed Hugh Dalton, minister of economic warfare, to set up a secret organisation with the objective of supporting a resistance movement in France. We are part of that organisation, the SOE – Special Operations Executive. You have been carefully watched since that interview and we believe you are right material for us.' He made a slight pause. 'Now, before I go any further, are you interested?'

'Yes, sir,' Gabrielle answered without hesitation.

'Right. Any questions you want to ask?'

'Does this mean you want me to go to France?'

The brigadier gave a little chuckle. 'No, there's no chance of that – well, not at the moment. There are those who consider the sort of work you would have to do over there as being too dangerous for women.' He gave a shrug of his shoulders as if he didn't entirely agree with that opinion. 'But who can tell what will happen in the future? We might decide to use women agents. I believe women are just as capable as men in most situations and I do think that they would be able to move around over there with a greater degree of safety than a man. But I am only a small cog in a large wheel, though my opinion of the capabilities of the recruits passing through here is always sought. No, for the time being we need your skill in French to receive and send messages to agents on the other side of the Channel.'

'By wireless?'

'Yes.'

'But I know nothing of that.'

'You'll soon learn. You'll have to become proficient in Morse code. That will be your initial training. If you can't master that to the required standard, then you will have to revert to being an intelligence officer. But I have no doubt that you will make the grades. You will now be taken to Cornwall House in Waterloo Bridge Road, where you will begin your training.'

The rest of the day was the only settling-in period for Gabrielle and the other twelve girls whom she joined at Cornwall House.

For the next fortnight they received intense training in Morse code from the three WAAFs who, Gabrielle learned, had been given honorary commissions so that their expertise could be used in the training programme. They put the new recruits under pressure with a steady efficiency and a ruthlessness which would stand no slacking. Their pupils were there to learn and learn fast. If they could not take it or fell below what was expected of them, they were off the course and sent to another unit under a dire warning not to say anything about what they had been doing.

At the end of the fortnight Gabrielle had reached the expected proficiency and, along with the other members of her course, reported to Fawley Court, Henley-on-Thames, for training as a radio operator.

Facing a three-month course with some apprehension, their spirits rose on seeing the elegant country house designed by Sir Christopher Wren, set in magnificent grounds beside the river with views to the Chilterns. Here they were to be billeted and work. This was a marked change from London and the girls revelled in the comparative luxury, even though life was not easy. They learned that after the course they would be posted to different units where most would be maintaining contact with agents who had been spirited into occupied Europe, though some would be in contact with others throughout the world.

This meant intense training in sending and receiving coded messages in Morse at a speed of twenty-five words per minute.

Gabrielle found she had a natural flair for the work and looked forward to the day when she would be posted to an operational unit.

It always amused her when she received a letter from Jean, who always sympathised with her for having a mundane job as an instructor in Windermere. One such letter sent on from there had just arrived.

RAF Waddington
14 February 1941

Dear Gabrielle,

I am slowly getting over Mum's death and the latest news has helped.

You may already know, Colin has passed his course. Got his wings! Got a commission! And will soon be on his way home. I just ache to see him. Time can't go quick enough.

Hope all is well with you and that you are not getting too bored with instructing. Poor you! Don't think I could have done it – same old thing over and over again. Life here is fine. Very interesting being involved with operational bomber crews. Squadron life is something special. Naturally there are the bad times when crews don't return, but the resilience of everyone to such happenings is amazing. It's a case of there's a job to do and we get on with it no matter what has happened.

If our leaves coincide we must meet, though I expect you will want to go home. I'm sad that I can't. Dad has never contacted me so I take it that his ban still stands. Sometimes I feel like defying it, but if I do it will only lead to argument and trouble which I think is best avoided.

Hope we may meet soon. Maybe I could come to Windermere. I'll let you know when it is possible.

Take care of yourself.

Love,

Jean

Gabrielle slid the paper back into its envelope. She must scotch Jean's idea of going to Windermere. She'd write and suggest that when they did find time to meet they'd be better away from any RAF station. Probably it would be a good idea to meet in London. Maybe Liz could manage it as well.

Her suggestion interested Jean, but thoughts of trying to arrange it were driven from her mind when she received a letter from Colin.

My darling,

Read that name again. Yes, I'm in Harrogate. Just arrived and simply had to write and let you know. We will be here only two days. Tomorrow some formalities to go through and our postings allocated so that we can go to our next station straight from leave.

I'm longing to see you, to hold you and tell you I love you. Can you get some leave? I will have to report to my new unit, an OTU, on the nineteenth.

I know from what you have written and from what Gabrielle has told me that you don't think it wise for you to go to Robin Hood's Bay. So where can we meet? We must. I want to see you so desperately.

Write home and let me know.

It pains me that we are so near and cannot see each other. The distance seems as if it is still those thousands of miles which have separated us, with only our thoughts and love to bridge the gap.

They have always been there, every day that we have been apart. My heart has always been yours and ever will be. Till we meet, keep my love in your heart.

Colin

RAF Waddington
4 March 1941

My darling Colin,

There are no words to express the thrill of getting a letter from you posted in England. I'm so glad you are safely back on these shores. Time cannot go quickly enough to the moment when I see you and feel your arms around me and your lips on mine. I wish I could wave a magic wand and make it tomorrow. But I can't so we will both have to be patient.

I know you must go home first. Your mother and father will be longing to see you so we must be sensible about this. I am not due for any leave yet, so could you spend a couple of days in Lincoln on your way to your next posting? Seeing each other would then depend on operations. If there were any I would be on duty, but there might be time for me to slip into Lincoln. I'm sure George could wangle some time off for me. He's a dear. Let me know what you think as soon as possible.

Oh, it's so good to have you on the same soil as me. You say the distance still seems to be the same as when you were in Canada. I know what you mean but just knowing you are much closer means that I can think of possibilities of seeing you and that eliminates those thousands of miles. My thoughts and love don't have to think in thousands but only in a few and that brings you so much closer.

I love you, now and for ever.

Jean

She folded the letter, slipped it into an envelope and addressed it to Robin Hood's Bay.

Colin sat at the bar in a small hotel opposite the station in Lincoln. He glanced at his watch. Seven thirty. She would not be coming now.

It had been the same the night before. He had arrived

in Lincoln at five, hoping she would meet him, but disappointment had filled him as he walked to the hotel. It had deepened when he found no messages. He had eaten alone and then, when he heard the twin-engined Hampdens climbing in the night sky, he knew why she had not come.

He drained his glass and went to the dining room. As he sat down, he heard a steady drone.

'Sounds as if they're going again tonight,' observed the elderly waiter when he brought the soup.

Colin nodded. He went through the motions of eating his meal without any enjoyment. The two nights he had planned to spend with Jean were wrecked by the needs of war. Tomorrow he would be gone, with only her voice to remember from the few moments that morning when she had rung him to apologise for not meeting him and answered his question of 'Tonight?' with a noncommittal 'I hope so'.

Five miles away at Waddington Jean's hopes had been dashed that morning when word came through that the group would be involved in an attack on Kiel and the Waddington squadrons were operational. George had been sorry for her when two consecutive night attacks on Germany corresponded with Colin's visit, but she was needed at the base. The compiling of information for the aircrews regarding the target, the fighter strength and distribution, the placements of anti-aircraft guns and their calibre, among other snippets of useful facts, took most of the day. After the aircrew briefing George regarded it as a duty for the intelligence officers to be around in case any last-minute information might be of value.

318

As Jean watched the bombers take off, she felt miserable. A telephone conversation was the only contact she had had with Colin. It was too late to get into Lincoln now; besides, she would have to be back for the debriefing when the crews returned. Tomorrow he would be leaving on the twelve-o'clock train. Her heart was heavy. What a fiasco it had been for him to come to Lincoln! Of all the days to pick – two when she had to be on duty. If only there had been a stand-down on one of them. When would they be able to meet? It seemed fate was stepping in to keep them apart.

'Stand-down tonight,' called George Sugden as he came into the Intelligence Section. He saw Jean, who was poring over a map of Germany with one of the WAAFs, look up with a grimace of exasperation. He knew what was going through her mind – if only that had happened last night! He inclined his head towards his office, and, after a brief word with the WAAF, Jean followed him.

'What time did you say your boyfriend was leaving?' he asked as she closed the door.

'Twelve.'

He glanced at his watch. Ten past eleven. 'Ring up the Transport Section. There may be something going into Lincoln and if there is, off you go.'

Jean brightened. 'Thanks, George.'

He winked at her as she grabbed the phone. 'Can't stand in the way of love, must give it a helping hand if we can.' He had taken to this pretty girl. They got on well together and he had been pleased at her contribution to running a happy department.

'Assistant Section Officer Lawson here.'

'Ah, hello, Jean, to what do I owe the pleasure of a call from you?'

She recognised the breezy tone of Flying Officer Tim White. 'Tim, I want to be in Lincoln by twelve. Have you anything scheduled?'

'Hold on, sweetheart, see if there is.' There was a pause which seemed interminable to her. 'Truck going in five minutes.'

'Hold it, I'll be there.' She slammed the phone down and looked at George with a broad grin. 'Five minutes.' She swung round and was at the door before he could say 'Off with you'.

She dashed into her office, grabbed her hat and rushed from the building. She tried to hurry in a dignified way as befitted her rank when all the time she was dying to run as fast as she could.

She reached the Transport Section to find Tim standing at the door, his hat set at the jaunty angle he always wore it, revealing a wave of fair hair at one side.

'Sorry, sweetie, a delay of five minutes. Vital parcel to go into Lincoln.' He shrugged his shoulders with an 'I can't help it' gesture.

The driver came round the truck. 'If you'd like to climb in the front, ma'am, we'll be away as soon as the parcel arrives.'

Jean got into the truck. If she looked at her watch once, she looked at it twenty times in the next five minutes. Colin would be gone. She would miss him.

She heard a thud in the back. The parcel had arrived. The door at the driver's side swung open and the aircraftman climbed in. The engine kicked into life.

'We're away, ma'am,' he said with a smile. They swung out of the camp on to the road to Lincoln. 'Understand you want to be at the station?'

'Yes, please, by twelve.'

The aircraftman glanced at his watch. 'Should just do it. Going on leave, ma'am?'

'No, want to catch someone and he's leaving at twelve.'

The aircraftman smiled to himself. Having daughters of his own, he thought he had read the signs and now he was sure he was right. He pressed the accelerator a little harder.

'Might just do it,' he called as they turned in towards the station. 'Sorry about those damned cows just outside of Lincoln.'

'Not your fault,' replied Jean, her hand ready to open the door.

'How are you getting back, ma'am?' he asked as he pushed on the brake.

'Don't bother about me. I'll find my own way back.'

The truck stopped. She flung open the door, leaped out and raced to the platform. She stopped. There was no train. She was too late. Gone! Her heart was sinking fast. Dejection overwhelmed her and her eyes dampened. She became dimly aware of a figure along the platform, an airman in officer's uniform. Colin? Could it be? Her heart leaped. He was starting towards her, every step quickening. Her eyes brightened and her tears turned to tears of joy. She began to run, ignoring the glances of the few people on the station. To her there was no one but him.

'Colin!' She flung herself into his outstretched arms. 'Oh, Colin, Colin!' She hugged him tight as if to reassure

321

herself that he was really here, that the train had not taken him away.

'Jean, my darling!'

His voice was real. His arms were around her. Ecstasy flooded her whole being. She slackened her hold to lean back and look at him. Her eyes searched his face, wanting to remember it for ever at this very moment of reunion. 'Colin, my love,' she said in a low voice filled with the intensity of her feeling.

His eyes adored her as he bent to kiss her, a gentle, telling kiss which swept into a powerful passion and sent magical feelings racing through her.

'I love you,' he whispered.

'And I you.'

He glanced around. 'There's a seat.' He indicated one at the far end of the platform, and with his arm around her started towards it.

'But your train will be here any minute.'

He gave a little laugh. 'Engine trouble at Grimsby. It will be half an hour late.'

Jean's mind soared at the news. 'We've time together. Oh, Colin, I'm sorry about these last two nights. I so much wanted to be with you.'

'It's all right, love. I wanted you with me too, but that's war.' He squeezed her tightly. 'But you're here now, so let's make the most of what time we have.'

They reached the seat and sat down, turning towards each other.

She looked at him with adoring eyes. 'Oh, Colin, I'm so proud of you.' She fingered the wings above his left breast pocket.

'And I of you. Oh, there's so much I want to hear, so much to tell.' He frowned, frustrated by the little time they had.

She put her fingers to his lips and then wiped his frown away. 'Save it all. Time is precious now. Talk can wait.' She kissed him.

Their world stood still for the next half-hour. Passengers on the platform ignored them. This was wartime and two lovers were seeking precious moments together, for who knew when they might next meet, if ever.

A distant whistle rent the air. Jean started. 'It's coming,' she gasped with annoyance. 'Oh, Colin, I've just got you, I don't want you to go.'

He smiled. 'I must, love. We'll meet again soon.'

'We must, we must. I want you all to myself.'

'So do I, so much.' He kissed her hard.

They pushed themselves from the seat and, arms round each other, walked slowly along the platform.

The train hustled into the station, drawing to a halt in a clanging of metal and hissing of steam.

They found a first-class compartment and opened the door. He turned to her again. There was no need for words. They both knew the intense longing the other felt.

'Next time,' he said hoarsely.

'Next time,' she replied with promise in her eyes.

They kissed, lingering until the very last moment, when the cry of 'All aboard!' told them they could stay no longer. Colin stepped into the carriage and swung the door shut. He leaned out of the open window and reached out to hold her hand.

'Take care,' she said with an intensity which not only held her fear but her love.

'I will. I have you and want to be with you always.'

A whistle blew, a flag waved. The train started to move slowly. Jean walked beside it, holding on to Colin's hand, wanting to keep contact as long as possible. The train gathered speed, her steps no longer able to match it. Their fingers slid apart. Colin blew her a kiss. She raised her hand and let the tears flow as she stood watching the train taking him from her.

Chapter Fifteen

1941

Two days later, at OTU at Landow near Cardiff in the pleasant countryside of South Wales, Colin wrote in his diary:

> I have settled in quickly to my new station thanks largely to having seen you, my darling, even though it was for but the briefest of time. But I know now you are near and the next time we meet it will be for longer.
>
> Today I sat in a Spitfire for the first time. I was surprised at how little room there is in the cockpit and it seemed even smaller when I closed the canopy once I was airborne. But no doubt I'll get used to it. Besides, that first impression when sitting in the cockpit was far outweighed by the thrill of being in a Spitfire. My ambition is realised!
>
> The instructor walked me round the plane first. Though dull in camouflage green and grey, it is, nevertheless, beautiful. Slim, trim, smooth and tempting,

just like a woman. Maybe that's why we refer to our aircraft as 'she', or maybe it's because they are dear to our hearts, just as you are to mine.

Standing there on the grass, the Spitfire looks the essence of power, eager to be in the air.

I was just as eager to take her, but first the instructor, having explained the flight-control system, stood on the wing, while I was in the cockpit, and went through the various controls explaining what they did. He enlightened me on the handling characteristics of the Spitfire, its moods and idiosyncrasies. Finally he went over and over the procedures to be followed in various emergencies and reminded me again about taxiing. The Spitfire has a high nose and so the pilot cannot see directly forward. The aircraft must be swung from side to side while taxiing in order to obtain a good line of vision and so avoid any likely collision.

Then the magic words: 'Start her up!' I went through the drill meticulously and the Merlin engine burst into life with a power which sent a thrill through me. I had never experienced anything like it. It did create a moment of doubt; would I be able to handle her? But I banished the thought. She was mine. This is what I had trained for and I was going to make a success of it.

'Take her up. Good luck!' The instructor slapped me on the shoulder and jumped down from the wing. I was on my own.

I moved steadily across the airfield, stopped and carried out a final check before turning into the wind with the propeller in fine pitch. I wouldn't have got off the ground if I'd forgotten that. And that would have looked good!

I checked the circuit. No plane in sight. I turned into the wind, paused, but only for a very, very brief moment. This was it. I opened the throttle firmly but gently. The power came. Oh, the surge! Much quicker than I was used to. The feeling was tremendous as I accelerated faster and faster. Tail up. Check a slight tendency to swing. Airborne! Undercarriage up. Pitch control set coarse. Speed regulated to 200 mph climbing. Close the canopy.

The sky is mine. I am tempted to fly, way, way up in this huge open space, the home of this beautiful aeroplane. If you were with me we would never come down. Some day I must share this wonderful experience with you.

I carry out basic manoeuvres to get the handling right so that we move as one, never fighting. She handles beautifully. I am happy. Now regretfully I must return. I must land her.

Alas, I let her down. I came in too high, tried to correct this but found I was coming in too fast. If I didn't do something quick I was going to end up in a terrible mess. There was nothing to do but open up and go round again. This time my approach was better but I came in a bit heavy and bounced. However, I kept her down. I knew that I had been watched and my thoughts were a mixture of feelings as I taxied round to dispersal.

The instructor grinned as I got out on to the wing and jumped to the ground. 'You'll improve' was his comment. I felt elated that there was no stronger criticism of my landing. I expect he has seen it all before and probably worse.

I have taken off, flown and landed a Spitfire successfully! A great feeling! Now I look forward to the joy of
many hours in unison with her.

Colin could not get into the air often enough. He looked
on it as his home, where he was happiest. He practised all
the manoeuvres he had been taught and attempted more
besides to see what he and the plane could do together.
He learned fighter tactics and as the weeks slid by he
became more and more confident and looked forward to
joining a squadron.

On 17 April he wrote to Jean, telling her that he had
received a pleasant surprise when he was notified that he
was to join 92 Squadron, for they were at Biggin Hill and
he looked forward to seeing Liz again. He urged Jean to
think of meeting him in London so that the brief touch on
Lincoln station could be turned into a lasting embrace.

The next day when Jean read the letter, the words
Biggin Hill sent palpitations to her heart. They recalled
Scotty and his fate and she prayed hard that Colin would
survive. Nothing must happen to him. She must see him
as soon as possible. She wrote back by return, asking him
to let her know the moment he was able to get some leave,
even if it was short, and she would do all in her power to
get to London.

The same day as Jean wrote that letter, Gabrielle finished
her course at Fawley Court and was posted to Bletchley
Park. Here again, along with other girls newly posted,
she was reminded of the strict secrecy about their work
which must be maintained at all times. As far as her

parents, Colin, Jean and Ron were concerned, she was still instructing.

She had done well on her course at Fawley Court and now all the intense training was put into practice as she took up her post as a wireless/telegraphist making contact with agents in enemy territory. The work was exacting, demanding concentration for in the briefest of moments something of vital importance might come through. Each girl operated a transmitter/receiver and was adept in the use of the Morse key. Each agent's code name and call sign were listed on a board and beside them was a coded message which had to be sent immediately the agent's call note was heard. Once contact was made, information from the agent was taken, the receivers concentrating on accuracy, for a false letter or figure in a code could make all the difference to the meaning of the message when it was worked out by the decoders.

The operators at Bletchley Park became familiar with agents, recognising who was calling by their individual use of the Morse key. Anxiety would grip them if a call suddenly stopped. Was there trouble with the equipment or had the operator been caught? They became anxious when the time passed for an agent to call in, although they only knew him as a code name.

At first Gabrielle found the six-hour shift trying but gradually she got used to it. She became fascinated by her contacts, which were operating chiefly in occupied France. In her mind she became involved with them and often wondered what they were like and what they were doing.

She was still amused by Jean's commiserations that she was stuck instructing when she might have been doing something more interesting. If only Jean knew! She was pleased to hear the news of life in Lincolnshire and was delighted when her friend informed her that, armed with a seventy-two-hour pass, she was heading for a meeting in London with Colin.

Although the train from Lincoln kept good time, the journey seemed to drag. Jean was so excited, she could not even read to pass the time. She gazed out at the flat countryside but saw nothing. Other occupants of the carriage chatted but she did not hear them. Her mind was solely occupied with seeing Colin.

He had been with the squadron a month and now had a seventy-two-hour pass. The news had sent her racing to her superior's office, where her excitement in her request for leave left George Sugden in no doubt that she was preparing to meet her young fighter pilot. He gave his permission for the leave, and Admin processed her pass.

Jean was the first out of the carriage when the train pulled into Kings Cross. Her brisk steps took her through the barrier and into the arms of Colin, whose eyes had never left her since he saw her ahead of the stream of passengers.

'Jean!' His arms came round her waist. This was a moment he had been longing for.

'Colin!' She dropped her small bag beside her and flung her arms around his neck, looking up at him with adoration and delight to match his.

Their lips met and held as people streamed around them, some smiling at the unashamed expression of the couple's feelings, others wishing they had been met with such ardour.

'It's so good to see you,' said Colin, standing back to admire her.

'Oh, Colin, I've looked forward to this meeting so much.'

He smiled. 'Come on, let's go.' He stopped and picked up her bag. 'I've booked us into a small family-run hotel. It's known to the pilots from Biggin Hill and the proprietors ask no questions.'

'From that I gather one room?'

He glanced at her with cocked eyebrows. 'No qualms about that?'

She smiled. 'I was hoping that was what you would do.'

They checked into the hotel, an unpretentious building not far from Hyde Park. The room was small and cosy, dominated by the double bed. Two easy chairs were placed on either side of a fireplace in which a small electric fire was a supplementary source of heat when required. Bright, flowered curtains hung from wooden rings on a pole covering the tall sash window. The floor was carpeted in deep red, giving the room a warm feeling. A washbasin occupied one corner, the bathroom being further along the corridor.

'All right for you?' Colin asked tentatively as they looked around.

'Anywhere with you is just fine.' She came to him and slid her arm slowly round his neck. 'This will always be our room, precious to us. I love you, Colin Harland, this day and for ever.' Her lips met his gently but provocatively and lingered with sensuality.

His arms swept round her waist, drawing her tightly to him. His lips moved hungrily across her cheek and down

331

her neck. He murmured close to her ear, 'We have two hours before we eat.'

'Mm . . . mm . . .' Her eyes flashed teasingly. She wriggled against his hold. As it slackened she moved away from him, slipped out of her tunic, undid her tie and started to unfasten the buttons on her shirt. Her shy, demure smile enticed him to follow suit.

With clothes cast aside, their eyes devoured each other before he took her into his arms.

'I love you so very, very much,' he whispered as he swept her off her feet and carried her to the bed.

Their first-time lovemaking was a gentle exploration followed by contentment. They lay in each other's arms with the occasional kiss and caress and whispered love until passion swamped them and led them into greater fulfilment.

Jean stirred. Dawn was breaking over the rooftops and some of it filtered into their hotel room. She looked at Colin asleep beside her. His face was pale on the white pillow, but he looked contented, at peace, and so young. Yet he had had the destiny of lives thrust upon him and had accepted it unflinchingly.

Jean lay watching him and loving him more and more. 'Oh, keep him safe, don't let him die like Scotty.' The words formed silently on her lips offered to a deity greater than themselves.

He moved on to his back. She kept still. His eyes flickered, then opened to stare for one moment at the ceiling as if he was trying to grasp where he was.

'Hello, love,' she whispered.

332

He turned his head. 'Hello, pugnose.'

'Pugnose?' she said indignantly with the ghost of a smile, propping herself on one elbow to gaze down on him.

'I watched you after you had gone to sleep and decided your nose turned up a little.' He smiled disarmingly. 'Liz would say you had a Myrna Loy nose. It's pretty. I like it.' He reached up and pulled her towards him. He kissed her on the nose and banished her mock indignation. 'And I love you very much.' He paused and then added, 'You were wonderful last night.'

'I could be wonderful again,' she said coyly.

He pulled her slowly to him, kissed her on the mouth and held her tight, making sure she could not escape. But she did not want to and she returned kiss for kiss until their desires overwhelmed them.

When they lay quietly in each other's arms, Jean said, 'Now you know why I said no in Robin Hood's Bay. This time, this leave, it was right. We'll always remember it for it will hold a special place in our hearts.'

He smiled, kissed her and said, 'Yes, you were right.'

Their time together went all too quickly. They were surprised how London life went on as near normal as possible. People were determined not to let the war and the bombing they had endured get them down. Jean and Colin looked at the shops, sat in a darkened cinema and danced the night away in one of the clubs still providing entertainment. They were happy just to be together, but most of all they would recall their special room in their special hotel.

Whenever they could arrange to have leave at the

same time, they spent it there and left the demands of war behind. If Jean was on duty, Colin paid his parents a visit and found the peace of Robin Hood's Bay eased the tension which gripped his mind at Biggin Hill. He found respite from the horrors of seeing comrades shot down to crash and leave a rising plume of smoke as a vanishing mausoleum. He gained the same reprieve with Jean when she visited the White Hart. On the first occasion Scotty's fate loomed in her mind, but she prayed that Colin would survive and she let Scotty drift away as he would have wanted.

Together they were happy wherever they were. In London the next day was a certainty. At the White Hart it wasn't. Tomorrow Colin would be flying. With the German attacks more spasmodic, the fighters were now carrying the war to the continent: low-level attacks, known as 'Rhubarb', on whatever they found as suitable targets, or accompanying bombers, a 'Ramrod', or in a large 'Circus' when the bombers were bait to tempt Luftwaffe fighters into the sky, or an attack on coastal shipping known as a 'Roadstead', or a sweep, a 'Rodeo', by fighters alone. Jean knew that all these carried the gravest possible risk for Colin but, in the knowledge that death was close at hand, she found a love of greater intensity.

It was matched by Colin who, whenever he flew, fixed a photograph of the girl he loved in his cockpit. A face, in close-up, filled with all the joys of life, hair caught by the wind, and eyes which shone with a special love for him alone. Round his neck he tied a silk stocking given to him on that first stay in London, a reminder of the love they had shared.

As he soared in the freedom of space in his beloved Spitfire, his loves were united.

He wrote in his diary:

Oh, how I wish I could share with you, my love, the ecstasy of flying. No words of mine will convey adequately what I feel but I'll try because I want you so much to know what it is like and what I feel about it.

Today, for instance, we were on a Circus. The bombers lured the Luftwaffe up and we were ready for them. The battle was furious but I came out unscathed, having damaged a Me-109. Planes were scattered far and wide and I found myself alone. The sky's a big place and I could see no one. I turned for home and looking down saw I was above masses of white cloud glinting in the sunshine. They billowed upwards like the huge domes of some fairy city stretching towards the horizon. I skimmed close to one, turning as I did so to find I was gazing into a deep canyon. I plunged into it and flew with white walls towering above me. I turned and twisted with the imaginary flow of the river in the canyon's depths. Then I pulled the stick back and soared up and up and up, skimming through the misty parts of the upper canyon to burst into the bright sunlight and fly through the gossamer spray of wave upon wave of beautiful clouds.

The peace and beauty is indescribable and makes you think that if it could be shared by everyone we would never want to shatter it with war.

After he had reread this entry, he picked up his pen and wrote to his sister.

Dearest Gabrielle,

This is not merely a news letter, some of that will come later. It is a request. I should have made it before but it did not cross my mind. However, it is not too late. I am still alive.

I keep a diary, have done since I joined up, events, feelings and such because I want to share all my life with Jean. Today after making the entry I realised that if anything does happen to me, all my effects will go to my next of kin and that means Dad. My diary will not go to Jean. If I do not come back, please ask Dad to pass it on to Jean unopened. I would have sent this request directly to him but Mum would see the letter and one written in this vein would upset her. She would be alarmed even if I told her I intended to hand the diary over to Jean personally when the war is over, maybe as a wedding present.

We meet whenever we can and I cannot express adequately the joy of those meetings. When she comes down here we have great fun, great parties, with a great set of pilots. Oh, there are sad times when someone does not return but we drink to him in our way, then turn our thoughts to other things.

Liz is liked by everyone here. No serious attachment but friend to all. Sister Asher is being posted and we expect Liz to be promoted in her place as squadron officer and a new flight officer to come in. She gives me regular news of Martin so they must correspond fairly often, though when I ask her if there's anything serious between them she just smiles and says, 'You never know'. Martin, incidentally, has been moved to Grimsby. A bit nearer each other, so maybe they'll meet, though from something Liz said I think Martin is embarrassed by the fact that she is an officer and he is still in the noncommissioned ranks, though that is nothing to be ashamed of and he has been promoted through corporal to sergeant.

Have you news of Ron? The last you told me he was in the Mediterranean.

We all seem to be having our fair share of excitement while poor you are still stuck instructing. Are you likely to be there until this is all over?

Write soon. I love getting letters.

Please remember my request.

Love,

Colin

The letter arrived four days later at Bletchley Park, having followed the usual channels. Gabrielle shuddered to think that Colin was making arrangements in case anything should happen to him. For one moment she wondered if he had had a premonition, but pushed it quickly from her mind as being her own sensitivity at reading between the lines. Amused by Colin's remark about her being stuck in instructing, she wrote back:

Dearest Colin,

Thanks for your letter. Of course I'll do as you ask, but we must not think of anything happening to you.

So pleased you and Jean manage to meet and I'm glad to have news of Liz and Martin. Ron is still in the

Mediterranean as far as I know. It is worrying, with the news from that area not good.

You needn't sympathise with me. I feel that what I am doing is worthwhile.

Sorry this is just a brief note to let you know I had your request. I am on duty in a few minutes. Will write more later.

Take care.

Love,

Gabrielle

Gabrielle smiled to herself as she sat down in front of her wireless set and thought of Colin imagining her lecturing trainees.

Over the past months she had struck up a rapport with one of the agents in France. She had come to recognise his touch on the Morse key immediately his transmission started coming in. He acknowledged the efficiency and speed with which she dealt with him, and they started to add one brief note of recognition at the end of each transmission. Gabrielle knew nothing of him except that he was an Englishman. She often wondered what he was like and felt that he welcomed the added note as a touch of home.

Half an hour of listening, then Gabrielle caught the first dots and dashes of identification. It was her man. She responded quickly. Contact was established. His coded message started to come through speedily with his customary clarity. But there was something slightly different. For a moment Gabrielle was puzzled but then she sensed an urgency about the transmission. Vital information needed quickly? She did not know, but the decoders would. Her role was accuracy. The message speeded up, the output of letters and figures almost catching her unawares. He had never transmitted as fast as this before. She concentrated harder. The coded message flowed from her pencil. Suddenly it stopped. The rhythm of dots and dashes was replaced by a constant buzz.

For a moment she did not comprehend. She expected the message to start again, but it didn't. She felt numb. What had happened? She looked round to the senior officer on duty and signalled to him. He was by her side in an instant and listened out with her. The buzz continued. After a few moments he looked at Gabrielle and slowly shook his head.

Gabrielle knew the worst. She had heard of agents being caught in the middle of a transmission and shot on the spot, to fall forward on to the Morse key, leaving it transmitting a continuous buzz.

Over the following weeks she hoped that she would hear his call sign and identification code and know that her suspicions were unfounded, but none came. She wondered what he was like, who he was – was he married, had he a family, who were his father and mother? She realised she would never know the answers and could only ever admire an unknown brave man.

Haunted by these unanswerable questions, she grew restless and dissatisfied that she was in a comfortable, safe situation when others were risking their lives. Sure enough, her work was of vital importance, but it had an element of boredom about it, for the messages, sent and received, were merely a series of letters with no meaning for her. She began to crave more excitement. Maybe her fluency with French might be turned to greater advantage.

Accordingly, late in November when Gabrielle went to London, ostensibly to spend a weekend with Liz, she went a day early, having been granted a meeting with Brigadier Irwin.

She took a taxi to Mortimer Street and was still a hundred yards from the house when she asked the driver to stop. She paid him and waited until he had driven away before crossing the street. She remembered the house from its brass plaque with the name J. R. Hailey engraved in copperplate writing.

She was soon admitted to the brigadier's office. It looked more like a study, its bookshelves, along two walls, full, a large oak desk across one corner and two easy chairs placed on each side of the fireplace in which a coal fire burned cheerfully.

As she was shown in, the brigadier rose from one of the chairs. 'Ah, my dear, how nice to see you again.' He stepped forward to take her hand in a friendly clasp, precluding any salute she might offer in deference to his rank. 'Please do sit down.' He indicated one of the easy chairs and waited for her to sit down before he resumed his seat. He glanced at the clock on the mantelpiece as he did so. 'I've ordered some tea for three o'clock.'

'Thank you, sir. That will be pleasant.'

'Please dispense with the "Sir".' The brigadier found an informal atmosphere relaxing and helpful whenever members of his organisation requested a meeting.

'Thank you for agreeing to see me,' said Gabrielle appreciatively.

'Gabrielle, the smooth running of this organisation depends on people being able to listen to one another and exchange ideas. I believe that no request for a meeting should go unheeded. The type of people we employ are not coming here to waste time. They have something constructive to say, some special request concerning their work or some such thing. Whatever it is, it will be important either to the organisation or to themselves, but generally to both. It is part of my job to listen to them.'

His eyes had never left her. She knew she was under scrutiny. The brigadier was making assessments all the time.

'Now, my dear, what can I do for you?'

'When you interviewed me you said you had a strong belief that women could be extremely useful as agents, but that higher authority was, at the time, against it. I wondered if there had been any change of opinion.'

The brigadier hesitated thoughtfully, then said, 'The short answer is no.' Seeing disappointment cloud her face, he raised his hand to stop the comments and questions he saw coming. 'Before I say any more, let me ask you, are you happy in what you're doing?'

'Yes,' she replied. 'But I'd like something more useful and exciting.'

Before she could elaborate, there was a knock on the door and after a moment's pause it was opened by an ATS corporal bearing a tray with two cups and saucers, milk, sugar and two tea plates with knives to butter the scones. She placed the tray on the low table which stood between the two chairs.

'Would you like me to pour, sir?' offered the corporal pleasantly.

'I'll see to it, thanks, corporal.' He leaned forward to the table and started to pour the tea as the corporal left the room.

'Right, my dear, carry on. Why do you want to change?'

As he passed the cup to her, he listened intently to what she had to say.

'I feel I could serve the organisation and my country better in a more active role. As you know, my French could get me by as a native and you yourself said you believe women could move around more easily and have better reasons for doing so.'

He looked up quickly. 'Give me some,' he snapped.

Gabrielle was almost taken aback by the sharpness but, realising it was a test of her reactions, remained calm and answered him in the same steady voice she had been using. 'It's more natural for a woman to go shopping, to visit neighbours when a man would be working, to visit relatives outside the neighbourhood, to be seen chatting to friends, to fraternise with Germans if the job demanded it.'

The brigadier smiled and, seeing that Gabrielle was supplied with a scone, sat back in his chair. 'You're not thinking of using this as a means of contacting your maternal relations in Paris?'

'No.' There was a touch of indignation in her voice that he should have thought of such a thing. 'It never crossed my mind.'

He raised a hand with a gesture of apology. 'I'm sorry but I had to ask.'

'Look,' Gabrielle went on earnestly. 'I'd like the chance to become an agent, but if the authorities are blinkered to

342

what women can do, then there is no use my pursuing the matter. I hoped that by now your views might have broken through.'

'I'm afraid they haven't – well, not completely. But I believe I, with the backing of others, may win the day.'

Gabrielle's hopes soared. 'And would you recommend me?'

The brigadier smiled benevolently. 'My dear, I think you're just the type of person we would look for.' He waited until her enthusiasm subsided and then went on, 'I must warn you that if we do decide to recruit women into the role of agents, you will have to undergo a very rigorous training. We will need to get you super-fit, train you in the use of various types of firearms, how to use explosives, how to react under fire. Those are the most dangerous aspects of training. You would also be taught how to organise resistance groups, how to gather information, what type of things we need to know, how to distinguish between genuine supporters of our cause from those who may well be in the pay of the Germans, and so on.'

'As I would expect,' replied Gabrielle.

'Right. Now all I can advise you to do is to go back to the job you are doing and if and when a decision is made I will contact you. Oh, it may not be face to face, but you will receive instructions in what we want you to do.'

'Thank you very much. I hope the authorities agree with you.'

'Good. Now, my dear, relax, enjoy another scone and some more tea and tell me about yourself, your family, your friends and what they are all doing.'

Although he had a good knowledge from the vetting

343

when Gabrielle had been recruited, by the time she left he had a much fuller picture of her and was even more convinced that she could serve them well in the role of an agent.

Gabrielle was walking on air as she made her way to the hotel where she had arranged to meet Liz the next day.

Liz brought apologies from Gabrielle's brother, but, with daily sweeps over France, Colin was unable to get away even for a brief visit.

'How is he?' asked Gabrielle with some concern as they entered the hotel room they were sharing.

'He's fine,' replied Liz. 'In very good form. Promoted to flight lieutenant last week, but I expect you know.'

'Flight lieutenant!' gasped Gabrielle. 'I didn't know. Tell him I'm hurt. He should write more often.'

'Writing time's taken up with letters to Jean, you should know that.' Liz grinned at her.

'He could spare one for his sister. Jean manages it.'

'You hear from her regularly?'

'Fairly.'

'That's good. I believe she missed you when you separated, but from what Colin tells me she settled down well at Waddington. Likes it.'

'Yes. I'm pleased,' said Gabrielle.

'Room all right?' asked Liz. She had laid her small case on the unused bed and now looked round with critical eyes. The pink-flowered wallpaper matched the pink carpet and the heavy curtains lined with blackout material. 'Tried the Junior Officers' Club but they were full up. Took this on the recommendation of one of the pilots.'

'Colin?'

'No. Dare say he could have told me. He and Jean do meet in London. Now, did you know that?'

Gabrielle smiled. 'Yes I did, and I approve.'

'Good.' Liz changed the subject. 'I'll freshen up, then I suggest we have a walk, tea in the Lyons Corner House, back here, leisurely bath, dinner and then a good chat in the lounge over a drink.'

'Sounds good,' agreed Gabrielle.

'Do you hear from Ron?' asked Liz as she unpacked her few belongings.

'Occasionally,' replied Gabrielle, flopping down on her bed. 'It won't be easy for him to post letters, particularly the way things are going out there.'

'I got one this morning.'

'Must have been in port somewhere. Maybe there'll be one for me when I get back. How is he?'

'Seems OK. Indicates that he is being recommended for a commission, but that will have to follow certain routine which will be conducted when next they are on Home Station. Reading between the lines, I think that won't be long.'

'Good for him. I look forward to seeing him.' But with her mind obsessed with the possibilities of serving as an agent in France, Gabrielle wondered if she would be around when he came home, and, if she wasn't, did she really care?

Liz noticed the lack of real enthusiasm of a girl in love. She knew that Gabrielle had not wanted to commit herself to her brother in Robin Hood's Bay. Maybe her attitude had cooled even further.

* * *

After an enjoyable weekend, Gabrielle returned to Bletchley Park to find a letter from Ron awaiting her.

15 September 1941

Dear Gabrielle,

I hope all is well with you and that the instructing is not too boring. We have seen a lot of action, as you will no doubt have guessed from the news from the Mediterranean. Fortunately our ship has been lucky and we have not fared too badly.

We have put into port, I cannot say where, so I am taking this opportunity writing to you.

Letters from home take some time catching us up. I got one from you which was old, early this year, goodness knows where it had been but it was good to get it all the same. I was sorry to hear about Mrs Lawson but was glad you were there. Your presence would be a comfort to Jean. Have she and Colin decided to get married? Hope all turns out well for them. Colin will be in the thick of it, as I understand from Liz in a letter much more recent than yours. Fancy them both being posted to the same place. Liz will be able to keep an eye on him for Jean!

I'm saving my important news until last. I could be in line for a commission. I think I will get a strong recommendation when we get home. If I get one I may even think of staying in the navy after the war. As you know, I always wanted to go to sea. This war gave me the opportunity. I like it and would probably be a fool to throw away the opportunity of making a good career out of it.

How would you like to be married to a peacetime officer in the Royal Navy?

Love,

Ron

Gabrielle stared at the last sentence. The words bit into her mind. Was this really a proposal?

Her thoughts tumbled back to Robin Hood's Bay. She and Ron had had some good times together. They got on well and she liked him a lot. If there had been no war, things would have been different. Their lives, maybe together, would most likely have been carved out there. But the future was still uncertain. Their lives were changing, their attitudes and outlooks too. Certainly hers were and this visit to Brigadier Irwin might change things even further. Ron had agreed to no commitment until the war was over and maybe it was best to keep it that way.

She picked up a pen to write, glanced again at the letter and noticed it had been written two months ago. She laid the pen down. By the time her answer reached him, Ron might be home. He could be in England already. She would have to wait until she heard from him again before she gave him an answer.

She pursed her lips, contemplating her dilemma.

Chapter Sixteen

1942

Since receiving Ron's letter, Gabrielle had been torn between two courses. She had convinced herself that she would be recruited as an agent, but that belief was wearing thin. She had heard nothing and the new year had moved into spring. Ron's offer became more and more tempting. She was still in an uncertain frame of mind when, on 28 March, she was told to report to the CO's office.

There the lieutenant colonel acknowledged her smart salute and permitted her to sit down. 'I have received a communication from Brigadier Irwin. I have to ask you one question: "Are you still interested?" '

Excitement gripped her. This was what she had wanted when she went to London, a more active role within the SOE. But now there was doubt in her mind.

'Do you require my answer now, sir?'

'I'm afraid I do, Harland.'

Gabrielle knew he was right. Decisions like this could

not be held up. But what should she do? From the way the lieutenant colonel was eyeing her, she reckoned her hesitation made him suspicious. She realised she had judged right when he advised, 'If you have any doubt at all, you should say no.'

'It's a personal matter which has arisen since I saw Brigadier Irwin last year, sir, but it can easily be resolved.' Gabrielle firmed her voice. 'The answer is yes, sir.'

'Good. You have done well here, Harland. You're a first-class operator. I'll be sorry to lose you. I know what you're going in to but that's all. You're a brave girl to want to be so involved.'

'Thank you, sir.'

'Beyond that I know nothing. I don't even know what is contained in this envelope.' He picked up a large white envelope which had lain in front of him. 'They are instructions for you. You are to read them here and now, memorise them and then I have to watch you destroy them.' About to hand over the envelope, he paused and added, 'You realise that everything from now on is top secret?' He handed over the envelope and slid a paperknife across the desk.

Gabrielle slit the envelope and drew out two sheets of paper and a smaller envelope. She read through the type-written instructions, then read them a second time, committing the contents to memory. Her commanding officer waited patiently.

'You're sure of the instructions?' he asked when she looked up.

'Yes, sir.'

'Certain? Read them again if you wish.'

'That's all right, sir. I have a good memory.'

349

'Good. Then let us destroy them.'

She passed the two sheets to him. He pulled a cigarette lighter from his pocket, flicked it sharply to light the wick, and held the flame to one corner of the paper. The flame licked at them, caught, and as the papers burned, the officer turned them, holding them over a metal wastepaper bin. The remnants floated down into the container to leave only charred wisps crinkling on the metal.

'What about that?' He indicated a small envelope in Gabrielle's hand.

'I am to go on immediate leave for two weeks. This should contain my passes, sir.'

'Check.'

Gabrielle opened the envelope, examined the contents and said, 'Two passes, that's all there is, sir, and they give nothing away.'

'Very good, Harland. You get off as soon as possible. No one here will ask questions, but as far as they are concerned you are posted back to Windermere, instructing.'

'Yes, sir.'

He rose from his chair and came from behind his desk. He held out his hand and Gabrielle felt sincerity in his grip when he said, 'I wish you well, Harland. Take care of yourself.'

'Thank you, sir.' Gabrielle saluted and left the office.

'Miss Gabrielle, how nice to see you.'

'And you, Mr Newton.' She smiled as she walked across the station platform at Robin Hood's Bay. Placing her two cases on the ground, she fished in her greatcoat pocket for her pass.

'Long leave?' he asked as he glanced at the paper she handed to him.

'I have a fortnight,' she replied, turning up the collar of her coat as a protection against the cold wind which blew off the sea.

'Oh, congratulations on your promotion!' He glanced at the stripes of a flight officer on her coat.

'Thanks.' She picked up her cases.

'No one to meet you?'

'Don't know I'm coming. Just got to know myself this morning.'

'Then they'll get a pleasant surprise.'

'Guess so.' She started off towards the exit.

'So will Ron Johnson,' he called after her, remembering how the six friends used to go about together.

The words hit her like an arrow. She stopped and turned. 'Ron here?' she asked in amazement.

'Yes, arrived yesterday. Looks well. Tells me he's in for a commission. Sounded confident of getting it.'

She nodded and set off once again, but now her mind was a jumble. How long had Ron been in England? Why hadn't he contacted her? Would it have made any difference to the decision she had made?

There was no mistaking the delight and surprise felt by Sam Harland when he opened the door to find Gabrielle standing there.

As he hugged his daughter, he called over his shoulder, 'Colette, a surprise for you!'

The tremor in his voice brought his wife hurrying into the hall.

'Darling!' she cried, holding her arms wide for her

351

daughter. As she hugged her tight, silent tears of joy flowed down her cheeks. 'How long?' she asked.

'A fortnight.'

Colette and Sam were delighted. This was the longest leave she had had at home and they were going to make the best of it.

Because she had brought all her things home, she had to explain that away by saying that she was being sent on a course before returning to her instructing duties at Windermere and therefore they should continue to write to her there. She did not like deceiving them but there was no other way. She knew how vital secrecy was. Besides, it would only bring her parents worry and anxiety if they knew for what she had volunteered.

'You'll be pleased to know Ron Johnson is at home,' said Colette.

'He looks well in his uniform, makes a good-looking sailor,' added Sam. 'And a possible commission in the offing, I'm told.'

Though they had wisely never pushed things, they had hopes that Gabrielle and Ron would 'make a go of it' as Colin and Jean seemed to be doing.

'I'll look him up tomorrow.'

The following morning Gabrielle, pleased to have a change from uniform, dressed in a close-fitting black woollen dress which flared slightly from the waist. The high neck was trimmed with delicate white lace. She slipped a pair of black court shoes on her feet in black silk stockings, saved carefully from before the war, and viewed herself in the long mirror. She ran her hands through her short hair, giving its natural wave an extra bounce. Satisfied, she stopped and stared herself straight in the eyes.

'What's the idea?' she asked herself quietly. 'You'd think you were going courting your best beau. Are you trying to impress Ron? Is it fair to him? Haven't you made your decision?'

She shook off the criticism. It felt good to be in civvies again and to take pleasure in feeling smart and attractive, so why not?

It was mid-morning when she set off for the Johnson house. The sun had little heat in it but it was bright. To combat the sharp air Gabrielle had donned a long, loose-fitting topcoat in red, with matching gloves. She turned up the large collar and snuggled down inside the coat as she stepped outside.

As she walked, she gazed across the red roofs of the fishing village glowing in the sunshine. The cliffs rose like sentinels across the bay, imparting a sense of security in spite of the depressing news of setbacks in all the theatres of war. The sea was calm, seeming to tell her she should be the same.

She smiled to herself at the butterflies in her stomach. She was a little nervous at facing Ron, yet she was about to embark on something that could take her into terrible dangers and it had not caused her a flutter.

She rang the doorbell and heard a muffled 'I'll get it' beyond the closed door. Ron. Her heart beat a little faster. Was it telling her she really was in love with him? Through the patterned glass she saw a figure bounding down the hall. The door opened.

Ron gasped. He stared wide-eyed, unable to believe who was standing there.

'Hello, Ron.' She laughed at the amazed expression she had caused.

'Gabrielle!' He swept her into his arms and swung her round. 'It's good to see you. You wangled some leave after getting my letter. That's great!'

'Letter? I never got a letter.'

'What?' He looked at her in astonishment. 'I got back to England three days ago. Wrote to you straight away telling you I was coming on ten days' leave and hoped that you could manage some as well.'

'I never got it.' She did not enlighten him that there were delays in letters going to Windermere before being forwarded to her at Bletchley, for as far as he knew she was at Windermere.

'Well, what does it matter? You're here. Come on in.' He stood to one side and allowed her to enter the house. 'Mum,' he shouted, 'look who's here.'

Mrs Johnson was soon greeting Gabrielle and ushering her into the front room. Here everything was so neat and tidy, not a thing out of place, that Gabrielle knew the Johnsons used this room only when they had visitors.

'Cup of tea?' Mrs Johnson asked.

'Please.'

When his mother had gone to the kitchen, Ron said, 'It's great to see you. And you're looking so gorgeous, black suits you.'

'Thanks.' Gabrielle acknowledged the compliment with an appreciative smile.

'When we've had a drink, how about a walk?' suggested Ron, eager to have Gabrielle to himself.

For one moment she thought of making excuses but she knew that she would have to face being alone with him some time. They had been thrown together on this leave and she must be straight with him. It was only fair.

'Right,' she agreed. 'Where?'

'Along the cliffs?'

'Then we'll go via home and I'll change into something more practical.'

'You look fine as you are.'

'But I need something different for the cliffs.'

Gabrielle saw admiration in his eyes and it remained there while they had their cup of tea.

As they climbed way above the village, Ron slipped his hand into hers. Their step was brisk in the sharp air. Gabrielle had changed into a warm skirt and jersey with a duffel coat on top. Her feet were snug in a pair of walking shoes.

Their breath clouded on the cold as the path steepened. Reaching the top, enjoying the exhilarating effect, they stopped. They had chatted easily about their life in the forces, Gabrielle careful in what she said, allowing him to do most of the talking while she tried to weigh him up. She was puzzled. He was different. She had detected it even before they had left the house. He was still the same handsome Ron and his dark-blue eyes still drew attention, but the kindness she had once seen there had gone. In its place was self-importance. The firm jaw now had the set of a man determined to have his own way.

His talk of the navy was all of himself and she sensed a touch of arrogance in his attitude. She felt she would not like to be one of the ratings under his command. The war had changed him and not for the better.

They looked back to distant houses and the sweeping bay.

'I love that view,' Gabrielle commented.

'I've seen better.' There was a touch of disdain in his voice.

'I thought you liked Robin Hood's Bay?'

'It's all right.' Ron was offhand. 'But there's a better life out there. I'm taking it and I want you to share it.' His words had become charged with the enthusiasm of one who expects a favourable answer.

'I can't.'

He stared at her, unable to believe she was turning him down. 'You mean you still want to wait until after the war?'

'I've a job to do.'

'But you're only instructing.'

Gabrielle bristled at his derisive tone. 'And you think that's not important?' she rapped indignantly, an edge to her voice.

'Well, compared to the rest of our gang of six . . .'

Words sprang to her lips to reveal what she was really doing but she held them back, not only because she must but, if Ron could not accept instructing as vital, then he was a lesser man than she had thought. 'It might be mundane compared to what you've been doing, but, let me tell you, without the training I'm giving there are lots of jobs wouldn't be filled, essential jobs at that, so I think I'm doing very important work, and that means I can't marry you.'

Ron's face darkened. 'Can't? Don't you mean won't?'

'Can't, won't, what difference does it make?'

'There's someone else?' There was a snap of annoyance in Ron's voice.

'No,' replied Gabrielle firmly, 'there isn't.'

'Then marry me.' He grabbed her by the shoulders and looked deep into her eyes, challenging her to defy him. 'I've got a great future ahead. I know it. I'll get this commission and then the world can be mine. We'll get married next leave and then you'll be able to come out of the forces. You'll have a good life with me.'

'But I don't want to leave the WAAFs. I have a job to do. Besides, I don't love you.'

Astounded, Ron stared at her. 'You don't mean it?' he gasped.

'I do,' she answered firmly. 'We've changed.'

'You might have,' he snapped, 'but I haven't.'

She drew back from telling him how he had. 'When we went into the forces we had no commitment,' she reminded him.

'Not in so many words,' he said sharply, 'but I thought there was an understanding.'

'You shouldn't have done.'

Ron's face darkened with a mixture of anger and disappointment: disappointment at being turned down, anger at her for refusing and so denting his pride. His lips tightened. 'There must be someone else. You could have told me.' His voice rose angrily and his eyes blazed. 'I hope he doesn't let you down like you've done to me.' He swung on his heel and strode towards the village.

She watched his figure getting smaller and smaller, her

357

mind in turmoil. She hadn't meant to hurt him. Had he really changed so much? Had she misjudged him? Confusion held her as she returned home, but later that night she realised that a sense of relief had replaced the sadness and uncertainty.

A fortnight later Gabrielle, on her way to Surrey, called at Waddington, where Jean, delighted by this unexpected visit, snatched an hour off.

'I'm on my way back after some leave,' explained Gabrielle. 'We haven't seen each other for some time and I have some news which I would rather you heard from me than from anyone else.'

Jean, her curiosity raised, was all attention. 'Well?' she prompted when Gabrielle hesitated.

'Ron was at home. He proposed.'

'You're getting married? I'm delighted.' Jean's smile was broad as she moved to give her friend a congratulatory hug.

'No. I turned him down.'

Jean stopped. The smile vanished, leaving a look of bewilderment. 'But . . . I thought you and he . . .'

'No,' Gabrielle cut in, and went on to explain the circumstances and how Ron had changed. 'The marriage would never have lasted,' she concluded.

'Well, whatever is for your happiness,' said Jean.

'Thanks. Now what's life like for you?'

'Fine, thanks. I've come to terms with Mum's death. Colin helped enormously.'

'You see him often?'

'As often as we can.'

'Why don't you two get married?'

'We had decided to wait until after the war, but I think the next time we meet, planned for the third of May, we'll decide otherwise.'

'Good, I'm pleased. What has changed your minds?'

'The last time we met we were looking in a bookshop in London and picked up a small volume called *The White Cliffs* by Alice Duer Miller. It's in verse and there were two which moved us:

> 'We went down to Devon,
> In a warm summer rain,
> Knowing that our happiness
> Might never come again;
> I, not forgetting,
> "Till death do us part",
> Was outrageously happy
> With death in my heart.
>
> Lovers in peace-time
> With fifty years to live,
> Have time to tease and quarrel
> And question what to give;
> But lovers in war-time
> Better understand
> The fullness of living,
> With death close at hand.'

For a moment there was silence, then Gabrielle hugged her friend. 'I understand, and I hope you and Colin will be very happy.'

'Oh, but we are. The strain of knowing the danger he is in is sometimes unbearable but I cope, remembering those last four lines. When we're together we live as if there was no tomorrow. You know, in a strange way, being here on an operational station, it seems to help. I'm involved with men who may not return tomorrow. I see how they face the possibility and realise I must do likewise and not let my fears for Colin get the better of me. Life here is good. I realise that there's no life like squadron life. Oh, there's sadness and grief when crews go missing but there's a lot of fun – has to be, otherwise the crews would go barmy. And it's been all go here.'

'Why, what's happening? Or shouldn't I ask?'

'I don't think it's a big secret now. It can't be. One day last September we were all surprised to see a strange aircraft circling the airfield. We thought at first it was a Manchester coming to join 207 Squadron but then we saw that, although it had some Manchester characteristics, it had four engines.'

'A new bomber?'

'Yes, a Lancaster. It tested out the airfield for suitability. 44 Squadron got the first three on Christmas Eve and others have been arriving since. Sadly, we lost the first on March twenty-fourth.'

'The crews like it?'

'I'll say. I've not heard one bad thing against it. They are really enthusiastic. A few teething troubles but they say it flies like a dream, is roomier and will carry a greater bomb load. I think it's beautiful for a bomber. With seven crew it means more aircrew and apparently more ground-crew, so it was hectic to accommodate this greater influx.

It's all so exciting! I wish you were doing something more interesting than instructing.'

'Oh, I'm all right. I enjoy it.' She glanced at her watch. 'I must be going.' She stood up, pre-empting any more explanation.

They left the anteroom and collected their greatcoats and hats. Jean walked with her to the guardroom, where Gabrielle booked out. As they left the building, a staff car drew up. Jean saw Tim White was driving an empty car.

'Hello, sweetie,' he called as he climbed out of the car to check out. 'Who's the dish beside you?' He grinned and winked at Gabrielle.

Jean laughed. 'This dish is Flight Officer Harland.'

'She'll have another name,' he protested as he came round the car.

'Gabrielle.'

'Then I'm pleased to meet you, Gabrielle. Coming to join this happy throng?'

'Alas, no.'

'Our loss,' moaned Tim. 'A dishy number like you could do wonders for this station.'

'Are you heading for Lincoln?' asked Jean.

'Sure am. Couple of squadron leaders to pick up. The Lancs are sure creating havoc around here.'

'Then can you give this dishy number a lift to the station?'

Tim grinned. 'It will be my pleasure. Maybe we'll ride off into the blue, never to be seen again. Fancy doing that, Gabrielle?'

'Maybe it's not a bad idea,' she replied, playing along. 'But I should hate to think of a couple of squadron leaders

361

having to walk all the way to Waddington and then working off their bad tempers on the personnel here.'

'Maybe you're right. Very considerate of you. I wouldn't have an easy conscience if folk like Jean were in hot water while we were having an ecstatic time. Better just run you to the station.' He swung into the guardroom.

'Lively type.' Gabrielle smiled.

'Tim's OK. Good fun. Take care, Gabrielle. You're a dear friend.'

'So are you.' They hugged each other. 'Love to Colin when you see him.'

'Something big in the offing, Jean.' George Sugden made the observation as the 44 Squadron Lancasters took off on another daylight formation exercise. 'But the CO's keeping tight-lipped.'

Over the past fortnight local formation flying had developed into cross-country flights at low level which had increased in distance each time they were airborne. Rumours of what it was all about increased when it was learned that 97 Squadron at Woodhall Spa, the only other squadron flying Lancasters, were doing the same. When the two squadrons rendezvoused and flew together, speculation increased.

That guesswork ceased when the crews assembled for briefing at eleven o'clock in the morning of 17 April.

The ribbon on the large map at the end of the briefing room traced a route to Augsburg deep in the heart of Bavaria.

Augsburg! From their training they now surmised they

were going in daylight at low level. So far! The crews gasped. A suicide trip!

Jean felt for them as she waited her turn to brief them with the information she and George had assembled – a detailed assessment of the target and the aiming point, using a model of the MAN factory which made vital parts for submarines, at this time the scourge of British convoys. She showed them a large target map identifying the factory situated in north Augsburg and, to help them make a correct judgement, an artist's impression of how the precise aiming point would look on their approach. She gave them information on enemy fighter distribution, likelihood of anti-aircraft fire and any other salient points she thought would help the crews to accomplish and return safely from their mission.

The crews listened carefully to the pretty intelligence officer, absorbing all she and the other briefing officers had to say, for they knew success and survival may hang in their words.

Shortly before three o'clock, Jean was among the group of well-wishers gathered beside the control wagon at the end of the runway. The Lancasters, with their Merlin engines shattering the uneasy peace, had been checked and double-checked, each in its own dispersal point around the airfield. Now, with engines ticking over, they were taxiing around the perimeter track towards the runway from which they would take off.

The first Lancaster reached the end of the runway, paused while the pilot carried out his final checks, then turned on to the runway and stopped. A green light signalled from the control wagon. The aircraft was held on its brakes until the engines reached the necessary power. Released of its restriction, the Lancaster started to roll forward. Jean and all those around her waved and received acknowledgements from the crew.

All eyes were fixed on the heavy bomber as it roared down the runway faster and faster. It seemed it was never going to take off. Jean held her breath. Was something wrong? She felt relief as the aircraft rose gracefully from the ground and started to climb, gradually turning away from the airfield.

The second bomber was already in position, its engines screaming for release. The light flashed and the Lancaster started to move. Then another, and another, and . . .

Darkness clung to Waddington like a heavy cloak. The hush across the airfield had an uncanny feeling to it. People who could have been in bed weren't. It was nearly midnight and their aircraft should be nearing home.

Jean stood at the door of the briefing room with George, ready to debrief the crews once they held a steaming mug of cocoa, drawn by the WAAFs standing by the urns. They strained to catch the first sound of distant engines, the dull throb which would herald a Lancaster safely back. The minutes dragged. The idle chatter gradually ceased, and with the silence came tension. Six had gone so six must come back, but it had been a daylight raid at low level – the worst possible scenario.

The minutes moved on. Still no welcoming sound. Uneasiness filtered through the groups around the airfield. The groundcrews grew anxious for the planes they so lovingly maintained and especially for the crews that flew them, with whom they had a close rapport. The WAAFs in the watchtower were listening for the first news of approaching aircraft, ready to talk the planes down. Everyone from the commanding officer to the lowest rank on the station grew anxious.

Time passed. No aircraft approached Waddington and everyone knew in their heart of hearts that tragedy had struck, yet all hoped that their beloved fliers had been forced to land at some other airfield.

But, when the news broke, only one had done so, the squadron leader who had led the raid. Despondent, people drifted to their billets. The urns of cocoa were taken away unused by the WAAFs who only a short time ago had brought them in high spirits, ready to exchange banter with returning crews. Now they spoke in whispers. Lights were switched off, doors were closed, the locker room, which should have been full of jocular airmen changing their flying clothes, was silent.

Jean felt heavy hearted. Her eyes were damp as her mind ran through the names chalked on the blackboard in the Ops Room. Stunned, she recalled their faces, the broad smiles, the serious eyes, the determined chins, all with that sense of solid reliability and belief in what they were doing. Though she guessed that all had had a touch of fear when they saw that ribbon stretched to Augsburg, none had shown it; they had got down to the job as if it was a big adventure which could do them no harm. She felt for them, and for their mothers, wives and sweet-hearts who would feel the pain of loss. She wondered how they would cope and could she do so if ever anything happened to Colin?

The sense of shock at the enormous loss was evident the next day. It hung over the airfield like an oppressive pall. People went about their tasks subdued and talked in hushed voices. Hilarity was absent.

Jean felt her beloved squadron would never recover, but eventually it did, with the arrival of new Lancasters and new crews. Life came back to the station. New friends were made, even as old friends were remembered.

Gabrielle relaxed in the train heading out of London for Scotland's west coast. The strain and pressures of the last fortnight had been immense and there had been times when she had almost been on the point of despair and wishing she had never volunteered for the SOE, but she had known she was being tested and was determined not to give way.

She had marshalled her resolve as she faced yet another interview, by a different officer. The questions had come quick and fast to test her concentration, her ability to stick to her story and relate the same facts over and over again. They had checked her aptitude to speak French fluently. They had tried to undermine her morale, but she had rallied.

She never got to know any of her interrogators. They were elusive figures who came and went without a friendly word. She never met them socially, nor at meals. The only fraternising was between the handful of girls on the same 'course', but there was little time even for that and at the end of the day they were so mentally exhausted that all they wanted to do was fold up and sleep.

Now it was all over. There had been no word of praise,

no indication that she had passed the trial, but she assumed she had when she was instructed to go by train to Oban. None of the other girls was with her and she did not know what had happened to them, for they had drifted away, posted when the authorities were satisfied or, in some cases, dissatisfied with the outcome.

She settled back for the journey, relaxed, pleased and looking forward to Scotland.

The journey was long and it was late afternoon by the time she reached the tiny port for the islands. She had no idea where she was going and she hoped that she was expected. As she left the station, looking about her for someone who might be there to meet her, an army sergeant moved from the staff car parked nearby.

'Flight Officer Harland?' he asked pleasantly.

'Yes,' she replied.

'Sergeant Henderson, ma'am. Can I take your things?'

'Thanks, sergeant. Glad you were here.'

'We don't slip up on these matters, ma'am.' He took the cases and put them on the back seat, then opened the front passenger door for her.

Gabrielle climbed in and settled herself. When the sergeant climbed in, he removed a rug from his seat and passed it to Gabrielle. 'Tuck yourself up, ma'am, there's a nip in the air.'

'Far to go, sergeant?' she asked as he started the engine.

'About forty-five miles, ma'am.'

'Good gracious! Where are we going?'

'If you don't know this part of the world, it will mean nothing to you. Suffice to say it's a beautiful place. I think you'll appreciate it.'

They threaded their way out of Oban.

'First time this way, ma'am?'

'Yes.'

'Then enjoy the ride.'

The spring sun cast a sheen across the landscape and sparkled the snow-capped mountains into a fairyland. It sent ripples of light dancing across the water of the lochs, moving with every twist of the road. Gabrielle fell into silence, lost in the magic of a land and a time at peace and far removed from war. The only reality was that she was in uniform sitting beside a soldier, and she was bound for a life which might thrust her into the worst of the conflict. But she would not allow those thoughts to intrude on the wonder around her.

The sergeant respected her desire for silence and he too enjoyed the beauty of the countryside against the mountainous backcloth.

'Ballachulish Ferry.' He eventually broke the silence to indicate the small car-carrying ferry drawn up at the shore. 'Way across the other side to Fort William.'

'Are we going there?'

'No, keeping on this side of Loch Leven.' He motioned to the loch on their left. 'Not far now.'

The mountains on the right rose high and glowering. Even the snow on their tops did nothing to alleviate their grimness and it seemed that the sun was fighting a losing battle to brighten their depths. It appeared as if the mountains were throwing a cloak of mystery around themselves as if warning the intruder, whether man or nature, to beware.

As Gabrielle gazed at the awesome bulk of rock, she shivered.

The sergeant noticed. 'Glencoe, ma'am. Haunted by the souls of the Macdonalds.'

'The massacre,' she half whispered to herself. She shivered again. The sergeant had said 'not far'. What was she coming to? Surely not to this stricken land, not after the fairy magic through which they had travelled.

She breathed a little easier when they did not turn into the glen but went on beside the loch.

They turned through open wrought-iron gates supported by huge stone columns surmounted by two griffins. The gravelled drive led upwards, then levelled to swing in a large circle in front of an enormous mansion.

The sergeant stopped in front of the main entrance, which was approached by wide steps giving on to a portico running the full length of the building. He got out of the car quickly and opened the door for Gabrielle.

'I'll get your things, ma'am, and show you in.'

'Thank you, sergeant.'

He led the way to the main door, where he rang the bell three times.

A few moments later the thud of bolts being drawn back sent a shiver down Gabrielle's spine. The huge door swung back noiselessly and another sergeant stood to one side to allow the arrivals to step into a dimly lit vestibule with no windows. They waited while he closed the door and opened another which let into a huge hall with a wide staircase curving upwards from the left in an elegant sweep.

The sergeant who had admitted them crossed to a desk at one side of the hall, his footsteps echoing on the mottled marble floor. Going behind the desk he examined an open notebook. He glanced up.

'Flight Officer Gabrielle Harland?'

'Yes, sergeant.'

'May I see your identity?'

'Certainly, sergeant.' Gabrielle unbuttoned her great-coat, took her identity card from the breast pocket of her tunic and handed it to the sergeant.

'Thank you, ma'am.' He glanced at it and back to Gabrielle. Satisfied, he handed it to her and asked her to sign in. When she had done this she glanced up to see that the serious officialdom had slipped from him. 'Welcome, ma'am. I hope you had a pleasant journey.'

'Yes, thank you, sergeant.'

He turned and pressed a bell.

The sergeant who had driven her from Oban had placed her cases beside the desk. 'Bill, I'll put the car away.'

'Right, Mike.'

As Mike turned to go, Gabrielle thanked him for the ride.

'It was a pleasure, ma'am.'

A WAAF in battledress appeared, Gabrielle presumed in answer to the bell.

'Flight Officer Harland, this is Aircraftwoman Joyce Leggat. She'll be your batwoman and will show you to your room and round the building. Dinner is served in half an hour at seven thirty.'

Joyce, a short, tubby girl with a pleasant smile, said, 'Pleased to know you, ma'am.' Her soft voice was toned with a charming Scottish lilt.

'And you.' Gabrielle smiled. She turned to the sergeant. 'Thank you, sergeant.'

'Follow me, ma'am.' Joyce picked up the cases and led the way to the stairs. Gabrielle admired the decor as they climbed to the second floor. The white of the hall gradually gave way to a light green. Paintings of Scottish glens hung in heavy gilt frames. The sweeping banister was supported by black wrought-iron work in the shape of thistles. Reaching the second landing, they turned along a well-lit, heavily carpeted corridor. The whole place spoke of money and luxury. Gabrielle was surprised to find such trappings still there when it was being occupied by the military.

'Who owns this place?' asked Gabrielle.

'One of the Campbells, ma'am.'

'And he left it just as it is?'

'Insisted, ma'am. Said the military people deserved a bit of luxury. I suppose he was reassured about the type of people who would be using it.'

They had reached a door at the end of the corridor. 'Your room, ma'am,' said Joyce, throwing the door open and standing back to allow Gabrielle to enter.

She raised an eyebrow in surprise when she walked in. The room was large, with a high ceiling. The wallpaper depicting intertwining plants matched the cushions and upholstery of the two armchairs. The deep carpet, a single shade of peach, lightened the room and thick curtains, matching the carpet, were drawn. A dressing table with oval mirror stood to the right of the bay window with its window seat. Glancing at the bed, Gabrielle knew she would luxuriate in its size for she liked a big bed.

Joyce had put the cases on a bench which stood just inside the doorway.

'A quick tour, ma'am, before your meal?'

371

'Please.'

By the time they returned ten minutes later, Gabrielle knew where the dining room, the lecture rooms, the anteroom, the drying rooms and the CO's office were and she realised that the trainees were being treated as something special. As she freshened up ready to go to dinner, she felt that she was going to enjoy it here after what she had been used to so far in her WAAF career. But she had a little niggling doubt about the enjoyment when the CO addressed them before the meal.

She walked into the anteroom at seven twenty to find a mixture of people of both sexes and widely differing ranks, standing in odd groups, guarded in their conversation lest they give away information best kept to themselves. She chose a glass of sweet sherry from a tray offered by a steward and fell into conversation with a WAAF of similar rank. A few moments later a major, accompanied by a captain, walked purposefully into the room, his entrance attracting everyone's attention.

The major was tall, broad-shouldered and exuded an aura of toughness. His eyes were sharp, roaming as if he was sizing up each individual. The captain also had the air of a man who would stand no nonsense, but there was a softer light about his eyes and his face bore a gentler look.

The major stopped so he could take in all the occupants of the room in one glance. He straightened, his chest tightening his jacket with its highly polished buttons. His trousers with their razor-edged crease were of perfect length to the tops of his shiny shoes. His appearance spoke of expecting everyone else to be equally smart when the occasion necessitated. He was a man who worked by and showed an example.

'Good evening, everyone. Welcome to Scotland.' His voice was deep, almost with a boom to it. 'I'm Eric Cole, in charge of this unit, and this is Graham Ferguson, my second in command.' He paused slightly to let everyone take in this information. 'You will notice I did not use ranks. You can observe them for yourselves. I did this on purpose. We are all one here. Your own ranks differ. Of the twenty on this course, we range from army major to WAAF assistant section officer. You will all be treated exactly the same, male and female, irrespective of rank. You will go through the same training, no quarter given. For all these reasons I prefer to dispense with rank identification. In training we use surnames so you will take no offence when sergeant instructors use them.

'The only segregations I make are between instructors, whatever rank, and trainees in off-time. Each has different dining rooms and anterooms. I organise it this way so that there is an opportunity for both to escape from the other and relax without the other's presence.

'The training is comprehensive and will involve you in handling weapons, learning how to live off the land, how to use dynamite, the art of sabotage. You will improve your adoptive language, learn how to act as a native of France, for you are all part of the so-called French School. There are those among you who have been trained in the use of Morse code, receiving and sending messages. They will keep up that efficiency and improve on it. Those who haven't will have special training.

'No corners will be cut in any part of your training. Do

373

that and you could be endangering not only your lives but the lives of others. You will not leave here until you have attained a very high standard, or you may be rejected altogether if you don't measure up to the high standards I set. There is no set time for the course, some may finish before the others. That depends on the extent of the training we determine is required for your eventual particular work. But whatever the length, it is our job to turn out highly efficient and capable agents.

'That is the overall picture, but the first thing we do is to get you fit.' He gave a little smile. 'I know you're all thinking, "I am fit". I'm afraid you'll be disillusioned when we start on you. I warn you it will be tough. We will spend a fortnight doing PT, cross-country expeditions and so on. You will be issued with kit tomorrow morning and then after lunch we will start in real earnest.

'There is one aspect of life here I haven't given you. I've said it's tough but we do compensate by living in luxury. Your rooms are above the class you meet in the forces and we have top-class chefs. You may think this is not right, considering that everyone else is tightening their belts in time of war, but I look at it this way; you are destined for hardship and high risk and should have some compensation for what you may have to face. One wag once called out, "Last meal for the condemned man" – well, view it as you like, I hope your stay here, though tough, will be enjoyable and memorable for the right reasons.

'If you have any problems, come direct to me; if I am not available, then see Graham.' He inclined his head towards the captain. 'One of us will always be around.' He paused. His eyes swept the room. 'Any questions?'

None were forthcoming. 'Good. After your meal, please go to your anteroom where I will bring the instructors, officers and sergeants, and introduce them to you, describing their specialities. Thank you for your patience. Enjoy your meal.'

'C'mon, Harland!' The sergeant's voice cut sharply through the pouring rain. Gabrielle reached the sergeant standing by the side of the quagmire of a path which cut across the lower slopes of the mountain. He fell in alongside her. 'Keep Jenkins in sight. Crossing the Pyrenees into Spain you wouldn't want to lose sight of your guide.'

Gabrielle, her chest heaving from the exertion of reaching this height, where the path skirted round the side of overhanging cliffs, nodded and tried to quicken her pace. This was an individual exercise at the end of the 'get fit' period. Only three of them were on the mountain; Sergeant Jenkins, who was acting as hare; Gabrielle; and the sergeant beside her, the cajoler, assessor and judge of her capabilities at the end of this part of her training.

It had been a gruelling two weeks. Hard grind of physical training designed to test every muscle in the body and increase stamina before moving into the open with cross-country runs increasing in distance every day for a week, followed in the second week by stiffer tests, in full kit with pack, across rough terrain and going higher and higher on the mountain. They had been above the snow line and today were destined to do the same. The temperature was dropping and this unceasing rain could easily turn to snow, especially when they got higher.

She pressed on, slipping and sliding in the mud but

determined to keep Jenkins in sight. She needed to close the gap, for the rain was thickening, threatening to obscure the man in front. If it turned to snow she would have to be nearer still in case of a white-out.

Gabrielle's muscles were beginning to ache. The rain lashed harder, stinging her face and beating a tattoo on her waterproofs. What foolhardy decision had brought her to such a situation when she could still have been cosy at Bletchley Park?

It was 3 May. The date struck her as she tried to take her mind off the trials and discomforts of her present position. The day Jean had said she was going to meet Colin in London. She would be sitting comfortably on a train heading south. Lucky, sensible girl!

Chapter Seventeen

1942

Jean settled herself in the train. She felt the satisfactory tingle of excitement at seven days' leave with Colin, based at their own special hotel where they had spent those wonderful days of first physical love.

'Lucky you, going on leave,' said Liz, as she met Colin coming out of the mess.

'Yes.' He grinned. 'Seven glorious days.'

'London? Same hotel?'

'Sure is.' Colin's grin broadened and he gave her a knowing wink.

'Give my love to Jean.'

'Will do,' he said breezily. 'Going to be a bit later than expected, though. Just been told Tubby's in SQ with a heavy cold, unfit to fly, so I'm to take his place on this afternoon's Circus.'

'Take care.'

'I will – extra care knowing Jean will be waiting for me. See you.'

She watched him hurry away with a light step. He was well thought of in the squadron, a first-class pilot who was always willing to pass on his knowledge to the newcomers. She was pleased that his relationship with Jean had never wavered. They made a good couple.

The sky was clear. The squadrons from Biggin Hill were flying at 25,000 feet, giving high cover to the American-built Boston light bombers whose mission was to strike at airfields, marshalling yards and power stations in France. Other escorting fighters were stepped up to 20,000 feet in a planned arrangement to give maximum cover to the bombers and at the same time prepared to do battle with any German fighters, luring them into the sky when the imminent attack had been plotted.

They headed out over the Channel, Colin positioned to the left of his leader. Ever watchful, he scanned the sky. No sign of the enemy. Maybe they would not be drawn into combat today. It was a glorious day for flying. His heart sang with the sheer joy of it. If the Luftwaffe spoiled it, so be it, he would match them man for man, but at the moment he would revel in the delight of flying in his beloved Spitfire. He glanced at the photograph of a smiling Jean on the side of the cockpit. He winked at her and silently mouthed the words 'Love you'.

Vapour trails began to stream out behind them. The leader took his squadron down until the telltale signs disappeared.

As they crossed the French coast, the radiotelephone crackled in his ears.

'Hello, Cartwheel, bandits in your area.' The sector commander's voice came clear from base. The radar had picked up the enemy fighters.

'Thanks,' the leader acknowledged and, although he knew his pilots would have heard the message, he put in his own word of alerted caution, 'Eyes peeled, everyone.'

Colin's nerves tingled. He kept up his meticulous scan of the sky, hoping that his rear was being protected. A touch of white some distance off caught his eye. Someone had left the merest touch of a vapour trail, must have realised it and lost height. But it had been sufficient for Colin. He focused his eyes on the distance, trying to see who had made it. There! Ten Me-109s swinging round in a curve to get behind the British fighters.

'Hello, Cartwheel, bandits, five o'clock, slightly above, four miles.' Colin's words were precise, given without any strain of anxiety, but his palms were sticky, his forehead marked with beads of sweat, and his stomach had butterflies.

There was a slight pause before his observation was acknowledged.

'Right, Colin, got them. Hold tight, everybody. Stay. Wait for it, wait for it!' The leader's restraint was crisp. He was in full control, judging the position of the enemy, waiting for the moment to put themselves in the most advantageous position.

Colin made a quick check – reflector sight on, gun button in the firing position. He was tense, waiting for the next order.

It came sharp and clear, introduced by a moment of preparation. 'OK, everyone, ready . . . Now, break!'

Colin saw his leader throw his plane into a steep turn, and followed instantaneously. They swept round together, straightened, and then planes seemed to be chasing one another all over the sky, guns chattering. Colin saw a German ahead on the tail of a Spitfire. He swung his plane round, caught the Me in his sight, pressed the gun button. Eight Brownings spat destruction. Colin saw his bullets hit. Smoke burst from the Me. It broke off its attack. Colin followed it, gave it another burst and broke away as the German's wing disintegrated and the plane went into a spiral towards the earth. Colin caught a glimpse of a parachute and was thankful that the pilot had escaped.

He started to turn, looking to get back into the fight.

'Colin, look out!'

He had no time to react to the warning. The cacophony of sound was shattering. Bullets tore through metal. The instrument panel exploded around him. The aircraft jerked as if the engine had been dynamited. Black and white smoke poured into the cockpit, then tongues of flame licked at him. His muscles strained to prevent the aircraft from going into a dive.

'Bale out! Bale out and let her go!' The words pounded at his mind. He reached for the canopy release and pulled at it. Nothing happened! He pulled harder. It refused to move. Panic gripped him. He fought hard to free the control. The plane dropped its nose. The flames engulfed the cockpit. Colin instinctively flung his arms across his face, then, in a desperate effort to extricate himself, pulled hard on the control column. It was no use. The plane did not respond. The dive steepened. The Spitfire plunged towards the soil of France.

Colin, his face contorted with pain and horror, screamed, 'Jean!' The ground rushed towards him. 'Jean, I love—'

Jean hummed quietly to herself. She had unpacked her things for the week but had decided to stay in uniform for Colin's arrival. He had always liked them to be seen that way when they dined together the first night. She had bathed since arriving at the hotel and was dressing to await Colin's arrival. She sat on the side of the bed and carefully rolled her silk stockings on to her legs. She stepped into her tight-fitting blue skirt and tucked her blue shirt into the top. Her black low-heeled shoes were highly polished and after fastening the laces she went to the mirror where she knotted a black tie around her neck and adjusted the collar of her shirt. She glanced in the mirror, this way and that and, satisfied, turned her attention to a final flick of her hair.

All the time she hummed Bing Crosby's hit 'Only Forever' in happy anticipation of Colin's arrival and the week they would spend together.

> 'Do you think I'll remember
> How you looked when you smiled?
> Only forever,
> That's putting it mild.'

The words formed as she hummed. She could see his face now with that cheeky, loving grin which he kept only for her.

She glanced at her watch and frowned. He was a little late, but they really had no set time for meeting, it depended on the demands of the RAF. Still, it was generally about teatime.

She looked at herself again in the mirror and adjusted a wisp of hair which seemed determined to be unruly. She turned to the bed on which she had laid her uniform jacket and brushed an imaginary speck of dust from it. She fidgeted, unable to settle, anticipating Colin's arrival.

Five minutes seemed an eternity. A knock on the door brought her turning sharply to rush across the room. She flung the door open.

'Col—' The word died on her lips. Her broad, welcoming smile, so full of love and pleasure, vanished in an instant when she saw Liz standing there. 'Liz?' she gasped, the unspoken query of 'What are you doing here?' behind her intonation. For a moment the scene seemed to be frozen. Then Jean, staring disbelievingly at Liz, backed slowly away from the door. Her face drained of all colour.

Liz stepped into the room and closed the door, all the time looking at her friend with a sorrowing expression of 'I wish I wasn't the bearer of this news'.

'Colin?' The word came as a hoarse whisper from Jean.

'I'm afraid he won't be coming,' replied Liz quietly. 'I'm sorry . . .'

'Why? What?' A desperate demand for answers came with her questions.

'The squadron went on escort duty this afternoon.'

'But he told me he wouldn't be flying today.'

'He shouldn't have been, but one of the pilots went sick and Colin took his place.'

382

'Oh, no!' The long sigh changed to anxiety as she pressed. 'But he's all right, isn't he?' Her eyes widened, willing the right answer from Liz.

Liz swallowed. 'I'm sorry. He was shot down over France.'

'But he baled out?' Her cry of hope was like an arrow to Liz's heart. How she wished she could say yes!

She shook her head. 'One of our pilots followed him down. Colin did not get out. He perished with his plane.'

'No!' The cry resounded from her very soul. She sank on to the bed. This hadn't happened. Not to her Colin. There must be some mistake. It wasn't him. He must have landed somewhere else. But when Liz sat on the bed beside her and took her hands and said, 'I'm so sorry', she knew it was true. She turned and looked at her with eyes damp with sad tears. 'I loved him so much.' The words jerked in her throat.

'I know, love, I know. And he loved you just the same.' Liz put a comforting arm round her shoulder. 'And I'll miss him too.' Jean sank against her and they shared tears. Liz couldn't imagine Biggin Hill without Colin's friendly presence and she knew that life at Robin Hood's Bay was never going to be the same.

Jean sobbed the immediate pain away and neither spoke until she straightened.

Jean took a handkerchief from her sleeve, wiped her red-rimmed eyes and blew her nose. They shared an understanding silence until Liz felt she could speak.

'Colin knew the risk and didn't shrink from it. So did you and you were prepared to face it, no matter what the outcome. Because you did so together, you gained a strength which would help if the worst happened. Because of the strong love between you, you will cope, come to terms with the loss and go on into a bright future because you know that is what Colin would want you to do.'

Jean nodded again, swallowed hard and drew a deep breath. 'I know,' she said quietly.

Liz smiled lovingly at her and drew her into a cocoon of understanding sympathy.

Jean returned a wan smile and said, 'Thanks for coming. It wouldn't be easy for you.'

'I couldn't leave you here wondering. After all, the official notification will go to his parents.'

'You're a true friend, Liz.' Jean stood up, straightening her shirt and skirt with a firm grip as if she had made up her mind to take her future in hand right away. 'When have you got to be back?'

'Would you like me to stay the night?' She answered question with question.

Jean's face brightened. The one thing she had been dreading, though she hid it from Liz, was staying alone in this room which had meant so much to her and Colin. 'Oh, yes, please.'

'I arranged it so I could. What will you do with the rest of your leave? Do you want to come to the White Hart?'

Jean shook her head. 'Too many memories,' she replied quietly with a catch in her throat.

'I understand. So?'

Jean pursed her lips thoughtfully. 'I think I'll go back to my bomber boys, forgo my leave or most of it. May take a day or a couple of days and go to see Martin in Grimsby.'

'Might be a good idea to get back into the swing of things as soon as possible,' Liz agreed. 'And if you see Martin, give him my love.'

'I will.'

'Don't forget, if ever you need me . . .'

'I won't,' replied Jean appreciatively.

'You may not feel like eating much but I think you ought to have something.'

'Right, nurse,' she said, forcing a smile, and picked up her jacket.

Jean gazed out of the carriage window as the train rattled north. Only twenty-four hours ago she had been heading south, her world full of joy in anticipation of seven days with Colin. Now that world was destroyed for ever.

In the small hours of the night she had lain awake and let silent tears fall. Her mind, full of Colin and the times they had spent together, seemed to pick up a message from him, a message of hope for the future, willing her to go on. A voice in the night struck at her heart: 'Mourn for me little but never forget me.' In the darkness she had silently mouthed the words, 'I won't, my love.'

In this frame of mind she resolved to face the heart-aches of a bomber station but she determined never to get intimately involved with a flier again. First Scotty, now Colin – she must be jinxed. Any aircrew who got close to her was doomed. She must not cast the spell of death on anyone ever again.

Jean had left London early so there was still some daylight when she reached Waddington. As she walked into the airfield, she had a strong sense of coming home.

Here she would find the strength to see her through days when she knew she would feel the loss of Colin so much it could break her heart. But she would not succumb, Colin wouldn't want her to, and she realised that, as part of a squadron, she would find great comfort in the companionship. Here were friends from whom she could draw strength and in their escapades in the mess, in their parties and drinking sessions, they would endeavour to ease her pain.

Before going to her billet, she walked to the edge of the airfield. No wind stirred the grass, the windsock hung limp on its pole beside the control tower. The black fingers of the runways stretched into the distance. A hush hung over the Lincolnshire landscape as if it was drawing in a subtle peace even on the brink of an upheaval which would plunge it back into the war. The black shapes of the Lancasters stood silent. There was no movement anywhere. The stillness was charged with expectancy. She stood drinking in the atmosphere.

She heard a door open and looked in the direction of the noise. It was the door of the briefing hut. Someone appeared, stopped, turned and called out. Jean could not catch the words, the figure was too far away, but she could guess what they were as figure after figure, dressed for flying, carrying equipment and parachutes, appeared and walked ungainly in their boots to waiting wagons.

Life had come back to the airfield, but it was the life of war.

As the aircrews climbed into the transports to take them to their aircraft, she caught their exchanges.

'See you tomorrow.'

'Saracen's Head?'

'Sure.'

'Leave tomorrow, Johnny?'

'Seven days!'

'Which WAAF this time?'

'That'd be telling.'

Jean shivered. They went innocently, unflinchingly, to a fate which might be the same as Colin's.

An engine started, then another and another. The transports moved off, picking up speed as they motored round the perimeter track towards waiting aircraft. Two crews whose Lancasters were nearby walked to their planes, drawing reassurances from their closeness. She watched them reach the aircraft and saw them making their inspections. The pilot was checking ailerons, rudders, undercarriage and every other item on his list before taking over the aircraft officially from the groundcrew. The bomb aimer moved under the belly of the aircraft where the open bomb doors enabled him to assess that the bomb load was in order. The gunners made sure their guns were uncovered. Satisfied, the crew climbed on board, where Jean knew they would be stowing their parachutes and meticulously checking their equipment and instruments.

A splutter rose to a roar and was joined by others around the airfield as pilots and engineers checked their engines. The air was filled with a pulsating crescendo until one by one the engines fell silent, but it was a silence charged with tension.

All around the airfield, crews had left their aircraft, each with their own thoughts. Some laughed jocularly, others chatted to take their minds off the events into which they would soon be pitched; yet others stood silent, thinking of loved ones or the date they had tomorrow night if they were not flying again. And all kept looking at their watches. Zero hour was approaching.

The first positive movement came towards the open door in the side of the Lancasters. Jean stiffened. The time had come. The crews clambered on board and a few moments later an engine shattered the uneasy peace.

One by one engines sprang into life across the airfield until it seemed to shake with power. They quietened to a steady drone and the Lancasters moved into a queue on the perimeter track heading slowly towards the runway in use.

The first Lancaster paused. A green light flashed from the control truck at the end of the runway. It turned on to the long black finger. The light flashed again. The engines roared as they were opened up. The pilot held his aircraft on the brakes until the necessary power for takeoff was reached. Released of its restraint, the Lancaster rolled forwards and moved into full-throated power as it gathered momentum down the runway until the pilot eased it into the air.

The second Lancaster had already turned on to the runway and, at the signal from the control truck, followed the first.

Across the airfield Jean stood watching the big black shapes leave the ground and follow the procedure laid down to climb steadily away towards an unknown fate. The numbers lessened, the noise abated until the last one took off and started a climbing turn on to the prearranged heading for Germany, its engine noise fading into the distance. Once more the airfield was silent.

Jean sighed, said a prayer for 'her crews', picked up her bag and went to the mess.

The dining room was empty. She helped herself to some food, which awaited the arrival of the ground staff, then went to one of the tables and sat down. Unseeingly she looked at her plate as the weariness of great loss suddenly hit her.

The sound of voices approaching jerked her back to reality. She hurriedly tried to straighten her shoulders and wipe the telltale dampness from her eyes, but she was not quick enough.

George Sugden's step faltered and his chatter with Wendy Carter stopped when he saw Jean. He exchanged glances with the WAAF admin officer and they both went straight to her.

'What are you doing here? Thought you were on leave?' he asked with puzzled concern, as he and Wendy sat down, one on each side of her. They sensed something terrible must have happened. Jean had gone on leave in such a mood of exuberance that nothing short of tragedy would have brought her back.

She glanced pathetically at each of them. Before she could answer, George said, 'Colin?'

'Yes.' Her voice was hoarse.

'Missing?'

She bit her lips and blinked her eyes. She must not cry. Other officers were coming in. She shook her head slowly. 'No.'

'Oh, my dear, I'm so sorry.' George felt he wanted to reach out as a father to help this young girl.

Wendy was too shocked to speak but she reached out

and took Jean's hand. 'But your leave? Wouldn't you like to go home?'

Jean found herself pouring out her whole story to sympathetic listeners. 'So you see,' she concluded, 'I really have no one to turn to. But here I've found companionship and understanding and a host of friends, especially among "my boys". Waddington and 44 are home to me.' She glanced at them apologetically. 'I'm sorry. I'm spoiling your meal with all my troubles.'

'Not at all,' Wendy reassured her. 'We're only too pleased to listen. It'll have done you good.'

Jean gave a small smile. 'You know, I think it has.'

'Still take that leave if you want to,' suggested George.

'Thanks, George, but I think I'd be better working.' She paused momentarily. 'Oh, wait a minute. I just might take a couple of days off to go and see my brother Martin. He's with Air-Sea Rescue in Grimsby.'

'Do that. It will do you good.'

Gabrielle was on her way to her room to freshen up after a lecture on weapons training when she picked up her mail. Two letters – she glanced at the writing – one from Dad and one from Jean. Pleased, she hurried up the stairs.

By the time the door of her room clicked shut behind her, she was flopping on her back on her bed. She held a letter in each hand. First she ripped open the one from her father.

Dearest Gabrielle,
How do I begin this letter? How can I break terrible news gently? I can find no way. Colin was killed . . .

Gabrielle stared at the words. They couldn't be true. But there they were in blue ink, stark on the page, with only one meaning. Her body went cold. Colin dead! 'Oh, no!' The cry in whispered tone expressed all the hurt which gripped her. She swung herself up slowly, sat on the edge of the bed and continued to read.

Colin was killed – shot down over France yesterday. There is no hope. No one saw him bale out and one of the other pilots saw him crash.

We are devastated. It is going to be difficult to come to terms with the loss but we shall have to cope even though it won't be easy. We wish you were near. Any chance of some leave? Your mother would love to see you, as I would.

I know you will feel the loss as much as we do. You were close. I know there is nothing I can say which will ease the pain for you, but remember we are always here if you need us. We love you very much and look forward to the day when this tragic war is over and you are back with us.

Take care of yourself. You are very precious.

All our love,
Dad

Gabrielle sat staring at the letter. How difficult it must have been for her father to write! It would have given him a lot of heartache. She knew how much the loss of Colin would hurt. He and Colin had been much more than father and son, they were friends, and she knew that he had dreamed of his son taking over a successful business after they had finished running it together. Now he probably saw no reason to carry it on except to keep himself occupied.

Suddenly she started. 'Oh, my God, Jean!' She ripped open Jean's letter.

My dearest friend,

You will probably already know the terrible news that Colin is dead.

What can I say to ease your pain when mine is as bad? The only way that I can see to bear this tragedy is to immerse ourselves in what we are doing. That is what I am trying to do. As you know, Colin and I were to spend seven days' leave together. I was at the hotel when Liz brought the terrible news. It was sweet of her to do so rather than let me hear some other way, but it must have been hard for her. She stayed with me the night and then I came back to Waddington. It is my home now and my life is here with my bomber crews. I wish you had such a fine bunch to help you in this trying time.

I would love to see you if ever you get the chance to be this way. I would say that I might get over to Windermere to see you but I want to be here. Being among aircrew I feel nearer to Colin. I hope you understand.

You are in my prayers.

Love,

Jean

Numbed by the news, Gabrielle laid the two letters down. Reality and disbelief mingled as she got ready to go to lunch. She must go, otherwise she would be missed and someone might come looking for her. And straight after lunch she would begin practical arms training. As she washed, she wondered about that training, and about the whole course.

Should she resign? Was it fair to her father and mother to run the high risks that might lie ahead, risks from which she might not return? With the loss of Colin, did she owe it to them to move back into a comparatively safe job? Her mind was in torment. More than ever she desired a more active role – a chance to hit back at the enemy who had killed Colin.

She could not turn back. If she met the same fate as her brother, she hoped her father and mother would understand.

Still hurting inside, as she knew she would for a long time, Gabrielle went to lunch.

Chapter Eighteen

1942–43

Jean took three days of her leave. The first she spent writing letters to Gabrielle and to Colin's mother and father, plus one of thanks to Liz. She contacted Martin on the phone and arranged to see him at Cleethorpes the next day, arriving there by train at noon.

He was at the station to meet her. As she walked to meet him she felt a flush of pride at seeing his tall, upright figure, smart in his uniform. Life in the service had taken him sharply into adulthood and given him an air of self-confidence.

He opened his arms to her and she was reassured to feel the brotherly love as he held her tight.

'It's good to see you, sis.' He released her to look more closely with an appraising eye. 'Shouldn't I be saluting you?' he added with a twinkle in his eye.

'Get on with you!' She gave him a smile and hugged him again. 'You look well.'

'I am. This life suits me.' Concern banished the brightness. 'How are you? When you gave me that awful news over the phone, I just wanted to be there to help you.'

'Thanks, Martin.'

'I'm glad you're here now. Let's go and get something to eat, and then maybe walk before you have to go back. What time's your train?'

'Five.'

They found the Queen Alexandra Dining Room serving a midday meal and as they waited for the soup to be served, Jean looked seriously at her brother. 'Martin, you're my only contact with home. Please keep in touch always.'

'Of course I will, sis.' He sensed a yearning in her for the security of knowing there was a loving base to which she could turn. 'You miss Mum?'

'Oh, yes,' she replied with heartfelt sincerity, revealing that she wished she had her mother to turn to at this time of terrible loss.

'You've had no word from Dad?'

'None, not even when Mum died.'

'He certainly should have written then and he could have done so now. He must know. News like this would soon be known all over Robin Hood's Bay.'

Jean shrugged her shoulders and grimaced with resigned acceptance that her father still held a grudge.

'Stupid man,' said Martin with disgust. 'He wants some sense knocking into him.'

'Martin, you are in touch with him?' she asked.

'Yes, and I'll certainly tell him off for not writing to you.'

'Please don't. It'll only cause more trouble. It might

even lead to breaking the link you have. I wouldn't want that. Some day everything may come right.'

Martin looked doubtful but after a moment's consideration said, 'If that's what you want.'

'It is. How was he the last time you were in touch?'

'Well. He misses Mum. He's wrapped up in his job with the coastguard, so I'm pleased about that. But he's a lonely man – and that's his own fault.'

They were enjoying steak pie when Jean brought up the subject of Liz.

'How was she when you saw her in London?' Martin asked.

Jean detected more than a passing interest.

'She was in good spirits. Sad about Colin, of course. She'll miss him being around. She sends her love.' She looked keenly at her brother. 'You and her?'

He gave a little smile, knowing what was behind the question. 'We're in touch.'

'Nothing more?'

'We have an understanding.'

'Wait until after the war, for it may change your attitudes?'

'Yes, but we remain very good friends.'

'I believe you both feel more than that.'

'Maybe. Well, I know I do. I think my feelings for her have strengthened but I'm not so sure about hers. After all, she's among a lot of glamour boys.'

Jean smiled. 'You think that makes a difference?'

'It could. I thought it had.' He went on to tell her about Alec.

'If there ever was anything between them, I think it's

gone. She never mentioned him to me and I think she would have if she was serious about him. But, you know, Martin, you should tell her how you really feel. Arrange to meet her in London.'

'I'll think about it.'

'Don't waste time, love. Colin and I didn't and I'll never regret it.'

'But you've a whole life before you. You can't live on memories alone. You should find someone else. I'm sure Colin would want you to, and you'll meet plenty of attractive men in your squadron.'

Jean gave a wry smile. 'I'll not get involved seriously with a flier again.'

She was reminded of that ten days later when a package arrived for her by post. Curious, she found the contents were two notebooks accompanied by a letter from Colin's father. She had received a letter of sympathy immediately after Colin's death, so she wondered what this was about. She read:

15 May 1942

Dear Jean,

We have received Colin's effects from the adjutant at Biggin Hill. Among them were these two loose-leaf books which we were told about by Gabrielle on Colin's death. Apparently he had mentioned to her that if anything happened to him, and his effects were sent to me, I was to send these notebooks to you unopened and unread because they were for you and you alone. I forward them to you as he requested.

We hope you are well and that your work helps you in your loss. You know we would love to see you if ever you are in Robin Hood's Bay, but we know it is difficult for you to come. I am sorry if anything I have done in the past has caused the rift between you and your father, but I assure you that what happened so long ago was not intentional on my part.

Incidentally, your father looks well, but I think he's a lonely man. I bumped into him a couple of days ago. He gave me the cold shoulder, then stopped after he had passed me and called out, 'Sorry about your loss.' I turned but he had gone on his way. I hoped that it signalled a breaking of his stubborn enmity but, alas, it was not to be. If it had been, then something good might have come from Colin's death.

We had hoped that Gabrielle might have got some leave under the circumstances but she said it was impossible. The course she is taking is very important and nothing should break its continuity.

Our best wishes and love,

Sam Harland

The last paragraph caught her eye again and she was puzzled. It seemed strange that Gabrielle could not get some leave at this time. She had never known a training course that demanded such continuity from one of its instructors, since there was always someone else who could fill in if circumstances demanded it. But she supposed Gabrielle knew what she was doing. She turned her attention to the books.

They were marked 1 and 2. She opened the first at the

first page and drew a sharp breath when she saw Colin's writing.

The Diary of Colin Harland, RAF

I have kept this diary of my life and feelings from the first day I joined the RAF so that my beloved Jean can share all my experiences and miss nothing of my life. Hopefully they will be handed over by myself at the end of the war, but whenever they do come to her, they come with my undying love. If I should not hand them over, Jean, weep not for me but remember me and the love we shared, for it made me deliriously happy.

Colin

Jean could not prevent the quiet tears which flowed for a few seconds until she recomposed herself. For a moment she had a dread of reading these notebooks, for she felt sure it would bring heartache. But she knew Colin had not intended that. She idly turned a few pages, reading a few words here and there. Then, wondering when the last entry had been made, she turned to it in the second book. It was dated the day before he died.

3 May 1942

Today was another good day for flying, sharp and crisp and clear. Another Circus escorting Stirlings attacking marshalling yards in France.

The German fighters came up and there was a swift engagement. I got a burst in but the Me escaped. All our aircraft returned safely, one pilot reporting a kill and two others probables.

The fight over, I saw no one to form on to for the flight back to Biggin Hill. I was high, 25,000 feet, the sky was blue, the engine purring nicely. I climbed higher in the sheer ecstasy of flying, of being alone in a wide expanse that stretched to infinity and beyond. I began to feel that my Spitfire no longer held me there but that I was borne up by some superior power, taken to see the sheer beauty of the space around me and see the futility of war. It was as if I was being shown some meaning to life, that we were on earth to achieve this goal if we wanted it. I felt I had touched the hand of God and that our love, Jean, was blessed by Him.

I love you and tomorrow we will be together and I will be able to share this new experience with you.

The entry ended. Jean was moved. She sat staring at the words and loved Colin all the more, and her eyes dampened at the thought of that meeting which never took place. She laid the books aside. She could take no more now. They were for the future when, with the passage of time, previous recollections would cause less pain.

Jean threw herself wholeheartedly into the life of the squadron and found that her work and the contact with aircrew helped her to come to terms with life.

As the year moved on, life assumed a routine which was only marred by crews succumbing to anti-aircraft fire, fighter activity or tragic accidents while training. Although she was saddened when familiar faces were no longer there, her feelings for others helped her bear her personal loss.

She began to enjoy the parties again, realising that she

could not stand aside. They were part of aircrews' lives and she knew that in joining in she gave some measure of comfort to men who might face death the next day. But she was careful with her own feelings. She did not want to experience again the hurt which had come with losing someone with whom she had a close relationship. Besides, she had it in her mind that she was a jinx – first Scotty, then Colin. She wanted no one else on her conscience.

Whenever she had leave she met Liz or Martin, but was a little hurt that Gabrielle always seemed to make some excuse when she suggested they meet or that she visit her in Windermere. Jean had hoped that Gabrielle would be able to manage a few days off at New Year, so that they might see 1943 arrive together.

She did not know that on New Year's Eve Gabrielle was crawling across a Scottish mountainside to blow up a mock target.

Gabrielle's training had continued throughout the year. She had learned to live off the countryside, to handle high explosives, to fire all sorts of weapons, kept up and improved her efficiency with Morse code, learned to recognise faults in transmitters and repair them. She was taught unarmed combat, how to deal with interrogators, how to pick locks. She mastered the art of disguise, and learned the customs of the people among whom she would be living when she was in France.

The course was tough, the instructors unrelenting; nobody was given any quarter. There were times when her body ached, when her mind was numb with application, when she felt she could absorb no more, physically or mentally. But determination drove her on. They had been warned that they might be killed in action, captured and tortured by the Gestapo, or sent to concentration camps or the gas chambers. But she refused to contemplate such a possibility.

During the third week in May, ten of the course, their training complete to the demanding standards required, were sent to RAF Ringway, Manchester, for parachute training. Gabrielle was among them, a little apprehensive. Her doubts still lingered even after the intensive sessions in the gym learning to fall and roll from a vaulting horse on to coconut matting. She found it difficult to coordinate the movements: tuck the head well in, keep the chin on chest, absorb the shock so that it transferred naturally along the side of the leg, the thigh, the shoulder and back, no matter whether it was a left-side roll, a backward roll or a right-side roll. Having mastered it, she went to her first jump.

She climbed into a basket suspended from a balloon and rose slowly in the still air to 800 feet. Her tension led her to notice the eerie silence as if it was anticipating the worst possible happening. She glanced over the side. The ground didn't look far enough away – the parachute wouldn't open in time. 'Why don't we go higher?' she wanted to ask the instructor. He gave her a broad smile as if to say, 'I've seen it all before. Everyone's like you on their first jump even though they try to put on a nonchalant attitude.'

He indicated a hook in the framework above their heads. Gabrielle looked up and clipped her static line to it. Satisfied with his examination, the instructor nodded towards the single iron bar which acted as a barrier. Gabrielle shuffled over and stood in front of it. She swallowed hard and concentrated, everything she should do rushing into her mind. She saw a hand reach out and remove the bar. A voice shouted in her ear, 'Go!'

Hesitation. Then she stepped into space. 'My God, it's not opening!' A tug. She was swinging slightly, falling steadily. Gabrielle looked up and felt a great surge of relief at the sight of the white canopy billowing above her.

'Correct landing position!'

Someone was shouting. Where?

'Correct landing position!'

There was more urgency in the shout and Gabrielle realised it was meant for her. She glanced down. A sergeant with a megaphone. The ground was near. Rushing at her. 'Feet! Bloody hell! Get 'em together!'

Everything she had been taught assailed her mind. Instinctively her feet came together. She braced herself ready to roll, to transfer weight, but the instructions from her mind were too late. She was down, crash, bang, bump. The parachute floated around here. She gasped back the breath which had been driven from her. A little dazed, she started to struggle to her feet. Then exhilaration surged in her. She had done it! She had jumped!

The sergeant was beside her. 'Well done, but a bloody messy jump.' He grinned at the disappointment on her face. 'But you'll be all right,' he added with a nod of approval.

After four more jumps Gabrielle felt easier and was almost looking forward to jumping from an aircraft; at least there would be more height, more time to prepare for the landing. But that enthusiasm was dented when she and those who were to jump on the same flight were given instructions about leaving the aircraft.

403

'You leave through a hole in the floor. Your static line is clipped to a fixture on the aircraft. You must drop through the hole in a straight, stiff attention position. Failure to do so might result in your getting tangled in your shroud lines with disastrous results – falling all trussed up or being towed behind the aircraft at a hundred miles per hour. So remember, attention! Now, getting into position. You are sitting on the floor of the aircraft near the hole. Red light comes on. Shuffle to the hole and sit alongside it. Green light comes on. Swing your legs over the hole. I'll shout "Go!" and when I do, bloody well go. Don't forget at that point, *attention*!'

All these instructions streamed through Gabrielle's mind as the plane climbed higher and higher. No one spoke. Some gave a sheepish grin if they caught a glance from someone else. Gabrielle was the first to go.

Once the green light shone, everything happened very quickly. After feeling a tug, she found herself floating gently in space, dropping steadily towards the green below. She landed successfully, winning praise from the sergeant on the ground.

She recognised him as the man who had been on duty when she had made her first jump from the balloon. And he recognised her.

He smiled. 'Good jump! I told you you'd be OK.'

Gabrielle was pleased, and was even more so when, after six more jumps, she was passed as proficient in parachute jumping. Her course completed, she was now ready to be employed in whatever SOE operations were required.

That came on 2 June, when she was directed under her code name Yvette to link up with an Englishman, code named Girard, who was organising an active Resistance group west of Dijon. She thought it ironic that after all her parachute training she was to be flown in by Lysander and not dropped by parachute, but the nature of the operation, with special transmitting equipment to be taken, made it necessary.

The night was dark with high cloud. Takeoff was on time and the pilot judged his speed to coincide with the expected time of arrival over the landing field in France. Near the site, he lost height to 500 feet and both he and his passenger strained to catch a glimpse of the expected signal. He flew over the area, banked and came back. Nothing but blackness. He flew on, then turned on to his original heading.

'There!' Gabrielle shouted at the sight of a flash from the edge of a wood on their starboard side.

The pilot dipped a wing and saw it himself. He straightened on to level flight and gunned his engine twice, his signal that he had identified the watchers below. He circled and in a matter of moments was landing between torchlights held by two rows of men marking the landing area. As soon as he had stopped, the door was flung open and a tall man wearing a beret was reaching up to help Gabrielle out.

'Welcome, Yvette,' he said quietly in perfect English.

She knew him to be Girard, the man with whom she was to work, for only he and the man she was replacing would know her code name. 'Thanks,' she said.

She glanced around. A dozen men were swarming round the plane, eagerly unloading it and taking the equipment away into the wood.

Girard turned to a man beside him. He held out his hand. 'Goodbye and thanks for all you've done. Don't forget the messages.'

'I won't.'

They shook hands. The stranger patted Gabrielle on the shoulder – a well-wishing touch – and climbed aboard the Lysander.

The plane was unloaded without any delay. Figures and goods disappeared into the wood. Satisfied, Girard waved to the pilot.

'Come.' He started for the wood at a brisk pace and Gabrielle followed. In the protection of the trees he stopped and together they watched the Lysander take off into the night sky.

'This way.' Girard turned and, with Gabrielle following, threaded his way between the trees.

There was no sign of anyone, nor of the goods from the plane. Gabrielle curbed her desire to ask questions.

They reached the far side of the wood and stopped, still under cover. A road ran alongside the trees.

'Wait here,' he whispered and slid away from her.

She lost sight of his shadowy figure. Even though all her senses became finely tuned to the situation around her, she still received a surprise when Girard emerged from the gloom close to her. She had had no indication of his approach.

'All clear,' he whispered. 'German troops use this road occasionally.'

They crossed the road quickly and moved across a field, keeping close to the hedge. They negotiated several fields this way, Girard moving at a fast pace. Gabrielle, thankful now for the testing training in Scotland, found no difficulty in keeping up with him. After about an hour he stopped and indicated a rise in the land ahead.

'Vézelay,' he said. 'Our base. Good position on the hilltop. Gives us good views of the surrounding country-side, especially from the tower of the basilica of La Madeleine. We shall be reporting any German troop movements and I'm organising the Resistance in the area, ready to take action once the Allies make their invasion. There are a few Germans stationed in the village. In their usual way they've overlooked the importance of this village as an observation point. Militarily it lies on an obvious route for a sweep into Vichy France and on a route to Lorraine and Alsace and the southern Rhine. So any movements in this area are of importance to the powers back home.'

His information was delivered crisply but his voice was soft. Gabrielle sensed that she was in the presence of a gentle man and she became curious how he came to be taking part in such dangerous activities. But more than that, she was interested to see him in the light, for the only distinguishing features she had been able to make out in the dark was his height – six foot two, if she judged correctly – his athletic build, and an outline of classical forehead, nose, mouth and chin which made her feel that he would be a fine-looking man.

'Any questions before we move on?' he asked.

'Curfew? How do we get—'

Girard interrupted her with a little chuckle. 'The few troops there are, about twelve of them and their officer, are a lackadaisical lot. You know how it is, they get into a routine, with a feeling that they've been forgotten in the war and so they drift into an easy time. When we're active we see that they have entertainment to keep them occupied – we've got enough girls willing to help us this way. They're being entertained tonight. All the men you saw at the landing will be safely back in their homes by now, the rifles and ammunition stored away, your equipment at Madame Cossart's.'

'Madame Cossart?'

'That's where you and I live. And we don't have to go into the village. She has a vineyard just outside, away to our right. I pass myself off as Bernard Debray, Madame Cossart's nephew, here because I'm medically unfit, but able to help her in the vineyard because there are few men to do so. The Germans vetted me but she had kept them happy supplying them with wine so they weren't too inquisitive.'

'Debray? That's the name I've been given. Wife or sister?'

There was an amused lilt in his voice when he replied, 'Sister, and I suspect you were briefed that way in England. So, sister Marguerite, let's go and meet your aunt.'

They passed along the edge of some vineyards as they approached a three-storeyed, solid-looking house, each tier with four windows at the front, the topmost being dormers in the roof. Girard circled to the rear, all the time observing and listening carefully. Satisfied, he quickly crossed an open space to the back door.

The door swung open silently. He stepped inside, held the door for Gabrielle, locked it behind her and shot the well-greased bolts without a sound. He found a switch and a dim light came on to reveal a stone-flagged passage. It gave on to a square hall, austerely furnished with a table and a small chest of drawers. On the right-hand side a staircase led upwards. Girard touched another switch and a light illuminated the landing for them to climb the stairs. He turned to the right, knocked on the first door on the left, and opened it on hearing a voice. Gabrielle followed him in.

She found herself in a large room at what she guessed was the front of the house. It was cosy, in contrast to the austerity she had felt when she first entered the house. A fireplace with elaborate surrounds and a large oval mirror dominated one wall. On either side of the fireplace, at right angles to it, were two settees, and facing the fire, so that the whole formed a square, were two large easy chairs. A low table on which there was a cup and saucer and a coffee jug stood in the square. A dark oak table with two high-backed chairs on either side stood against one wall. Another wall held a bookcase and in the fourth was a second door, which was closed. The walls held several landscape paintings in oils.

'Madame Cossart, this is my sister Marguerite.'

'I am pleased to know you, mademoiselle.' There was a twinkle of knowing amusement in Madame Cossart's eyes as she extended a hand to Gabrielle.

'And I you, madame,' returned Gabrielle.

She saw a tall woman who held herself erect, exuding authority. The only relief on her plain grey dress was a marquesite brooch in the shape of a butterfly, pinned above her left breast. A small cream silk scarf was tied at her throat and she wore grey stockings and black court shoes. Her dark hair, greying slightly, was drawn back tight and fastened in a bun at the nape of her neck, adding to the severity of her appearance. But Gabrielle judged this to be a wrong impression. The severe look could be there in an instant when she wanted it, but in the oval face, small nose and small mouth there was gentleness, kindness and understanding. The eyes were a deep blue and shimmered like the sea caught in the sunlight. Behind their penetrating gaze was a shrewd judgement. Gabrielle knew she was being sized up.

'Bernard, go and make some more coffee. There are sandwiches prepared on the kitchen table along with some scones and some cake. I'm sure you are both hungry.' She glanced at Gabrielle. 'I'm sorry it's not more substantial but it was difficult not knowing what time you would be here. However, there is plenty, you'll not go hungry.'

'Thank you, madame.'

'Off with you, Bernard, off!' She waved a dismissive hand at him. 'I'll have a chat to Marguerite.' As he hurried away, Madame Cossart said, 'Take your jacket off and sit down. I'll explain a few things to you and then show you your room.'

'Thank you.' Gabrielle slipped out of her leather jacket, unwound the woollen scarf from around her neck and placed them, with the gloves and beret she had removed on entering the house, on a chair and then sat down opposite Madame Cossart.

'Now, Marguerite.' She leaned forward slightly, her voice soft. 'I know why you're here. I am part of the team by allowing you to use my house, apart from keeping my eye on local happenings. Contrary to what you may hear and see, I have no love for the Germans who are desecrating my beloved land with their presence.' Her eyes hardened. 'The sooner we drive them out, the better, and I'll do anything to further that day.' She paused, and when she resumed, her voice flowed like rippling water. 'Bernard will have explained our assumed relationship.' Gabrielle nodded. 'We must be careful to keep it that way. As I am your aunt, we must be seen together in the village from time to time, and if on those occasions we are approached by Germans, leave most of the talking to me. You see, I'm on good terms with them and there are times when I invite the two officers in charge to dinner. There are villagers who don't like it, they say I shouldn't fraternise, but they don't know the real reason behind it. Keeping the Germans happy makes a perfect front for your operation. Use the garden, walk in the vineyard, but don't stray too far from the house on your own. After all, you are supposed to be visiting your aunt and we haven't seen each other for a considerable time, so naturally we want to spend time together. In the roles of niece and nephew, you and Bernard dine with me. I have a cook, who has been with the family for years, totally reliable. Her hatred of the Germans matches mine, for they took her husband and son away, she knows not where. A girl comes in to clean twice a week, a grandchild of the cook.'

'Any family, madame?'

Madame Cossart gave a small, sad smile. 'Alas, no. I am a widow. My son was killed when the Germans invaded France, and my daughter was taken away by them; they tell me she committed suicide. Whether that's true I can't be absolutely sure, but I think it most likely after the way they threatened her. So I'm alone, trying to maintain as much of a civilised life as I can with hatred in my heart.'

'I'm so sorry,' said Gabrielle softly.

Madame nodded. 'That is war.' She turned to the door when it opened. 'Ah, Bernard, bring it over here.' She indicated the table between the settees.

He pushed the door shut with his foot and carried the tray, laden with cups, saucers, plates, food and coffee, across the room.

Gabrielle watched him, the first time she had really had time to observe him. He was even more handsome than his profile had revealed in the dark. His black hair had a slight wave along the temples, which gave him a debonair look. There was a casual air about him but Gabrielle saw the steel behind it. He had removed his jacket and pullover and was in his shirtsleeves. She judged that there was not an ounce of flesh on his muscular body and sensed a man fanatical to keep it that way. His eyes were dark, alert for the unexpected. They rested on Gabrielle. She caught his look and he smiled to reveal a perfect row of white teeth. She felt they would work well together and she would be comfortable with him.

They chatted while they ate. He was eager for news from England and then he and Madame filled Gabrielle in on the situation locally.

When they had finished, Madame stood up. 'Now, Marguerite, I will show you to your room.' They stepped out on the landing. 'Bernard is at the far end of this corridor –' she pointed to the right – 'on the right-hand side. You, my dear, are up another flight.' She led the way and

412

Bernard followed behind Gabrielle. Reaching the top corridor, she turned to the right and went to the room immediately above Bernard's. 'Easy for you two to communicate being one above the other,' she explained, 'and the extra height will give you better reception when using your wireless.'

Gabrielle found herself in a good-sized room which held a comfortable-looking bed with a bedside table. A dressing table and stool occupied the space below the dormer window and an easy chair fitted into one of the corners. A wardrobe stood on one wall beside a door. 'I think you'll be comfortable here,' Madame said.

'I'm sure I shall. I wasn't expecting such comfort on this assignment.'

'They aren't all like this,' Bernard smiled. 'Some are very rough.'

'Then I'm lucky.'

Madame crossed to the wall beside the wardrobe and pressed it. After a very faint click, a well-camouflaged door opened. 'See in here,' she said.

Gabrielle gasped when she saw another room, small but not the cupboard she had expected. In it was a bench on which the transmitting and receiving set she had brought out from England was already in place beside the old one. The men Bernard had employed had been quick and thorough. A chair was the only other item in the room.

'What more could I want?' she said.

'One more thing,' said Madame and stepped back into the bedroom. 'Keep this door locked. We three and the two men who brought the equipment – trusted men, I may add – are the only ones who know what is here.

Neither the cook nor the granddaughter, who will be cleaning your room, know about it; they don't know the room exists.'

'And you should know about this.' Bernard opened the wardrobe door and felt in the bottom four corners. When he straightened, he pushed the wardrobe with ease so that it covered the entrance to the hidden room.

'Marvellous,' said Gabrielle. 'How was that done?'

'Something I picked up from a joiner back home. He'd been testing ways of making wardrobes easier to move and experimented with this idea of having hidden castors which could be lowered when required. Push the knob in each corner down and the castors take the weight. Pull them up and the legs of the wardrobe settle back on the floor.'

'Ingenious!' said Gabrielle, amazed at the simplicity.

'So you don't want a lot of weight in the wardrobe, but do have some flimsy items or shoes on the floor so that the knobs won't be discovered, though a search is unlikely.'

'Well, I think that is enough initiation for now,' said Madame. 'I think a sleep will do you the world of good. There's a bathroom across the corridor. I'll bid you good night.'

'Thank you, madame. I'm sure I'll be very comfortable here.'

Madame Cossart paused at the door. 'Since we're supposed to be related, you'd better call me Aunt Stéphane as Bernard does.' With that she was gone.

Bernard, his hand on the doorknob, looked back, winked and said, 'Sleep well.'

As she undressed, Gabrielle wondered about him.

414

What was his real name? Where was he from? She knew she would never ask and that in all probability she would never know. As she lay down in bed, she thought of Jean and smiled to herself. If Jean could only see her now, she would not be concerned that her friend was facing a drab war as an instructor.

For three weeks life ran smoothly even amid the tensions of their situation. Ever watchful and alert to anything that might give their real roles away, the three occupants of the house outwardly followed a normal, relaxed life.

Behind the façade Gabrielle regularly sent information gleaned by Bernard and received requests from England on which he acted as quickly as possible. His sources were spread over a wide area and he accumulated vital knowledge of German troop movements and the attitude of Vichy France. Sometimes he was away two or three days and she worried for his safety. Her initial concern was for him as a member of the SOE and her working companion, but as the second week came towards its close she realised that her anxiety was for the man himself. She was drawn to him and she sensed he was seeing her as a woman, not merely as an agent.

He had up to now always worked with male wireless operators, to have a woman beside him was new. He had been doubtful about the change when he had been informed from England but within a couple of days he had realised that she was as efficient and alert as anyone he had worked with before. But as the days progressed and they were thrown more and more into each other's company, he felt the physical attraction becoming intolerable.

One evening at the beginning of the fourth week, after making the regular contact with England, they strolled in the vineyard. The evening was pleasantly warm, a stillness in the air, the birds singing their retiring song, the war far away. Their conversation drifted away from war and they strolled as two lovers might. His fingers brushed hers. They both felt a quiver run through them. They touched again but this time they did not draw apart. Their fingers entwined. Gabrielle experienced an exciting urge. He stopped and turned her to him. Without hesitation he bent and kissed her, moving quickly into a passion which she did not resist. Then suddenly she broke away and glanced round anxiously.

'What is it?' he asked, concern in his voice, alarm in his eyes.

She looked back at him, her eyes expressing a hope that he would understand what she was about to say. 'We shouldn't. If anyone saw us they would be shocked at a passionate kiss between brother and sister.'

'But there's no one . . .'

'Who knows? Eyes are everywhere. Besides, if your training was like mine, you'll have been warned about getting emotionally involved.'

'Yes, but you and me—'

'No buts. You know I'm right.' Her voice was forceful. As much as she wanted to be in this man's arms, to be loved by him, she knew it could prove a fatal attraction. One thing could lead to another and one of those would be the exchange of real names and that would not do. If either of them fell into German hands and was made to talk, information of that sort could be more than useful to the enemy.

416

Bernard shrugged his shoulders in a gesture of reluctant acceptance. 'You're right,' he agreed with a shake of his head. He hesitated a moment, then added, 'I shouldn't have put you in this position. I'm a married man with two young children. I'm sorry.'

Gabrielle reached out and touched his arm in a sympathetic gesture. 'Don't be. I'm flattered that you find me attractive. You miss your wife. I understand.'

The incident was not mentioned again and they resumed the amiable working relationship they had had before, even though they both knew that beneath their calm exterior were passions longing for release.

The following week word came through to Bernard from a small group of the Resistance that German troops were being moved south from the Paris area. He and Gabrielle set out to investigate and from their observation point were able to note that there were a considerable number of troops involved as well as some heavy tanks and armour. Bernard was puzzled as he searched for a reason for the relocation towards the south.

Suddenly he snapped his fingers. 'Got it!'

Gabrielle looked at him eagerly for an explanation.

'Vichy France. They're moving to bring pressure to bear on Vichy France. The Germans don't want it to become a regime to which French men and women would rally. This massing of troops is a reminder that any move in that direction will bring invasion and occupation.'

'That will be of immense interest back home,' said Gabrielle, excitement creeping into her voice.

'It will. I don't think the Germans will occupy. There are rumours coming out of Vichy France that it's moving towards a police state with an agency specially created to hunt down sympathisers with the Allied cause. That will suit the Germans and these troop movements will send a sign to Vichy that it should remain in full collaboration with the Nazis.' He started to move away from their vantage point. 'Come on. We must make contact with Bletchley as soon as possible.'

As they neared the house, Bernard suddenly stopped, grabbed her and swung her into the cover of some outbuildings. Though she was startled by the sudden action, her training had taught her not to cry out. Something was wrong and Bernard had seen it. He put a warning finger to his mouth. Gabrielle waited, ready for any action that might be needed.

They heard a car driving away.

'The two officers from the village, but they had someone else with them, higher rank by the glimpse I got of the fuss they were making. Madame was on the steps seeing them off.'

With the sound of the car fading, they hurried to the house.

'So glad you're back,' Madame greeted them with a grave face. 'I've had visitors.'

'We saw them leaving,' said Bernard.

'The area is being flooded with German troops in a couple of days.'

'We've seen them moving south,' said Gabrielle.

'My house is being commandeered as staff headquarters.' She spread her hands. 'There was nothing I could do about it. The two officers we've had in the village mentioned my nephew and niece were here but I quickly reassured them that you had planned to leave in a couple of days to see your mother. They seemed to accept that, and insisted on establishing this house as their headquarters with accommodation for the commander and his staff.'

'So that's the end of our cover,' mused Bernard.

'I'm afraid so,' said Madame Cossart with regret. 'But if ever the situation changes and there's anything I can do to help get rid of these invaders, I hope you will remember me.'

'You can be sure of that,' said Bernard. 'And they'll hear in England what you've done.'

Madame gave a dismissive wave of her hand and a shake of her head as if to say what she had done was nothing.

'I think we had better get that information through to England as soon as possible.' Bernard led the way to Gabrielle's room, where he rolled back the wardrobe.

Gabrielle sent out her call sign hoping that, though it was not their normal transmission time, someone would pick her up among the welter of messages she knew would be flowing in from agents around the world.

Five impatient minutes passed before she got an acknowledgement. She passed the information as Bernard dictated it. At the end of her transmission she was told to listen at the usual time for further instructions.

They came on time and once Bernard had deciphered the coded message they knew they had alarmed the powers in England. They were ordered to abandon their position as quickly as possible. Bernard was to see to covering their tracks and get the wireless equipment to a reliable Resistance leader who would be contacted with the code word 'Catspaw' in future. Gabrielle was to be airlifted out of France the following night, and after he had seen that had been successful, Bernard was to go to a small village near Caen in Normandy, where he should contact and assist an agent with the code name Pepin.

In the next twenty-four hours Bernard, with Gabrielle's help, had carried out his tasks. The room behind the wardrobe had been stripped of all evidence of its illicit use, the castors from the wardrobe had been removed, and all signs of occupation by anyone other than Madame Cossart's nephew and niece had been eliminated. Madame, realising that she would be in a unique position to glean information, insisted that she was put in contact with Catspaw. Dubious about putting her into more danger, Bernard at first resisted her request but eventually was worn down by her persistence.

Under cover of darkness Bernard escorted Gabrielle to the field where she would be picked up. They spoke little and arrived in the wood beside the field ten minutes before the allocated time. They stood in silence, hugging themselves against the sharp night air. Although she had seen no one, Gabrielle knew that men of the Resistance were also waiting in the wood.

These were anxious moments. Would the plane arrive on time? Would it make a successful landing? Had the Germans any knowledge that might lead them to forestall this operation? Gabrielle felt this tension and more besides. She and Bernard were parting, maybe never to see each other again. She had grown fond of him and in another time, another place, their relationship might have developed into a passionate affair. She sensed the physical tension in him and now had some regret that she had not allowed that kiss to go further.

She was about to voice her thoughts and make it possible in the future when the drone of an engine broke the silence. It came nearer and nearer. Bernard drew a torch from his pocket and awaited the moment when the pilot gunned his engine. He pointed the torch upwards and made two flashes. The aircraft droned and started to turn. Bernard called, 'Now!' Several figures darted quickly out of the wood and marked the landing zone with torches.

The plane landed, turned and taxied back to the end of the field ready for takeoff. Bernard grabbed Gabrielle's hand as she was about to run. He turned her to him. 'Thanks for all your help, you've been great to work with. Take care.' He bent and kissed her quickly.

'And you, be careful.' She kissed him with lips which told him of her regret. Then she turned and ran towards the plane. He controlled his urge to hold her back and came up beside her to help her into the plane.

She was in her seat. The door was closed. The pilot opened the throttle. The engine roared and the plane started to move. Gabrielle looked out of the window. Bernard was there, his hand raised in a gesture of farewell. She waved, her eyes damp. The plane was moving faster. 'God go with you,' she mouthed silently as the figure on the ground disappeared from view.

Chapter Nineteen

1943

After being debriefed and passing on valuable information about the situation in France, Gabrielle was given two weeks' leave. On her way to Robin Hood's Bay she called at Waddington.

Jean was surprised and delighted to see her friend, but admonished her for not taking up her offers to meet before now.

'Believe me, Jean, I wanted to, but I just couldn't manage it,' she apologised.

'I thought I could have spent some leave in the Lakes and been near you. I had nowhere else to go.'

'I'm truly sorry it couldn't be arranged, especially when I knew you were needing company after Colin's death.' She hesitated and then said, 'I've been involved in some special courses and subsequent follow-ups. I can't say more but, believe me, it was service commitments that kept me back. So please forgive me.'

'There's nothing to forgive. I knew I'd see you when it was possible.'

'How are things with you? The loss of Colin must still hurt.'

Jean sighed deeply. A sadness came to her eyes. 'It's been almost a year now and I still miss him terribly. You must too.'

Gabrielle's lips tightened and she nodded. 'Yes, I do, but I got so wrapped up in my work that it helped to keep my mind focused.'

'I've done the same. The crews here have been terrific; in fact, everyone on the station has.'

'No one else yet?' Gabrielle asked.

'No. I don't know if there ever will be.'

'Jean, there must be. You can't mourn Colin for the rest of your life. Remember him, yes, but mourn him, no. He would want you to find happiness elsewhere. And I agree with him.'

'Jean, come into my office,' George Sugden called to her as he walked through the Intelligence block. 'Sit down,' he said as she closed the door behind her.

She was puzzled. He was neither light-hearted nor deadly serious and she detected a touch of disappointment and regret in his eyes.

'44 Squadron are moving to Dunholme Lodge, just the other side of Lincoln.' George was a man who came straight to the point when the necessity merited it.

'What!' Jean was stunned, hardly able to comprehend the news. This was something totally unexpected. She had thought that the squadron was settled at Waddington until the end of the war. Now she was going to lose her beloved crews. The shattered expression on her face told George everything.

'I feel the same,' he said. 'It means the breaking-up of our team. You and I will have to separate.'

'Oh no, not that as well!' Jean protested.

'Afraid so. The CO has just had me in his office. One of us will have to go with the squadron and start the Intelligence Section there. Dunholme is a new station, 44 will be the squadron to open it. There are no plans for a second squadron yet but I suppose that will be inevitable, stations generally house two squadrons.' He made a momentary pause, then said, 'So one of us goes, the other stays.'

'And who did the CO decide should go?'

'He didn't. He left it to me.'

'And you've decided?'

'No. I want to know what you would like to do. I know how attached you are to 44, but you would be moving to a station built in wartime – Nissen huts, less comfort. Here you're already established and have the comfort of a permanent station. I leave the choice to you.'

'But what do you want? You're senior to me.'

'In time only, since your promotion.'

'But you were here before me. It's only right that you should choose.'

George gave a small smile and a slight shake of his head. 'I would like you to have your choice.' He met her look with one which said that was that and he would hear no more arguments.

She hesitated, then said, 'I'd like to go with my boys.'

George's smile broadened into one of approval. 'I thought you'd say that. They're a great bunch and you're liked by them. They admire the way you take the losses and they're jealous when you're giving more attention to some than others.' He grinned. 'They'd never forgive me if I said I was going to Dunholme.'

After a few frantic days of preparation for the move, the time came for Jean to leave.

There were tears in her eyes when she said goodbye to George. He had been more than the intelligence officer with whom she worked. He had become something of a father figure, someone to whom she could turn for advice when she was in need.

'Thanks, George, for all your help and for all you have taught me. I'm most grateful. I couldn't have faced setting up this new post if you hadn't offered me all your knowledge.'

'That was nothing.' He brushed aside her praise. 'I know you'll do well. I'll miss you. You brightened my life.'

'I'm sure at times I wasn't easy.'

'You were never hard. I'm glad to have known you. Please keep in touch.'

'Of course I will. I'll never forget you.'

'Got a parting kiss for an old man?'

'You're not old, but you can have your kiss just the same.' She let it linger affectionately and knew she was bringing a touch of joy to him.

At the door she paused and looked back. 'Be at the control wagon to see the boys off.' She winked and was gone.

Many of the permanent staff were at the end of the

runway to wave goodbye to a squadron which had graced Waddington with honour. George was among them and he was certain that the person occupying the mid-upper turret of Lancaster T-Tommy was a certain WAAF intelligence officer going to take up her new post.

The squadron settled in quickly and made its first raid on 11 June to Düsseldorf. Jean had organised her section with the help of a newly trained assistant section officer, a WAAF corporal and two aircraftwomen. The quarters and mess seemed spartan after what she now considered the luxury of Waddington. The wet weather did not help: in places the new station was a quagmire. Nevertheless the spirit of squadron life prevailed and everyone coped with their new surroundings.

A week later Jean walked into the mess about five o'clock in the afternoon intending to relax with a newspaper. The squadron had been stood down. It was quiet. Only a couple of officers were sitting in easy chairs reading. The rest were in their billets or away in Lincoln for the evening. She went to the bar to get a drink and found a stranger leaning on the counter nursing a beer and exchanging a few words with the steward.

'Evening, ma'am.' The steward turned to her as she came in.

'Evening, Tom. Gin and orange, please.' She turned to the stranger, for she felt his eyes on her. 'Good evening,' she said.

'Hello there.' He straightened. 'Peter Wallace.' He held out his hand.

'Jean Lawson.' She felt a friendly grip. Tom placed the

gin and orange on the bar. 'Thanks,' she said with a side-ways glance.

'Put it on my account,' said Peter.

'Right, sir.' Tom moved away to make the record.

'No, please, you shouldn't,' protested Jean.

'And why not?' said Peter. 'It's a good way to get you to join me and start off on friendly terms.' He spoke easily. 'And no doubt we'll be seeing each other again.'

'You're posted here?' asked Jean.

'Yes, as from today. My crew's all gone into Lincoln but I decided I wanted to get to know a few folk. Seems I picked a bad time. Oh, I'm sorry.' He raised his hands in a gesture begging forgiveness. 'No, I probably picked a good time. With so few here, I've met you. If the mess had been crowded I might not have done so, well, certainly not so soon, and I wouldn't have had you to myself.'

Jean smiled. 'Do you flatter all the ladies like that?'

'Only the special ones.'

Jean already found herself liking this tall flight lieuten-ant with the ribbon of the DFC and bar sewn to his uniform. He was easy-mannered, relaxed, and had the abil-ity to put strangers at ease. His brown hair was well groomed, his fingers long, his nose straight. His strong jaw marked a confident air which was not objectionable. His eyes were a deep, soft brown, shrewd, with an ability to judge quickly. There was a steeliness about them but with-out a cutting edge. They held attention and Jean had the impression that they were kind, but she also saw a look there which came when a man was interested in a woman. That it had come so soon in their meeting flattered her and she found she liked the feeling, something she had not experienced in this intimate way for over a year.

'You?' he prompted.

'Intelligence officer. Came with the squadron from Waddington. Do you know any of them?'

'No. First tour was with 49 Squadron.'

'You'll like them. They're a great bunch.' She spoke with enthusiasm and admiration.

'You're obviously fond of them. Anyone special?'

'No. There was. A fighter pilot. Killed over France just over a year ago.'

'I'm sorry.' His voice was soft and gentle and his words sincere.

Jean found herself talking about Colin as she had not done since his death. She felt at ease with Peter and saw him in the role of a confidant.

Later that night Jean lay awake in bed thinking about him and wondered what it was that had made her talk so much about her feelings for Colin. She was puzzled by an awareness of exorcism. Something that had haunted her had finally been met head on. Gabrielle's words came back to her. Maybe this baring of her soul to Peter was a turning point. Maybe her memory of Colin was to be held only in the background. She fell asleep with two men filling her mind.

When she awoke the next morning she had a sense of pleasant anticipation at seeing Peter again.

During the next fortnight they enjoyed meeting in the company of others. She met Peter's bomb aimer, Flying Officer Dave Rowlands, in the mess and the rest of his crew when he invited her to an evening out with them in Lincoln. She took to them immediately and, from her experience of observing other bomber crews, recognised them as efficient, confident and reliable, with a deep trust that every other member of the crew knew his job thoroughly. She was pleased, for she had been hoping that Peter would not be endangered through a weakness in his crew.

Peter observed the esteem in which she was held by the crews of 44. He wanted to ask her out but after what she had told him about Colin, he knew the timing had to be right.

That moment came two weeks after he had joined the squadron.

He had operated four times and Jean felt a tension she had not experienced with any other crew. She had always been concerned for their safety, hoping they would return, but with Peter she found a deep anxiety building up every time he flew. She had been fearful of Colin flying but it had never been as intense as this. She had never known when he was operational, except on the few occasions when she was at the White Hart. But now she knew every time Peter left on a mission from which he might not return and she began to feel tortured. The intensity of her feelings told her she must be falling in love. She fought the idea at first, thinking it nonsense. No one could ever replace Colin. But each time Peter took off she had a dread feeling in the pit of her stomach, an anxiety which was only relieved when she saw him touch down, safely home. On his fifth flight she became fully aware of how she really felt about him.

She had been at the end of the runway to see the

bombers go. She waved to Peter and received in reply a broad smile and a thumbs-up sign. Her gaze never left the Lancaster as it roared down the runway. Her whole body was tense as it approached its lift-off speed. 'Up! Up!' The words hammered her mind. The plane rose, climbing gently. Jean breathed more easily. In spite of the thunderous roar close at hand as each Lancaster took off, her eyes watched Peter's plane turn away from the airfield and set course for Germany.

She watched until it was but a speck in the evening sky. She said a prayer for their safe return and, with the last bomber airborne, walked slowly back to the briefing room. In the silence she packed her documents with care and left for the mess. There she found some coffee and biscuits and decided to settle down for a long vigil. She did not feel tired, did not feel like going to bed, and established herself in an easy chair to await the bombers' return.

There was an uneasy atmosphere in the mess whenever the aircrews were absent. Their boisterous banter was missing. The ground-staff officers seemed to speak in hushed tones, and, with thoughts on their crews, their conversations were stilted. As the night wore on, most of them drifted away to their billets to set their alarms for the hour when the bombers were due back.

Jean had chatted idly, drunk more coffee, read the papers, tried a book and dozed.

Her head jerked. She started, rubbed her eyes and glanced at her watch. It was two in the morning. She looked around. The gunnery leader and bombing leader were playing cards. She stretched and stood up.

The gunnery leader glanced at her and smiled. 'Good sleep, Jean?'

'Never know whether it's better to go to bed or not,' she replied, running her hands through her hair.

She left the anteroom to freshen up and on her way back went via the kitchen, where she knew that the cooks would be getting bacon and eggs ready for the returning crews.

When they saw her coming their way, armed with a pot of fresh coffee and a plate of sandwiches, the two officers immediately stopped their game.

'Ah, this is more like,' said the bombing leader with enthusiasm. 'Food and a pretty girl to serve it.'

They enjoyed the cosiness of the little group, warmed by the coffee, sustained by the sandwiches. Though no one voiced their thoughts, all were wondering what hazards the squadron had met and if they would all return safely.

Three quarters of an hour later they left the mess and walked towards the airfield.

It was a pleasant night. The shallow moon shed only the faintest of glows, sometimes obscured by clouds drifting lazily on the breeze. A low mist swirled patchily without being a hazard on the runways.

'They'll get in all right,' remarked the gunnery leader, a man of experience after two tours, though still only twenty-three.

Jean made her way to the control tower after the two officers had gone to the briefing room. It had become her habit, after her first invitation to do so, to listen to the returning squadron, and after four or five had landed she would return to the briefing room for the debriefing.

She entered the control tower and climbed the stairs to the watch office.

Two WAAFs sitting in front of their transmitters, their earphones on, glanced round as she came in. She smiled and nodded to them. From previous visits, she knew them as efficient, calm even in traumatic moments, their voices cultured in their enunciation, clear in their delivery. She knew how the aircrews heard their voices as soft caressing tones, encouraging them with their landing instructions.

'Hello, Jean.' The moustached flying control officer welcomed her with a warm smile. 'No contact yet, but shouldn't be long now. No one early.'

'No one landed away, Jack?' she asked.

'No. So we're expecting them all back.'

Jean had great respect for Flight Lieutenant Jack Cuthbertson, who had been with the squadron almost as long as she had. He exuded confidence to his team and was always ready with an instant answer should anything untoward happen when planes were returning. Here at Dunholme he had found the situation a little more hazardous than at Waddington, for the airfield was very close to others and circuits tended to overlap. However, he coped with the situation and had overseen the guidance of 44 Squadron's aircraft with expertise.

Keeping out of the way, and with only an occasional word with Jack, Jean settled down to wait, hoping that she would know that Peter was back before she left to start the debriefing.

'Hello, Tumbleweed, this is March Tune A – Apple. Permission to land.'

The words crackled over the speaker. Jean started. Her

mind had been wandering, wondering, where was Peter?

'March Tune A – Apple. Permission to join the circuit.'
The WAAF's voice sounded heartening.

'Thanks, Tumbleweed.' A few minutes' silence, then,
'A – Apple, upwind.' The controllers knew the position of
the first returning Lancaster.

'Hello, Tumbleweed, this is March Tune S – Sugar.'

'Hello, March Tune S – Sugar, join the circuit.'

'Thanks, Tumbleweed.'

'A – Apple, crosswind.'

'S – Sugar, upwind.'

Each pilot gave his position.

'Hello, Tumbleweed, this is March Tune Y – York.'

'Hello, March Tune Y – York, join the circuit.'

Three planes were in position and following the landing procedure.

'A – Apple, downwind.'

Jean knew that A – Apple would be losing more alti-
tude, ready to turn in through the lead-in lights, the
funnels, to the runway.

'S – Sugar, crosswind.'

'Y – York, upwind.'

So they came back one by one. The circuit was full.

'Hello, Tumbleweed, this is U – Uncle.'

Peter! Relief flooded over Jean. He was back, safe. Joy
filled her heart. She offered up a silent prayer of thanks.
Jack turned and gave her the thumbs-up sign. The station
knew of the rapport building up between the likeable
flight lieutenant and the pretty intelligence officer.

She hardly heard the instructions telling him to circuit
at 1,200 feet. The acknowledgement crackled over the

loudspeaker. Peter would do a circuit of the airfield at that height and when he was over the funnels he would seek permission to descend and join the landing circuit. C – Charlie ahead would be approaching that position now and U – Uncle was next.

'Look out! Lanc—' A piercing cry came out of the night. Cut short in its warning, it tore in earphones and rattled in the loudspeaker in the control room.

Almost in the same instant a vivid flash rent the sky above the funnels. Flames plunged earthwards to crash with a fiery explosion and remain scattered between the lead-in lights, burning fiercely, devouring what but a few moments before had been massive bombers containing men happy to have returned safely from the hell of enemy skies. Now, C – Charlie would not call Tumbleweed again and an unknown aircraft – was it from one of the nearby bases? – would never reach home. All that remained was a funeral pyre of fourteen airmen who had survived the distant horrors only to find the sky's brutality extended to their homeland.

'Bloody hell!' Jack's sudden reaction was immediately under control. His eyes swept across the WAAFs, their faces pale. There must be no panic, no hysterics. He was about to utter a calming word when he heard one of the WAAFs say, 'This is Tumbleweed calling March Tune aircraft. Land as normal. Repeat, land as normal. U – Uncle, permission to join circuit.' Her voice was steady, reassuring, exuding confidence to the airborne crews who, in order to land, would have to fly just above the flames. She turned to Jack. 'The fires are beyond the end of the runway, sir. The crews should get in all right.' She had weighed the distance up quickly and Jack verified her decision with, 'Well done, May. Keep them coming in as if nothing had happened.'

The WAAFs continued to talk their beloved crews down, knowing that on them depended their safety. The terrible sight was nerve-shattering but they must keep tight control. If they succumbed they could cause further disasters.

Jean was staring, transfixed by the flickering flames, her eyes wide with horror, her mind pounding with dread.

Jack saw her and came across. 'You all right?' he asked with concern.

Jean nodded. 'It could have been Peter.' The possibilities behind her whispered alarm terrified her. 'He was next, behind Charlie!'

'But it wasn't,' said Jack firmly. 'You must never think like that. Peter will be all right. Second tour, he'll only do twenty.' He tried to reassure her.

She started and tore her eyes away from the flames. 'I'm sorry,' she apologised in a fluster. 'I'm taking you away from your job.'

'That's all right.' He patted her comfortingly on the arm and went back to supervise the safe landing of the remainder of the squadron.

Jean waited, marvelling at the cool efficiency of the WAAFs, for she knew the strain they were under after the crash. She should go to the debriefing but tonight she must wait to hear Peter down safely. She knew the rest of her team would be ready for the returning crews.

By the time Peter had landed, they knew that all the squadron's aircraft, with the exception of C – Charlie, were back, either on the ground or on the circuit. The other victim must be from one of the nearby airfields, fatalities of overcrowded airspace.

Jean left the control tower when she knew Peter was safely down. She had a sudden urge to run to U – Uncle so that she could hug him as soon as he emerged from the plane, hold him tight and reassure herself that he was there, safe and sound. But she knew that to do so would embarrass him.

As she walked towards the briefing hut she realised that that impulse meant one thing – she was in love with him.

His debriefing over, Peter waited until Jean was finished. 'Walk to the mess?' he asked.

'Yes,' she replied. 'Unless you want to take the transport?'

'I'd rather walk. I'd like to stretch my legs and breathe the fresh air.'

They glanced across the airfield, where only the faintest glow remained of the holocaust that had littered the Lincolnshire countryside.

Peter stopped and turned her to him. She met the loving look in his eyes with one of equal intensity. Their lips met and moved into an overwhelming passion.

'I love you, Jean. Have done ever since the first time I saw you, but I didn't want to encroach on the love you had for Colin.'

'Oh, Peter, you darling!'

'But I can hold back no longer. I just had to tell you and hope there's a chance for me.'

'There's every chance. I wasn't sure how deep my love for you was until tonight. That could have been you out there. It told me something. My concern was so intense that I knew I loved you and want you to be mine.'

Colin no longer intruded.

Peter said nothing but his lips told her everything.

Over the next fortnight their relationship sparkled with a love which knew no bounds. Every time Peter took to the air, Jean's nerves were on edge until he returned, and then she loved him all the more. Scotty, Colin . . . Peter? Was she still a jinx? Surely not? He couldn't be taken from her. She lived for the moment, loved him every minute and found joy in the intensity of their love.

> 'But lovers in war-time
> Better understand
> The fullness of living,
> With death close at hand.'

Jean recalled the words and thanked Colin for discovering them. She knew the love she wanted for Peter must match that which she had given to Colin.

'Leave on Friday.' Peter broke the news when they met in the mess for lunch. 'You get some and come home with me. I'd like you to meet my mother.'

Pleased at the prospect of seven days away from Dunholme, away from the roar of Lancasters and all the anxiety they signified, Jean agreed happily.

It was late afternoon when they approached the house on the shore of the Menai Strait. Though the journey had at times been slow, their pleasure in each other's company eliminated the tedium.

Jean had heard how in 1937 Peter's father and mother, then in their fifties, had been left the house and some money by a distant relative. They had decided to retire and enjoy the new surroundings of Anglesey, the Menai Strait and North Wales. Mr Wallace had been in local government in Wolverhampton, so the change had been marked, but they had taken readily to their new life. Alas, their enjoyment had not been long, for his father had died two years later, when Peter, an only child, was twenty-one.

He had talked a lot about his mother and Jean realised how devoted they were to each other, especially since his father's death. She saw it as a situation where the mother could be jealous of any girlfriend her son might bring home, but that thought was dispelled immediately she met Rowena Wallace.

They were halfway to the house along the garden path, which curved between neatly cut lawns, when the front door opened and a woman of medium build, dressed in a cream blouse and a tweed skirt, stepped out. Jean knew she was being watched with some curiosity but with no hostility, a little apprehension perhaps, which she accepted as only natural. Jean's heart gave a little flutter. She hoped she was going to be liked. Things would be so much easier if she hit it off with Peter's mother.

She glanced at him and saw a son's love and admiration in his eyes. Oh, she hoped for his sake she didn't do or say anything that would upset the lady who awaited them.

Rowena Wallace smiled and opened her arms in welcome to her son and his friend as they quickened their steps towards her. They looked a handsome couple in their uniforms. Rowena envied that trim waist, belted tightly. Air-force blue suited her and her hat was set straight – no, on a closer glance it was slightly tilted, giving a jaunty look to the light-brown hair which was swept up and rolled around the back of the neck. Her black tie was neatly knotted, her buttons highly polished, matching the shine on her low-heeled black shoes. She walked with confidence and in the smile and shining eyes she read a desire to please.

Jean saw her hopes matched by similar ones in the kindly face. Care lines, no doubt drawn by worry, disappointment and the loss of her husband, competed with the delight and pleasure at having her son home. Her thick brown hair was brushed back across her temples and tumbled in waves to the collar of her blouse. It framed a round face, a little pale, from which brown eyes sparkled, reaching out to everyone, no matter what company she was in. They reached out now to embrace her son and the girl he was bringing home. She smiled with full lips, dimpling her cheeks.

'Welcome,' she called.

'Mother!' Peter's stride lengthened. He embraced her with a loving hug as he kissed her on the cheek. He straightened and with his arm still round her turned to face Jean. 'Mum, this is Jean Lawson.'

The older woman smiled and slipped away from her son's arm. Nothing must impede the welcome she had to give this girl, for she had sensed a special love between these two people.

'Jean, I'm delighted to meet you. You are most welcome.' They embraced and kissed each other on the cheek.

439

Jean felt a warmth in the contact, a friendliness which augured well for their future relationship. 'I'm pleased to meet you, Mrs Wallace. Peter's talked so much about you.'

Rowena laughed. 'I hope all good. But I'll bet he's not told you as much as he's told me about you in his letters.'

'Oh, I didn't know he'd . . .' There was a touch of alarm in her voice.

'My dear, you needn't worry,' trilled Rowena, 'it was glowing.'

'Oh, dear.' Jean smiled with relief but with a touch of nervous concern. 'I hope I shall live up to it.'

'I'm sure you will. Now come along in.' She linked arms with Jean, who appreciated the friendly gesture, and they went into the house followed by Peter, happy at the way his two 'best girls' appeared to have immediately taken to each other.

The hall was square with a wide staircase. In the wall at the turn of the stairs was a large window flooding the hall with light.

'I'll take you to your room.' Rowena started up the stairs. 'We were extremely fortunate having this house left to us, as Peter has no doubt told you.'

'It must be quite old,' Jean remarked.

'It was built by the previous owner's father, who made money in the cotton trade. He chose the site and you'll see why when we reach your room.'

She turned left at the top of the stairs, followed the corridor to its end and turned left again. She opened a door on the right and as they entered the room, Jean judged that she must be at the opposite side of the house to the door by which they had entered.

She gasped. 'What a beautiful room!' It was large. Even the wardrobe, two tables on either side of a double bed, tallboy, dressing table, two high-backed chairs and an easy chair did not overcrowd it. The chintz bedspread matched the curtains and cushions and their flowered pattern gave a lightness to the room which was matched by the pale background of the ivy-patterned wallpaper.

'I hope you'll be comfortable here,' said Rowena.

'Of course I shall,' cried Jean with expectant delight. 'Luxury with a capital L after our Nissen hut. Thank you, Mrs Wallace!'

'Come and see why our distant relative chose this site.' She walked to one of the two windows.

Jean joined her. 'My goodness! Yes.' She gazed wide-eyed at the view.

The ground sloped away with lawns and flower borders to the waters of the Menai Strait. Across the strait stood the town of Caernarfon, its castle prominent to the eye, and beyond, the backcloth of the mountains of Snowdonia were bathed in the late-afternoon sun.

'Beautiful,' whispered Jean. They were both lost in the silence of the scene.

'Hey, you two, snap out of it. I'm hungry.' Peter's remark jarred their shared tranquillity.

'Philistine!' said Rowena as she turned from the window. 'But I suppose you too must be ready for something to eat. It's nearly ready.' She started for the door. 'Bathroom's next door, Jean. Fifteen minutes.'

Peter paused at the door and looked back. He winked at Jean and mouthed the words, 'Change, informal.'

When Jean arrived downstairs she found him in a pair

of old grey trousers, thin pullover and open-necked shirt. He looked thoroughly at home, and this would all be his one day. He had never spoken of his ambitions or what he wanted to do after the war. He would tell her in his own good time and she would wait patiently, knowing that there might be no use planning so far ahead.

Peter sprang from his chair when she entered the room. His eyes widened with admiration. He came to her, took her in his arms and kissed her. 'Welcome to Abermenai House,' he said. He stepped back and held her at arm's length. 'This is the first time I've seen you in civvies.' He gazed at her with deep admiration. 'And you look just as lovely as you do in uniform.'

Jean was pleased with his praise, for she had carefully chosen good but casual wear, a grey skirt and V-necked red jumper with the collar of her white blouse turned over at the neck. A silk paisley cravat was tied at her throat. 'Thanks,' she said with a smile. 'Where's your mother?'

'In the kitchen.'

'I'll go and see if I can help.' She started for the door but stopped and glanced at the second door. 'Which way?' she asked.

'This way.' He grinned and held out his hand to her. She took it and he led the way through the second door.

Jean found that they were in the dining room with a long table down the middle. It was set at one end for three. Soup plates stood on an oak sideboard. Landscape paintings adorned the walls above the waist-high oak panelling. Peter hurried her through a door at the far end. The kitchen was square, a scrubbed white-wood table in the centre, a Welsh dresser on one wall with a large range

442

opposite. Two pans were bubbling on the top and Rowena was examining the contents of the oven.

'Can I help, Mrs Wallace?' Jean offered.

'No, thanks, dear,' she replied appreciatively. 'It's nearly ready.' She glanced at Peter. 'Give Jean a quick look round the house, then she'll feel more at home. Five minutes,' she called after them.

It was a whirlwind tour but it oriented Jean and she appreciated what a lovely house had come into the Wallaces' possession. She sensed it was a friendly house and she knew she was going to enjoy her leave there, even apart from the fact that she was spending it with the man she loved.

The days were idyllic. Precious, carefree days of living were theirs. They walked the shores of the strait, strolled inland to Dwyran and Brynsiencyn, or around the dunes of Newborough Warren. They sailed the strait or took the dinghy across the water to Caernarfon from the small wooden pier at the bottom of the garden. They enjoyed the wind and even the rain and felt in them a freedom untouched by the bloodbath of war. Uniforms were forgotten and, with them, aeroplanes, flying and operations. They lived for the day and the love they shared.

Rowena saw that love and was happy for them. She had taken to Jean and did not see her as a rival for her son's affection. Each had her own special love from him.

At breakfast on the fifth day Rowena announced that she had a Red Cross meeting followed by a WI meeting in Caernarfon, would be taking the dinghy and would be away all day.

They accompanied her to the pier, where Peter helped her cast off. 'Wouldn't think she'd had nothing to do with boats until she came here. We took sailing lessons soon after we arrived,' he commented as they watched his mother head across the water. 'Threw herself into life here with great enthusiasm – a big change after the town.'

They waited until she was three quarters of the way across the strait and then, hand in hand, strolled towards the house.

Not a word was spoken. The touch of their fingers said it all. There was a silent rapport between them which recognised the mounting desire in them both. As one they moved to the stairs. Step by step they climbed slowly. They reached the landing and made only the slightest hesitation. 'My room, please,' she whispered. She wanted the reassurance of the familiar. That night she would sleep in the bed in which she had given herself to the man she loved and in doing so would feel the giving had a permanence. Anywhere else, in unfamiliar surroundings, it could be perceived as a spur-of-the-moment happening. That she did not want. The coming moments must be charged with a fulfilling love, nothing must mar them.

They closed the door and, still without speaking, undressed each other. He straightened, swept her into his arms and devoured her lips with passion. Still locked in each other's arms, they sank slowly on to the bed.

She loved him with an intensity which was overwhelming and he returned it with a hunger which would not be curbed. They loved again and again and, their passion spent, fell asleep in each other's arms.

Jean stirred. She looked at her watch. One o'clock! They had been in bed three hours. She glanced at Peter. He was asleep. He looked at peace, contented and happy as if their loving had dispelled the weariness of war.

> 'But lovers in war-time
> Better understand
> The fullness of living,
> With death close at hand.'

She mouthed the words silently and, with joy in her heart, slipped from the bed. She blew him a kiss and hurried to the kitchen. When she returned with sandwiches and glasses of milk, he was awake.

He smiled at her. 'Put that down, and come and love me as you did before.'

She needed no second bidding.

They lay in each other's arms, contented.

'Will you marry me?' he whispered.

For one moment she lay there savouring those words. Then she twisted over to face him.

'Yes! Yes! Yes!' she cried and in the joy of her laughter smothered him with kisses.

'Peter, you go and busy yourself. Jean and I want a little chat.'

Those words might have sounded ominous, but Jean knew otherwise. The proposed chat would contain only kindness, for when Peter broke the news to his mother on her return from Caernarfon, she was delighted.

The mid-morning sun was pleasantly warm when they

strolled to the garden seat near the water's edge. Across the strait, clouds were gathering around the mountaintops.

'My dear,' Rowena began, half turning to face Jean, 'your news yesterday came as no surprise, for I've seen, ever since you first arrived, how in love you two are. I had a talk with Peter after you'd gone to bed last night – a mother's privilege. He told me you want to marry the next time you have leave. I won't say, wait until after the war. Life is too precious to wait. I think you both know that you have my blessing, but I wanted you, alone, to hear that from me.'

'Thank you, Mrs Wallace.' Jean leaned forward and kissed her on her cheek.

'Peter also told me something of your story. I'm sorry about your mother and also that you're estranged from your father. I take it, therefore, that you won't be marrying in Robin Hood's Bay.'

Jean gave a sad shake of her head. 'No. Two brothers are in the merchant navy, they won't be able to come. Martin is in Air-Sea Rescue and if he can get leave I know he'll want to be with me. Apart from him, my two friends Gabrielle, who is in the WAAFs, and Liz, who is in Princess Mary's Royal Air Force Nursing Service, will do their utmost to be there. I'd also like to invite Flight Lieutenant George Sugden, who was my senior at Waddington. He was like a father to me. I'd like him to give me away. There's no one else, so if you don't mind I would like a quiet wedding.'

'Here in Anglesey?'

'Yes, if that's possible.'

'Of course it is. I'll be only too delighted. And we have

few relatives. My husband was an only child and I have only one sister and she's in Canada, so it will be as quiet as you wish. Leave everything to me. Look on me as your mother.'

'You're so kind!' Jean reached out and took Rowena's hand in hers in a gesture of appreciation and love.

'There's one thing I want you to do and I think you ought to do,' said Rowena, eyeing her seriously. 'Tell your father. Ask him to give you away and invite him to stay here for the wedding.'

Jean hesitated, then, seeing Rowena's advice was well meant, said, 'I will. If he won't come, then George will take his place.'

'Good,' said Rowena with a reassuring smile. Then she became serious once more. 'I'm so pleased that you're to be my daughter-in-law. All I ask of you is that you make Peter happy. He is all I have in the world but I'm willing to share him with you.'

Jean squeezed her hand. 'I'll never take him from you, and thanks for being my mum.'

Chapter Twenty

1943

As soon as she was back at Dunholme Lodge, Jean wrote to Gabrielle.

2 June 1943

Dear Gabrielle,

This will come as a great surprise to you. I am engaged to be married!

Peter is a pilot with 44 Squadron on his second tour. He is a wonderful person – I think so, naturally.

Oh, Gabrielle, I hope you don't mind. I thought there never would be anyone after Colin but I have found out that there is. And I had in mind what you said – there's a life to be lived and Colin would want me to live it. So I've fallen. I only hope God blesses us with Peter's safety. I could not bear to lose someone else.

We have just come back from leave, having spent it with his mother in their beautiful house in Anglesey.

She is a widow and the sweetest person. We get on so well considering I'm marrying her only child.

We want you to be bridesmaid. Please say yes. Will let you know the date as soon as I have it. I'm asking Liz too.

Be happy for me.

Love to my dear friend,

Jean

She wrote a similar letter to Liz and one to Martin, telling him her news and expressing a hope that he would be able to get leave to attend the wedding. She ended the letter to him:

Do try and come for, with John and Jim in the merchant navy, goodness knows where they are, you are the only member of the family who is likely to be there. I'm asking Dad if he will give me away but I don't suppose he will even come.

Liz and Martin answered by return, expressing their pleasure at her news, accepting her invitation, and eager to know when the wedding would take place.

Ten days later she received another letter from her brother:

Dear Jean,

I have just come back from seven days' leave at home.

I'm sorry to tell you that Dad won't come to the wedding – stubborn old fool! I did all I could to persuade him but I couldn't budge him. He still believes that Mum would have been alive if you had stayed at home and so he blames Colin and Gabrielle for enticing you into the WAAFs, and of course that takes him harping back to Aunt Mary's death. His reason's still blinded by that obsession.

I nearly left after my first night at home but I saw how lonely he is, and hoped by being with him I might make him see sense and persuade him to see you wed. But it was no good.

I'm sorry, sis. Try not to let it spoil things for you. You deserve all that is good.

Take care of yourself.

Love,

Martin

She shed a silent tear but the news was no more than she expected. She was hurt, but not more so than by the fact that she did not receive an answer from Gabrielle. She had been sure that her friend would have been gladdened by the news of the wedding, but now she wondered if Gabrielle had, in some way, been offended. Had she seen it as a betrayal of Colin? Surely not. Jean wrote again and still received no reply. She toyed with the idea of writing to Gabrielle's parents but dismissed the urge. If Gabrielle felt like that, then so be it. She was sorry to lose a friend she had held so dear, but at least she still had Liz and Martin.

'We've got to re-establish the escape route,' Gabrielle insisted. She glanced quickly at each of the four men sitting round the table in a small, sparsely furnished room on the outskirts of Paris. They stared back impassively, all except the middle-aged man she knew by the code name of Chasuble. She fixed her eyes on him, for she knew the rest would take their lead from him.

She had been in France three weeks, ordered to contact Chasuble to act as his wireless operator and re-establish his contact with England. He was a power in the Resistance in the Paris area and south of the capital. It had become essential to keep an eye on his activities and encourage him to channel them in the direction most useful to the Allies. Gabrielle had been given that task and was also under instruction to re-form the escape route through France to the Pyrenees and into Spain. A link in Vichy France had been broken by a betrayal to the Germans. It took out two operators but the rest of the line in France remained intact. She needed Chasuble's cooperation for this but knew that that might be difficult since he was obsessed with striking hard at the Germans. He saw his sole objective as blowing up bridges, attacking supply trains and military installations, and was blind to the usefulness of anything else.

Chasuble did not speak. He poured himself another glass of wine. Gabrielle could read the disdain in his face.

'It's important to provide the means of escape for any airmen who are shot down,' she pressed.

'They can fend for themselves. We've more important things to do.' He dismissed her idea with a wave of his hand.

Gabrielle's lips tightened. She admired his bravery and understood his desire to kill Germans after she heard how they had raped and murdered his wife and shot his ten-year-old son, who had witnessed the atrocity and could have identified the perpetrators.

He stood about six foot two, his face gaunt, lined by the tragedies. His sunken dark eyes held no pleasure and she had seen them sparkle only after a successful raid had struck hard at the Germans. He was a determined man, a fearless leader who asked nothing of his men that he would not do himself. He had created a chain within the area of his operations through which he could quickly muster a substantial force by the use of a single code word. That code word changed constantly and whatever it was, its meaning was clear to the men who received it. Gabrielle had never been able to discover how Chasuble arranged it but she admired his organisation. It was that organisation which she wanted to harness now.

'Getting fliers back to England is important,' Gabrielle emphasised. 'They can return to their squadrons and attack the enemy again.'

'It takes time to get them back to England.' He threw up his hands in a gesture of hopelessness. 'Besides, how do we know they return to flying? How do we know the Spaniards don't keep them rotting in jail?'

'But they do get back and rejoin their units,' she insisted. 'I know they do. You'll be doing an important job if you help me in this.'

'It'll take too much time.'

Gabrielle glanced at the other occupants of the smoke-filled room, hoping to find at least one ally, but she saw them all nodding their approval of Chasuble's statement. 'Look,' she said, an edge to her voice, for this was not the first time she had raised the subject and met resistance, 'we're all Allies together. We're all fighting the Germans. These airmen who are shot down were doing just that, they deserve to be helped. When your wireless operator got killed, you wanted a replacement. My organisation was willing to help by sending me. All right, Chasuble, I know you were disappointed when I dropped out of the sky, you wanted a man. But have I let you down? Haven't I worked with you? Haven't some of my suggestions been helpful? Hasn't some of the information I've gathered been of good use? Haven't we fought side by side? Aren't we such thorns to the Germans that we have a price on our heads?' She knew this always brought admiration for her. 'Now all I'm asking is your help in this task I was told to do by my superiors in England. They see it as important and asked me to do it alongside the work I do for you. They saw you as a very knowledgeable man, someone who has travelled through France and would therefore be able to help enormously in re-establishing this escape route which can be so vital.' She had pressed home her case, knowing that Chasuble was susceptible to a bit of flattery.

She saw him considering her words, and knew she had said enough. She had gone further than at previous times when she had broached the subject, but she regarded those occasions as a softening-up, increasing the pressure each time. Today she had made her final plea. If Chasuble refused again, she would have to seek instructions from England and she feared they would be, in effect, 'You're on your own.' If that happened she knew the task would be very difficult with greater risks, but she would do it.

She waited. She could learn nothing from the inscrutable faces of Chasuble's lieutenants.

He took another drink of his wine and placed the glass down slowly, stared at it for a moment, then looked up at her. She could read nothing in his dark eyes. Then he spoke.

'True, I thought it ridiculous to send me a woman, but you have proved yourself. You are brave, fearless. I'm grateful for what you've done and I can see that with more careful planning and selection of targets, as you suggest, we can inflict more harm on the enemy. I suppose, even though I am not wholly in favour of taking time to re-establish an escape route, I should help you.'

Gabrielle smiled with relief. 'Thanks, Chasuble.'

'It must not interfere with any other work we have to do.'

'Very well.' Gabrielle had hoped that he would curtail all other activities until this task was completed, but she knew better than to protest. That would only bring his withdrawal of help.

'First of all, it will mean travelling throughout France. You have your identity card as Marguerite Debray but you will need travel passes as well. That can be arranged. One of my men will accompany you, he will pass as your fiancé. He knows some of the contacts, and I will tell him others. You see, I know of this escape route. I knew the weak links. There's another in Paris who could break at any moment.'

'You knew and did nothing about it!' Gabrielle fought to keep her anger under control. 'The whole line was in danger. You should have done something. Fortunately only two contacts were taken and they committed suicide rather than suffer torture by the Gestapo and risk endangering others. Now you say there's a traitor in Paris. Tell me who it is. He must be eliminated before others can be taken.'

Chasuble hesitated to reply.

'Come on, tell me! And tell me where I can find him,' she urged.

Chasuble eyed her solemnly. 'You'd kill him yourself?' he asked tentatively.

'Yes, if it saves the lives of others who risk theirs by being part of an escape chain. And yes, if it saves the lives of our aircrew who take the war to Germany, yes.'

'No matter who it is?'

'No matter.'

'Even your own brother?'

Gabrielle, speechless for a moment, stared at him. 'Yours?' she whispered.

He nodded, tightening his lips into a thin line of regret.

'Oh, Chasuble, I'm sorry.'

He shrugged his shoulders.

'How long have you known?' she asked.

'Last week.'

'Then we must act quickly. The Germans may have taken him already.'

'They haven't.'

'Tell me where he is.'

Chasuble shook his head slowly. 'No, I won't let you risk yourself. I will see to it. A brother who collaborates with the race who murdered my wife is no brother of mine.'

'You're a brave and honourable man, Chasuble.'

He raised his hand. 'Enough. His passing will create a gap which will need to be filled. You go to this address and contact Michel Buffon. But wait until my brother is no more.'

Gabrielle felt a chill grip her. She only half heard the

address. She already knew it, for Michel Buffon was her cousin.

She nodded, acknowledging Chasuble's information impassively.

'Michel has been keen to join the Resistance in the field but he was too valuable to us as an information supplier in Paris. He will be totally reliable in the role you want, a strong link in passing airmen through Paris.'

Two days later, when Chasuble returned to the house outside Paris, he told her, 'You had better contact Michel as soon as possible.'

She knew Chasuble's brother would never talk. She offered no commiserations for she knew that to him it was as if his brother had never existed.

Gabrielle made her way into Paris with some apprehension. She had avoided contacting her relations for fear of compromising them. She did not want to bring the Germans to their door through any action of hers. Yet all the time Michel had been working with the Resistance!

She remembered him from her visits before the war as someone she liked to be with, who enjoyed sharing outings with her whether with parents when they were young or by themselves when teenagers. She had seen him develop from a plain child into a handsome youth who loved to keep her French polished to Parisian standards and make sure she was up to date with Paris life. They visited the pet market, took coffee at one of the terrace cafés or dreamed as they window-shopped in the glamour of the Champs-Elysées district.

She recalled one summer when they were fourteen and

staying at her aunt's country cottage close to the forests of Compiègne, northeast of Paris. They had gone cycling and had picnicked by a small secluded lake. The day was stifling hot, the sun beating down with the intensity of a fireball. Michel had suddenly jumped up and shed his clothes.

'I'm going to cool off!' he shouted and ran to the water's edge, his firm, lithe body flowing across the grass.

Gabrielle's immediate shock at his actions was replaced by curiosity. It was the first time she had seen a naked male.

He ran into the water, sending spray tumbling around him. He half turned, his face wreathed in innocent laughter. 'Come on, it's lovely!'

She hesitated, then, drawn by his splashing and the swirl of water, scrambled to her feet, stripped and, unabashed by her nakedness, ran to the lake.

In joyous abandon they splashed water at each other and swam without a care in the world. There was laughter in their eyes when they eventually emerged from the lake and ran to their belongings. They flung themselves on the grass, feeling it tickle their spines while the sun dried the shining drops of water which still clung to their young bodies.

'Enjoy that?' Michel asked, turning on to his stomach to look at her.

'Lovely,' she answered, smiling with the pleasure of feeling the sun on her nakedness.

He leaned forward and kissed her, an impulsive, innocent kiss.

She said nothing, made no reaction, but she had held that kiss, her first, in her memory.

She thought of it now as she walked casually through

the Paris streets and she was curious to know how he came to gather information for the Resistance. The last time she had seen him was in the spring of 1939, when Paris was reluctantly preparing for war. As an eighteen-year-old he had grown to six foot. His tanned face showed his love for the sun and, with his dark hair and slim eyebrows, gave him an attractive look. His *joie de vivre* communicated itself to her whenever they were together, and she wondered if he still held that intense love of life in occupied Paris.

She was careful in her approach to the house, without being secretive, and knocked on the door as if she was there for a purpose. Two passing German officers gave her only a casual glance.

The door was opened by a small woman dressed in a light-grey skirt and matching blouse held at the throat by a stag's-head brooch. Her fair hair was turning grey but still held its bouncy wave. If she had been standing beside Gabrielle's mother, there would have been no mistaking that they were sisters. Her eyes widened at the sight of the girl on the doorstep.

'Good day, Madame Buffon.' Gabrielle reacted quickly to prevent any exclamation of surprise attracting the attention of a passer-by. 'Can you spare me a few moments on a personal matter?'

Madame Buffon, quickly alert to the situation, suppressed her surprise and said, 'Yes, certainly, do come in.'

She stood back, allowed Gabrielle to enter the house and then closed the door. Free from prying eyes, she gave way to the shock of seeing her niece.

'Gabrielle!' She flung her arms wide and embraced her.

Emotional tears flowed. 'I can't believe it. What are you doing here? The danger!' Alarm rose in her cry and was reflected in her eyes as she stepped back to look at her niece, still holding her by the hands.

Before she answered, Gabrielle asked quietly, 'Anyone here?'

Her aunt shook her head. 'Only Michel. He's upstairs. I'll get him. He'll be pleased to see you. He often talks of your visits before the war.' She called to him from the bottom of the stairs and then took Gabrielle into the kitchen, where a pot of coffee was simmering on the coal-fired stove. A scrubbed white-wood table with four kitchen chairs occupied the middle of the floor and a sideboard stood beside another wall. The cream paint was showing signs of wear and Gabrielle could see the effects of war in the lack of materials to keep the house as she had known it.

'Take your things off and sit down.' Madame Buffon reached out for Gabrielle's jacket and beret.

As she was hanging them on a peg beside an outside door, Michel came into the kitchen. He pulled up short at the sight of his cousin. He stared unbelievingly, his eyes straying to his mother for confirmation that he was not seeing things.

'Yes, it is,' she said with a smile.

'Gabrielle!' Michel hugged her with a deep affection. 'It's good to see you. But what are you doing in France?' His delight turned to troubled concern. 'The risk!'

'And it's good to see both of you. We've been worried about you, not knowing how things were.' Gabrielle's eyes roved from one to the other, searching for any telltale signs of hardship, but she saw none. Her aunt had changed little. She still held herself erect and composed, with a lightness about her presence. Michel had matured, a process quickened by war, but she was glad to see the sparkle had not left his brown eyes, though they were now touched with a cautious streak. He was dressed in a grey suit, well cared for, or was it new? A white shirt had a blue tie at the neck and his black shoes were highly polished. It made him look older than his twenty-three years and she would have classed him as a typical French businessman but she knew he had no business. So why was he dressed like this? What was his job in German-run Paris and how was it connected with the Resistance? There were so many questions she wanted to ask but they were pre-empted by her aunt.

'Sit down and tell us what you're doing here,' she said. 'To my mind it can only mean one thing and I tremble at the danger.'

Michel, attentive as ever, pulled out a chair for her and Madame Buffon poured three cups of coffee.

Gabrielle's explanation of what she was doing in France brought a nod from her aunt. 'I thought so. It's too dangerous. If the Germans capture you, you'll be taken by the Gestapo . . .' She let her voice slide away and shuddered with a vision of the consequences. She glanced at her son for support but he was studying his cousin, marvelling at how this beautiful young woman could risk everything this way. He wanted to reach out and protect her.

'I haven't contacted you before because of the consequences for you if you were found to be in touch with an undercover agent,' she went on, 'but it couldn't be helped this time.' They both stared curiously at her, waiting for her to explain. She told them of her operational work with Chasuble and of the break in the link in the escape line which she had to repair. She told them of the need for a fresh link in Paris and that Chasuble had recommended Michel.

'Good!' He sounded enthusiastic. 'I've wanted a more active role. Gathering information for the Resistance is well enough but this sort of duty will be better.'

'You'll be right under the Germans' noses,' Gabrielle pointed out.

'That's all right. I'm well in with them.' He grinned at the shock on Gabrielle's face. 'I run an export-import business.' So that's the reason for the suit, thought Gabrielle. 'Well, really it's collecting goods for transport to Germany and distributing those brought back for the occupying forces and some for French civilians. It enables me to travel around freely with German approval, for I gather information for them – that which is true is of little consequence and that which is false they think has been a turn of events. Besides, I keep certain officers supplied with wine and cognac.' He gave a little chuckle. 'They think I have contacts. Oh, I have, they're contacts with the Resistance who raid German warehouses for the supplies.' Gabrielle laughed at the picture he created. 'Moving freely with men in authority, I'm able to glean information for the Resistance.'

'You're playing a double game!' gasped Gabrielle with alarm.

'Don't worry, it's safe enough. So you see,' he went on, 'filling this link will work very well.'

'It'll bring more danger.'

He waved a dismissive hand. 'What's that when there's a war on? I won't be running the same risks as you.'

'If any airmen need a hiding place, they can use this house,' Madame Buffon offered.

'No, Aunt, that's too risky,' Gabrielle objected.

'Nonsense,' replied Madame Buffon firmly and swept aside any more objections. 'I'm already sharing dangers with my son so I may as well share them with my niece. Enough of war! Now tell me about my sister, your father and brother,' she added, putting an end to any more protests.

After expressing their sorrow at Colin's death they spent the next hour exchanging news. Before she left, Gabrielle gave Michel the names of his contacts on either side of his position in the chain and promised to visit them again when she could.

Over the next few weeks, apart from passing information back to England and operating with Chasuble's Resistance group in destroying railway lines into Paris, Gabrielle travelled with Jacques Diderot, Chasuble's trusted man, re-establishing the escape route and reassuring the contacts that the chain was now stronger than ever.

Jean stood at the end of the runway. U – Uncle turned, paused and got ready for takeoff. The green light flashed. The pilot's head turned and a broad smile spread across his face. He blew her a kiss, gave the thumbs-up sign to the rest of the watchers and then, with engines shattering the air, headed down the runway. Jean watched as Peter made his climbing turn and set course for Stuttgart.

* * *

'Navigator to bomb aimer, the markers should be going down soon.'

'Thanks, navigator.'

The Lancaster droned on. The outward flight had been uneventful. Peter knew each member of his crew was alert. He had every confidence in them. They had clicked as a team, operating the deadliest bomber in the world. He shuffled more comfortably in his seat and allowed himself a moment to think of Jean. How lucky he had been to be posted to 44 Squadron and find this pretty intelligence officer there. In ten days' time he would be heading for Anglesey and marriage.

'Markers going down now.' The observation came from the bomb aimer.

Peter acknowledged. He noted that the target area was covered by cloud but the sky markers were clear. They should get a good run on to them. The master bomber, having assessed the markers were accurate, called the bomber force to bomb.

Peter kept the Lancaster steady. 'Pilot to bomb aimer. It's all yours.'

'OK, skipper.' The bomb aimer's voice was confident. He was now in charge and Peter would obey his instructions. He made a quick judgement and gave an alteration, ready for the final run in. 'Right.' His long-drawn-out inflection told Peter that a considerable alteration was required. He turned to starboard and then turned back on to the correct bombing heading.

With the Lancaster back on level course, the bomb aimer reassessed their heading on the markers. 'Right, right, steady.'

Peter made the slight alteration as indicated by the speed of the words.

'Steady. Steady. Bomb doors open.'

'Bomb doors open,' Peter repeated. He compensated for the drag on the aircraft as the belly opened to expose the bomb load.

'Right. Steady. Steady.' The bomb aimer concentrated on the markers, viewing them through his bomb sight. 'Steady. Left – steady.' The sharp intonation meant a slight alteration for Peter. 'Steady – steady – steady.' There was a note of satisfaction in the bomb aimer's voice. Peter knew they were on a good run in on the markers. He concentrated on keeping the Lancaster at the correct speed and height and on the designated heading, oblivious to the shells from the anti-aircraft guns bursting in the path of the bomber force.

'Steady, steady.' A brief pause. 'Bombs gone!' A hesitation. 'Bomb doors shut!'

'Bomb doors shut!' repeated Peter and he banked the Lancaster away from the pounding sky above Stuttgart. Home and to Jean!

He dived to the allocated height and swung on to the designated course which would take them west to cross the French border, then north over France to the North Sea, East Anglia and finally Lincolnshire.

'Two going down over the target,' reported the rear gunner on seeing the sudden bursts of flames in the sky which held their height for a brief moment, then plunged earthwards.

'Thanks, rear gunner,' Peter acknowledged.

The Lancaster roared on. The steady note of the engines

was music to the crew for it took them ever nearer home and safety.

'Navigator to crew. Should be over France now.' He knew it was something they liked to hear. Though they still had considerable flying to do over enemy-occupied territory, there was something reassuring about leaving Germany and being over a country where there were some Allies.

'Pilot here. Thanks, navigator. Everyone keep alert.' Peter knew he had no need to remind his crew but he liked to keep contact with them as a unit and would also call them up individually at intervals to make sure everything was all right.

Isolated by the cloak of darkness, the bomber headed home.

The knowledge that they were in a bomber stream did nothing to alleviate the feeling of loneliness. Blanketed by the dark, the bombers had the anonymity of the unseen, until—

'Someone hit!' The report came from the rear gunner, who had witnessed the burst of flame and fiery plunge earthwards. 'Fighters about.'

Lancaster U – Uncle of 44 Squadron droned on, the crew alert for danger.

'Dive, skipper, dive! Dive!' The unexpected shout, filled with fear and urgency, crashed into Peter's thoughts.

His reaction to the rear gunner's warning was instantaneous. He flung the bomber into a diving turn but the night fighter, which had moved in on them under the cover of the black night, got in its burst of cannon shells. They ripped into U – Uncle even as the gunners fired their less powerful Browning 303s. Holes were torn in the side of the aircraft, the wireless operator's compartment was blown apart and the navigator's table disintegrated. The Lancaster lurched. Its nose dropped, though Peter fought to prevent it. The altimeter needle swung faster and faster: 20,000 feet, 19,000 feet . . . 17,000 feet. Peter strained on the controls. He felt bathed in sweat in spite of the cold air blasting into the aircraft through the yawning gaps in the metal.

'Fire, starboard wing!' The cry came from the engineer.

Peter glanced across. The flames were threatening to take over. In that glance he saw that his engineer's left arm was shattered. He pulled hard; he must get level flight and give them a chance to bale out. The Lancaster responded at 14,000 feet but Peter realised that it was doomed. There was no way he could fly this mortally wounded bird back to England. It was taking him all his time to maintain some semblance of flight.

'Check in,' he called with urgency.

'Rear gunner. Hit in the right leg, otherwise OK.'

'Mid-upper. OK.'

No reply from the wireless operator, nor from the navigator.

'Engineer. Shattered arm. Wop and Nav both dead.'

'Bomb aimer. OK.'

Peter held on. Was there a chance of getting back? As if in answer, the Lancaster plunged again and he only managed to straighten it out at 10,000 feet. Immediately he had done so, he screamed over the intercom, 'Bale out! Bale out!' He felt an extra blast of cold air sweep up from the bomb aimer's compartment and knew the bomb aimer had jettisoned the escape hatch in the floor of his compartment.

'Bomb aimer going.'

'Rear gunner going.' He knew his gunner had swung his turret so he could drop out.

'Mid-upper going.'

Peter glanced at his engineer. He motioned towards the escape hatch in the bomb aimer's compartment.

'You?' yelled the engineer, knowing the effort it was taking to keep the Lancaster in flight.

'OK. I'm coming.'

The engineer clambered down into the bomb aimer's compartment. Peter gave him a few seconds, then prepared to make his own exit. He would have to move smartly before the aircraft took its final death plunge. With everything fixed as well as he could to keep it flying for the few seconds he needed, he slipped from his seat and scuttled into the bomb aimer's compartment. His parachute caught on the step, but he yanked it free and dropped through the hole in the floor.

The rush of air took his breath away. He was falling, falling, resisting the temptation to pull the rip cord. He wanted to be well clear of the aircraft. There was a roar and a swoosh and he was aware of a big black shape with flames streaming behind hurtling past him. It was gone in a fiery glow earthwards.

Now he pulled the metal handle on his parachute. He felt a sharp tug and jerk and realised his fall had been halted. Above him, white against the night sky, was a life-saving canopy of silk. From the shattering horrors which a few moments ago had attempted to destroy him, he was floating peacefully towards the ground.

A violent explosion sent a burst of flames reaching

upwards. This marked the end of his beloved aircraft and would remain for a few minutes as a funeral pyre to two of his friends. He hoped the rest made safe landings. Then he concentrated on his own.

'Hello, Tumbleweed, this is March Tune B – Bertie.'

'Hello, Tumbleweed, this is March Tune S – Sugar.'

So 44 Squadron returned to base one by one after a successful raid.

Jean waited in the control tower, listening to them calling, counting them back. They landed, Y – York, T – Tommy, A – Apple. Jean grew anxious. V – Victor, C – Charlie. Fourteen out of the fifteen despatched were back. Only one was missing, U – Uncle.

An anxious silence descended on the control tower. The WAAFs, still listening out, were hoping for the call that would lift the gloom, willing the likeable Peter Wallace to call in. Jack Cuthbertson glanced anxiously at Jean. He saw a white, drawn face and fear in her eyes.

'How much longer, Jack?' she asked, a catch in her voice.

'Who knows? But don't think the worst. He may have landed away.'

'How long before we know that?'

'Within the hour. We'll have a report from Group on the losses.'

That hour was an eternity to Jean. She tried to occupy herself at the debriefing, but all that brought was more worry when crews reported four aircraft on fire: two over the target, the others on the way back. That was confirmed when word came through that only four Lancasters were missing on the raid. Every other aircraft had returned safely, though six had reported engagements with fighters over France.

Jean was numb, her mind not comprehending. She could not remember getting to her billet, but could recall her assistant section officer plying her with coffee and uttering hopeful suggestions.

Jean sank on her bed and sobbed. 'A jinx! You're a jinx! You killed him just as you killed the others!' The accusation pounded in her head until she fell into a kind of sleep, and then it turned into a nightmare.

She took her leave and went to Anglesey.

As they embraced on the doorstep, Rowena and Jean wept without saying a word, each drawing strength from the other.

'Thank you for coming.' Rowena dabbed her eyes and they walked into the house.

'I just had to be with you,' replied Jean. 'Being together, I think we both feel nearer to Peter at this moment.'

'And this time should have been such a happy one for you both!' said Rowena, leading the way into the drawing room where she had a light tea ready. 'Is there any chance that he may have survived and been taken prisoner?'

Jean shook her head as she took the cup of tea from her. 'Reports have come through that the two gunners, the bomb aimer and the engineer are prisoners, and from them we know that the wireless operator and the navigator were killed in the attack. But there's no word of Peter. It seems most likely that he went down with his plane.'

* * *

Peter had made a successful landing near an extensive wood. He had gathered his parachute and hidden it in the undergrowth. Deep among the trees he found a hollow where he reckoned he would be safe until daylight. Having slept fitfully, he felt a little refreshed, though cold, at daybreak. He ate some of the aircrew-issue chocolate and assessed his situation. He could orient himself by the sun, but first he must try to establish where he was.

He moved to the west edge of the wood and saw that he was looking at a farming landscape of nothing but fields and the odd farmhouse. Using the wood as cover, he moved towards its north side. A road ran alongside the wood and to the north, about two miles away, a small village stood on a rise in the land. He lay on the edge of the wood, surveying the area.

He was patient. Though he had an urge to be making his escape, he knew he was more likely to be successful if he was ultra-cautious.

Half an hour later he saw a cart pulled by a thin-looking horse rumbling slowly from the direction of the village. As it got nearer, he saw two elderly men sitting on the cart, casually allowing the horse to make its own pace. He shrank back in the wood but kept in earshot, hoping that his French was good enough to pick up a snatch of conversation which might be helpful to him.

When he caught what they were saying he was thankful that he had been able to understand it. The word 'Lancaster' riveted his attention and by the time the cart had passed beyond his hearing, he knew that the other four members of the crew who had baled out had been

470

captured by the Germans, who had concluded that the other three had perished in the crash.

This brought some measure of relief to him since it meant that the Germans would not instigate a search for any more survivors. He would still have to be cautious but the heat was off.

For ten days he moved only at night, fearful of making a contact that would lead to his capture. He lived off the land, on berries and root vegetables, and eventually took risks by stealing eggs and loaves of bread from isolated farmhouses. He knew he could not go on like this. He was beginning to look dishevelled, and would attract attention if spotted. His beard felt scruffy and he longed for a bath and clean clothes which had not been soaked and then dried on him. He must take the plunge and make some contact soon with the hope of reaching an escape line which would get him back to England.

One day before bedding down in a small wood he kept a farmhouse under observation and came to a decision that at dusk he would venture to it and seek help. With luck the old man and woman and three younger women, who he concluded were their daughters, all of whom he had seen going about their farming chores, would be friendly.

He woke late in the afternoon and, after eating the last of the bread he had stolen a couple of days before, he settled down to watch the farm again and judge the right time to make his move.

The light was fading and he was about to break cover and run to the farmhouse when he heard the noise of a car on the road about a mile away. He waited for it to pass beyond the wood but was startled when it turned along the rutted track towards the farm. He shrank back in the undergrowth, making himself as inconspicuous as possible, for the vehicle would pass within a few yards of him. He received a severe shock when he saw that the car contained three German officers, laughing as they passed by. He could not make out their rank nor identify their uniform from the glimpse he got.

His heart raced as he watched the car pull up at the farmhouse and he saw the three women rush out to greet the Germans with great warmth. They had obviously met before, for there was no doubting who partnered whom. Quick kisses were exchanged and with arms round each other and with raucous laughter at some joke, they entered the house.

Peter let out a long sigh of relief. He had been so near to being wrong. He must move on. He saw no reason for the Germans to suspect his presence, he felt sure no one from the house had seen him, but he would be better away from here.

He was about to move when he felt something hard and cold pressed against the back of his head. He froze in horror. He had been so preoccupied that he had heard no one approaching. His mind raced. So he had been seen! After all this time he would still end up in a prisoner-of-war camp. He cursed his luck and his own carelessness in not staying alert.

The person holding the gun called in a low whisper. Immediately Peter drew a small measure of relief. The language was French and the man was attracting someone's attention. The Resistance! He was safe!

A second person appeared. 'Who the hell's this, Charles?'

'Came across him here, Albert. Still!' he added with a snap when Peter started to ease himself from his crouching position.

Albert peered more closely at Peter. 'Who the hell are you and what are you doing here?'

'I am an English airman. Shot down nearly two weeks ago.' He realised it was no use trying to outwit these men. They were heavily armed and he reckoned they would have no qualms about shooting him. They were roughly dressed in grey trousers and grey shirts. Charles was bareheaded, his dark hair long and unkempt, his stubbled chin adding to the sinister look imparted by his hooked nose and sunken eyes, which were cold and merciless. Albert looked little better with his thick hair jutting out at the sides of his black beret, and eyes that seemed to penetrate the very soul. Peter wondered into whose hands he had fallen.

'Stand up,' rapped Albert.

As he did so, six other men emerged from the undergrowth and gathered round.

Albert looked at the pilot's wings on Peter's uniform and gave a grunt.

'What are we going to do with him?' asked Charles, a note of hostility in his voice. When Albert hesitated, Charles pressed, 'Get rid of him. We can't let him see what we're going to do. He could betray us.'

'He's an ally,' Albert emphasised strongly.

Charles grunted. 'Maybe, but he's English and no doubt a bloody capitalist.'

Peter started at this last remark. He knew there were many factions within the Resistance, though with the help

473

of British agents, some unity was being organised. But this reference to capitalism sent a shadow of doubt through his mind. They must be members of the Francs-Tireurs et Partisans Français, the military wing of the Communist National Liberation Front. They operated almost entirely on their own and were notorious for their exploits. Peter had fallen in with extremists for whom nothing and no one must stand in the way of their objectives. He knew his fate hung on a thread.

'I say shoot him and dump him with the rest,' Charles pressed.

Albert's lips tightened into a thin line as he considered the situation. Peter realised he must be the leader of this band of heavily armed men bound on some mission.

'There are three German officers in that house.' He offered the information in the hope that he might win them to his side.

'We know, so shut up,' hissed Charles, pressing the gun harder against Peter's side.

Peter stiffened. They knew! So were they here to kill the Germans?

'Come on, come on,' urged Charles. 'We're wasting time.'

'He comes with us,' said Albert firmly.

Charles grunted with disapproval. 'So he becomes a witness. He's taken, talks, and we're marked men.'

'Aren't we that already?' returned Albert.

'Yes. But after what we have to do, he'll be able to point a finger at us for a particular crime and that could make us dead men.'

'Then he stays with us to the end of the war,' said Albert. 'We have a common enemy. He's fought them.

See, he has medals.' He pointed to the ribbons below the wings. 'He's a brave man. He has a right to live.'

Some of the others murmured their approval.

Charles shrugged his shoulders and lowered his gun.

'Right,' said Albert. He looked at Peter. 'You've seen us. We cannot let you go. You'll have to come with us and that will mean staying with us. Agreed?'

Peter nodded. He was in a tense situation. Though he did not want to get involved with their activities, he saw he could do nothing else. At least he was with allies, hardly friends, certainly not Charles, but he would have food, drink, shelter and maybe fresh clothes. He was about to ask them to pass him to an escape line but thought better of it. This was not the moment. That could come later.

Albert fished a pistol from his belt and thrust the 9-mm Walther P-38 at Peter. 'You might need this.'

Peter took the weapon, having no doubt how these men would have gained German army issue.

Albert looked round and indicated two young men. 'These two will be outside at the front. You stick with them. If anyone comes out, you kill and make no mistake.' Without another word he set off with Charles, muttering his disapproval under his breath, beside him. The other six followed and Peter fell in step with the two men who had been indicated to him.

After clearing the wood they broke step and, crouching, kept close to the hedges on either side of the lane leading to the house.

Fifty yards from the buildings, they stopped. Albert signalled. Two men broke away and circled to the back of the house. When Albert judged they would be in position, he signalled to the men assigned to the front of the house. They moved away with Peter and positioned themselves so that they had the front door covered from close range.

Once they were there, Albert, Charles and the remaining two men hurried to the front door. They kicked it in and rushed inside.

Although he was expecting it, Peter still flinched at the sudden blast of six Sten guns. The bursts seemed never ending. Then they stopped and a deathly silence seemed to hang over the house.

The figure of a woman staggered out of the front door, blood streaming from her. The man beside Peter raised his gun and fired. The woman jerked against the doorpost and slid to the ground.

Albert, Charles and the other two men stepped over her as they came out of the house. Charles stopped when he reached Peter and glared close to his pale, shocked face. 'Like it?' he hissed. 'That's what we do to Germans, collaborators and,' he added meaningfully, 'traitors.'

Chapter Twenty-One

1944

'Albert, I must get home. It's my duty to try to rejoin my squadron. You've got to put me in touch with an escape route.'

Albert shook his head slowly. 'I don't know of one.'

'I don't believe you.'

'We have nothing to do with any escape route.' Albert was adamant.

'I know you haven't directly but in the nine months I've been with you I've learned sufficient to know that, with your contacts, you could direct me to one.'

Peter had often pleaded his case during the time he had been with Albert's group but had always been rebuffed.

'I'm sorry, my friend.' Albert pushed himself from the rough table at which he and Peter had been sitting in a hut deep in the forest which was used as a meeting place pending an operation. They were now awaiting other members of his Resistance group prior to a raid on an ammunition dump. Peter had decided to make his plea once more before the others arrived.

'Albert, wait.' He reached out and grasped the Frenchman's arm. Albert sat down again. 'I'm grateful for all you've done for me. I would never have survived the winter on my own. As it is I've had food, shelter and clothing and companionship.' Peter had got on well with all the group, except Charles, once initial suspicions were doused. Charles had never come round even though Peter had proved himself in the field.

'And you've done well with us. You are a brave man.'

'Then grant me this request, Albert.'

Before he could reply, the door opened and Charles, accompanied by two other men, walked in. From the expressions on Albert and Peter's faces, he knew what had been going on.

'Trying to get round you again, is he?' sneered Charles with a contemptuous glance at Peter.

Peter's lips tightened. 'What is it with you?' he snapped. 'All I want is to get back flying again—'

'You stay here,' replied Charles firmly, wanting to impress authority on Albert. He knew his leader had a liking for the Englishman and might give way to his wishes, and Charles feared betrayal of the group.

'You've seen me fight alongside you. Have I let you down? If I got caught, do you think I would betray men who have helped me, men who have become my friends?'

'There's no telling what a capitalist would do.' Charles bared his teeth. 'You see us communists as a menace to your lifestyle. You'd betray us to the Nazis to save your skin and get rid of us in the process.'

Protests came to Peter's lips but, before he could utter them, Albert intervened. 'He's right, my friend. We can't take the risk of you breaking down if you were captured. You've seen how much damage we do to the German war effort; we can't risk our work being wrecked. You stay with us to the end of the war, then you can go home.'

'When will that be?' cried Peter in despair.

Albert shrugged his shoulders. 'Who knows? But it will come one day.'

Peter knew there was no more to be said. He glared at Charles's look of contemptuous triumph. The only way he was going to get back to England was to escape from these men. That was a risk, not only from Charles, who he knew watched him like a hawk, but also from the Germans. But he would have to make an opportunity and take it.

Jean and his mother must think him dead. He paled at the thought of the agonies they would have gone through. He must risk escape to bring joy to the two persons he loved most in the world. The thought that Jean might have found someone else haunted him until he thrust it from his mind.

On her next leave, in April, Jean again arranged to spend it at the house in Anglesey. The memories of Peter were precious and she felt so near to him there. And she knew from her regular correspondence with Rowena that she brought comfort to her.

'Bring someone with you,' Rowena suggested. 'You don't want to spend all your time with an ageing fogey like me.'

Jean took up her suggestion and invited Martin. She also extended the invitation to Liz and was delighted when both, unbeknown to each other, arranged to have some leave at that time.

Jean had agreed to meet Liz off the London train at Bangor, due to arrive ten minutes after the train from Manchester which she and Martin had caught. On Jean's excuse that they were meeting a friend of Rowena's, they waited. Only a handful of people alighted from the train.

'Liz!' gasped Martin when he saw the trim figure, smart in RAF uniform, coming along the platform, searching for a familiar face. 'You trying to be a matchmaker?' he hissed as Liz, a smile of pleasure chasing that of surprise, spotted them and quickened her step.

Martin watched her intently.

Her delight embraced them both. She dropped her case and hugged Jean with a greeting that meant so much. Without a word it expressed sorrow at her loss and pleasure at being with a dear friend.

She turned to Martin. 'Hello,' she said. 'Didn't expect to see you.' He couldn't read excitement in her greeting, nor could he hear any sign of displeasure. It was a wary greeting as if she was unsure of her feelings, or was it that she was not sure how he felt about her?

'Nor you,' he replied. He hesitated a second and then added a kiss on the cheek to his words.

She gave him a smile which revealed nothing, then turned to Jean. 'It was so kind of you to invite me. I'm ready for this break.'

'Good. You'll love this place and Peter's mother.'

She made them more than welcome. She loved having

the young people with her and, though they brought back memories of Peter, she enjoyed being reminded of the son who had filled her life so much.

Martin was glad that they had brought casual clothes with them, for he was somewhat embarrassed that he, a sergeant, was accompanying two flight officers. He talked endlessly with Rowena about the sailing around the island and visualised the joy of having a motor launch to sail these waters.

Jean contrived to let him and Liz have some time together, hoping that the magic of the island would rub off on their relationship. But something held them apart. Who could put a finger on it? Was it the uncertainty of war? Jean was puzzled. Why did they hold back from committing themselves? Were they uncertain of their own feelings, of the other's feelings? Why couldn't they clear the air? They seemed to get on so well together and enjoyed each other's company.

Rowena guessed that Jean was trying a bit of match-making. When there were no signs of success, Rowena whispered to Jean when they were leaving, 'Bring them again. They'll be more familiar with the surroundings, know me better and that might do the trick.'

Amused that her motive had been spotted, Jean thanked her for making a further invitation.

'In fact,' Rowena added as she said goodbye, 'any of you, together or by yourselves, are most welcome at any time. I mean that. You've done me the world of good.'

As they travelled to Bangor where they would catch different trains, Liz expressed her delight at such a wonderful leave and then put the question, 'Gabrielle has

481

never been mentioned so I must ask why. And have you any news of her?'

Jean frowned. 'I've never heard from her since I wrote inviting her to be my bridesmaid. She didn't answer either of two invitations. I have no news at all. Maybe she didn't like the idea of my marrying when Colin and I had been so close.'

'Surely not,' Liz protested. 'You and Gabrielle were such friends. I don't think she would object to you marrying someone else.'

Jean gave a tiny shrug of her shoulders. 'There's nowt so queer as folk, as my mother used to say. And Gabrielle's a Harland – you know my dad's opinion of them.'

'Don't you get like him,' Martin put in. 'I'm sure there must be some good reason.'

'Ever the tactful and generous Martin.' Jean smiled wanly. She appreciated his steadying influence.

'What about when Peter . . . ?' Liz let the sentence slide away.

'I wrote to her but again no reply.'

'Strange.' Puzzled, Liz shook her head thoughtfully. 'Did you try her parents?'

'I put off doing so but I did eventually make an enquiry. They were worried for they too had not had a word and could get no satisfactory answer from the RAF – just that their daughter was still in the service and doing her job.'

'There you are then,' said Martin.

'But it doesn't answer the question, why hasn't she acknowledged Jean's letters?' Liz pointed out.

* * *

Gabrielle was satisfied with the way things were going. Chasuble had come to admire her organising skills and her tact in bringing individuals and small groups to work under him rather than by themselves. In it he saw the Resistance could achieve greater things and when finally the Allies returned to Europe, they could be a formidable force ranged against the occupying Germans on the inside.

She was grateful for his help in restrengthening the escape route for British airmen and she saw to it that the links were kept strong, although she recognised that a chain could still be broken by a careless word, a collaborator or someone who could be turned by bribery, blackmail or persuasion. For this reason she was worried about her aunt and cousin and became a frequent visitor to their house to make sure all was well.

They dismissed her concern. Passing as his girlfriend from the country, she saw the advantage of accompanying Michel when he mingled with German friends on social occasions. These visits excited her. To be so close to the enemy, talking to them, laughing and drinking with them, gave her a thrill, but it also meant that she and Michel spent more time together, often in a relaxed, convivial atmosphere when they wined and dined with German businessmen and officers of the occupying forces. Together they enjoyed Paris nightlife, which went on as if there was no war, yet there were times when Gabrielle could sense the current of unrest beneath the surface, with collaborators and betrayers not far away. She had to keep alert against one careless slip which would jeopardise her work and put lives in danger. But two sets of ears were better than one, and she gleaned information that Michel could not. She admired his ceaseless role which took him from German confidant to British spy, from information gatherer to rescuer and guide to escaping fliers. Sharing danger drew them closer and in their work and pleasure they found a compatibility which was rooted in the past and was blossoming into a love they feared to express in the circumstances.

She sorted out the vital information from the mundane, despatched it by wireless to England and implemented the instructions from her headquarters there. She acted as courier for Chasuble as well as his wireless operator and oversaw the passing of airmen in the chain through and beyond Paris. She became familiar with the procedure and knew the contacts for a hundred miles beyond the capital. When she escorted escapees herself, she followed a strict rule that she should not know their names nor they hers. This way one could not betray the other if ever either was caught.

The year moved into April and expectancy of an Allied invasion strengthened, born in the hope that liberation would come soon. The Resistance continued their activities and also held themselves ready to set Europe ablaze once the signal from England had been given.

Gabrielle was ready to play her part but received a jolt one day when she was visiting her aunt. Michel returned with disturbing news. She read deep concern on his face when he greeted her with, 'Thank goodness you're here! It will save time. We need to work fast.'

'What is it?' she pressed.

'The Germans have been rounding up suspects – one of their regular exploits, but this time it endangers the escape route.'

'Oh, no!' Gabrielle's lips tightened in exasperation. 'Just when it was strong. What's happened?'

'I thought nothing of the Germans' action – just routine – but then I was called to "Mitre", the link south of Paris. She had an airman she wanted to pass on. When I arrived, Mitre's house was silent. As I searched through it, I had an uneasy feeling. I found her body upstairs. She had been beaten and shot. I feared it might have been the Germans who had found out her role and had taken the airman prisoner. But it turned out it wasn't. I knew the secure hiding places Mitre used and I found an English pilot in one of them.

'He was reassured of my friendliness immediately. He lost no time in telling me that it was not the Germans who had killed Mitre but a member of a Resistance group.'

'What?' Gabrielle couldn't believe what she was hearing. 'Resistance killing someone working as closely with them as Mitre?'

'It seems this airman baled out over nine months ago. He was picked up by a group operating within the Francs-Tireurs et Partisans Français.'

Gabrielle's lips tightened. She knew of this communist organisation but had never had anything to do with them for they preferred to operate on their own.

'The airman asked them to pass him on to an escape line but they refused. One in particular, a man called Charles, was opposed to it. The group insisted that the airman remain with them until the end of the war.

'He accompanied them on some of their raids but eventually escaped. After ten days he made contact with someone who led him to Mitre. Unfortunately this

Charles believed that, if caught by the Germans, the airman would betray them, and was determined to kill him before that happened. He must have trailed the Englishman to Mitre's and tried to make her reveal the hiding place. Unsuccessful, he remained watching the house, figuring that the Englishman could not remain hidden for long.

'I came along and played into Charles's hands, but with the airman's warning I was ready. Charles is no more. The airman is now in our cellar, brought in from the outside passage and waiting to be passed on. With the Germans rounding people up for questioning, we should move him quickly.'

'Right, I'll take him with me now,' said Gabrielle.

'One more thing. To make matters worse, I learned that there has been another betrayal to the Germans, the next three sections of the line towards Spain have been broken.'

'So we're isolated?'

Michel nodded.

'Right, first things first.' Gabrielle's voice was forceful, taking command of the situation. 'I'll take the airman with me, return to Chasuble and report to England. I think they'll want me out.'

Michel bit his lip with regret. This was not what he wanted. He would miss her. They had worked well together, but she had come to mean more to him than an efficient undercover agent. Now he found there was so much he wanted to say to her but he merely nodded and left the room. He returned a few moments later with the Englishman.

Peter's worried look was mingled with the relief of feeling that he was in good hands.

'This is the person who will look after you from now on,' said Michel, indicating Gabrielle.

'I'm—'

Gabrielle halted him quickly. 'No names. I don't want to know yours and you don't want to know mine. It's safer that way if either of us should be taken by the Germans.'

Peter nodded.

'But you can call me Marguerite.' Gabrielle paused thoughtfully for a moment. 'And we'll have papers made out for Auguste Fourie for you.'

Peter smiled. 'You admire his paintings?' The severity which had come to haunt his features through his experiences was broken by his smile.

Gabrielle raised an eyebrow at his knowledge and gave a little nod. She glanced at her aunt and cousin. 'It will be better if we leave immediately and let you return to your outward respectability without the added risk of me.' She gave her aunt a hug and when they parted there were tears in the older woman's eyes.

'Take care of yourself,' cautioned Madame Buffon.

'I will. This is probably goodbye until after the war.' She hugged her aunt again, then turned to Michel. Their eyes met and held each other, his trying to impart his real feelings for her, hers full of admiration. 'Goodbye and good luck! Keep up the good work but walk carefully.'

'I will. How will we know what happens to you?'

'Chasuble.'

Michel nodded and took her into his arms. 'Be careful,'

he said with concerned sincerity as he held her. He straightened to look down into her eyes. 'May God go with you.' He bent and kissed her and whispered close to her ear, for her alone, 'I love you.'

Gabrielle's mind raced. But this was no time to consider that statement, nor examine her feelings for him. She turned to Peter. 'Come on, Auguste, we'd better get moving. Follow me, keeping about twenty yards behind. Act naturally. If I stop for anything, walk on by and then stop on some pretext until I pass you.'

Peter nodded. 'You speak good English, Marguerite.'

'Father English, mother French. That's enough explanation.'

She slipped her jacket on, placed her beret at a jaunty angle and gathered up her shoulder bag.

' 'Bye.' She kissed her aunt, met Michel's concerned look, went to the door and was gone.

Peter, about to follow, was stopped by Michel who looked out, saw it was safe, signalled to him and gave him a reassuring tap on the shoulder as he stepped outside. In return Peter gave him a smile which expressed all his pent-up feelings of gratitude for the help he had been given.

Peter matched his pace to Gabrielle's. Alert to things around him and to people going about their normal business, he tried to merge in and become as inconspicuous as possible.

Alarm seized him when two German soldiers stopped Gabrielle. What should he do? His instinctive reaction was to stop. She had said walk past, but did that mean if she was stopped by the Germans? He kept walking, trying hard not to stare at her. As he neared the tiny group, Gabrielle turned and, raising her arm, pointed at something in the distance. The Germans nodded, smiled, saluted her and went on their way. Peter breathed a sigh of relief. They must have been asking directions.

They reached Chasuble's house without any further mishap. She quickly acquainted him of the breakdown of the escape route and of the stepped-up activity of the Germans, and then contacted England with the same information.

When she had interpreted their return message, it was as she had suspected. 'Chasuble, they want me out. I know too much and they fear the Germans' persuasive powers might be turned on me.'

Chasuble threw up his arms in disgust. 'I know you would never talk, Marguerite.'

Gabrielle shrugged her shoulders. 'Be that as it may, I'm to go. Tomorrow night they will parachute a straight wireless operator to keep your contact with England.'

'Why not a landing and take you out at the same time?' asked Chasuble.

'Too risky with the present German activity.'

'So how are they taking you out?'

'I have to report to an agent in the Tours area for instructions.' Not wanting to be questioned more about this, Gabrielle changed the topic quickly. 'I have a message for you, Chasuble. Your leadership and the control you now have over a large part of the Resistance in this area is highly valued. They want you to hold yourself in readiness for the invasion when it comes and in the meantime to concentrate your activities on disrupting the transport system.'

Chasuble nodded and pulled a face. 'I'll be sorry to see you go.'

'And I to leave you. We have worked well together.'

'You want escort to Tours?'

Gabrielle smiled her thanks but shook her head. 'Might be too conspicuous. But what we do want is papers in the name of Auguste Fourie for my Englishman.' She glanced at Peter, who had been sitting listening in amazement to the conversation.

'Shall be done,' said Chasuble. 'Ready by the morning.' He rose from his chair and left the house.

She turned to Peter. 'We will travel as cousins going to visit your mother who is ill. I am her only other relative.' She went on to fill him in on details. 'Those are just so you have an answer should we be questioned, but leave as much of the talking as you can to me – your French is passable but has a foreign accent.'

Peter grinned. 'Sorry it isn't better.'

'Don't worry about it. We'll get through all right.' She smiled back, already feeling a rapport with this Englishman who was not trying to impose any ideas or suggestions but who was willing to trust his fate to her.

She had time to study him as they were talking. She knew only that he was a bomber pilot, and it was evident that even in his 'captivity' he had kept himself fit. He showed no signs of the fatigue or stress often seen in airmen she had helped to escape. She was sure his confidence and alertness would be assets in the days ahead, and his strong jawline marked a determination to win through. Beneath the steeliness, which had been honed finer during his time with the communists, she detected a

490

gentle, considerate man. She found herself attracted by his eyes, whose soft brown colour reminded her of autumn bracken close to home, but more than that she was drawn by a sexual magnetism.

She reined her thoughts in sharply. Only a short while ago Michel had whispered that he loved her. It had set her thoughts wondering about her feelings for him, but she had had no time to give them serious consideration. Their relationship was different, deeper, born in childhood, lasting. The circumstances of war played havoc with feelings, and this pilot, suddenly plunged into her life, needing help, raising a desire to see him safely to freedom, had roused other instincts in her.

She clamped her mind. Nothing should get in the way of caution, nothing should deviate the mind from the objective of getting them back to England safely. The way and the time might be long, for she had a feeling that they would be directed to cross the Pyrenees into neutral Spain.

Peter was struck by her confidence. He wanted to know more about this remarkable, attractive young woman who had obviously been in France some time working with the Resistance, in contact with England – an underground agent, who seemed to have no thought of what would happen to her should she be unmasked.

'We'd better get some rest and be ready for an early start. Chasuble will have your papers back tonight. But before that I would like all the information about the group you were with before you were contacted by Michel. It may be valuable to the powers in England. It can form my last transmission from here.'

Peter told her all he knew and then watched as she

made contact with England, passed the information on and signed off. She sat back on the chair with a sigh. He could not tell if it was one of relief or regret.

She looked up at him. 'Well, that's that. Now food and sleep.'

They had cold meat pie, cheese, bread, apples and coffee. He noted that she asked no questions of him. Following her example, he did not pry.

On leaving the outskirts of Paris, Peter was apprehensive. He had not been used to moving about among people as if he was one of them and had a right to be where he was. For over nine months he had been a fugitive and now, as he accompanied Gabrielle, it was not easy to hold down the sense of being stared at and scrutinised.

Boarding the train for Tours, he almost panicked when his papers were examined by a German soldier on duty at the station. Gabrielle had warned him that this would happen but even so he was unprepared for what seemed to him an extra-long scrutiny. Relief swept over him when the German thrust the papers back at him. He climbed on board and felt Gabrielle's comforting touch as they sat down.

The journey proved to be uneventful and after leaving the train at Tours they caught a local bus out of the city, southwest to Villandry.

Peter was silent by the window watching a fertile countryside slide by. The wide plain, stretching as far as he could see, was lush with green cultivated fields, tree-lined lanes and well-tended vineyards. From the bus it seemed the war was far away. But it was occupied by an alien people and beneath the surface smouldered hatred and hostility. For all the appearance of safety, Peter knew that danger lurked and that he should be ever on his guard. He began to feel a tension and wariness which he realised must have been part of Gabrielle's make-up ever since she had come to France as an agent. He admired her all the more.

After alighting from the bus, Gabrielle led the way to a well-kept house on the bank of the lazily flowing Loire. Behind it stretched an extensive vineyard and to the left and right healthy-looking orchards.

Peter was surprised. If this was their contact, it was not what he expected. This seemed too open, too conspicuous to be in tune with undercover activities.

Gabrielle rang the bell at the imposing front door. A few moments later it was opened by a young girl dressed in black with a white apron tied at the waist.

'Monsieur de Staël?' Gabrielle enquired.

The young girl's eyes switched from Gabrielle to Peter and back again. Peter thought he saw a flash of recognition, tinged with one of query at Gabrielle, as if she was clearing his right to be there. Though he did not see it, he realised that Gabrielle must have given her some sign, for the girl said in accent-free French as she stood to one side, 'Come in, Mademoiselle Debray. It is nice to see you again.'

She showed them into a large room, comfortably furnished with settee and four easy chairs. Three walls were lined with books, and windows looked out on a well-kept garden.

'Monsieur de Staël will be with you in a moment.' She closed the heavy door and was gone.

Gabrielle smiled at Peter's amazement as he looked

round the room. She guessed his thoughts. 'The Allies have friends in all walks of life, some more active than others. The Germans cultivate Monsieur de Staël as a supplier of fine wines and he is pleased to let them do so. It provides a cover for activities they would not tolerate.'

Before Peter could make a comment, the door opened to admit a tall man, his pointed features accentuated by his goatee beard. He was a striking man, one who would command another glance from the ladies and knew it. As he strode across the room, his broad smile of welcome drew them both in, and Peter knew that whatever room he entered would be filled with the presence of his personality.

'Ah, Marguerite, it's good to see you again.' He threw his arms wide, kissed her on both cheeks and turned to Peter.

He felt he was scrutinised in the lively blue glance. The Frenchman raised a querying eyebrow at Gabrielle.

'This is Auguste Fourie.'

Before she could go on, Monsieur de Staël let out a chuckle which disturbed Peter for behind it he read a touch of mockery. It was so slight that he immediately thought he must have imagined it.

'An English airman, more likely,' he said. He had seen through the disguise. Was that the reason for the slight contempt?

'As you say, an English airman,' replied Gabrielle quickly. Peter sensed a touch of annoyance in her voice, but once again it was so minute that he wondered if he was right.

'Then what is he doing here, my dear? You know I am

not part of an escape route. Too risky, with my reputation with the Germans to keep up. I thought you must be on one of your information-finding missions. But an English airman?' He threw his hands up.

From that moment on Peter did not like this man in spite of his outward charisma. He was treating Gabrielle as if she was a mere courier, and he knew that she was stung by his criticism.

'Monsieur de Staël, the escape route has been broken in three places. I had this airman and there was no one to whom I could pass him. Besides, my last contact with England ordered me to leave and to come here to await further instructions about my return to England. I could not leave this man. I had to bring him with me.'

Monsieur de Staël's lips tightened with exasperation. 'I've had no word about you from England.'

'Then we'll have to wait until you get one,' Gabrielle observed tartly.

'Impossible! I cannot have an English flier in my house. If he was discovered, puff –' he threw his arms wide – 'everything gone, my home, my livelihood, and me – slave camp.'

Peter was fuming at the conceit which had come out. He got a warning glance from Gabrielle to say nothing.

'Monsieur de Staël,' started Gabrielle. The determination in her voice warned the Frenchman of a storm but he forestalled her by cutting in.

'Marguerite, let us not come to disagreement over this.' His charm was oozing again. 'I shall arrange for you both to move on to a Madame Rideau, she is a widow, has a cottage further along the river.'

'I do not know of this Madame Rideau,' replied Gabrielle with some doubt. Since working with Chasuble, her sources of information had been wide and she had never heard of this woman. She knew she could not know of everyone who was sympathetic to the Allied cause and the liberation of France, but she thought it strange that Monsieur de Staël had never mentioned her before.

'She is a new worker for us. I recruited her. You'll be safe there until I receive instructions from England.'

'Very well.' Gabrielle was terse, but she realised she could do nothing but comply.

Monsieur de Staël issued instructions on how to find Madame Rideau's cottage and told them to say that they had been sent from him.

'I don't like him.' Peter voiced his opinion firmly as he and Gabrielle followed the riverbank downstream. 'Can he be trusted?'

Gabrielle frowned. 'I noticed a change in him, but he has worked well for the Resistance in the past. I have no reason to suspect that he has changed and we were instructed by England to contact him for our next move.'

The small cottage was close to the river, with an untended garden running up to the road. Their knock was answered by a woman in her fifties. Dark, thick eyebrows arched above dark eyes which were cold and suspicious. Her mouth was wide, her nose rounded and her chin jutted with a determined thrust. Dark hair was tied in a tight bun at the nape of her neck, giving her a hostile appearance.

Gabrielle sensed distrust but felt she may have prejudged too quickly when some of the outer shell cracked on hearing the password.

Madame Rideau ushered them into a room which served as both a living room and a kitchen. A black open range was built into one wall and a sink stood beneath the window overlooking the river. A wooden table and four chairs occupied the centre of the room while two rocking chairs and a dresser piled with pots were the only other furniture in the room.

Gabrielle explained why Monsieur de Staël had sent them. The woman accepted this without question. 'You don't know how long you'll be here?'

'No, but it shouldn't be long – just until Monsieur de Staël receives instructions about us.'

Madame Rideau grunted. 'I have little room here. My room is there.' She indicated a door on the left. 'You must share this one.' She opened a door on the right.

Gabrielle and Peter found themselves in a small room with a double bed covered with a blanket and a grubby quilt. One wooden chair and a small table, on which stood a ewer and a bowl, were all the other furnishings in the room. A window gave a view of the river. The walls were whitewashed but not recently.

'Instructions while you are here,' said Madame Rideau with a tone which would brook no questioning. 'You will remain in your room at all times except to use the privy. At no other times will you venture outside the cottage. I will bring your food, you will eat in here.'

Gabrielle knew it was no use protesting. It was dangerous to harbour enemy agents or shot-down fliers and there were always prying eyes. When she recalled the comfort she had experienced at Monsieur de Staël's on other visits, she was annoyed that now, because she had an airman with her, he would not offer them the safety of his house. However, she had slept in worse places than this, but never with a man of whom she knew so little. Yet in the short time she had known him, even in strained circumstances, she had felt the pull of attraction. She wanted to know more about him, but knew she must not ask questions until they reached England. Now they must adjust to the situation in which they found themselves.

'I'll bring you something to eat in twenty minutes.' Madame Rideau left them to sort themselves out.

'Strict rules,' observed Peter.

'Understandable when there are those who would betray for their own ends. If we were seen here, someone would talk,' explained Gabrielle.

Peter examined the room while she turned the blankets back.

'At least the sheets are clean,' she commented.

'There's water in the ewer and a tap in this corner,' he informed her, pointing to a corner of the room next to the window. 'So I'll take this corner next the door,' he added.

'You'll do no such thing,' Gabrielle called over her shoulder as she removed her beret and shrugged herself out of her jacket. 'You'd get no rest down there. We'll both need to be properly refreshed, for we have no idea what faces us. You'll share this bed with me.' She glanced round, curious to see Peter's reaction to her offer. For a moment she caught a flash of embarrassment. 'In the cause of war,' she added, with a mischievous twinkle in her eyes.

He wet his lips. 'You're the boss. I'm in your hands.'

'You'll sleep well in this feather bed,' she replied.

As he poured some water into the ewer and washed his hands and face, Peter marvelled at this young woman who could take risks so calmly. She was good-looking, and he had found her nice to be with in the short time they had been together. Under different circumstances, who knew . . .

But the circumstances were here and now. They were different when he was with Jean. Jean! She must think him dead. Maybe she had found someone else.

It nagged at him as he stripped to his underpants, aware that Gabrielle's eyes had noticed his firm, strong thighs and the muscles rippling in his back. He sank into the feathers and surreptitiously watched while she, on the other side of the bed, her back to him, undressed to her bra and panties. He admired the smooth back, the tiny waist and firm bottom. As she turned and slipped into bed, he caught a glimpse of small breasts taut beneath the bra.

'Comfy?' she asked casually as the feathers folded around her.

'Yes. A while since I slept in a feather bed.'

'Me too.' She turned her back to him, taking some of the tension out of the sexually charged atmosphere.

He made no move and she sank into a deep sleep.

Waking the next morning, she found him already up and dressed. It was something of a relief that he was not still beside her in bed, for in the sleepy moments of returning to consciousness, desire churned deep in her.

'You slept well,' he commented, his eyes drinking in the pleasure of seeing her stretch.

'Mm. So comfy in these feathers. You?'

'Not bad. Woke several times but not for long.' He

could not tell her that in the small hours of the morning he had had an intense desire to wake her and take her.

In the week that followed, tensions mounted in the tiny room in the cottage on the banks of the Loire.

They had expected to move on quickly. Each time they saw Madame Rideau, their enquiry brought rebuff. 'I know nothing. I await orders.' The desire to be on their way, the longing for action, the craving to break the bonds of their tiny prison, put a restive strain on their emotions. They needed release.

To keep fit, they exercised as best they could in such a confined space. They invented games to pass the time; they lazed, trying to relax. They talked, but Gabrielle still insisted that they should know nothing about each other – their origins, background or service life. Yet each knew the other was longing, even needing, to know more.

They were both aware that the small confined space in which they had been thrown together had become charged with sexuality. They tried to ignore it but that only heightened desire. The precariousness of their survival made them want to live life to the full while they could, for who knew what lay ahead?

Peter stirred. Something had disturbed him. He looked at Gabrielle. She was asleep, her head turned towards him. She had twisted on to her stomach in her sleep and in doing so her hand had come to rest on his shoulder. Did instinctive longing lie behind her sleeping action? Was it a sign that she wanted him as much as he wanted her, needing to find a release of the tensions which bound them together?

He watched her in the dim light which filtered through the window from a waning moon. Her face, pale against the pillow, seemed lost in tranquillity and yet there were signs of disturbance. Her hair spilled across the pillow as if reaching out for him, wanting him to draw closer.

His mind drifted into another world, one in which only they existed. He leaned across and kissed the corner of her mouth. She moaned. He kissed her again, lingering this time. The moan was prolonged, full of the desire surging through her body. She stirred, turning instinctively towards him. He kissed her full on the mouth, his hands sweeping caressingly across her skin. An electric storm burst in her mind as her body was suffused with sensations she had never experienced before. She felt swamped with the need to be taken. Her eyes opened, focusing on the soft brown eyes so close to hers, and she was lost in their depth as they searched for her response to his desires.

She smiled and arched provocatively, tempting him, teasing him. She was drawn to sigh contentedly by the touch of his fingers gliding over her skin. He fumbled with the fastenings of her bra and they fell away, leaving him free to fondle her breasts and heighten her desire. She could wait no longer. She slipped easily into nakedness, matched by his urge to feel the same freedom. Her arms came round his neck and held him tight in a prolonged kiss as her body closed on his. Desire, craving and lust united in an explosive union.

Peter woke. It was daylight. He saw her watching him from her pillow. The memory of what had happened flooded into his mind. He sat up and turned to look down at her.

'I'm sorry,' he mumbled, half apologetically.

She smiled at his embarrassment. 'Don't be. I'm not. I needed that.' She reached up and wiped her fingers across his brow. 'Don't ever regret it. Thank you for it.'

He bent and kissed her lightly, a thank-you kiss. 'And I needed it too.' He paused, his brow knitting again into a frown. 'Us . . . if we get out of this . . .'

She stopped him. 'That's not for consideration. We needed each other here and now. If it happens again . . . *c'est la guerre*. It has no hold on our future.'

They passed the rest of the day without further references to the incident, but both wondered what the night might bring. They were never to know.

When Madame Rideau brought their evening food, she informed them that they were to be ready to leave at ten o'clock that night.

Gabrielle was surprised at this sudden notice. 'What's supposed to happen? Where are we going?'

Madame Rideau shrugged her shoulders. 'How should I know? You be ready.'

'On whose instructions?' asked Gabrielle.

'Monsieur de Staël's.'

She left the room quickly.

Gabrielle frowned at the door.

'You worried?' Peter glanced at her as he broke some bread.

'Puzzled,' replied Gabrielle thoughtfully. 'Madame was in a hurry to leave. Wanted no more questions.'

'Nothing wrong in that,' Peter pointed out.

502

'No, but she seemed agitated. You know, it has just struck me, Monsieur de Staël said that he recruited her, but what for? He wasn't expecting us.'

'You think that all is not straightforward for ten o'clock?'

'You have to trust in this game, yet you always have to remain suspicious.'

Peter raised his hand. 'Listen,' he whispered. He had heard a click of a latch. Now they both heard another click, different in tone, with a ring of finality about it. Then fleeting footsteps, as if they were trying not to be heard, moved away from the cottage. 'Madame Rideau. She's never gone out at this time.'

'And she's locked the door,' commented Gabrielle.

'To keep others out while she's away.'

'Or to keep us in.'

Peter looked anxiously at her. 'For what purpose?'

'Who knows?'

'Let's take a look around.'

Their examination of the cottage did not take long but it was thorough. Gabrielle reckoned she knew all the likely hiding places from experience but they found no arms or other evidence of Resistance involvement.

A worried doubt clouded her face as she considered the situation. 'So why didn't de Staël want us in his house? It would have been much more convenient for instructions.'

'Because of me,' Peter pointed out. 'He didn't want an escape line connecting with his house. It might have endangered his other activities.'

'Double-dealing?' mused Gabrielle.

'You don't mean . . . ?'

'Betrayal.'

'But you said he contributed so much.'

'Yes, he did, but people can turn. You've seen his lifestyle. We don't know to what lengths he would go to preserve that. And there's a price on my head.'

'I didn't like him, but surely—'

'You know what I said, trust no one and always be suspicious.'

'So what now? Leave?'

Gabrielle considered the situation thoughtfully. 'The instructions might be genuine. If we leave, we risk losing our escape route.'

'And if we stay and have been betrayed . . . ?' The consequences needed no words of clarification.

Peter saw Gabrielle lapse into deep thought and knew better than to interrupt. The clock ticked relentlessly on towards ten o'clock.

At half past nine Gabrielle stood up. 'Madame has not returned, I'm even more suspicious, and ten o'clock may not be the deadline. We leave. Take only what is necessary.'

They stuffed the pockets of their jackets with some food. Peter picked up a kitchen knife.

'No weapons,' Gabrielle ordered. 'Armed, you can be shot.' She looked round. 'We'll use that window. It's closest to the river. It'll be a tight squeeze but we can do it.' She indicated the sash window over the sink. Peter started towards it. 'Wait a minute,' she said. 'Listen carefully. Make straight for the river. We'll hide near the water. If the instructions were genuine, then we can reveal ourselves at ten o'clock; if not, we can be away before they realise we've gone. If we get separated, don't attempt to find me. You'll be on your own and all I can advise you to do is head south for Spain.'

'Right.' He looked at her with gratitude. 'Thanks are inadequate.'

She brushed his words aside. 'Take care.'

He bent to kiss her but she turned away with a whispered, 'No. Keep the memory.'

'Where will I find you if . . . ?'

'Knowledge is a dangerous thing. Now out with you. Straight to the river.'

'You first.'

'I give the orders, remember. Go!'

He scrambled over the sink, raised the window and got stuck halfway. Delay could be fatal. He struggled, moved an inch or two, then felt a hefty shove and plunged head first to the ground. He scrambled up and turned to help her.

'Go!' she hissed and slipped through the window after him.

In a crouching run he headed for the river.

The explosion rent the air and bowled him over. As he rolled, he was aware of a mass of flame where the cottage had been, and imprinted on his vision was a slender silhouette, arms flailing, tossed into the air.

'Marguerite!' The name he knew her by screamed in his head. He wanted to run back and find her and hold her shattered body, no matter what else happened. But he knew that would be betraying what she had done. If only he had insisted she leave first! He felt a pain in his arm and knew something had ripped through his sleeve. His right leg felt numb. He struggled to push himself forwards. Though it seemed like an eternity, everything had happened so fast. He stumbled to his feet and lurched towards the riverbank.

Rifle fire tore through the air. He managed a few more yards before the pain struck the side of his head. He pitched forwards into blackness and rolled down the bank into the water, where the river took charge.

Chapter Twenty-Two

1946

The seascape unfolded before Jean's appreciative eyes. Even from the train it seemed to send out its soothing touch, just as it had done when she walked the beach at Robin Hood's Bay so long ago. It sent her mind drifting over the last two years.

She had come to terms with squadron life without Peter. She had been offered a posting away from the squadron, a compassionate gesture by her commanding officer, but she had turned it down. The memories and heartaches were vivid as she mingled with the aircrews, but they were her boys and she could not leave them. She wanted to live the rest of the war as near to Peter as possible.

The dark days she had endured, along with so many more, became worthwhile on 6 June 1944 when the Allies returned to Europe. Although there were still sacrifices to be made in the hard battles ahead, the end seemed in sight.

When that end came on 7 May 1945, Jean felt a deep

hurt even among the joyous celebrations, for now life was more certain and she had to face it without Peter.

That was brought poignantly home to her when, in October of that year, she received a letter which brought delight, yet opened wounded memories.

RAF Hospital
Halton
5 October 1945

My dearest friend Jean,

Getting a letter from me must come as a surprise and a shock.

You must have wondered what had happened to me. All I can say is that I would have been in touch if I could but circumstances prevented that. Please believe me. As you will see, I am in hospital. I have been seriously ill for some time but I am pleased to say that I am now on the road to recovery, though the doctors say that I am not likely to be released before Christmas. If my demob cannot be arranged for then, I may be allowed home for a few days.

I am dying to know all about your wedding. I have just got your letter and invitation after all this time. I am so sorry that I was not able to be your bridesmaid. What must you have thought of me not answering your invitation? I hope everything went off all right. Of course I didn't mind you marrying. It's what Colin would have wanted. Now I am longing to know all about him and look forward to meeting him. I hope you are blissfully happy and that you will have a long life together.

508

Write to me here. Please. We will try and arrange a meeting, but that may have to wait until you are de-mobbed and we are back in Robin Hood's Bay. Oh, but maybe you won't be coming there now that you are married.

It is so good to be in touch again.

Love,

Gabrielle

Jean had written back by return, expressing her joy at receiving that letter, but had told her sadly of Peter's death. She was concerned for Gabrielle's health and hoped she would soon recover and that they could meet before long. She expressed curiosity about what Gabrielle had been doing but it had brought no response from her.

Looking out of the train window, Jean hoped she would soon find out, for she knew that her friend was back in Robin Hood's Bay. Since that exchange of letters, they had not been able to meet and they both looked forward to the day when Jean was demobbed, though Jean knew her homecoming could be stormy when she faced her father.

The train slowed. Her heart beat a little faster. The familiar station came into view and the engine huffed and puffed as it came to a halt, with carriage buffers ringing out as they were jerked into contact.

'Robin Hood's Bay! Robin Hood's Bay!'

Mr Newton! As Jean heard his call she felt as if she was back six years, as if the intervening period had never been. She opened the door and stepped out of the carriage.

She paused after shutting the door and looked both

ways along the platform. Nothing had changed. The flowerbeds were as bright as they had been when she last saw them. The fire buckets still hung red against the station wall. And there was Will Newton standing beside the exit, collecting tickets from the passengers who had alighted from the train. It was as if the momentous events of the past six years had made no mark on Robin Hood's Bay.

But she knew that was not true. Outwardly things might appear the same but people's lives, even in this tiny Yorkshire coastal village, had been affected in many different ways. She was not the naive girl who had left to join up. She was confident, mature, could accept responsibility, and she had been scarred mentally by the loves she had made and lost.

She walked towards the exit. Mr Newton looked up as he held out his hand for her ticket.

He stared. For a moment he thought his eyes were deceiving him. Then his face broke out into a broad smile. 'Why, it's Jean Lawson! My, you do look well, and grown up from the lassie I saw leave here.'

Jean smiled. 'Mr Newton, it's good to see you and you don't look a day older.'

'You're only flattering an old man.'

'Old? You'll always be young to me.'

Will Newton grinned fondly.

'And the railway let you see out the war,' she added.

'Aye, but I expect they'll retire me before long.' The touch of regret in his voice was dismissed when he went on, 'But I'm grateful to have had those six extra years. I think I'm ready to retire now.'

'And if I know you, you'll enjoy it.'

'I mean to.' He paused, looking at her with approval. 'Well, all my young folk are back. Gabrielle's been home since Christmas, Liz arrived last week, Martin was here a fortnight ago but left again after four days, saying he'd be home for good in two weeks. Ron's been back and forth, but a month ago he was home before sailing for foreign parts. Said he was making the navy his career. Cut a fine figure in his uniform.' He paused. His face saddened. 'There's only Colin missing. You and he were such good friends.'

Jean gave a wan smile as memories came flooding back. 'We were, Mr Newton, we were.'

'Aye, a brave lad.' He shook his head sadly. 'A terrible waste of a fine life.'

'Don't look at it that way, Mr Newton. He helped his country and he died doing what he liked doing – flying.'

He watched her as she walked away from the station, thinking on her words. 'Aye, maybe you're right,' he muttered to himself.

Jean walked at a steady pace, looking around her, taking in the familiar scenes as if they might bring stability to what she thought would be a stormy reception. The buildings of the new part of the village on top of the cliffs were unchanged. She was tempted to go to see Gabrielle but she must go home first, if she could call it home. She had left with her father's words of exile pounding in her mind. Would they ring out again when he saw her? Should she have come? But where else could she have gone? Rowena would have welcomed her in Anglesey, she had said so but had also advised her to go home. There was some making-up to do, she had to try. If she failed, then Anglesey could be her home.

She paused at the top of the hill above the old village. The red roofs tumbled towards the sea which lay calm in the bay, lapping the stretch of sand gently. It was a fine day to be coming home. The sky was a bright blue with only the odd puff of cloud. Everything was so peaceful, and Jean hoped that peace would not be shattered when she reached the cottage in Sunny Place.

She started down the bank, her footsteps cautious on the worn stone flags. Glancing along the snickets and alleyways, she recalled how as young children they played chase along them. Some of the cottages and houses needed a coat of paint and repairs to woodwork, but that would come now the war was over.

She paused for a moment at the door of the cottage in Sunny Place, and glanced at the windows. 'Curtains need washing,' she muttered. 'Mum wouldn't have had them like that.' She pulled herself up, realising that that statement was an oblique criticism of her father. She should not enter the house in that state of mind.

She knocked on the door and at the rapping sound her heart started to flutter with apprehension. She had made the break six years ago. Should she have left it that way? But this was where her roots were, this was home to her.

The door opened. For one moment brother and sister stared unbelievingly at each other.

'Jean!'

'John!'

John stepped forward and enveloped her in his arms and she drew comfort from their reassuring strength.

She hugged him back with delight, her head buried against his chest.

'Oh, it's good to see you, John.'

'Here, let me look at you.' John stepped back, holding her at arm's length. 'My, my kid sister's grown up! That uniform suits you. Officer, too. I should be saluting you.'

Jean laughed through the tears of pleasure which ran down her cheeks. 'What did you expect? Time doesn't stand still.'

'Here, come away in with you.' John picked up her case and ushered her into the cottage.

As she slipped out of her tunic, she looked round. A shiver ran through her. It was almost as she had left it. A litle untidier – a woman's touch was missing – but the furniture was the same, the table and chairs, the sideboard and black range, which was in need of polishing. A duster wouldn't come amiss and the carpet needed a beating. Jean was already seeing work in her quick glance around the room. Was she going to be caught in a trap like her mother? She had seen independence, another world, was she going to slip back into the net of drudgery? Times had changed, the world had moved on, but she could easily get taken into the backwaters she had left if she did not resist.

'Sit down, sis. I'll get you a cup of tea.' John went to the range where a kettle, hanging over the fire, was puffing steam. 'You back for good?' he asked as he poured some water into a teapot. He stood it in front of the fire to brew while he got two cups and saucers.

'Who knows?' replied Jean. 'Much depends on Dad. How is he? What time will he be in from work?'

'He isn't at work. He's in bed, sick with bronchitis.'

'What! I didn't know.'

'How could you?'

'I must go and see him.' She started to rise from her chair.

'No, wait. I've just been up. He's sleeping soundly. Let him have the rest.'

Jean sank back slowly on the chair. 'How ill is he?'

'He's been pretty bad, but he's over the worst. Doctor says he'll be OK now. It was as well I was here.'

'How long have you been home?'

'Three weeks. Nearly stayed in the merchant navy but Robin Hood's Bay pulled. Not so for James, he decided to make it his career. He'll do well.'

'You've seen Martin? Mr Newton told me he'd been here.'

'Yes. He's well. Filled out. Air-Sea Rescue suited him. He'll be home on Friday.'

John poured the tea and opened a tin to offer Jean a cake.

She raised her eyebrows as she took a fairy cake. 'Home-made,' she observed. 'You didn't make these, John Lawson. Which lass is your sweetheart?'

John laughed. 'No lass. Mrs Harland made them.'

Jean gave a little wry smile. 'And Dad allows them in the house?'

'Doesn't know.' John laughed. 'Thinks I have a black-market contact.' A serious expression clouded his face as he sat down opposite Jean. 'Don't know what he's going to say when he hears the news I learned a couple of hours ago. Waiting the right moment to tell him.'

'What's that?'

'Mr Harland wants me to go into the business with him.'

'What? How?' Jean's brow furrowed with curiosity.

'His business thrived with war work but he has no one to leave it to. Gabrielle isn't interested, though if the arrangements go through she will have shares in the business. Naturally he had hoped that Colin . . .' His words trailed away. 'Sorry, sis.'

Sorrow clouded her eyes. Resignedly she said, 'What had to be, had to be. We can't alter it. Is Mr Harland seeing you as a replacement for Colin?'

'I suppose something like that, but he also doesn't want to see the business disappear. He encouraged me before the war, said I was an excellent mechanic and now wants me to put some capital in and become a partner. I've saved some money so it's possible.'

'You're going to do it?' There was enthusiasm in her question. 'You must!'

John smiled. 'Aye, I am. It's too good an opportunity to miss. Though what Dad will say I don't know. Maybe turn me out like you.'

'If that's the case, go. Don't let him persuade you otherwise. I never regret leaving, in spite of losing Colin and then Peter, except that I wasn't here when Mum died.'

'He should have let you know,' said John with a shake of his head.

Any further discussion was stopped by a sharp rap overhead.

'He's awake,' commented John.

515

'Then let's get this all over together,' said Jean firmly. 'It's no use dallying about. Then we can get on with our lives.' She stood up and straightened her skirt with a sharp tug.

She led the way into the small bedroom on the right of the tiny landing. She stopped at the foot of the bed and looked at the pale, drawn face, thin against the pillow. Her heart cried out in sympathy for the man who was but a shadow of the robust man she remembered. In that instant she made a vow, a pledge for her mother's sake, that she would see him built up and on his feet again before she left even if there was no welcome for her.

'Hello, Dad,' she said softly.

The response was a puzzled frown as if he was trying to recall who it might be. He tried to raise his head to see who spoke.

John had come to the side of the bed, close to his father. 'Dad, Jean's here.'

'Jean?' There was a catch in his throat as the name brought memories flooding back of the young girl who had brought so much joy to him and Sarah after three boys. Then those recollections were darkened by a nineteen-year-old daughter who had defied him and followed the urging of the Harlands when she should have been at home for her mother. 'The last time thee was here, what did I tell thee?' It seemed he had purposely gathered strength to make that pronouncement, for his words came firmly, piercing her mind with their implication.

Jean stiffened. 'I remember all too well.'

'Then what are thee doing here?'

'Dad, I came to see you. I thought after all this time

516

you'd be reasonable; besides, I need a home. I'm asking you to—'

'Thee made thy bed so thee must lie on it,' Jonas cut in.

'But, Dad,' protested John.

'Thee keep out of it. If Jean hadn't left, her mother might have been here now.'

'Thee knows that's not true,' rapped Jean. 'Can't you face up to the fact that she died of cancer and nothing I could have done would have saved her? You're just being a stupid, pig-headed old man. And I'll tell you another thing. You'll maybe go the same way if I don't help you.' She glanced at her brother, the look in her eyes signalling that what she was about to say was no criticism of him. 'You need the care and attention that only a woman can give. You need looking after. John can't be here all the time.'

'He is,' Jonas put in sharply, only to start up a rasping cough.

'It's not fair to him. He has a job to think about. And look at you, look at the untidy state your bed's in. The whole house needs a spring-clean and brightening up.'

'There's been a war on.'

'You don't have to tell me that,' returned Jean with some bitterness. 'But that's no excuse. You missed Mum, naturally, and you weren't used to housework.' She looked hard at her father, who lay wheezing, and set her expression into one of no nonsense. 'No matter what you say, I'm staying now. Mum would never forgive me if I walked out on you, leaving you in this situation. When you're better and up and about again, if you don't want me here, then I'll go. It'll be up to you.'

Jonas said nothing. His face was grim at the defiance he saw but deep down he admired her spunk and he saw a lot of his beloved Sarah in her. He gave a little nod of resignation without approval.

'Another thing, you may as well know while we are about it.' She glanced at her brother. 'Tell him now. He's got to know sooner or later and better sooner.' She looked back at her father. 'John told me something downstairs which you've got to know.'

John damped his lips and met his father's gaze. 'Mr Harland wants me to work with him in his garage and haulage business, take me in as a partner just as he would have done his own son, had he lived.' He put the information forcefully, with enthusiasm.

Jonas's face darkened. 'Will I never hear anything about this family that isn't connected with the Harlands?' The sinews in his neck stood out with the tension of anger. 'He took Mary from me, now he wants my son.' His look was scathing. 'That thee should ever think of it!'

'Dad, don't talk so daft. Mr Harland isn't taking me away from you. I'm only going into partnership with him. He's remembered my ability before the war and this is a golden opportunity for me.'

'Maybe, but he'll come out of it all right,' rasped Jonas.

'And so will I. And you.'

'Me? How the hell will it affect me?' There was a sneer in his voice.

'Oh, Dad! Can't you see that this chance will earn John good money? And because he'll be here, you'll benefit. And I'll tell you this.' Jean was bristling like a fighting cock. 'John is going to take this opportunity. And you

518

should be grateful to Mr Harland for giving it to him. What else is there to keep John here? Nothing. The fishing's gone. You'd rather have him here than elsewhere.' She looked at John. 'You get yourself off to see Mr Harland. And don't let on I'm here. I want to surprise Gabrielle.'

John glanced at his father.

He said nothing.

Jean had taken charge just as her mother would have done, and Jonas recalled that once she had her head set she would go to any lengths to achieve what she thought was right and best. Hadn't Sarah done just that when Sam had offered to teach John all about engines? Now Jean was doing the same. Maybe she was right too.

John left the bedroom without another word.

'Now that's settled, let's get you straightened up.' She started to adjust the bedclothes and pillows and, though he said nothing, Jonas felt much more comfortable when she had finished. 'A little fresh air will do you good.' She opened the window a little and the tang of the salt air brought him memories of days spent fishing in the bay. If John was around, maybe they could do it again, but this time just for fun, for Jonas had not left the coastguard.

Jean stood beside the bed and looked down at him. 'Comfortable?' He gave a slight nod and she smiled to herself. 'Right, now I'm going downstairs to see what I can rustle up for your meal this evening. When John returns, I'm going to see Gabrielle.'

As she reached the door, he stopped her. 'Jean?'

She turned to face him. She had detected a softer tremor in his voice.

'I was sorry about Colin and . . . the other chap.'

'Peter.'

'Aye, Peter. It must have been hard for thee. I'm sorry I wasn't any help.'

Jean came slowly back across the room. There was a lump in her throat and tears were brimming in her eyes. 'I needed you then, Dad. I need you now.'

A hand came from under the bedclothes and reached out to her. 'I'm here if thee wants me.'

She took his hand and sank on to her knees. 'I do, Dad, I do.'

There was a catch in his voice as he said, 'I wronged thee, lass. I'm sorry. Can thee forgive me?'

'Of course, Dad.' She laid her head on the pillow and hugged him.

Jonas could sense Sarah approving. He felt nearer to her than he had for a long time.

Jean walked to the Harland house with a lighter step than she had had a few hours ago when she arrived in Robin Hood's Bay. The early storm at her arrival had been calmed and a future she had feared might have little to offer now seemed much brighter, even if she had to spend it as home-maker to two men, her father and brother. She would miss the air-force life, the comradeship, the fun in the midst of tragedy. She had been tempted to sign on but realised the WAAF in peacetime would not be the same.

Her ring at the doorbell was answered by Mrs Harland, whose eyes widened with surprise on seeing her.

'Jean! How nice to see you after all this time.' With a

hug and a kiss she ushered Jean into the house, calling, 'Sam! Sam! See who's here.'

Sam came hurrying into the hall. 'Jean!' He held out his arms to her. 'It's good to see thee.' After his kiss he held her at arm's length and looked her up and down. 'Thee's grown into a fine lass. Colin would have been proud of thee.'

Jean's smile of greeting faltered a little. 'Thanks, Mr Harland, that's a nice thing to say.'

Colette took her arm and led her into the lounge. 'And we were sorry about your other young man.'

'Thanks, Mrs Harland.' She glanced at Sam. 'And thanks for what you're doing for John.'

Sam waved the thanks aside. 'It's a pleasure to have him. He'll be an asset. I think there's a good opportunity for him. When petrol rationing ends, folks will be flocking to buy cars. You know there's—'

'Stop, Sam.' Colette halted him with a knowing smile at Jean. 'Set him off on that topic and there's no stopping him.' She looked back at her husband. 'Jean's here to see Gabrielle, not to hear about your lorries and cars. You'll find Gabrielle in the summerhouse, my dear. You slip down there and see her. I'll bring a tea tray down in half an hour.'

'Thanks, Mrs Harland.' Jean glanced at Sam. 'You built that summerhouse you always said you would?'

'Aye, thee knows the spot from which I used to watch the sea and your father fishing, remember?'

'Yes, I do.'

'How is he? I hear he's got bronchitis.'

'He'll pull through,' said Jean and added with a smile, 'Still as stubborn as ever – well, not quite.'

'You mean you and he . . . ?'

'Yes.'

'I'm pleased. Maybe he'll see sense about another matter.'

Jean grimaced. 'I wouldn't count on it, but I'll work on him.'

Sam grinned. 'You do. Nothing would give me greater pleasure than for him and me to have one of those nights out in Whitby that we used to have before we were both married.' He gave a half-laugh of contempt at his thought. 'But that was long ago, a pair of old-timers like ourselves couldn't do it now.'

'I'll bet you'd have a jolly good try,' Jean said with a laugh.

'Aye, maybe we would, lass, maybe we would.' He opened the french windows and Jean hurried across the well-cut lawn bordered by rosebeds. Reds, pinks and yellows tumbled like a sparkling waterfall towards the summerhouse.

The side of the small building facing the sea was almost all glass, only the stout oak frames marring the expansive view. Jean saw it was a place which could be used in all weathers, cosy on a day like this, warm even when there was a fresh breeze outside, and somewhere to watch the sea in all its moods and wonder at the storms as they lashed the mighty cliffs.

As she went down the steps on the right of the summerhouse, she saw Gabrielle lazing in a deck chair, her eyes shut. She received a shock when she stopped and looked at her friend through the glass. Gabrielle had aged. Though there was a lot of the young girl left, there were lines which shouldn't be there and her hair, nicely waved, had the odd touch of silver. Her face was pale and drawn as if the cares of the world sat heavily on its owner. If instructing took its toll this way, Jean was thankful she had merely had the stresses of squadron life. She opened the door slowly, closed it behind her and stood for a moment.

'Wake up, lazy-head.' Her voice came sharply in the small space.

Gabrielle stirred and, sensing a presence, sat up, eyes widening. Then, with a delighted scream of 'Jean!', she sprang from her chair.

With laughter tumbling from their lips, both firing questions at once, they hugged each other in the delightful reunion of a deep friendship.

It was only when Mrs Harland brought a tray set with two cups and saucers, two tea plates, milk and sugar, a plate of scones and one of fairy cakes, butter and jam, and a teapot, that Jean realised that she had been talking of her war and still knew very little about Gabrielle's. In the excitement she had not even enquired about her friend's health. 'You are all right?' she asked.

'I'm recuperating, coming along fine. I've been rather ill but I'll be OK,' replied Gabrielle, pouring the tea.

Jean was curious. Her friend made no offer to say what had been the matter.

'Instructing too much for you?' Jean teased, hoping she might draw more information about Gabrielle's illness. When her friend merely smiled, she went on. 'You should have asked for a transfer, got something more exciting and in keeping with your talents. You were wasted—'

'I saw my aunt.' The words came quietly, stopping Jean in full flow.

'Pardon?' Jean felt sure she hadn't heard correctly.

Gabrielle met her surprised look with directness. 'I saw my aunt,' she repeated in the same tone. 'Ask no more questions, get no lies. I can't say any more. And please, on your honour, tell no one.'

Jean's mind was in a turmoil trying to figure out what might lie behind those words. Had Gabrielle's aunt left France? Or had Gabrielle been there? If she had . . . She was longing to pour her questions out but from Gabrielle's rigid stare she knew she should not. 'Of course I won't,' she said reassuringly, and watched Gabrielle closely. If she hoped to find some answers in her expression, she was mistaken.

As Gabrielle reached for the plate of scones, her blouse sleeve caught on the corner of the table. The button was torn loose and the sleeve pulled up her forearm.

'Oh, dear, you've—' The words froze on Jean's lips. She stared in unbelieving astonishment at the numbers imprinted on Gabrielle's arm. 'You weren't . . . ?'

Gabrielle nodded, quickly covering her arm.

'But . . .' Jean floundered in her bewilderment.

'I am lucky to be alive. I wouldn't be if the young German officer who had been sent to my cell to shoot me hadn't taken pity, when they were evacuating the camp in a hurry, saying, "What's the use of killing you? The war's over." He fired his shot into the ceiling and left. An hour later British troops arrived.'

'Oh, Gabrielle!' Jean's countenance expressed concern for her friend and regrets at prejudging her when she had not heard from her. 'And I thought you . . .'

'Think no more about it. I'm sworn to secrecy about my war. I've told you more than I should but you deserve the little explanation I can give you. You must say nothing. As far as anyone else is concerned, my war was spent instructing.'

'Your mother and father know?'

'Yes, but only what you know. Don't even mention it to them.'

'I won't.'

When Jean left the Harlands, she made another joyful reunion with Liz.

'You're back for good?' Liz asked.

'Seems like it. Dad and I have patched things up and he needs me. I'll think again about the future when he's well again.'

'You might leave?'

'Don't know. Robin Hood's Bay pulls.'

'I know what you mean. It attracts me like that but I've a good career in the nursing service if I sign on.'

'Might you?'

'Like you, I don't know, but I'll have to make up my mind before I go back next Monday.'

'Then you'll see Martin, he's home on Friday.'

Liz was thoughtful as she walked along the beach on Friday evening.

In spite of the horrors she had witnessed at Biggin Hill – maimed pilots, burning aircraft and exploding bombs – she had had a good life, experiences she would not have missed. Although it would be different in peacetime, she

525

reckoned she could take to the life around air-force stations. It was tempting to sign on, but as she looked around the bay, peaceful in the evening sun, the waves rolling in to run up the sand sending tiny fingers of foam reaching for her feet, she wondered. She slipped off her sandals and let the water tickle her toes as she walked slowly, deep in thought.

She stopped and let her eyes sweep round the bay up the great towering cliffs climbing to Ravenscar and then in the opposite direction to the cottages and houses spilling down the cliffside, their red roofs bright in the sun. They clung together as if in that closeness they could survive storm and war, as indeed they had done for centuries. There was a permanence about them. Did she want that and was Robin Hood's Bay telling her this was where she would find it?

The drone of an engine caught her attention, at first a low throb but getting louder. Her eyes flicked towards the horizon and she identified a fighter heading north. It brought back memories of how she had stood here when Biggin Hill was in the midst of battle and watched two Hurricanes heading in the same direction. Then she knew where her future lay. Was this lone aircraft telling her the same?

She walked slowly on, lost to the world.

'Hello, Liz.'

The voice behind her was quiet, hardly piercing her thoughts. For a moment she thought she was imagining it. She turned to make sure.

'Martin.'

'Liz.' He came the last few steps. 'We said we'd meet here.'

She nodded. 'I wondered if you'd come.'

'I wondered if you'd be here.'

In the moment's silence their eyes searched each other, trying to interpret feelings, and neither could read the expression offered. It was as if they both held a veil before them, frightened to cast it aside lest they revealed what the other did not seek.

'Does coming mean anything?' Liz broke the silence.

He nodded. 'Does being here mean anything?'

'We kept a pact, that must mean something after all these years.'

Martin reached out and pulled her closer. He looked into her eyes and cast his veil aside. 'Marry me, Liz. I love you. I always have.'

'Oh, Martin, I love you too. I was always afraid you didn't feel the same.'

There was no need for words as his lips told her his feelings. And she responded with equal revelation.

An aircraft engine faded in the distance and then was gone.

When they returned to climb the hill between the cottages, Liz knew that Martin, encouraged by his father, intended to join the coastguard. When she returned to Diggin Hill on Monday she would hand in her resignation and put in an application for a position at Whitby hospital, where she had left to go to war.

The Saturday morning's post brought a letter for Jean. She was pleased when she recognised Rowena's writing, for they had kept up a regular correspondence and had become close.

9 June 1946

My dear Jean,

I am so glad that you decided to go home and I hope that there has been a reconciliation between you and your father. Family ties are always precious and it hurts if they are broken for whatever reason.

I need to see you urgently as there are matters concerning the future of my property and other assets that I would like to discuss with you. I know that you have been at home only a short time but I would appreciate it if you could come as soon as possible.

No more news now as I hope to see you in a day or two.

Love,
Rowena

Jean was puzzled. Why should Rowena want to discuss her affairs with her? She read the letter again but it gave no hint that she might have overlooked.

When she showed the letter to her brother, he put no obstacle in the way of her going. 'You must go as soon as possible. There sounds to be some urgency about it. Dad will be all right. He's so much better, much chirpier. I'll ask Mr Harland for some time off and see Dad's OK. You get off to the post office and send Mrs Wallace a telegram telling her you'll see her on Monday.'

Jean told her father and, though he grimaced at the thought of losing the comforting attentions of his daughter so soon, he did not object as he might have done once.

Jean and Liz left by the same train from Robin Hood's Bay early on Monday morning.

Martin's announcement had been greeted with joy by both families. As she sat opposite Liz, Jean felt a little envious. Liz knew where her future lay, but as yet she didn't. What did she really want? She knew even in this short time that her father hoped, probably expected her to settle down with him. The life of an old maid? She was young. There was a long future ahead, but could there be anyone after Colin and Peter?

The two girls parted at York station, Liz catching the London train, and Jean heading across the Pennines, North Wales and the Menai Strait to Anglesey.

Clouds were bubbling up over the Snowdon range but the island was bathed in sunshine when Jean got down from the bus to walk that last few hundred yards to the house overlooking the strait, a house with so many memories of the man she had loved. They were happy ones and she knew Peter would not want her to be saddened by them.

Carrying a small suitcase, dressed in a grey three-quarter-length suit sweeping from square shoulders to hug her waist, she opened the gate and started up the path to the house. Her boxy skirt had three pleats at the front and her white blouse peeped from the lapelled neckline of her jacket. Her small round hat, swept up at the front, emphasised her well-proportioned features and allowed her light-brown hair, still air-force short, to peep provocatively at the sides. The heels of her shoes were of the right height to set off her silk-clad legs to perfection. She was glad she had managed to find such a pair of stockings, for this visit presented an opportunity to feel smart which would be rare in the life she seemed destined to lead in Robin Hood's Bay.

As she walked between the bright colours of the scented stocks, snow-in-summer, dwarf lavender and columbines, she wondered why Rowena wanted to discuss the future of this house with her.

The front door opened and a smiling Rowena came out to meet her.

'Welcome, my dear! It's so good to see you.' She opened her arms to the girl she had hoped would be her daughter-in-law. 'I've been looking out for you.'

Jean returned the greeting warmly and as they turned towards the house, Rowena linked her arm through Jean's. 'I'm so grateful that you could come so soon after my request. I hope you were able to leave home without any inconvenience.'

'Oh, yes. Everything is all right between Dad and me now.'

'Oh, I'm so glad.'

'Your letter sounded so urgent.'

'What I want to discuss is—'

Jean stopped in her tracks. Her body went rigid. Rowena gripped her arm more tightly as if steadying her against shock. She saw Jean's face had drained of its colour and her eyes were wide with disbelief.

A figure stood in the doorway.

Jean's mind screamed. A ghost! This wasn't what she wanted. She had never seen this house as being haunted. Any moment she expected the figure to vanish but it didn't.

530

'Peter!' The word came in a long-drawn-out whisper of incredulity. She turned to Rowena, her eyes demanding, Is this true or am I . . . ?

Rowena, her face radiantly happy, smiled reassuringly at Jean. 'It's Peter.'

Jean gasped and turned her gaze back to the house. Peter was running towards them. Jean dropped her case. Rowena let her go and she sprang forward to fling herself into Peter's arms.

Tears were streaming down her face as he hugged her to him. Oh, it was so good to feel his arms around her, holding as if they would never let her go. Her mind was awash with joy and disbelief. 'Peter, Peter!' She said his name over and over again to reassure herself that he was really there.

Then he pushed her gently from him to look longingly at her. 'It really is me,' he said, his soft brown eyes sparkling with joy at seeing her again.

She gulped, wiping away the tears with her fingers as a wide smile broke across her face. 'How? What? Where?'

Peter laughed. 'All in good time. There's so much to tell. Come on, let's go inside. Tea's ready. Oh, it's so good to see you!' He slipped his right arm round her waist and held out his other for his mother.

When they were settled with a cup of tea and a piece of home-made cake, Jean had time to assess Peter. His face bore lines of hardship and his short hair suggested that his head had been shaven. But she figured that rest and good food would soon restore him to the Peter she remembered.

She listened intently as he told his story.

'. . . When the Germans closed in, this agent saved my

life and lost hers.' He shook his head sadly at the thought. 'And I don't know who she was. I only knew her as Marguerite, her code name. I can't even contact her family.'

Jean reached out and held his hand. 'If it's any consolation, I'm grateful to her. She will always be remembered by me.'

'Even as she saved my life, I nearly lost it. I remember this pain in my head and falling into blackness. I learned afterwards that it was a bullet wound and I fell into the Loire. There good fortune was on my side, for the shock of the water must have brought back some instinct for survival, even if only for a brief moment, and I must have grabbed a floating branch and was taken downstream. I can only surmise this for the next thing I knew was that I was in bed in a peasants' cottage, being tended by a middle-aged couple. They told me they had dragged me out of the river.

'They nursed me for a month at great risk to themselves. When I was well enough I left them so as not to endanger them further. I was on my own and moved carefully south towards Spain. There's no need to go into all the details now – some of them would horrify you – suffice to say that after a long time I managed to reach the Spanish border. Crossing it was hazardous, a game of patience and choosing the right moment to avoid patrols. I made it and then was faced with more hardship crossing the Pyrenees. Again I would have perished but I was picked up by two men who gave me shelter and said they would see me over the mountains. I learned nothing about them, not even a name. Once safely across, I was on my own again.

'Safe in neutral territory, I thought it was only a matter

of time before I would be in contact with British officials and brought back to England.' Peter gave a half-laugh of derision. 'How wrong I was! I made myself known to the first Spaniards I met in a tiny village. The rumpus that caused! They flung me in a small wooden hut unfit for chickens and I was there for a week with a meagre helping of food. Then a truck arrived with two police who hand-cuffed me and took me away. What they had been told by the people of the village, I never knew, but I was treated roughly and taken to an internment camp. There I nearly rotted. No one took any notice of my pleas for someone to contact the British embassy. They seemed to doubt my story that I was a British airman. So there I stayed. And it was only after the war that I was taken out and someone contacted the embassy.

'Eventually I was flown home, debriefed and sent to hospital. When I had recovered sufficiently, there were a lot more questions about what had happened and the people I had been in contact with in France. In all this time they would allow no contact with relatives. They let me come home only last Monday.'

'The day I left the WAAFs. Oh, Peter, why didn't you get in touch with me?'

'I didn't know where you were. I didn't even know if you had got someone else. I wouldn't have blamed you if you had – after all, you thought I was dead. Besides, I wanted to get myself oriented to life again. And I hoped Mum would be able to give me news of you, I hoped you two had kept in touch though there was no reason why you should. The rest you know. I got Mum to invite you over here because this is where I felt I would be most at ease

533

meeting you again. If I had come to Robin Hood's Bay, it would have been strange to me. I hope you don't mind.'

'Of course not. I agree with you, this was the best place.'

'Now, you two,' said Rowena, rising from the chair. 'I'll clear these things away and then prepare an evening meal.'

'I'll help you,' offered Jean.

'No, you won't. You two have a lot of time to make up.' She started to gather the teacups, glanced at Jean and said with a half-smile, 'My ruse in the letter to get you here was not untrue: the future of this house is in your hands.'

Jean and Peter strolled across the lawn towards the Menai Strait. The water was calm. Caernarfon was catching the sun while the mountains rose majestically in a backcloth topped with billowing white clouds.

Peter turned Jean to him and looked at her with loving eyes. 'Will you marry me?' he asked.

'Oh, yes!'

Their lips met in a long lingering kiss which sealed their future.

'In Robin Hood's Bay?' he asked.

'Oh, no. I want it to be in the place we had planned originally. It'll have more meaning, and this house has special memories of our previous visits.'

He kissed her again, a kiss of thanks for keeping her memories of him precious to her.

As they strolled back to the house, Jean asked, 'How long are you home for?'

'A month. Then I report back and will take demob.'

'Then you'd better come and meet Dad.'

'Love to.'

'Right. How about if we spend a few days here and go to Robin Hood's Bay next Saturday? Then, when you come back here, you'll have at least another week with your mother.'

'That sounds perfect.'

Chapter Twenty-Three

1946

As Jean and Peter left the train in Robin Hood's Bay in the late afternoon of the following Saturday, they were welcomed by the cry of seagulls wheeling around the high cliffs. The sun filtered through thin cirrus clouds and there was a gentle breeze.

'Hello, Mr Newton,' cried Jean happily. 'I'd like you to meet Peter Wallace.'

'Glad to know you,' said Will, holding out his hand.

Peter felt a broad, firm grip. 'Heard about you,' he returned with a smile.

'All good, I hope?' Will cocked an eyebrow at Jean.

'Couldn't be anything else, Mr Newton,' she replied, squeezing his arm affectionately.

'Watched her grow up, favourite of mine,' Will went on, turning back to Peter. 'So take care of her.' He had guessed from Jean's effervescent demeanour that this handsome RAF officer with ribbons on his chest had captured her heart.

'I will. She's special to me too.' He nodded reassuringly. 'Here for long?'

'Maybe a week, then home again before reporting back for my demob.'

'Then enjoy yourselves.' He watched them walk away, thankful that Jean had got a fine handsome young man, a brave one too. She deserved him.

At the top of the hill Peter stopped to let his gaze wander over the scene. The wide sweep of the bay, the rampart of cliffs rising to Ravenscar from the lower erosions closer to hand, captured his attention before he turned it to the tumbling red roofs of the cottages spilling down the cliffside towards the sea.

'Beautiful!' he murmured.

Jean hugged his arm tighter. 'I'm so glad you like it.'

'Would you want to live here?' Peter put the question tentatively.

When Jean looked at him, the serious expression in her eyes was matched by the tone of her voice. 'I'm marrying you, so wherever you are, I will be.'

'I've got something in mind,' he said mysteriously. 'I'll tell you later. We'd better get on to see your father.'

He made to move but Jean stopped him. Her curiosity had been roused too much to be kept waiting. 'No, tell me now.'

He saw she would not be put off. 'Well, you know I'm not badly off. The house in Anglesey will be mine one day and I'd like to take up Mum's offer to share it with us, living our own lives without getting on top of each other. But I see no reason why we can't buy a cottage here and divide our time between both places.'

537

This suggestion sounded good to Jean. 'But what will you do?'

'Write.'

'Write?'

'Yes. It has always attracted me. And I have a lot of material from my experiences which I can use. There'll probably be some restriction on factual books about the war for a short while, but that will disappear. In the meantime I could use it as background material in fiction.' His voice was filled with a visionary enthusiasm. 'I'd like to write about my experiences as a pilot. There'd also be a wealth of material in my escape story, and I'd like to do some research into the girl who saved my life.'

'Marguerite?'

'Yes. I think there will be a story worth telling and I don't think it should go untold.'

Jean had been carried along on the wave of his fervour. What he was suggesting sounded ideal, and between them they could make it work. 'There's a surfeit of history around here you could use,' she offered helpfully, 'smuggling, fishing, whaling, the haunted moors . . . the coastal villages and Whitby are very atmospheric. I could help you with your research. I'll learn to type properly. Let's try it! We've everything to gain.' She hugged him. 'Oh, I love you so much!'

The joy in her heart received a further boost when they reached the house in Sunny Place, for they found her father setting the table for tea.

'Dad! It's good to see you up,' cried Jean, giving him a kiss. 'Are you all right?'

'Aye, lass, I'm on the mend. Doc says I've made a

538

good recovery. Must be you coming home that did it. Now come on, introduce me,' he added, turning his gaze on Peter.

'Dad, this is Peter. His survival was miraculous.'

'Pleased to meet you, Mr Lawson.' He smiled broadly as he held out his hand.

Jonas felt a grip which said, 'I hope we'll be friends.' He viewed this young man with a critical eye and approved his daughter's choice, and he had no doubt the impression would be strengthened with time. The only blot on the horizon was the fact that he would be losing Jean so soon after her return, but these fears were allayed when, over tea, they told him their plans. She would be near for at least part of the year and he couldn't grumble at that. Life would not be so bad after all. He had his job in the coastguard, Martin would be joining him, Jean would be close by, and John would be at home even though he was working with Sam Harland. That stuck a bit in Jonas's craw but if that was what John wanted, then so be it. He didn't have to meet Sam, and woe betide him if this was an attempt to take his son from him as a replacement for his own loss.

'Peter can have Martin's room,' said Jonas when they had finished tea. 'When we got your telegram yesterday saying you were bringing someone to stay, Martin said he was sure the Johnsons would let him have Ron's room for a few days.'

'Thank you for all your trouble, Mr Lawson, I didn't expect—'

Jonas waved aside the thanks. 'Thank Martin when you see him.'

'Right, I'll show you the room and then you must come and meet my dearest friend Gabrielle.'

Ten minutes later, with Peter changed into grey flannels, open-necked white shirt and blue pullover, they walked up the hill towards the Harland house.

Peter remarked on the quaint, narrow streets running along the cliffside with houses and cottages standing almost one on top of another, and sensed the atmosphere which made Robin Hood's Bay dear to Jean's heart. He could enjoy a life shared between here and Anglesey.

'A fine house,' he observed when they turned in the gateway on the top of the cliffs.

'It is,' agreed Jean. 'A pity Dad created the ill feeling between himself and Mr Harland, he's missed out on so much friendship.' She had told Peter about her father's hostility to Sam Harland when she was briefing him about her family.

'Maybe something will turn up to show him he was wrong,' suggested Peter, mainly as a comfort to Jean, who he knew bitterly regretted the situation.

'What, after all this time? You must be joking. Thank goodness I didn't allow it to mar my friendship with Gabrielle.'

'She must be some girl.'

'She is,' replied Jean. She wanted to say more but she would not break Gabrielle's trust.

After introductions to Colette and Sam were over, Colette informed them, 'Gabrielle is in the summerhouse. She spends a lot of time there recuperating. I think she finds peace there after the traumas of her war.'

As they went down the garden, Peter asked Jean what Colette had meant.

'I don't know any details but I think she had a rough time.'

Peter had to rein in his curiosity. Jean went on ahead by a couple of strides so that she reached the steps before him. She paused and held a finger to her lips and then mouthed, 'She's asleep.' They started gingerly down the steps but he accidentally sent a stone clattering down them. Gabrielle came wide awake.

Jean flung open the door. 'Gabrielle, I've brought Peter—' The words stopped, cut short by her astonishment at the look which had come to her friend's face. She glanced at Peter. He too was gaping disbelievingly at Gabrielle.

'Marguerite!' The word escaped in a long breath charged with unreality.

The name penetrated Gabrielle's disbelief. With a cry of 'Auguste!' she was out of her chair and in his arms, hugging him tight, her joy evident to them all. Then she stood back, tears in her eyes, and looked at him. 'I wondered if you'd escaped.'

'I thought you were dead,' gasped Peter. 'Oh, it's so good to see you again.' He stepped forward and hugged her once more as if to reassure himself that she was real. But in the midst of surprise and pleasure his thoughts were in confusion. Marguerite – Jean's dearest friend! The last night in the cottage by the Loire came vividly back to lend its own turmoil. He battled against it as, with his arm still around her, he turned to Jean, who stood bewildered and astonished at what was going on. 'Jean, this is the girl I told you about who saved my life.'

541

'Gabrielle?'

'I knew her as Marguerite.'

'But how? What?'

Peter glanced at Gabrielle. 'How much can you tell us? I'm dying to know what happened to you. I thought I saw you blown up.'

Gabrielle looked thoughtful for a moment, then said, 'Sit down.' She looked at them in turn before she spoke. 'I think explanations are necessary, but what I tell you must not go beyond this summerhouse. So much is still secret and we were told not to talk.' She looked at Peter. 'Jean knows I was in France and that I was . . .' She loosened the button on her sleeve and rolled the cloth back.

'Oh, my God!' Peter gasped when he saw the numbers on her arm. He looked at her questioningly.

She nodded. 'And Jean knows why I'm alive but she knows no other details.'

'But you two, how . . . ?' asked Jean. There was so much she wanted to know.

Gabrielle went on to tell her how she and Peter had met, how they came to be in the cottage by the Loire and how they were betrayed and made their exit from the cottage just in time. 'I was badly injured in the blast. I knew Peter was heading for the river. I heard rifle fire followed by a splash. I didn't know whether that was a deliberate escape or a body falling into the river.' She glanced at him. 'I often wondered and remembered.' She saw the implication behind the last word had not gone unrecognised by him and she also saw the almost imperceptible shake of his head and knew that Jean did not know how much they had shared in that cottage by the Loire.

'I was taken prisoner but was so badly wounded that I hovered between life and death for a long time. Probably saved my life. The doctors wouldn't allow interrogators near me, said it would kill me if they tried to elicit information too soon, and they wanted the information so they wanted me alive. Then the invasion took place and I kept getting moved from place to place. I was stronger by now and interrogation had begun, but I held out and was eventually sent to a concentration camp. There I would have finished my days if it hadn't been for a sudden sweep by the British. There was panic in the camp and the Germans made a hasty retreat.' She smiled. 'There you have it.' She looked at Peter. 'Now you?'

He quickly told her his story.

When he had finished, Jean reached over and hugged Gabrielle. 'Oh, thank you so much for saving my Peter,' she said with all the sincerity in her heart.

When they reached the house in Sunny Place, Jean could not hold back the news that Gabrielle had saved Peter's life. 'Don't ask any questions, Dad, but it's true. Isn't it amazing?'

He shot a querying look tinged with doubt at Peter.

'It's true, Mr Lawson. What a coincidence! But strange things happen in war.'

'But that means Gabrielle was in France,' said Jonas.

'You've made a conclusion. Ask no more. Don't mention it to anyone,' said Peter. He then added, risking Jonas taking offence, 'Might I say, without any attempt at interference, that it strikes me as unlikely that someone as brave and likeable as Gabrielle would

543

come from stock who deliberately meant to harm Jean's aunt Mary.'

Jean and Peter could sense her father bristle. Peter knew he had risked turning Jonas against him but he thought it worth the risk if it could heal a rift which he knew troubled Jean.

'So thee knows,' he grunted.

'Dad, I'm going to marry Peter and I want no family secrets between us.'

Jonas sat for a moment, then grunted again, leaned forward, picked up his pipe and started filling it. He looked up at Peter. 'Feel like a beer?'

The tension fled from the room.

'That would be nice.'

'Thee'll find a bottle in the pantry. We'll have it while Jean gets the meal ready.'

Jean and Peter went into the kitchen together.

'Hope I did some good,' he whispered.

'Might make him think. He didn't fly off the handle so that could be a good sign.'

Peter did his best to concentrate on things around him but Gabrielle's Marguerite kept appearing in his mind. She became even more vivid in the silence of his room and the thoughts which pounded confusion in his mind would not let him sleep. She had saved his life – he owed her. Marriage? Would she expect it? Clear the air by telling Jean everything that had happened in that French cottage? He risked losing her, maybe them both, and it would break up a long friendship between them. If he married Jean, could he live with Marguerite living nearby? They could turn their backs on Robin Hood's Bay and escape to Anglesey, but that would break Jean's heart, especially after the excitement she had shown for his plans. Peter's mind was torn in two, his loyalties divided.

Confusion still reigned the following morning. He seized the opportunity to go for a walk on his own while Jean saw to the housework. Wanting to know Gabrielle's feelings, he climbed the hill to the Harland house. She was pottering in the garden when she saw him approaching. She went to meet him.

'Good morning, Peter,' she greeted him brightly, her disposition matching the warm, friendly feeling of the day.

'Hello, Marguerite.' He shrugged his shoulders. 'I will never get used to calling you Gabrielle.' He frowned, his face serious.

She smiled and ran a finger across his brow. 'Once before I had to wipe a frown away.'

'Marguerite?' His voice was charged with emotion. In it there was the desire for answers.

'Let's walk along the cliffs,' she suggested. As they turned, she said, 'It was a shock to find you had slept with Jean's best friend?'

He nodded. 'What do we do?' There was a cry for help in his voice.

'She doesn't know?'

'No.'

'Then there's no problem. She will never know from me.'

'You don't regret what happened between us now you know that Jean and I . . . ?'

'No. I never will. It helped then and will always be a treasured memory, but it was of the time and that cottage. It has no place in the present or the future.'

'But you saved my life. I owe you for that.'

'You owe me nothing. The past is the past. Your future is Jean's.'

'But you? What . . . ?'

'Spending time in that summerhouse has given me time to think what I want to do with my life.'

'You've decided?'

'Dad wanted me to work in his business but I'm not really interested. He's taken Jean's brother as a partner, as you probably know. Dad's given me shares in the business so, as long as those two make money I don't mind.' She looked thoughtful for a moment. 'I think I may go to France.'

'France?' Peter was surprised. 'Hasn't it too many bad memories for you?'

'We've got to cast such things aside and get on with living now. Madame Buffon is my aunt.'

Peter raised his eyebrows in astonishment. 'I didn't know. Then Michel is your cousin.'

'More than a cousin.' Gabrielle smiled. 'When he learned from Chasuble that I had been taken by the Germans, he was torn by anxiety for he knew what the Gestapo could do. He so desperately wanted to try to locate me and help. He had friends in the Resistance who he knew would be willing to attempt a rescue, Chasuble among them, but fortunately better sense prevailed. It could have jeopardised a great part of the Resistance movement.

'In any case it was some time before his enquiries bore fruit. He had to be very discreet, otherwise his role of double agent could have been unmasked.' She explained the part Michel had been playing. 'He eventually found which concentration camp I was in and he feared the worst, for no one had ever left there alive, and systematic executions took place every day. He was desperate to try to do something to help me, even to the point of walking into that camp and giving himself up. Again he was persuaded it was foolhardy and would gain nothing, for he might not even see me – SOE agents were segregated from the other prisoners. As the Allies swept eastwards, his role of agent ceased and he attached himself to some British troops as interpreter. He was with them when they swept into the camp and liberated us.

'My joy at seeing him was overpowered by his at finding me alive, but only just. He stayed with me when we were taken away and finally was instrumental in getting me quickly into a British hospital in Paris. Such devotion! His love is so strong.'

'And yours?' asked Peter, amazed at this story.

She nodded. 'I had grown very close to him through our undercover activities before he brought you to my aunt's, and after my capture I was obsessed with a desire to stay alive for his sake and for the love I was feeling for him.'

'Then it's Paris for you?'

'Yes.'

He stopped and took her arm. 'Whatever is for your happiness, Marguerite.'

'I like that name.' She smiled wistfully. 'It's ours, and no one else will share it.'

He bent and kissed her, a kiss that brought back memories of a time in a cottage in the midst of war, but also put them firmly in the past.

* * *

Jean came into the room where Peter was reading. She carried two notebooks carefully tied with ribbon.

'Peter, these are Colin's diaries which he kept from the moment he joined the air force. He wanted me to share every moment with him. I read some of them when Mr Harland sent them to me as Colin had requested, and then I tied them up with this ribbon and put away the hurt they were causing. Last night when I went to bed I got them out and read some of them again. You said about being a writer – I think these would make excellent material.'

He stood up and took them from her. 'You sure you want me to read them?' he said gently.

'Yes. I'd like you to know Colin and I'm sure he would want you to, and if you can use them I'd like it if his memory was kept alive.'

Peter spent some time reading the diaries and knew he had the makings of a moving story in his hand.

'Tear yourself away from them,' called Jean, breezing in to interrupt his reading. 'It's got out a lovely afternoon, I want to walk along the beach.'

'Come on, you two, where have thee been?' There was an urgency in Jonas's tone as Jean and Peter returned to the house in Sunny Place.

'Walking on the beach, Dad. What's the matter?' Concern clouded her face, chasing away the happy-go-lucky attitude which had filled her during the walk with Peter. All had seemed well with the world, but now she wondered.

'Never mind, come with me.' He started out of the house.

Jean and Peter exchanged puzzled glances. They

followed Jonas, who went up the hill at a quick pace without speaking. They recognised his desire for silence and respected it, for he seemed to be turning something over in his mind.

They looked askance at each other when they realised he was making for the Harland house but they did not question his decision.

His loud rap on the door – not for him to use these newfangled bells – was answered by Colette. She stared speechless when she saw Jonas.

'Sam in?' he asked gruffly.

'Yes,' she spluttered.

'Then can I come in and see him?'

'Yes.' She stood to one side and Jonas strode past her to stop in the hall and await further directions. As Jean and Peter entered the house, Colette looked questioningly at Jean, but realised from the shake of her head that she did not know why her father was here. Gabrielle, who was coming down the stairs, got the same signal.

'This way.' Colette opened a door on the right and as she entered the room she said, 'Sam, visitors for you.'

Sam pushed his big frame from an easy chair which had its back to the door. When he turned, his eyes widened with astonishment at seeing Jonas.

In the brief moment before speaking, Jonas registered the comfort of this room with its pleasant furniture and large windows looking over the garden to the sea, and his thoughts went to Sarah. How she would have loved a place like this! He had let her down. He swallowed hard for he sensed her shaking her head at that thought and smiling approvingly at what he was doing.

'Before thee speak, Sam Harland, listen to me,' he said brusquely before Sam could get over his surprise. 'I'm here to apologise and say how sorry I am for all the misunderstanding and ill feeling I caused over all these years.'

Everyone stared in astonishment at him. What had caused the stubborn Jonas Lawson to come here with apologies?

'Thee no doubt know that the life of my future son-in-law was saved by thy daughter. When he discovered this, he said to me that such a brave girl as Gabrielle could not come from stock that had deliberately harmed Mary. He made me think. Sam, thee also had a brave and honourable son and he couldn't have come from bad stock either. And I've always remembered how kind Gabrielle was when Sarah died. A war's just ended; I think another one should too. I'm sorry for causing it. And another thing, my thanks for what you're doing for John. I was lucky, I lost no one in the war. If I can share John with thee, then I am glad to do so.' He held out his hand.

Sam stepped forward and took it firmly in his. The years rolled away in that grip. They were friends about to enjoy a night out in Whitby.

'Oh, Dad!' Jean kissed her father on his cheek. 'Mum would be so pleased.'

He nodded. 'Thank God thee found two airmen who made me see sense.'